IT'S A DEVIL OF A JOB...

I waited until I stopped shaking, got into
my car, and drove very carefully down into
Hollywood. I had gone without sleep before,
of course, but I had gotten to that age where it
wasn't a trivial matter anymore. Still, had to
warn the robot and the crawling eye that the
gremlin was going to kill them.

And then hate the fact I lived in a world where
such a sentence was said with a straight face.

PRAISE FOR CITY OF DEVILS

"Robinson crafts a uniquely interesting world that is sure to
please horror, science fiction, and mystery fans alike."
—*Minneapolis Books Examiner*

**OTHER CANDLEMARK & GLEAM BOOKS
BY JUSTIN ROBINSON:**

Mr. Blank

CITY

OF

DEVILS

JUSTIN ROBINSON

Candlemark & Gleam

First edition published 2013.

For information, address
Candlemark & Gleam LLC,
104 Morgan Street, Bennington, VT 05201
info@candlemarkandgleam.com

Library of Congress Cataloging-in-Publication Data
In Progress

ISBN: 978-1-936460-49-6
eBook ISBN: 978-1-936460-50-2

Cover art and design by Kate Sullivan

Book design and composition by Kate Sullivan
Typeface: Marion

Illustrations by Fernando Caire
www.artofernando.com

Advertising design by Alan Caum

Eye icon by Ayesha Rana, from The Noun Project

Editors: Kate Sullivan and Sarah LaBelle
Proofreaders: Aliza Becker and Aaron Sikes

www.candlemarkandgleam.com

For Lauri.

I'm so glad those evil eye charms
didn't work on you.

ONE

The man knocking on the outside of my office window had the head of a fly.

I sighed. Not another one.

I wanted to shoo him away, but I didn't have a newspaper big enough. Were they even scared of newspaper? I'd have to check with the human-only apothecary on Alameda. The human flies were supposed to be pretty strong, just like their insect brethren, but I'd never arm-wrestled one. Better to be careful. Just in case. I dug the insecticide sprayer out of the desk, finding it under more wolfsbane than any man should ever have to see in his lifetime, and turned back around. He was still there, stuck to the glass, plainly visible even through the venetian blinds. One of his legs was a fly leg. Must make getting around fun.

I waggled the sprayer at him, making sure those big red compound eyes saw it. He licked the window with that horrible tongue thing. I cringed. Was that really necessary? I opened up the window next to him and got a whiff of whatever he'd had for breakfast. Sweaty garbage, judging by the smell.

"What?"

"Bzzzz. Bzzz."

"I'm sorry—"

"Bzzz! BZZZ!"

"I don't... uh... I don't speak... fly." Why didn't they understand that? They were still newish; I couldn't remember them showing up before about six months ago. I wondered what had spawned them—pretty sure no one was keen to take the credit on that one. Safe bet it was a brainiac or mad scientist fiddling with something or other. Still, you'd think the human flies would have figured out that no one understood buzzing, no matter how slow or loud it got.

I could almost see him sigh. He was in a shirt and tie, wearing a pair of slacks with one leg torn off at the thigh to reveal a skinny greenish insect leg covered in stiff hairs, all topped off with a lab coat. Of course he was wearing a lab coat. He was probably with JPL or some other outfit. All the human flies seemed to be.

"Bzzz."

"Yeah."

Wings like cellophane unfolded from his shoulders and he jumped off the window into the sky over Flower Street, nearly slamming into a witch speeding along on her broom. She almost lost her cat, catching the little black-and-white fella by the scruff of its neck and shouting something decidedly unladylike.

Just another traffic snarl in the former City of Angels.

It was the tail end of a lousy summer day, with the desert sun baking us like cookies. I had already sweated through my undershirt and was getting some nice rings under my armpits, and this stupid bowtie was starting to feel like a piece of spaghetti wrapped around my neck. The rickety little fan on the top of the filing cabinet wasn't doing much more than floating the ribbons threaded through its tines. Even that was taking more effort than it should've; the ribbons moved sluggishly through the soupy air. It would have been nice to chalk the whole shebang up to hell finally coming to earth, but the fact of the matter was, this was typical of summer in Los Angeles. Just another windless day spent cowering under the punishing heat, and wishing every public swimming pool in town wasn't monsters-only.

I leaned the insect sprayer against the leg of the desk and collapsed into my chair. There *was* a desk under there somewhere. Under the files and papers, and that little corner of the actual blotter. I don't even know why I had a blotter; either my secretary bought it under the sweetly misguided sense I'd use it, or else the thing came with the office. Two filing cabinets were shoved against one wall, vomiting up paper; my private investigator's license hung, framed, on the other. Across from me sat two more chairs for clients. The office was so cramped that anyone in them would have to scoot forward if the door opened.

I saw my secretary's shadow on the frosted glass, eclipsing my name, a second before she poked her head in. "Mr. Moss? You have a client." Last names when there were clients. We had to look professional.

I peered at my watch before remembering it no longer told time. "It's a little late, isn't it?" I jerked a finger at the sun setting over my shoulder and hoped I wasn't gesturing at another human fly crawling on the window.

She squinted past me, her eyes enormous behind her goggles—which wasn't too unexpected, since they contained seawater. Something about her eyes; she couldn't see properly in air. One time she had come in to work with a tiny fish swimming around in there and was horribly embarrassed when I pointed it out. Didn't stop her from eating it, though. "We're still open."

I sighed again. "Send him in, Miss Sargasso."

"Her," she corrected.

"Well, then, kick her the hell out."

"What?" Her eyebrows, which were little blackish green fins, shot up.

"I'm joking, Miss Sargasso. Send her in."

My secretary, Miss Serendipity Sargasso, gave me a nervous smile. On her, that was a little terrifying, since her mouth was stuffed with razor-sharp teeth—rows upon rows of the bastards, too. As long as she kept that thing shut, she was just your standard blue woman with pretty yellow stripes, and webbed hands and presumably feet to match. Open it, though, and she could give you some serious second thoughts about nearly anything. Nice quality in a secretary; pretty on the outside, yet intimidating when you needed the extra security.

She poked her head out into the reception area and I heard her slightly muffled voice say, "Mr. Moss will see you now."

The woman who came through the door was clearly not the kind that heard "no" very often. She was almost six feet of imposing ice queen, platinum blonde hair in a series of immaculate rolls, and an outfit that didn't just say money, it screamed it loudly, repeatedly, and directly into my face.

I'd seen this movie before. Femme fatale saunters into a private dick's office on gams taller than he is, offers a job, and pretty soon the dick is in dutch up to his eyeballs. As a matter of fact, not only had I seen the movie, but it starred the woman presently looking at me like I was a talking badger. It's why she wore that face around town; it was the one that made her famous.

I popped up out of my chair, scampered around the side of the desk, and banged my knee.

"Ow! Son of a—hi, I'm Nick Moss."

She looked down at me imperiously. "Imogen Verity."

I knew that already, but it was still kind of impressive to hear spoken out loud by the star herself.

"Miss Ver—is it Mrs.? I feel like it should be... I'm Nick Moss."

"You already said that."

"Did I? Oh, well, sit down," I gestured at one of the chairs and quickly cleared it off, sticking the files on top of the cabinet in front of the fan. Not like it was doing that much for anyone. I ran back around my desk and hit my other knee. They'd have matching bruises now, so that was something. I successfully bit off the yelp of pain.

"How can I help you?"

"You're a private investigator." Her voice was smooth and powerful, like good scotch with a gasoline chaser.

"Yes, I know." I pointed at the license on the wall.

She didn't look. "Mind if I smoke?"

"No, no, of course not." I reached into my jacket for my lighter, but only found a rosary and a vial of quicksilver. I tried the other side, near the mirror and the gold coin with a picture of Queen Victoria on it. There it was. I flicked open the cover, caught the flame, and held it out. She had already expertly removed a slim cigarette from a silver case and was holding it to cherry lips. A single puff and she had it going.

I fished the pack of cigarettes from my jacket and shook one out. I didn't technically smoke yet. They'd given us each a carton before dumping us out over France, but I never got the hang of it. I always ended up trading the things for chocolate bars. Still, it was expected of me to smoke, being a private dick and all, so I gave it a good faith try. Took three attempts to get the damn thing to light and I had to swallow two coughing fits, but at least I looked the part, clicking the lighter shut and leaning back.

"It's a pleasure to meet you. I know your movies, of course. I, uh, I really like the one where you were, you know, a kid." I coughed loudly. "Excuse me."

She flashed her canines, delicately resting her cigarette on the ashtray. She sat straight up, shook her hair out just a bit, and then it happened. Her features ran like melting wax, her head shrinking while the liquid flesh poised like frozen waves over the bare skull. When the skull had stopped changing, the flesh came back up, layering blood vessels, muscle, and, finally, skin and even hair. The platinum blonde ice queen was gone, replaced by the little girl from *Marion.* She was sitting in Imogen Verity's expensive, and now gigantic, outfit. The cigarette ruined the image even more, especially when she plucked it from the ashtray, took a long pull, and exhaled a stream of smoke.

"That's the one," I said, trying to keep the quaver from my voice. The sight of the little girl in the chair made me suddenly self-conscious. Even though she was smoking, and in point of fact wasn't a little girl at all, I wanted to stub out my cigarette and tell her to get back to school. Or at least hide her from Constable Gisbourne, who had to be nearby.

"It's always lovely to meet a fan," she said in a little-girl voice, setting the cigarette back in the ashtray.

Her features ran again, dripping off the skull before dripping back up, and she was Sister Mary Olaf from *The Hills of St. Verence.* The iconic scar where the Nazi put out her eye was a dead giveaway. The nun took a drag on the cigarette, because it was apparently important to Imogen Verity that all beloved icons of innocence be sullied in my office.

"Oh. I had forgotten you were her, too."

She cut me off with another shift and she was the ice queen again. I managed to fumble the cigarette right out of my mouth and onto the floor, where I did my best to crush it surreptitiously. The constant shifting was pretty much guaranteed to get under my skin. Not that appearance was the most important thing, but it felt like you were talking to a different person every minute or so. Doppelgangers are tough to get used to. Make great actors, though.

"I can show you my identification if you like," she said.

"That's not... well, you know, for paperwork purposes... no, that's not necessary." I stopped, wondering what I was supposed to say to Imogen Verity, the woman who won an Oscar for playing the nun that thirty seconds ago was sitting in the chair across my desk. "Miss Verity, it's obviously an honor to meet you. You probably raised the tenor of the building by a whole... um... scale, I guess. But why are you here?"

She tapped some ash off the end of her cigarette. "I need a detective."

"So I understand, but what I'm trying to get at here is that there are other detectives in this city. Monsters, I mean. Last time I checked, I'm literally the only human detective in all of Los Angeles."

"Your humanity doesn't concern me."

"I don't quite know how to take that."

"Take it as a paying job."

"I could do that."

"I knew you were human before I arrived. My agent informed me when he recommended you."

"Recommen—who's your agent?"

"Vlad Bathory. You probably remember him better as..."

she paused, trying to summon the name from beneath studied monster contempt for their early human existences. "Richard Brower?"

"Oh, yeah. I remember Dick." His folks had hired me to find him when he had gone missing after a petting party. I found him a week later sleeping the days away in a mausoleum in Hollywood. That was a little over a year ago. Nice to hear the kid had a career to go along with the blood thirst and cross phobia. "How's he doing?"

She ignored the question in that practiced way only the very rich have mastered. "He informed me that you specialize in missing persons."

"Well, yes. But I *am* still human, and you're, uh, you're not. And it does beg the question."

"Get to the point, Mr. Moss."

"A werewolf."

"What, here?" She glanced around, more curious than scared.

"No, I mean you can afford one of the werewolf PIs. There's Baskerville, Gevaudan... I hear good things."

"I've never seen a man so intent on advertising his competition."

"Don't get me wrong, Miss Verity, I'm flattered. But you can afford a monster. Someone more... more attuned to the problems facing other monsters. Like yourself."

"I have my reasons, Mr. Moss. You are a missing persons specialist, are you not?"

I nodded. "Yes, yes I am. That's ninety percent of what I do here. But, um... the person sitting there, where you are now, is usually human. And she's usually crying. And her husband would be sitting there." I pointed to the empty chair. "They'd tell me about how Susie or Timmy or whoever went missing one night after a party that ran too late, and they'd hire me to find them. And nine times out of ten, the happy ending is that little Susie likes being a fish girl now."

"But still, you find missing persons?"

"Well, yes. They're not always still technically persons, but sure." I paused, meaning to search her baby blues, but found her far too pretty to actually look at. She was a little like the sun, and thus best appreciated in peripheral vision, so instead I began the long and arduous task of lighting another cigarette. "I take it you've misplaced someone?"

"My husband."

"And he's another doppelganger?"

"He's a mummy."

"Oh, it's a mixed marriage."

She nodded. "My husband is a city councilman. Juba II."

Never heard of him. "Sure."

She was the tiniest bit shakier now, her breath hissing slightly through her teeth. I couldn't tell if this was actual nerves or if a literal Oscar-winning actress was playing a part just for me. Those eyes were too blue, her skin too fair and smooth. She even smelled like Chanel rather than cigarette smoke. Of course, she *was* a shapeshifter. She could look and sound and even smell however she wanted. If I were a doppelganger, I'd make myself taller. And less hairy.

To cover the silence and the fact that I had already gotten lost in thought, I said, "Mrs. II—"

"Miss Verity, please. I prefer my rebirth name."

"Miss Verity, tell me what happened."

She nodded again, concentrating on the wispy thread of smoke slowly rising to the ceiling. "Last night, my husband got home after dark, which is normal. He's been working hard lately and is under a lot of stress. I had returned an hour earlier. At any rate, by the time my husband arrived home, our maid was preparing dinner. My husband went upstairs to his study, which is, again, normal. When our maid rang the bell, I came down to the dining room, but he didn't. I sent her up to find out where he was. She told me he wasn't there. We searched the house top to bottom. He was gone."

"Under a lot of stress for what reason?"

"He's looking to run for mayor soon."

I noted that down. "On the night in question, what did you do next?"

"I called the police."

"You were sure something was the matter?"

She nodded. "My husband, for all his faults, is not one to leave suddenly, especially after he has come home for the day."

"What did the police say?" I was honestly curious. You don't really get monsters going missing. Humans, sure, all the time. Call the cops, and after a little cursory sniffing around, they'll tell you that your—wife, husband, child, parent, what have you—was out after dark and what happened was totally aboveboard. With a monster... who would want to kidnap one of them? If that was even what had happened.

"They dismissed me. Called me hysterical. Until one of them found a little bit of sand on the windowsill, that is."

"Your husband was wounded?"

Her answer was a tiny sob, instantly blocked off by an immaculately gloved hand. I didn't know whether to applaud or offer a tissue. I almost did both.

"Was there a trail?"

"Not that they found."

I thought it over. "Miss Verity, if this is a homicide or a kidnapping and you already called the LAPD, there's really not much left for me to do. I mean, I can make a citizen's arrest, but I can't interfere with their investigation in any way."

"No, Mr. Moss, you don't understand. They think *I* did it."

"Did you?"

"No!"

"I have to ask, you know, for legal..." I took a drag on the cigarette to cover and ended up coughing.

"That is precisely why I have to hire you, and only you, Mr. Moss. My husband has connections to law enforcement, given his job. It could be... complicated. Now, with the police suspecting me, I need someone with no links to them at all. And I need someone who will keep this quiet."

"Then I'm your man. So, what do you think happened to him?"

"I don't know," she said. "He might have run off and accidentally cut himself on a nail. I really don't know. That's why I wanted to hire a professional."

"Why would he do that? Run off, I mean."

"My husband is having an affair."

"That... um... that speaks to motive."

She glared at me through the gray web of smoke. "I had nothing to do with my husband's disappearance, Mr. Moss. If I had, would I be here?"

"Well, yes, actually. I'm human, sort of the perfect patsy, when you think about it, and... you know what, never mind, I shouldn't be giving you..." I cleared my throat. "Please, go on."

She gave me another dubious look. "I bear no ill will towards my husband, Mr. Moss. Our marriage is really more out of convenience for both of us. He gets a glamorous movie star for his arm. I get respectability and an aura of fidelity. He was considerate enough to keep his affair discreet, and so there was no problem. But him running off with whoever she is, that *is* a problem. And if he was, in fact, kidnapped or hurt in some way..." She trailed off, finding some comfort in her rapidly shrinking cigarette.

"I... uh... I see. Do you know who with?"

"Aria Enchantee. A phantom, as you probably could have guessed. She works at Visionary Pictures much of the time, composing movie scores."

"That's your place of employment too, correct?"

"Yes." Visionary was as big a studio as Pyramid or RKO.

"You've caught them together?"

"Oh, heavens no. I said he was discreet."

I waited for her to elaborate. When she kept smoking and staring at the ceiling, I had to prompt her. "Why do you suspect Miss Enchantee?"

"He spends entirely too much time at the studio. Visiting when he doesn't have to."

"Maybe he wants to see his wife?"

She let out a brittle laugh.

"All right. But this is a movie studio we're talking about. There have to be more people there than just Miss Enchantee."

"True. Though she is the one I see him talking to more than anyone else."

"Your husband is a politician. Could be he's just shoring up a vote? How can you be so certain it's an affair?"

She reached into her handbag. There was no awkward rummaging, just a single, graceful movement. She removed something and put it on the pile of papers in front of me. I picked it up. It was a matchbook, glossy black with a silver snake coiled up as some kind of logo. Opening it, I found several matches were missing.

"I take it your husband doesn't smoke."

"He's a mummy, Mr. Moss."

"Oh, right. I guess that would be a little like a gremlin

taking up sunbathing."

She paused, and I couldn't tell if she was sore with me or not.

I coughed. "Go on."

"That isn't the only one I've found. Every now and then, one will be in his pocket. The maid found the first one and after that, I asked her to keep her eyes peeled."

"Do you know what this logo means?"

"I was hoping you might know. I assume it's for some sort of club or hotel. Where they would meet."

I turned it over in my hand. "I'd agree with your assumption, but I can't say for certain. I'm not a member of any... that is, my kind is not the most welcome..."

"I understand, Mr. Moss."

"Well, if he has, in fact, run off with his paramour, he'd take something with him. Clothes, sundries, money. Was anything missing from your house?"

"There was a packed suitcase."

"Missing?"

"No. It was still in the room."

"So he packed a suitcase and left without it?"

"Apparently."

"That's odd, isn't it?"

"I thought so, but I'm not the detective here."

I sighed. "Have you checked your accounts?"

"There is nothing missing."

"You're certain of that?"

She nodded again.

"Well, he definitely wouldn't have left without the other woman. Has Miss Enchantee disappeared?"

"I don't know. When she's not at Visionary, she's usually downtown at the Ophelia."

The Ophelia was a new opera house. Very big, very grand, and very much outside of my price and interest range.

"Was there a note?"

She shook her head.

"Did you receive any telephone calls? Even if it was just heavy breathing or a hang-up?"

"No, nothing like that."

I stared into space, trying to put the pieces together into something that vaguely resembled anything, really. Kidnapping, disappearance, murder. Nothing. A packed bag, but it stayed behind. A little blood—well, sand—but no one heard anything downstairs. And no calls for ransom.

Sounded like City Councilman Juba II had vanished into thin air. Of course, I wasn't about to tell her that. She needed hope, and I needed money.

"I can look into it if you like. I charge te—fifteen dollars a day, plus expenses."

"That is more than fair. How do you usually begin these investigations?"

"I try to reconstruct the missing person's day, starting from where they disappeared and working backwards."

"So you'll want to see our home, then?"

"Yes, Miss Verity. I'll need to poke around there. And then I'd like to talk to Miss Enchantee."

"Very well, we can leave now."

I nodded to the setting sun behind me. "No, Miss Verity, we can't. I'll see you tomorrow, first thing."

She looked disappointed.

"That's the problem with hiring a human dick, ma'am."

There was a long silence while we stared at each other.

Finally, I said quietly, "It's just a figure of speech."

Imogen Verity

TWO

My new client left as elegantly as she arrived, and as soon as she was out out the door, I grabbed my stuff. A quick goodbye to Miss Sargasso later, I was down the stairs and on the street. Thankfully, I owned a car, an old Ford coupe that ran better than I had a right to expect. Traffic was always bad near dusk, as the city's human residents hurried home and the monsters came out for a night of hunting. Streetcars were stuffed with people, wires buzzing with every bump.

I drove into Watts, a little suburban neighborhood south of Downtown. Small houses, but cheap and in reasonably good repair. Plus, they still sold to humans here.

My street was quiet, a relatively wide avenue bordered by these little one-story numbers. Palm trees, of course, because it was Los Angeles. Mostly families on my street, with a couple of bachelors, plus Miss O'Herlihy, our neighborhood spinster. The men worked on assembly lines, or on streetcars, or as garbage men, or as janitors. The women, if they worked at all, were waitresses, with the occasional telephone operator and nurse for the human-only hospital in Boyle Heights thrown in. They thought I had the most glamorous job in the neighborhood, since they didn't know the actual specifics of the thing.

I pulled in right as the sky was turning from gold to red. Magic hour, they used to call it. Now it was the last minute you could get anything done. Across the street, Mr. Schroeder glanced up at the sky, stopped watering his rose bushes about halfway down the row and turned off the hose, not even bothering to coil it up. Mrs. Hammond called her boys in from riding bikes. All up and down the street, doors slammed. Locks thumped. Shutters closed. Charms swayed on their hooks. Clumps of herbs were placed on windowsills.

Just another night in the City of Devils.

I pulled into my driveway, waving to Will Hammond as he hung the crosses on his doors. He threw me a salute. Inside joke. While I was jumping out of a C-47 with the rest of the 101st, Will was driving a truck, since back then they wouldn't let Negroes hold guns. Of course, that stopped mattering once the fella next to you on the streetcar could turn into a bat. Or, more accurately, it stopped mattering to those of us who couldn't.

"Cutting it a little close, Nick?"

"Late client. My regards to the wife."

"This weekend, we're still fixing up Mrs. Mendoza's roof?"

"I'll bring the suds." Since her husband turned, Irene Mendoza didn't have anyone to help out with that kind of thing. And she had a blob that had been dissolving the shingles on the southeast corner of her house for about a month.

A quick once-over on the house said everything was more or less in place. Rose bushes flowering nicely under the windows. Crosses and mirrors at regular intervals. Wolfsbane at the corners, along with bundles of feathers. I lit the torches hanging from the little sconces on my porch. Then I got the allward from the spice rack in the kitchen and touched up the ring around the house. It smelled weird. Hardly surprising, considering all the stuff that went into the rusty brown powder.

Going back inside, I replaced the allward on the rack. Time was, something like that would've held actual spices. Now there was powdered silver, garlic, dried blood, salt—well, all right, salt might have been there before. But probably not to scare away zombies.

The sun was still going down when the first of the cars squealed to a stop down the street. A man in a suit got out. Normal, until you saw the angry line of stitches across his head and the greenish tinge to his skin. He leaned against his car, staring at Don and Camille Webber's place. Headlights at the top of the street said more were coming. And there were shapes wheeling overhead in the deepening gloom.

Time to close up shop.

I shut the door. Locked it twice. Windows, too, and the back door. It was illegal for them to come in without an invitation, but better safe than sorry, right? The house was a fortress now. All that remained was to wait out another night. I leaned against the barricaded door and sighed. From the couch, the cat took one look at me and yowled.

"Same to you, buddy."

It wandered into the other room, twitching its tail contemptuously.

I went into my small kitchen and made dinner, such as it was. A bologna sandwich with a little bit of potato salad on the side from the block party last Saturday, with a bottle of cheap beer. I sat at the cheap Formica table in my kitchen, listening to the nightly choir start up. Beer and bologna. This is what happens when you don't get married when you had the chance.

The scratching on the window over the sink didn't come until near the last bite. Bald head, big eyes, mouth full of sharp buckteeth. He was burping out little screeches. Batboy. Although I think they preferred the term "nosferatu." Who cares? I didn't much like getting called "meatstick," but it didn't stop every cop in the city from flinging it in my direction. And besides, I wasn't going to call the batboy anything, since there was no way he was going to get in. I put the dishes in the sink, showed him my middle finger, and got another beer out of the fridge on my way to the living room.

"Nick! Nick, you in there?"

Of course I was. This was getting really annoying.

I headed for the front door and peered out through the little porthole window, already knowing what I would find.

All along my street, monsters surrounded houses, slunk over rooftops, prowled through shadows. Looking for a way in, a way to entice the people inside to come out. Every monster shied from the things put out to baffle them. Zombies recoiled from the lines of salt, meat golems held their hands up to shield their faces from firey torches, vampires hissed at the crosses, witches hid from evil eye charms, werewolves bayed at sprigs of wolfsbane. There was even a crawling eye slithering over Miss O'Herlihy's roof. Didn't see those too often, since they were mostly uptown kinds of monsters. It hit something, and the bunch of tentacles coming out of the back swirled away as it glowered at whatever it was. Probably a sand trap. Good for you, Miss O'Herlihy.

This was what you got from that Fair Game Law. I mean, sure, people could walk down the street all nice and safe in daylight, but nighttime was a goddamn free-for-all. Plus, security was expensive, and this was all out of pocket. Not like monsters were going to vote for tax subsidies to protect the people they wanted to turn.

"Nick! Hey, Nick!"

The thing calling me was a pumpkinhead. About seven feet tall and dressed in a rather nice business suit, complete with a jaunty pocket square. What skin was showing was green and gnarled like a vine, with little thorns dotting the surface. His head was an actual grinning jack-o-lantern, complete with flames lighting the triangles of his eyes and nose, and the jagged line of his mouth. Of course, this was the nice form. His name was Sam Haine. "Nick! It's me."

"Sam."

"How are you doing?" He sounded almost nervous.

"Can't complain." I took a pull on the beer.

A headless horseman thundered down the street and jumped over Will Hammond's Packard, the hooves of his spectral charger kicking up sparks on the car's roof. Poor Will. That's a new paint job right there.

"Why don't you take down that line of chicken blood?"

The line was flaking, but it still ringed the house. I was going to have to replace it before the week was out, assuming it didn't rain. Never knew how folks managed it in Florida.

"I don't see myself doing that."

"Clean it up, I come in, I have a beer." He smelled like Halloween, even through the door.

"What was I, born yesterday? You don't want a beer. You want to turn me."

"Being a pumpkinhead is great."

"Your *head* is a *pumpkin!*"

He touched the orange rind of his face self-consciously. "It doesn't feel any different. Other than the wind inside your head."

"Wind inside your... I'm not letting you in, Sam."

"Have a heart, Nick."

"Have a non-windy head, Sam!"

At that moment, the batboy loped to the front of the house, probably hoping I hadn't put the guano out there. He screeched loudly and leapt for the door, but never really got the chance to land. Sam reached out, his body growing three times its size, skin turning green-brown, a massive viney tail exploding from his pants like the worst incontinence in history, and grabbed the batboy, slamming him down onto my lawn. The thorns on his arms were now the size of kitchen knives. "Find your own," he growled, the flames licking out from his jagged pumpkin grin. The stench of burned pumpkin wafted off of him, like Thanksgiving gone horribly wrong. The nosferatu screeched and nodded, scampering off as soon as Sam let him up.

Sam changed back to his less-threatening form, inspecting the parts of his suit the change had shredded. "You see what I do for you?"

"Pull the other one. It's got bells on." I paused, looking out at the chaos on Juniper Street. "What do you want, Sam?"

He followed my gaze to where a killer robot sparked and smoked on the Morenos' lawn, having tripped Hernando's elaborate electrical trap. Sam turned back and tried to smile, but he was trying it with no lips and a mouth full of sharp pumpkin teeth. Ruined the effect. "You. To be a pumpkinhead."

"Not going to happen."

"Nick," he said, "I know two things: vengeance and my specialty line of jams and jellies. And I think you would be an asset to both pursuits."

"Jams and... I don't cook, Sam. I had a bologna sandwich tonight. And some potato salad that I'm pretty sure went bad yesterday." I held my belly and let out a fragrant belch.

"Yeah, but the vengeance! Look, someone comes by my pumpkin patch..."

"Which is where, exactly?"

"San Berdoo."

"So you, what, commute every night?"

"I'm not here every—it doesn't matter." He took a deep breath, making the candleflame in his mouth flicker. Behind him on Mr. Yamamoto's lawn, a brainiac was doing doughnuts in his weird little cart. The brain bounced around in its bubbling green liquid while the arc guns threw sparks over the grass. We'd have to reseed that. "Someone who has been wronged comes to my pumpkin patch and invokes me, and I go—" Sam embellished with a couple gestures, "—extract vengeance. Pound of flesh, eye for an eye, that kind of thing. I'm bulletproof. I can lift a car. Don't you think that would make your job easier?"

"I'm not the car-lifting type."

"You know what I mean."

"Go home, Sam." I walked away from the door.

Sam called after me, "See you tomorrow."

"See you tomorrow, Sam."

I hauled myself to bed, drew the shades in the face of a gremlin with enormous white muttonchops, and got some sleep.

I had work to do in the morning.

THREE

I was up about a half-hour before dawn. When you only have twelve hours outdoors, you generally want to use every little bit of them. At least it was summer. In the winter, the short days were killers: human-run businesses shut their doors at four.

I peeked between the living room curtains. There were still a few monsters lingering on Juniper Street, trying to find a way in to someone's house. You'd think they'd use teamwork, but near as I could tell, that was some kind of taboo. I mean, if a vampire could just wipe away your line of salt while his buddy the zombie removed the crosses, you'd be like a debutante five minutes after her debut: open for business. So that was a little luck.

I shut the curtains and went back into the bathroom for a shower and a shave, for all the good the last would do me. I kept a short mustache, but by the end of the day, it had practically spawned a beard, no matter what I did. My hair grew like kudzu. And it's not like it was especially good hair. There was a lot of it, but it was a pretty nondescript brown. I wasn't what you called much of a looker. Thanks to the features and the lack of height, most people described me as looking like a weasel.

Almost as good a recommendation as the PI license on my office wall, in this business.

I pulled on a rumpled suit and a hat, then gathered my usual tools from the footlocker in my closet. The revolver loaded with silver bullets and the cold iron dagger went into shoulder holsters on the left and right. The wooden stake and the lighter went into special pockets on the inside of the jacket. The vials of salt, sand, and about twenty other powders, grains, and herbs each got their own tiny pocket, almost like a bandolier sewn into my jacket's lining. All told, it was an extra twenty pounds spread over me, but you could never be too careful. When I walked, I made little clinking noises.

Ready to face the day, I stood at my closed door, looking out the little window near the top, waiting to see the shadow of the weathervane in the middle of the street. Soon as the antler-like shadow appeared on the gray asphalt, I was out the door, turning around to see the sun winking at me from over my house. Daytime. Safe for another twelve hours.

A single zombie shambled past me toward his car, trailing his grave stench.

"Better luck next time," I said to him.

He turned, shot me the finger, and moaned, "Brains."

I got behind the wheel of my car and drove north, back through Downtown and toward the address Imogen Verity had given me on an immaculate white calling card. It was on Carroll Avenue, a street in the middle of Angeleno Heights, less than a mile from Echo Park. The route took me past Pharaoh Field on the corner of 42nd and Avalon. Before the Night War it had been Wrigley Field, and had even housed refugees during the darkest years. After the war, Pharaoh Bandages bought the place, slapped up some billboards over the outfield ("Pharaoh Bandages! Look Like a Pharaoh Every Time!"), and had the Hollywood Stars join the Monster Leagues. The Human League team—the LA Angels—played on a reclaimed field over in Lincoln Heights. Even if they could have afforded lights, they still wouldn't have played a single night game. The Angels were mostly picked-over talent, high school kids, and part-timers. Turk Lown had an arm on him, though, and I had tickets to see him pitch against the Caballeros a week from Saturday.

Normally, a big star like Imogen Verity would be in Hollywood somewhere, and for a minute I wondered what she was doing so far from actor territory. But Carroll Avenue was in a ritzy enclave close to her husband's office Downtown, and matched Imogen Verity rather perfectly.

I rolled up on the wide street under the morning sun, already a little hotter than was comfortable, and pulled to a stop in front of a huge Victorian. The whole avenue was lined with them, all rich and gorgeous, with smaller guest houses peeking from behind them. I got out next to an antique hitching post with a swan head and took Verity's place in. All blues and oranges, it had large windows, numerous eaves, and even a third floor. It looked like a haunted gingerbread house.

The neighborhood was deserted in the early morning light. The only person out was a meat golem walking his stitched-together wolfhounds. He sneered at my beat-up Ford with the kind of disdain meat golems usually reserved for angry mobs.

I made my way up the cement steps, rising between big rose bushes that leeched what they could from the cracked earth, and grinned. Guess the IIs didn't entertain many ghouls. The porch was wide, with a few wicker chairs in which to while away the hot summer days. I knocked on the heavy wooden door. Inside, as glimpsed through the little glass windows on the door, the house was dark, probably darker than it really had to be. Actresses. Always so dramatic.

The door seemed to open of its own accord. I focused on the blank space beyond, and sure enough, a translucent woman faded into view from nothing. Well, everything above her waist faded in, anyway; her skirt hid whatever legs she might have had. The maid's uniform seemed a little much. What looked like black blood was pouring in a thick stream out of her mouth when she opened it. Her head lolled to the side, and her haunted eyes focused on me. She raised a hand with cracked nails and pointed at me, leering.

"Hi, I'm Nick Moss? I'm here to see Miss Ver—could you please stop that?"

The ghost spoke, but because she was a ghost, her mouth moved, and then about three seconds later, her voice came to me as a series of whispers. "Miss Verity asked me to show you to the... *sitting room.*" She hissed the last two words with an air of spectral dread.

"Was someone killed in there? Because the way you said it... is sitting somehow ominous here?"

"Please, Mr. Moss... *come with me.*"

"All right."

She led me through the house. There were pictures on every wall, but none seemed more than ten years old. Normal for a monster household, I supposed. Imogen was in a great deal of them, looking as regal and imperious as she had in my office. There was a mummy in several, who I assumed to be the husband. Wrapped in bandages, usually under a nice expensive suit, he posed with studio heads, businessmen, police. One large picture featured a crawling eye, a gremlin, a phantom, and a werewolf, all dressed well except for the werewolf, who was a proper werewolf rather than merely a wolfman. They always looked strange when someone tried to put them in sweaters. The phantom was a woman, and I took a guess she was Aria Enchantee. The others were probably the cream of the crop in monster circles. My client hadn't been kidding; Imogen Verity's husband was a man with important friends.

"The New American Benevolent Society. They're... *philanthropists.*"

I shuddered. The maid led me to a nice room with large windows overlooking the street, outfitted with lots of very plush furniture. Light streamed in, making this one of the more pleasant haunted houses I'd ever visited.

"May I get you something... *to drink?*" she asked, right as the walls started bleeding.

"No, I'm fine." I settled into a nice armchair and took the notebook from my pocket, but I had to move an evil eye charm and a woman's compact to get at it. "What's your name?"

"Bloody Bridget. I'm... *the housekeeper.*"

"I think you got the scary-emphasis part backwards. So, pay well, does it?"

A lamp started to float around the room. "I like the... *job security.*"

"Right. Stop it. It's daylight."

"Fear has... *no schedule.*"

"That doesn't even make se—look, you can't do anything to me, and even if you did," and here I reached into my coat, found the bottle of holy water, and gave it a little shake in front of her bloodshot eyes, "You know what this is?"

The lamp dropped, nearly hit the floor, but swept upwards at the last second and alighted on the table next to me. The walls stopped any fresh bleeding.

"I'm sorry, Mr. Moss, it's just..."

"You eat fear and you thought I was the buffet... *at the Sahara.*"

Bloody Bridget nodded, her ghostly green-gray form slowly bobbing up and down. She looked at me speculatively, starting to consider me as a person instead of a snack.

"I'm here to look into your employer's disappearance."

"I don't know much," she said, sitting opposite me on a sofa. Or, more accurately, floating above the sofa at an approximately sitting height and position. The wooden scalloping of the couch's backrest was clearly visible through her head and made eye contact dizzying.

"Tell me the story."

"Miss Verity came home first and went upstairs to bathe. I started preparing dinner. Mr. II came home around seven, I think. Dinner was a little late, because while I was thawing the roast, I kept accidentally making cold spots."

"Why?"

"I was listening to *Buford and the Zombie,* and it was making me upset."

"Is that a show?"

"On the radio. It's about a golem and his best friend, who's a zombie. And Cheryl, his sister, is going to run off with..."

"Let me stop you right there. Okay, so Mr. II came home around seven."

Bloody Bridget sniffed, some ectoplasm running down her fishbelly face. I wasn't sure if she was annoyed at me cutting her off, or if this was distress over her missing employer. "He went upstairs to read in his study. At around seven-thirty, I took the roast out of the oven and rang the bell. Miss Verity came in, but Mr. II didn't."

"Where was Miss Verity?"

"She was in here, reading a screenplay."

"The whole time?"

"She went upstairs once, after Mr. II got home."

"When was this?"

Bloody Bridget shrugged; several lamps and knickknacks in the room levitated a fraction of an inch and came down with a wobbling clatter. "Sorry."

"It's fine." At least the walls had stopped bleeding. Would they scab? Seemed like that would be making work for herself, but I wasn't about to judge.

"Miss Verity went upstairs maybe twenty minutes after Mr. II came home and came back down shortly thereafter."

"And with no commotion to indicate that Mr. II was missing."

"No. She went right back to where you're sitting and read her screenplay."

I glanced at the end table next to me. On a lower shelf sat some loose pages, tucked inside a blue cover. The title blared, *Love is a Many-Splendored Thing From Another World*. So that story checked out.

"And what happened next? After you rang the bell?"

"Miss Verity came into the dining room, but Mr. II never did. So she asked me to go fetch him, and when I did, he was nowhere to be found. I called for Miss Verity and she phoned the police."

"And then...?"

Bloody Bridget opened her mouth so wide it looked like she was gearing up for another moan. At that moment, the front door opened. The dainty clack of heels on hardwood echoed through the cavernous house. Bridget stood up, or really started floating in more of a standing position, and smoothed out her maid uniform. I followed her lead and stood up as Imogen Verity walked into the room. She wore a large floppy hat and sunglasses to protect her from the Los Angeles sun, and adopted the perfect pose of pleasant surprise when she saw me. The hat and sunglasses came off and dropped, with Bridget stopping the fall before they hit the ground and floating them to their proper places.

"Mr. Moss," Imogen said, holding out a gloved hand.

I took it. "Miss Verity."

"Bridget, if you will put a pot of coffee on for Mr. Moss?"

"Yes, Miss Verity."

"That's okay, I don't... uh... that's... blonde and sweet, I guess," I said.

"Right away... *Miss Verity.*"

"Did you hear that? Can you get her to cut that out?"

"Oh, of course, Mr. Moss. Ghost housekeepers can be wonderful, but there are certain problems that you don't encounter with, say, a human. But Bridget can stay after dark. Not that we'd do anything to a human housekeeper, but they never seem to believe us. We're not interested in having children."

"Can you blame... um... I'm sure you and your husband are lovely people."

"Was Bridget helpful?"

"Very much so. Does she live here?"

Imogen Verity nodded. "We need live-in help. Another reason a ghost was the best choice."

"Why do you need live-in help?"

"The demands of my career do not give me time enough to run a household in an acceptable manner. Bridget has been a lifesaver." She realized what she'd said, and hastily added, "In that regard."

"And where does she live?"

"We had her mortal remains interred in one of the retaining

walls. Best way to maintain a proper haunting."

"Mmm. If it's all the same to you, I'd like to see the study?"

"Follow me."

I went back out into the hall and into the bandage-wrapped gaze of Councilman Juba II and all of his friends. It was a little intimidating. I felt underdressed. Thankfully, she took me up the wooden staircase and out of their judgmental view. The second story was somehow even more plush and classy than the downstairs. This wasn't just a Victorian home, this was straight from Victorian times. The wallpaper was better than most dresses I'd seen. The pictures were so classy I didn't even want to look at them. I felt like I would... maybe just a peek, right? No harm done.

One was a self-consciously old picture of two mummies, aged and staged to look antique when odds are it was taken within the last ten years. It's very hard to tell mummies apart, being primarily defined as people wrapped in old bandages. The color of the glow of their eyes helps, but not in a photograph. One was standing, and wearing a very gaudy headdress that had to be gold, an equally gaudy necklace, and some kind of skirt. He looked like a pharaoh burn victim. His hand was on the shoulder of the second mummy, this one in an expensive suit, arm resting outstretched on a table, which was decorated with a single lotus in an elegant vase. Chances are that was Juba II with his creator, probably Juba I. When mummies chose their rebirth names, they were suckers for that dynastic nonsense.

It took me a minute, but I found the matching shot, this one with two genderless entities. They were tall and slender, with blank stretches of skin where their faces should be. They stood next to one another, arm in arm, both dressed in what looked like christening gowns. "Is this you?" I asked Miss Verity, pointing to one.

"No. I am the other one."

"Oh, right. Of course. Don't know what I was thinking."

She opened a door at the end of the hall. "In here, Mr. Moss."

I nodded and went in. Bay windows looked out over Carroll Avenue. It was pretty obvious my battered Ford didn't fit on the street, like a mustache drawn on the Mona Lisa. Turning back from the window, I took in the rest of the room. The other walls were bookcases, with a very comfortable-looking chair sitting in the angle of the cases with an end table next to it. A desk stood by another wall. Unlike my desk, this one was immaculately clean. "Which window had the sand?"

Miss Verity pointed to the leftmost window in the bay arrangement. I went to it, looked out, and wondered. It would have been quite a fall, but as long as nothing was on fire, Juba could have made it just fine. He would have landed in the rose bushes, but what are thorns to a cursed pharaoh? "And there was no more sand out in the yard?"

"None that the police could find."

"Well, we can rule out spontaneous combustion, I suppose."

"Was that supposed to be funny?"

"Ye... um... no, of course not. I was just... is this a mummy neighborhood?"

She caught up to my train of thought. "Yes, mostly. There are also a few doppelgangers, meat golems, a vampire or two, and a few other varieties of monster."

"Block parties must be fun, huh?"

"Is there anything else you'd like to see?"

"Right. Uh... the suitcase?"

"Come with me."

She led me into her bedroom. It was probably the fantasy of more than a few humans and monsters to be in the boudoir of Imogen Verity. She was the face of how many sex symbols?

From the bathing beauty in *My Last Summer*, to that bit part in *All About Eve*, to her current starring roles, she was known for becoming every man's dream. Partially by looking like every dream, though there was an undercurrent to her roles, a strange worldly innocence that charmed seemingly everyone.

I was far too nervous being alone with a monster to be charmed at the moment.

As though to drive the point home, one of the walls of Miss Verity's boudoir was decorated with detailed porcelain masks, each one a perfect replica of one of her characters. They looked like death masks, only they all belonged to the same person.

"Mr. Moss... *your coffee*," a voice hissed behind me.

"Yaaah!" I jumped, turning around to find Bloody Bridget holding out a steaming cup while bleeding out of her eyes.

"Thank y... was that necessary?" I took the mug out of her hand and nodded a simultaneous thanks and dismissal.

The ghost smirked at me and faded through the floor.

"She's a charming woman," I said to Miss Verity.

She made a noncommittal noise and gestured to a suitcase on an ottoman. "There it is."

I set the cup aside, and she immediately hissed.

"Oh, sorry, is there a coaster or something?" Just my luck. I hadn't even wanted the coffee and yet here it was. Too hot for it anyway, even in a house as drafty as this one. I picked it back up and awkwardly opened the suitcase with one hand. Neatly folded shirts, some shorts, slacks, socks, sock garters. So he took clothes. No, he *packed* clothes. There was a difference between throwing stuff in the case and stacking it neatly as he had done. Several boxes of fresh Pharaoh-brand bandages nestled amongst the clothes. Mummy, right. Probably like underwear to them.

There looked to be several things missing. I sifted through

the contents a few more times before I was satisfied they weren't hiding under anything else. "Where are your husband's canopic jars?"

"In the basement."

"He wouldn't travel without those. He also forgot to pack a toothbrush." To be polite, I took a sip of coffee. It was really good. Maybe I wanted it after all. I frowned, considering. "Mummies have teeth, right?"

"My husband does."

"Does he, um..." I mimed the act of brushing.

She nodded.

It didn't help me, but at least my curiosity was satisfied. "Could I see the jars?"

"Right this way." As we descended the stairs, she said, "Do you think this has something to do with his canopic jars?"

"I have no idea what this has to do with anything yet. I still don't know if I'm looking for a living... uh... undead... active? Active. Man."

She led me to a door in the base of the stairs and opened it, releasing a wave of musty basement scent. "We're lucky to have a basement," she said. "Only this side of the street has them. Something about the natural topography."

"Topography?"

"The hill is higher on this side than the other. We have basements, and a higher vantage of the city."

"How nice for you."

"Does that have something to do with this?"

"Uh, no. I was just making conversation."

I was led into the basement by Oscar winner Imogen Verity, about to view the five clay jars that held her husband's powdered organs, all while trying not to think of how bizarre this was. She pulled a string and the light came on. I was slightly disappointed to see how normal everything was. Neat, too, everything on little shelves, just so. She gestured to a shelf in the back where five small clay jars sat, each with the head of something different: a dog, a crocodile, a hawk, a cat, and a man. Hieroglyphics covered the sides, and I couldn't help but wonder how authentic the writing was. Probably said things like "Today's Special" in Egyptian. Still, they were made of proper clay and probably lined in gold.

"There they are," she said.

I ran a hand over them, distractedly setting my cup on a shelf, less interested in the jars themselves than in the rest of the room. Something was bothering me about this basement, but I couldn't quite put my finger on it. I glanced up at the ceiling, then at the walls. The right wall would be butting up against the foundation of the house, but the left...

More shelves lined that wall. The things on them were not quite as neat as those on the other side. I knelt at the base. Scrapes marred the floor along one side. I went to the wall, reaching behind the shelf. There were no spiders. Even a place as clean as this should have a cobweb or two behind a shelf in the basement. I ran my hand along it. Tapped it. Oh, there we go.

"Mr. Moss? Is something wrong?"

I poked around the shelves, picking up the jars of nails and screws one by one until one didn't come up. I pulled it toward me.

The secret door swung open. Miss Verity gasped.

I went to the door and poked my head in. "Found your husband," I said, pointing to the mummy lying in the open sarcophagus inside. Then I frowned. "Wait. Was he always that busty?"

FOUR

I took a step into the room. It was pretty small, barely seven feet on a side, with the sarcophagus awkwardly crammed in there at a slight angle. The scrapes I had seen on the way in were still pretty fresh, suggesting sarcophagus storage wasn't the room's usual purpose. Imogen Verity came up behind me.

"I take it you didn't know this was here?"

"No," she said.

Other than the sarcophagus and the mummy, there was a single chair, and it was not up to the standards of the rest of the house, though its shabbiness fit in well with the ersatz squalor of this little room. The chair was still upholstered, but not with the two inches of thick stuffing the ones upstairs got. The finish on the wood was chipped and scratched. Scattered around the room were little pieces of parchment with black spidery lettering on them. I picked one up and had a look. The words were partially gone, a few arcs scattered over the scrap. The rest of the parchments told the same story. One I'd read before.

"What are those?"

"Hexes," I said. "I think your husband is an addict." I realized what I'd blurted and tried to cover. "Which is totally understandable. I mean, a city councilman, married to an actress—a movie star, really, and—oh no. Don't cry."

And she was. Prettily, too. Little artful tears, some sniffles, but no snot or drooling. She cried exactly the way the Venus di Milo might if you asked her to clap. I handed her a handkerchief before I realized it had the evil eye sewn into it. "Sorry. Um."

"No, no. It's all right. It's just..." and she fell into some more of her photogenic crying, even turning away for some possibly false modesty. With no real way to comfort her, I went back into the room and knelt by the sarcophagus. Something drew my attention from the corner of my eye: a single sheet of paper crammed up under the chair. I pulled it out. The hex was complete. Hadn't been used. Miss Verity was still turned away, either in the grips of grief or acting, her graceful shoulders shuddering. I pocketed the unused hex as well as a few of the used ones and turned my attention to the sarcophagus.

The mummy's canopic jars were in a compartment on the side. Cheaply made, the kind they sell to tourists in Little Cairo. I hefted one. Aluminum. I put it back and kept rummaging. From the back of the compartment, I pulled out a skirt, a blouse, some shoes, and a purse. That held her wallet and identification. Evelyn Farrell, a resident of Kansas City, Missouri.

"Miss Verity?"

She sniffed. "Yes?"

"Does the name Evelyn Farrell mean anything to you?"

"Is that... is that who this is?"

"Yes."

"No, I've never heard the name before."

"And you mentioned earlier that you and your husband

weren't planning on children?"

"No, Mr. Moss. Neither of us has the time for anything like that."

"We should probably call the authorities."

"Why? We don't know if anything illegal has happened."

"True, but trust me. They'll want to know about any possible leads. And the more you cooperate, the more innocent you look."

"I *am* innocent."

"I know. So it's important to look innocent."

"I don't look innocent?"

"That's not really... why don't you make the call?"

She telephoned the police, and we waited for them in the kitchen while I drank the coffee Bloody Bridget kept putting in my cup in between bouts of trying to frighten me.

"Would you like more... *cream and sugar?*"

"Stop tha—actually, yes. Please."

The cops didn't ride their siren. They knocked, too, which I thought was quaint. Bridget got the door and moments later, two detectives entered, both in relatively cheap suits, so at least they weren't visibly corrupt. No siren, a polite entry, and two honest cops—well, as honest as they came in Los Angeles, anyway—all said that if Imogen was guilty, she was still worth treating with kid gloves.

One detective was young and lean, his suit olive green. The other one was overweight, and his checkered jacket could most nicely be called a textile-related crime.

"Mrs. II. Unfortunate to see you again so soon," said the older one in a raspy voice.

She was already on her feet, smoothing a dress that didn't need smoothing. "Yes. Well, there's been something... someone else new in my husband's case."

"If you could show me to the offspring?" the older one said.

"Yes, of course. Please, come with me."

They left the room, leaving me with the younger of the two, who was eyeing me like a rare steak right at dinnertime. "Can... uh... can I help you, detective?"

He got closer, sniffing me, giving a nice view of his pockmarked face. "And who are you?"

"Nick, um, Nick Moss? I'm a private dick... detective. Miss Veri... Mrs. II hired me. To find her husband."

"The one she killed? You looking for a pile of sand and some bandages?"

"Well, if I were, a trip to the beach and the drugstore, and I could be paid."

He grinned wolfishly. "You're being funny."

"Thanks... I, uh, I thought so."

He leaned in. I looked for Bloody Bridget and nearly laughed out loud when I realized I was looking to a ghost for comfort. He sniffed my neck. I stayed very, very still. He moved away, his eyes flashing like embers in a campfire, and let out a growl that sounded like sheetmetal getting torn in half. "What's your pack?"

I reached very slowly into my jacket. He grabbed my wrist with a suddenly hairy hand, his fingernails sharp and curved. Before my eyes, his face turned hairy, his muscles bulged, his teeth jutted out from a now simian jaw. In that moment, I had time to reflect on one of the great philosophical questions of my time: had the person who named these monsters "wolfman" ever actually seen a wolf? They looked much more like apes or cavemen. The scent of dog filled my nostrils. Carefully, he pulled my hand from my coat, revealing the mashed-up thing in my palm.

"Luckies?" I said, showing off the only pack I had.

He growled. Werewolves were all the same. Cops, but you

got the idea they only really did it out of a pack mentality. He backed off a little, the change sinking back into his skin, though not all the way. At least he was one of the wolfman kind. The others walked around naked far too much for my taste.

"You're a dick."

I nodded.

"But you're not a werewolf."

I shook my head.

"Then what the hell are you?"

"Human."

"Well, that explains the smell," he said, wrinkling his nose a little. "What's a little human doing in a big-boy caper like this?"

"Like I said, Mrs. II hired me. Ask her."

"I'm asking *you*. And I can ask a lot meaner if that makes a difference."

"My specialty happens to be relevant. You mind?" I shook a cigarette from the pack, needing something to distract me from the pissed-off wolfman in front of me. Sure, it was illegal for him to actually do anything, but he was a cop. Would they bat an eye if he said I drew down on him?

"Go ahead," he snarled.

I retrieved the lighter, and my jacket decided to take that moment to completely betray me by flopping open. He wasn't going to ignore the stuff lining it, although his eye went to the snubnose .32 under my armpit. He sniffed, and the hair on his neck puffed out, changing back ino something much more like fur. "You got a license to be carrying silver?"

"I got a license for everything."

"Cough 'em up."

I found the sheaf of cards and fanned them out on the table. He picked through each one, pausing on the silver and my PI license. "Good boy. Looks like you have your papers. Didn't know there were any humans in your line of work."

"I'm the only one."

My hands were shaking, so I tried to calm down using a trick smokers employed: concentrate on the act of smoking and everything else could fade into the background. That, and maybe a little smoke wreathing artfully around my head would give me an intimidating aura. Or at least scramble that canine nose of his. Unfortunately, I managed to drop the cigarette out of my mouth while trying to light it, and tried to hide it with a quick cross of my legs. Of course, now I was sitting like a woman.

"You said your specialty was relevant. What is it, Moss?" he asked, looking out the window onto Imogen Verity's green backyard and, down the hill a few blocks away, Sunset Boulevard.

"Missing persons."

"You look for a lot of councilmen?"

"No, sir. I... uh... most of my cases are... well, they're human. Or were. Not so often once I find them."

"That how it is? You're some sad sack with a vengeance jones?"

"I have a not-dying jones."

The wolf was gradually going back into him. His suit wasn't much the worse for wear. They must have special fabric or something, because he looked like he put on about twenty pounds of muscle and five pounds of fur in as many seconds. "How good are you at your job?"

"Pretty good, I guess."

"Have to be if you're the only human. Ever thought about joining the force, then?"

"Have to be a werewolf, last I heard."

"Go out on a full moon, see what happens."

"Um... no thanks. No offense, but no thanks."

"There something wrong with being a werewolf?"

"No! No... nothing at all. Fine, upstanding peop—uh... well, you know. Citizens."

Approaching sirens cut off whatever he was going to say to that. He pushed through the kitchen door into the hall. I knew better than to move. He'd want me right where he'd left me and any movement would only arouse suspicion. I lifted my by-now-cold coffee and had a sip.

"Miss Verity... *would like to see you.*"

I jumped and swallowed a little squeal. Bloody Bridget was right next to me, her glowing green-gray face inches from mine. Her eyes were bleeding again.

"Why, Bridget, why?" The initial shock faded, and I could process what she said. "Where is Miss Verity?"

"She's... *in the hall.*"

"Thanks."

I got up and followed the detective through the door and found all three of them—both cops and Miss Verity—in the hall. The detectives manned—well, wolfed—the front door and the basement door as two white-clad meat golems came in with stretchers. Their skin was greenish, crisscrossed with angry stitching.

"The girl is in the basement," rasped the older cop from his position by the front door.

"Girl... good," rumbled one of the medics as he led the way downstairs.

"This is best for her?" Miss Verity asked.

"Ma'am, anyone discovered needs to be taken to the hospital. She'll do fine at Los Angeles General. The monsternity ward there is top notch."

Miss Verity nodded, dabbing delicately at a few errant tears. "I know. My husband donated it three years ago."

The two nurses came up the stairs, the mummy on the stretcher between them, her canopic jars resting awkwardly on her inert form. "Girl... good," rumbled the other medic, as though confirming what the other one had said earlier. As they trundled her out to the meat wagon, I kept waiting for one of them to trip and fall. Meat golems always seemed just on the verge of collapsing. All it would take is some shoddy stitching.

The older detective shut the door and put his back to it, and I realized now I was in a house with two werewolves, a doppelganger, and a ghost. "Son of a..."

And they were all looking at me.

I smiled and continued without missing a beat, "...carpenter, good thing that girl is going to be all right. Evelyn Farrell, right? Of Kansas City? Someone should... someone should call her folks. Find out why she's here. I mean, I could do that. That could be my job. That sounds like 'me' work."

The younger cop loomed a little closer. "Stay away from this, Moss. You'll just get your human stink all over a perfectly good trail."

"Or I could do that. That sounds a lot easier."

He got even closer, his dog breath washing over my face. "Remember what we talked about. The name is Garou. Detective Lou Garou. You see the light, you call me."

And Imogen Verity, bless her, chose that moment to speak. And the wonderful thing about Miss Verity, other than the gams, I mean, is that she has pipes. Maybe she modified those with her powers, maybe she was born with them. Didn't matter in the moment. "Detective Garou? Detective Moon? Are we quite finished?"

Garou started. Moon was a little smoother. In his rasp, he

said, "For now, Mrs. II. I wouldn't get too comfortable. Come on, Lou."

Garou had gotten himself under control. "Just a second, Phil." He glared at me. "Remember what I said, Moss. See you in the funny papers."

The two detectives left us alone. I let out the breath I had just noticed I was holding and turned to the immaculate Miss Verity. "Stay on the case and I'll pay you double," she said before I could speak.

I closed my mouth.

"Would you like... *more coffee?*"

And then I yelled.

FIVE

he problem with Evelyn Farrell is that there might not even be a crime there. Assuming she was nabbed on the up and up, there was no crime in changing her. Who knows? She might have even asked Juba II to do it. The picture on her identification was attractive enough, though certainly not the equal of his wife. Granted, put Imogen and Cleopatra next to each other and chances are the Queen of the Nile would end up looking like an old shoe.

Looks wasn't something mummies went for, was it? Vampires, sure. Witches, sometimes. But mummies? They always got covered up with bandages. A pretty kisser seemed like a waste.

I got out of their home as soon as I knew the wolves had gone. I didn't want to spend any more time with Bloody Bridget coming out of walls and offering me things in that sepulchral hiss of hers. It was exhausting.

I needed to focus on something considerably more relaxing, namely the case I was employed to solve. Two things were in my corner: the completed hex and the matchbook. Put those on the back burner for the time being and bring them out if the dead ends started piling up. Start with the wife's suspicions. Aria Enchantee wasn't going to come out and admit anything, but gauging her reaction would be helpful in determining if Imogen Verity was barking up the wrong tree.

Then I'd move on to the final day. Solving missing persons cases always came down to that, and this one would be no different. It just had a different ending than I was used to.

Maybe even a happy one.

Assuming "happy" meant returning one creature of the night to another creature of the night so they could keep up their marriage of convenience.

Beggars couldn't be choosers. This was as happy as my endings were going to get. First things first. I needed to stop by the office for a fresh shirt, since the werewolves and summer heat made me sweat through the first one. I pulled up in front of my office, went up the outdoor staircase, where I could see over the other businesses on Flower Street, and let myself into the reception room. It was cramped and, other than my secretary, devoid of intelligent life. She perked up from her gossip magazine, looking at me hopefully through her water-filled goggles.

She kept a large aquarium behind her desk full of bright saltwater fish. She caught them herself, and I'm pretty sure she did it with her bare hands. Whether it was the tank or Serendipity, the room always smelled faintly of the beach.

We had a single chair for waiting clients, but I'm almost certain it had never actually been used.

"Were you working on Imogen Verity's case?" she bubbled. "I could not *believe* when she walked in, just as pretty as she is on the silver screen, and actually asked to see you. You!"

"What's wrong with me?" I asked her, hanging up my hat.

"You don't hobnob with many stars, do you?" I thought it was a question, but Serendipity plowed right through it. "What did she say? Were you with her now?"

"I was at her home in Angeleno Heights."

Serendipity squeaked, her gills momentarily frilling outward, making it look like she was wearing a bright red Elizabethan collar.

"Yeah, it was a little like that."

"I've seen all her movies. Should I have mentioned that when she came in?"

"Don't forget to demand an autograph."

She squeaked again, this time her face contorting just a bit too much; all the water fell out of her goggles. "Oh, Judas priest," she muttered, standing up and sticking both her face and the goggles into the aquarium. The fish darted away, wheeling around and peering at her suspiciously. She was content to ignore them, pulling water and goggles over her eyes. She stood up straight with a slosh, adjusting the goggles and blinking both sets of her eyelids at me as saltwater ran down the front of her navy blue dress.

"You really think I should say something?" she said, water dripping from her to tap her desk.

"I'll tell her next time. And could you please get a towel? You'll attract ants."

"Ants like sugar, not salt."

"Fine, you'll attract... I don't know, lobsters," I said, going into my office.

"Lobsters are tasty."

"Lobsters are giant sea cockroaches, and these days, they probably talk." I took off my jacket, tie, and shirt. That was another problem I had. A little nervousness, and I was pouring sweat all over the place. It's a wonder Garou didn't think I was a swamp monster.

"They don't talk. You can trust me on that."

"Yet. They don't talk *yet*."

Serendipity was quiet for a moment. "Nick?"

"What?" I went into one of the file cabinets and found a spare shirt, neatly washed and pressed by the laundry downstairs.

"If you're going to spend all day on this case, do you really need me in the office?"

I knew that wheedling tone well. "Ser, you're not going to get discovered just by wasting time at the same drugstore Lana Turner did."

"It wasn't a drugstore," she shot back, "it was the Top Hat Cafe on Sunset. And can I go or not?"

I buttoned up the shirt. "I don't want to burst your bubble, but they don't discover anyone anymore. It's doppelgangers or nothing, and that includes sea hags."

"I *hate* that term. I'm a siren, not a sea hag. And they need singers. It's not just phantoms that sing, you know."

I worked the tie into a reluctant bow. "You sing?"

"Sure." A gravid silence followed, and I could just picture Serendipity in the waiting room standing up a little straighter, her hands linked, chin high, and who knows, maybe gills out? When her clear voice rang out in the hot little office, I picked out the first couple bars of "Jeepers Creepers." Good song, the kind of thing to listen to after a nice day at the beach; I could remember it on a perfect summer day when it had happened just like that, crackling out over the old motorola. The memories wove together, and I was listening to it at the beach, dancing through the lazy breeze. The sun was so bright, and the sand a cleaner shade of white than anything I'd seen. The sea and the sky were both an aching kind of blue: one hot, the other frigid. I was in the water, but it wasn't cold; it was so warm, I just wanted to sink into it forever and never have to worry about anything ever again. My mother was calling from the shore, but it seemed so far away and...

"I'm sorry, Nick." Serendipity's voice, coming from everywhere and nowhere.

I blinked. Serendipity's face was right below mine, looking extremely embarrassed, her fish eyes gigantic under the goggles. I realized I had her cradled at neck and waist, dipped low for a passionate flamenco kiss.

"Damn it!" I let her go. She caught herself on the desk, straightening her outfit with webbed fingers.

Her gills kept frilling outward, though she resolutely tried to keep them in her neck. "I'm sorry. I forgot what that does to your kind. Humans, I mean."

"Geez! Serendipity! That's not all right. I'm your boss."

"I know! I'm sorry. I didn't mean, I... you can't even breathe water... at all. Not even for five minutes."

"How is that the problem?"

Her gills were pretty much standing straight out now. "It's not! I mean, I'm not... It's also a moral lapse. Of which I am rightfully ashamed."

"You should make some calls. Make sure we've been paid for everything. And, um... file something." I grabbed my jacket and hat and went back out to my car.

Life in the big city. Did people in Kansas City have the same problems? Or did they just come here and get turned into mummies?

SIX

The Ophelia was Downtown, the first of several theaters planned for a new complex. With the Night War over, there was a sense of the monsters wanting to take back "their" city. It didn't really affect me much, since no human could afford to see whatever it was they put on there anyway. I pulled up in front, turning my car off. Not knowing what opera houses elsewhere looked like, I had no way of knowing if the Ophelia was really supposed to be that terrifying.

It had a baroque, gilded look that made me feel like I'd have to fight through a mob of angry French peasants to get close. The twin spires almost looked like they were assaulting the summer sky. The front entrance was a smaller door set into a false pair of giant double doors.

I went inside and immediately regretted it.

I'm not sure exactly what happens when a person changes. The body undergoes a metamorphosis, and since the brain is part of that, it would stand to reason that certain thought processes might get a little odd. For one thing, they have to adapt to a new body with new abilities, new dietary needs. New cranium shapes.

All of which is to say, I have no earthly clue what inspired phantoms to do what they did.

The floor of the lobby was a series of wrought-iron tiles looking like a fence laid flat. Below that, there was twenty feet of empty space and then glittering, razor-sharp spikes pointing upward, turning the entire entryway into a very clear threat. Gold curtains fell from the vaulted ceiling; high overhead, a chandelier shimmered. I knew the thing was rigged to collapse.

"Kind not welcome, human. Staying means your ruin."

I turned, already knowing what I would find. The goblin was a little over three feet tall, dressed in an immaculate tux. His pointed ears extending far over his head made me think of the front of the building, but his ridiculously long nose just made me think of zucchini. He bared sharp yellow teeth at me, green mitts at his lapels.

"I'm here to see Aria Enchantee."

"Don't care if here to see Kong. Meatstick leave now, or meatstick get gone."

And that's when I noticed two other goblins had appeared, one through a door, another from a mass of gold curtains. All were eyeing me hungrily.

"Listen, boys. I need to see Miss Enchantee, and... can you stop licking your lips, please?"

"Meatstick funny, can't wait to eat. Bet face taste yummy sweet."

"I really didn't want to do this." I reached into my jacket. The goblins charged me. I didn't know if they were planning on making good on their threat to eat me or if they would just rough me up and toss me out onto the street, but I wasn't really keen on finding out. I fished around for the little stoppered vial and pulled it out, shaking a few polka-dotted mushroom caps into my hand.

All three goblins came to a skidding halt as they saw it.

"Meatstick hateful, meatstick cruel! Eat his brains like rotten gruel!" the lead goblin howled, throwing his claws up over his face.

"Yeah, *I'm* the jerk here," I said. "Now, is Aria Enchantee here or not?"

The goblin pointed a trembling claw toward the double doors. "Beyond! Inside! Meet with diva, wish you'd died!"

"Right." I backed up toward the doors. The goblins kept up their wailing and protesting, but with every step I took away, they took one toward me. Still, the buffer of three paces was enough for now, even as I was going deeper into their lair.

And that's when the problem with wrought-iron floors caught up with me. My heel caught between the slats of the floor. I stumbled backward, desperately trying to keep my balance, but it wasn't going to happen. The mushrooms flew out of my hands, up into the air. I somehow had time to look at the faces of the goblins, staring upward in wonder, then looking back down at me and running black tongues over yellow teeth. The mushroom caps came back down, hitting the slats, bouncing once, and falling into the pit trap to be impaled on the spikes below. It was a fitting end for them, even if it likely wasn't the intended purpose of the pit.

From my place on my ass and hands, I looked over at the goblins. "Sorry about that."

They charged. And this time, I scrambled up and ran, hitting the double doors and pounding into the concert hall beyond.

The sound was the first thing I noticed, since it was all around me, reverberating off the cathedral ceiling, finding a new home in the back, taking up refuge in my brain, and making certain I would be annoying Serendipity in the coming weeks by whistling half-remembered bits of it. The source of the sound was a banshee, singing onstage. Her Viking costume looked a little odd, since it was formed of ragged strips of ectoplasm. She was in the middle of an aria, her mouth stretching unnaturally wide, showing off a black portal directly to hell.

I heard the goblins gibbering right on my heels as I sprinted down the carpeted aisle toward the stage.

"What is going on here?" The voice rang out from the audience, though with the acoustics, it was difficult to determine precisely where. "Oh, bother."

Chains rattled. A huge weight slammed into the ground behind me, my artillery-honed reflexes hurling me face-first into the carpet.

"Meatsticks not allowed! Security vowed!"

"The term is 'human.' Leave the the street words where they belong. Now, let's see this human."

I looked up. The goblins were inside an iron cage that had fallen from the ceiling. Lights blazed along its surface, confirming my suspicions that all the chandeliers in this place were multipurpose. The goblins had climbed the inner walls and were baring their teeth at me, jabbering indignantly. I rolled over to see who they were talking to.

She stood in the center of the aisle, turned partly away from us, knowing exactly how to make the theater work to amplify her voice and presence. She wore an elegant gown, her hair falling in loose curls around her shoulders. Her eyes bulged from blackened sockets. Her snaggleteeth looked like they were on the verge of falling out of her skull, and her cheeks were almost rotted through. She was actually rather pretty for a phantom.

"Hi," I said. "I'm the, um, the human."

"Perhaps you could find another theater to your liking, then. Something with more... familiar surroundings."

"Miss Eeeeenchaaaaanteeeeee?" the banshee wailed. "Shaaaaaaaall weeeeeee postpoooooone?"

Aria Enchantee waved a waxy hand. "Don't be silly, dear. This won't take a moment."

"I'm certain I would enjoy one of those establishments," I said, dusting myself off. "But I'm not here for the theater. I'm here about Juba II."

I think she raised an eyebrow, but she didn't really have those. Instead, a pale patch above one of her eyesockets twitched a little. "You know Juba? How lovely. Why don't we discuss this somewhere more private."

Aria Enchantee glided toward the stage without bothering to look back to see if I was following. Since the choice was that or stay with three goblins and a banshee, all of whom were glaring daggers at me, I thought it was in my best interests to do so. She opened a door, and I joined her at the foot of a carpeted staircase leading up into the guts of the theater.

"Now, what can I do for you, Mister...?"

"Moss."

"Enchantee," she said, holding out a hand. It was cold as a grave.

"Uh, yes. I know."

"No. *Enchantée.* As in, how do you do?"

"Oh. Very carefully, Miss Enchantee."

She might have tried a thin smile, but with those chompers, her bloodless lips didn't really close all the way.

"I'm a private detective," I said, watching her face without looking like I was. Good job skill, that.

"Oh?" I couldn't tell if I was seeing fear or not. *I* was a little afraid, but that didn't help.

"I don't actually know Mr. II. My services were retained by his wife. She's looking for him."

"Has she checked his office?"

"He vanished. She has some suspicions."

"About me?" Aria Enchantee could not have looked more surprised. But some of that was probably the lack of eyelids.

"Specifically, she believes that you two were having an affair."

Aria let loose a musical laugh. "An affair? With Juba?"

"So you weren't?"

"Heavens no, and I've a mind to slap you if you suggest it again, Mr. Moss."

"Why do you think she would think that you are?"

"You would have to ask her, I'm afraid. Juba and I are acquainted, of course, but that is where it ends. To put things simply, he's not my type."

I reached into my coat, and caught her flinch for just a second. Interesting. Probably marked her as being from the Night War, back when any human would draw on any monster. No law protecting either side. I held up the matchbook. "What about this? Have you seen it before?"

"No. I have not." Her tone had lost any element of playful half-offense. "Now, Mr. Moss, I'm auditioning a new singer, and I can't spend all my time assuaging the suspicions of jealous wives. If you have any more questions, do come for a performance. I believe I would be able to help you then."

I could tell she was grinning because her dry lips peeled back over the teeth and I had the intense urge to set her on fire. She left me on the staircase alone with her scent of mildew. I quickly made my way out, and as I returned to the lobby, I heard the clank of chains and the gleeful whoops of the now-freed goblins. I ran for daylight.

SEVEN

Before arriving home and vanishing into sandy air, Juba II had been at the office. That was where I needed to look next. Visiting Aria Enchantee hadn't done much but convince me they weren't having an affair and that the matchbook was important, as well as reinforce my dislike of goblins.

Reconstructing Juba's day was the beginning of finding him, so I left the Ophelia and drove the couple blocks to City Hall, parking up the street between a broom and a flying saucer. Despite the obelisk exterior, which was more Art Deco than Eighteenth Dynasty, I don't think the founders of Los Angeles exactly had mummies in mind when they designed the place. But ever since the Night War, City Hall looked like a burn ward. Mummies wandered to and fro, sometimes shadowed by secretaries and assistants, the odd vampire, or invisible person, or sea hag—sorry, *siren*—unmounted headless horseman, or even ghost. An ogre sat behind the central security desk, already sizing me up with piggy eyes. On top of the uniform tailored to fit his twelve-foot frame, he had chains crossed over his chest, and was leaning on a battle axe that looked like it could comfortably be used to hunt streetcars. Strings of drool ran from tusks jutting out of a lower jaw that should have been on construction equipment.

His name tag said KIZOK.

"Hi. I'm looking for the office of Juba II? Councilman for the first district?"

Kizok glared down, probably trying to decide if he should eat me or not. "Office is upstairs. Cause trouble and Kizok the Backbreaker hurt you."

"No trouble here, Mr... Mr. the Backbreaker. You know what? I'll just go find the office. That sounds best."

I went across the lobby, painfully sure that everyone in the place knew who I was, why I was there, and, most importantly, what I was. My eyes stayed glued to the polished marble floor, where the reflections of the monsters were vague enough that they could have been human. Their footsteps, either the clean and purposeful clicking of shoes echoing off the floor, or a disturbing shuffling, surrounded me. A large and winding staircase took me up, and the offices started past the mezzanine. Juba II's was close by, a little ways down a clean hallway.

In the office, behind a cluttered desk, a pair of cat's-eye glasses on croakies floated midair above an empty blouse that looked like it was full; papers shuffled just beyond the end of the sleeves. The papers settled gently to the desk and the glasses came down, shadowed by the blouse sleeves. I never could get used to invisible people.

"Can I help you?" The voice was young and unsure, tinged with fear, maybe. I couldn't be certain without reading her expression, and that would be impossible without throwing a sack of flour on her, which was considered rude in most circles. Anyone in my neighborhood would have been thrilled, because, hey, free flour.

"Hello, miss. I'm Nick Moss, and I'm a private detective hired by Mrs. II to locate, well, Mr. II."

"Have you found him?" she blurted.

I looked at the space immediately to my right, where no mummy was standing. "Um... no... if I had, I wouldn't be..." I cleared my throat. "How did you know he was gone?"

"The police visited me last night. A pair of detectives."

Garou and Moon, my friends from the II house. "Right. Well, they probably want to know the same things I do."

"They seemed to think he was murdered! Is that what happened?"

"I don't know, Miss..."

"Welles."

"Miss Welles. I'm keeping my options open. But I work for Miss Veri... Mrs. II, and my job, what she's paying me to do, is to find her husband, alive. So I'm working off the assumption that he's still... is alive the word? No one will tell... doesn't matter. Can I ask you some questions?"

There was a long pause.

I sighed. "Miss Welles, I can't see when you nod."

"Oh, sorry. I only turned this year. It takes some getting used to." She paused. "Yes, you may ask me as many questions as you like."

I sat down opposite her, removed the pad and pencil from my jacket, and got ready to write. "All right. Can you describe his day for me? What he did, who he saw, anything out of the ordinary?"

The sleeves jerked, probably signaling an emphatic and unseen hand gesture. "Of course! You're here about the woman."

"What woman? Evelyn Farrell?" I waited. "I also can't see

if you're frowning."

"Oh. I'm sorry, I didn't get a name."

"Miss Farrell's nineteen. Blonde hair, brown eyes."

"Oh, no. This woman was a little older. Early twenties, maybe? She had red hair, and lots of it."

"A witch?"

"Probably. She certainly looked like one. Patched dress, lots of pouches. She smelled like a spice rack. I didn't see a broom, but she might have parked that outside."

"Cat?"

"Toad."

"Did you get a name?"

"Why would you need the toad's name?"

"From the witch!"

"No. She just barged in, and when I tried to stop her, Mr. II told me it was okay and I sat back down. But it wasn't okay. He was scared of this woman. They were talking. Their voices were low, but it was strained."

"Did you get close enough to hear what they were saying?"

"Oh no. They would have seen me."

"You're invisible."

"I would have had to undress!"

"They wouldn't have seen anything."

"Mr. Moss! Still! I'd be... *naked*." The last word was a horrified whisper.

"Uh... you'd be invisible."

"Yes, but *I'd* know!"

I sighed. "All right, so you didn't hear what they were saying. How did it look?"

"The woman was leaning in like a heavy in one of those crime pictures, jabbing a finger at him. Mr. II had his shoulder hunched, and it's hard to read expressions on his face because of the bandages, but his eyes usually glow a sort of orangey-red, and while the woman was talking, they turned sort of indigo-blue."

My stubby pencil scratched to a stop. Wasn't sure how to note that. "So he was... um... scared?"

There was a pause. "Oh, I'm sorry. I'm nodding."

"How did it end?"

"The woman made some weird gesture, and there was the smell of burning hair, and she left."

"And what did your boss do then?"

"He was shaken, but his eyes turned a little closer to their normal color, and he shut his office door and made some telephone calls."

"To whom?"

"I don't know. He let me go around five, but the police told me he wasn't home until seven or so."

"That's right."

"Where was he?"

"That's what I'm trying to figure out. Anything else?"

"Well, he had lunch over at the Visionary Pictures lot. But that's not unusual."

"With whom?"

"Gortran. He's a director."

Serendipity would know who the man was. I wouldn't know him from Adam. Or Adamoid, considering that name. "Thank you." I got up, putting the pad and pencil back in my jacket, my fingers brushing the matchbook. I took it out, turned it over in my hand, and showed it to Miss Welles. "Do you know where this came from?"

I waited, hoping she was actually looking at the matchbook cover and not just inspecting her nails or taking a nap. Finally, she said, "I just shook my head no."

"Long shot anyway," I said, putting it back.

"It's so nice having a wolfman on this," she said, settling back into her creaking chair. "You'll sniff Mr. II out in no time."

I gave her a bland smile and didn't bother to correct her.

EIGHT

For lunch, I stopped by Castle Frankenfurter, a small silver diner a couple blocks from City Hall. It was a decent enough place. The humans-only lunch counter was passable, and no one really hassled us. The monsters, mostly second- and third-rung civil servants, ate at the tables and never so much as glanced at the line of meatsticks pressed shoulder-to-shoulder at the counter. My waitress was even human, though they had her in makeup to match the meat golem management, with crude stitches drawn across her tired frame. "Food good," she said wearily. "Substitutions bad."

"Frank, fries, coffee."

She wrote it down and left me to think about what I knew, which wasn't much. Connected councilman gets shaken down by a witch. Probably his hex dealer, come to think of it. Then he disappears. So either she made good on whatever threat she made in that office, or...

The plate slid in front of me. I looked up at the kitchen and saw their cook, another human in fright makeup, and threw him a little shrug. He threw it back. It was a common gesture with the humans in this city. Even if we never spoke, we were in this thing together, surrounded by monsters. I ate quickly, paid up, and went back out to my car, turning the used hexes over in my hand. The question remained as to what he was using. That would pin down his mental state, maybe tell me where he'd gone.

The drive to Hollywood was quick enough, especially now that half the traffic was airborne. The roads still had cars running along them, though, nice big Cadillacs and Studebakers gleaming in the Southern California sun, alongside the other machines monsters occasionally built. There were the wheeled carts of the brainiacs, their brain-bodies bouncing around in bubbling liquids. There were the spectral chargers of the headless horsemen, all glowing eyes and huffing smoke and brimstone. There were the tripods of the Martians, clanking along on tentacular legs, sweeping the streets with their bizarre pinging radar.

Overhead, the skies were never empty. Flying machines whirred past, everything from the saucers of the bug-eyed monsters, to the airborne step pyramids of the jaguar people, to the smoking and unpredictable contraptions of the gremlins that always looked ready to fall out of the sky and into a fireball. And then there were the beings that could just fly under their own power. Even on a cloudless summer day, shadows raced over the ground, distended and bizarre. If you looked up, all you could see was a dark shape flapping overhead. Pretty easy to remember the city was no longer human.

Before me, the Hollywoodland sign sprawled against the side of Mount Lee, the new letters shining like oil in the sunlight. Right before I shipped out for basic training in Georgia, the H had been destroyed by the groundskeeper in the middle of a drunken rampage. The Night War had ravaged it even more, and there had been a period of several years where it had read "ol y oodla." Just a year ago, Oculon, the unofficial mayor of Hollywood, had paid to have it restored. Of course, he had hired a gremlin, so the damn thing glowed iridescent green in the dark, exploded into sparks and rockets on the hour, and occasionally launched itself into the sky.

I wasn't heading for it, but rather a smaller and altogether dingier part of Hollywood. The club was dark and the neon signage wasn't lit in the daytime, but I could still read it: THE GLOOM ROOM, picked out in muted pink. Supposed to be a happening place after nightfall, but I had no plans to see if that was actually the case. It was a converted theater on Bronson, just off Hollywood Boulevard, and though there were no lines this early in the day, it was easy to conjure the image of ginned-up monsters out for a night on the town.

The front door was unlocked. Inside, deep curtains smothered what little light snuck in from outdoors. I went past the foyer, a densely carpeted room fitted with little ensconced lights, into the club proper. There was a low stage with tables arranged in front and a hardwood dance floor in the middle. A lone man, probably human, was mopping up between the tables.

Onstage were the Salem Sisters, all three of them, arrayed before a microphone, each looking like they were about to tell it a secret. It would probably be a good secret, because all three of them were knockouts, and the way they crammed their copious curves into those silk dresses only helped the look. They really could be sisters, except for the hair, which was predictably platinum blonde on one, raven black on another, and cherry red on the third, and all done up in elaborate and immaculate rolls.

They were who I was here to see. Specifically, the redhead.

Because I knew her.

They were trying to start up "In the Mood," the band playing percussion as backup. The musicians were mostly phantoms, though I spotted a single gill-man and a pair of zombies. Three little birds sat on a perch nearby—a red robin, a bluejay, and a white sparrow, whistling harmony for the three women. The zombies scraped and stomped; the phantoms added a layer of drums and a piano. The gill-man looked like he was waiting for his big part, but what that was, I had no way of knowing.

"Who's the lovin' daddy with the beautiful eyes," the Salem Sisters sang in close harmony. "What a pair of lips..."

I raised my voice over their song. "Daisy Mooney!"

The redhead stopped singing instantly, shading her big green eyes and peering into the audience through the stage lights. She focused on me as I wove my way through the empty tables toward the stage, smiling just a little. "My name is Lily Salem now, detective," she said.

The other two witches tried to stab me with the force of their minds alone. "Ladies," I said to them.

"Take a powder, why don't you?" the blonde suggested.

"I thought witch covens were supposed to have a maiden, mother, and a crone," I said.

"I'm a year older than her," said the blonde about the brunette.

"And I'm a year older than her," said the brunette about Daisy Mooney.

"And you know that full well, detective," Daisy finished, her hands on lush hips. "What are you doing here? Did my folks send you?"

"Nope, nothing like that. They know you're happy as a witch, and they're happy you're happy. At least, they were last time we spoke." I cleared my throat, focusing on the parquet dance floor. This next part was never easy. "I... uh... I need a bit of a favor."

"Oh, do you now?" said the brunette. The brunette, Verbena—Verb—hated me. I might have said a few things the last time we met. I might have used an evil eye charm. It wasn't entirely my fault. She'd tried to hex me, and a man in my line of work needed to defend himself. Especially because it happened in broad daylight. Not that any cop would take my word over hers, and that was *before* her coven backed her story up.

"Verb, please," Daisy said, sighing, which in that low-cut dress was practically a humanitarian mission. "Take five, boys." The band began to get up, stretch, and put aside instruments. The zombies didn't take to stretching very well; one popped his shoulder from its socket and flailed helplessly until his partner shoved it back into place. The birds relaxed on their perch, all six of their little button eyes on me.

The blonde—that was Hyacinth—narrowed her eyes. "What kind of favor?"

"Expertise."

"Hunting another witch?" Daisy—sorry, *Lily*, though I couldn't see the point in going from one flower to another—came down from the stage.

"Not exactly. Just looking to have a chat with someone. I was wondering if any of you ladies knew of a witch dealing spells."

"We all deal spells, honey," Verb said.

"I thought you were musicians."

"A girl can't do two things at once?"

"I... uh... I have no idea how to answer that."

Lily Salem, who used to be Daisy Mooney before she vanished after a house party on Bunker Hill eight months ago, was now right next to me. Monsters, no matter the type, were good at slinking. I didn't notice her until I caught her scent right next to me. Unlike most women, witches didn't go for perfume. They always smelled a little earthy, no matter how well made up. In Lily's case, her aroma was identical to her name. "Out with it, detective."

"Got a description of a witch shaking down a missing mummy. A witness said she had lots of red hair."

"Maiden," supplied Hyacinth.

"Yeah, I know. Which means there's a mother and a crone out there too, but as you ladies prove, those labels can be somewhat... ah... less than accurate."

Hyacinth and Lily had the good graces to blush, and only Verb, the mother, seemed annoyed by the fact. "Your point," she snapped.

"Well, if I find this maiden, she has backup, uh... you know, this is really beside the point here. Do you know this woman?"

"Not really much to go on," Lily Salem said to me.

"She was supposedly wearing a patchy dress?"

"Still not much. Hy?"

Hyacinth shook her head. "Almost any maiden could match that description."

"I was wondering," I said to Lily, "when they changed you, your hair changed colors, just like that? It's not... I mean... it's not dyed?"

"Don't be fresh," she chided, but there wasn't much conviction behind it.

Still, I blushed bright red, since that's not what I meant at all. "No, it's just my secretary, she's a sea hag—sorry, siren—and she won't tell m... and I was wondering what... you know... womae's mysteries, she said..."

Lily and Hyacinth laughed at me, but then the crone took some mercy. "If you had something of this maiden's, I might be able to help you. Since you're a friend and all. You *are* a friend, detective...?"

"Moss. And yes, very friendly. No ulterior motives with regards to the Salem Sisters whatsoever."

Verb made a rude noise. "Drop your charms, then. I can feel them in your coat."

"Come now, Verb. A man has the right to defend himself," Hy said.

"They're helpless otherwise," Lily said, smirking.

"I do have something," I said, trying to ignore the glowering woman onstage. It was tough. Those gray eyes were like thunderclouds, and the hairdo made her look all the more severe. I wasn't scared of her exactly, more disappointed in myself for hurting her last time. I tried to remind myself that it was self defense and she had it coming, but how could I have done that to such a nice, sweet lady who only wanted the best for me?

"You have something," Lily prompted.

"Right. Yes." I shook it off and reached into my pocket for the spells, but touched the matchbook first. Bringing that out, I said, "You wouldn't happen to recognize this, would you?"

Lily looked at the silver snake and shook her head. I held it up for mother and crone. Neither knew. "All right." I put it back and removed the sheaf of paper—a couple of the used-up hexes, plus the one complete one—and handed it over. Hyacinth trotted off the stage and took them from her sister, looking them over, starting with the incomplete ones. After a moment, she brought them to a table, sat down, and spread them out.

I sat across from her, Lily between us. Hyacinth layered them, trying to find the most legible words and symbols, a frown creasing her smooth forehead. After a moment, she looked up and fixed me with her baby blues. "These look like amnesia spells."

"Amnesia spells?"

"Mmm-hmm. Hard to be sure, because so much is missing, but it looks like your man was taking something to make him forget." Hyacinth collected the used ones and made a neat little stack before handing them back over to me.

"Is that common?"

She shrugged. "I don't sling hexes. I'm a singer."

Lily broke in. "We get the odd request for love spells here and there. We don't deal to hexheads."

It was hard to tell if she was telling the truth. I mostly saw how much she looked like her mom. The old pictures of Daisy Mooney with the long mousy hair and the doe eyes were pretty far from the bombshell she had become after the change. No wonder she liked being a witch. Still, the girl she'd been was there, lurking just under the surface, and apparent to those who knew what to look for.

Hy poked the remaining, complete hex with her finger. "This one is different."

"What is it?"

She turned it over, checking the back of the little brown square of parchment, then flipped it back. "It's a disguise." Hyacinth looked up, and as pretty as she was, I felt a little fear. Where Daisy had become desire, and Verb was someone I didn't want to disappoint, Hy was power, pure and simple. "Read this, focus on a face, and you change. Even baffles enhanced senses, like the scent of a werewolf or the sight of a crawling eye or the hearing of a wendigo. "

"Like being a doppelganger?"

"Not quite. A doppelganger can turn into anyone, but a werewolf can sniff one of them out. This, you only get to pick one form, but it's completely perfect. Better, but more limited.

This trumps them all."

"Unless one of you counterhexes it."

Hy shrugged and gave me a small smile. "Unless that happens, yes."

"So something like this, is it expensive?"

"Very much so. A hundred dollars, easy."

I let out a low whistle.

Lily grinned. "We usually get another kind of whistle in here."

"What with the wolves," Verb said testily. She still wasn't happy, but she had edged a little closer and was peering at the spell in Hyacinth's hand.

"What good is a disguise if it isn't used?" I asked the room, to which I got a bunch of blank faces.

Daisy-Lily batted her long eyelashes at me prettily. "Is that all you needed, detective?"

"You said you could... uh... if I had something of hers? Does this qualify?"

"Yes, definitely," Hy said.

Verb came up behind me. "You need to get up," she said.

"Oh, right. Sorry."

Verbena took my seat and the three linked hands: maiden, mother, and crone around the table. Heads bowed, they began to mumble under their breaths. The words, though inaudible, thrummed against my insides. I knew I should take a couple steps back. That circle was a center of power—of feminine power—and I had no place there. My hand crept toward the evil eye charm in my pocket before my conscious mind pointed out that the ladies were helping me, and pulling a weapon on them was not a proper way to show gratitude.

The paper with the disguise spell fluttered under a phantom wind. The chanted words grew louder, but their meaning was no clearer. I had the sensation of being watched, the hairs on the back of my neck standing straight up at attention. Something was in here with us, and that something was a being created through the synergy of the three women. The paper lifted off the table, flapping like a little bird, tumbling over and over, describing something close to a sphere in its playful dancing. A light radiated from this sphere, and all three witches looked up in unison, their voices still quiet, but their words growing more and more powerful, like thunder crawling over the Mojave.

The light began to take shape. Colors that were simple smears resolved themselves: an invisible camera twisting a lens into focus. And for a moment, I saw her, wind whipping through a huge mane of wavy red hair, perching demurely side-saddle on a broom, wearing a dress that looked more like a repurposed quilt draped over her thin frame. Her features were pugnacious and girlish, a snub nose and pink cheeks covered in freckles. She carried herself like she didn't even know what fear was and might punch you if you tried to describe it. As she rode, a frown creased her forehead. She turned slowly to look me directly in the face. Her emerald eyes flashed as she mouthed something I couldn't hear.

The hex caught fire in midair and the image winked out.

The witches gasped as the little firefly bits of paper fluttered to the ground.

"Wait... how could... she's a maiden, how did she..." I stammered.

"She got lucky," Hyacinth said.

"Caught us unawares," Verb said.

Lily was silent, patting her hair, making sure it was still in place. As if there were a force on heaven or earth that could muss Lily's style.

"You couldn't..."

"She severed the connection too quickly, detective," Hy said. "Nothing we can do, unless you find another of her completed spells, or better yet, something she owns."

"And ask real nice," Lily said.

"We can't help you," Verb said, caught between annoyance and pleasure.

"Well, thank you. You ladies have been very helpful." I paused, wondering. "Could you do that with the man I'm supposed to find?"

"Not unless he's a witch," Hy said.

"Thanks anyway."

"You should come to the show tonight," Lily suggested, having regained some composure, standing and smoothing a dress that couldn't get smoother without industrial sanding. "We'll put you on the list, give you the best table in the house."

"You know I can't do that."

"They protect humans in here. It's perfectly safe."

I smiled at Lily Salem, sure she was actually being sincere. "Even if it were safe in here, Lily, it's not safe out there. And I'd have to get all the way home."

"Where is home?" Verb asked.

"Watts. Just follow the conga line of monsters trying to turn me and my neighbors. You can't miss it." I immediately regretted smarting off to Verbena. She was so disappointed in me.

I stood up, the two witches who liked me doing the same. Lily said, "Let me walk you out." The red robin fluttered off the perch to alight on her shoulder. She reminded me of Snow White.

She walked me to the door, and I was the biggest sucker alive in admitting to myself I felt the tiniest bit safer with a witch at my side. The sunlight burst in as I opened the door. Standing in the shaft of gold, Lily looked a bit more like she did back when she was Daisy. The makeup was more obvious as that—makeup—and the styling on her hair seemed closer to falling out. "Thanks, Dais... Lily."

"Don't mention it, detective. You ever change your mind, we'll be right here."

"I wouldn't want to keep your sisters waiting when you're in the mood."

She smiled, which turned into an unguarded grin. "You seem to have found yourself quite a case."

"You don't know the half of it."

She looked me over, making up her mind about something. "One thing. That maiden... Hy wouldn't mention it because of the way Verb feels about you. But I know you were just trying to find me, and Verb tends to shoot first and ask questions if anyone is still alive later. That maiden of yours, she is *dangerous*. They were covering before, but she was powerful enough to slap all three of us away, and she did it easily."

"Oh. Oh, good."

"Be careful, detective. I'd hate to lose you before you got to see what my life is now."

"I'd hate to lose me, too."

NINE

Visionary Pictures was located on a former orange grove, bulldozed and covered over with cement. A series of massive sound stages like warehouses or airplane hangars was at the west, while a pastoral garden and offices were tucked away in greenery on the east, and all of this behind huge and ornate wrought-iron gates. Eyeballs were worked into the tines, and above, in a graceful Spanish arch, the studio name was written out in pure Hollywood glory. Small streets formed a cross-hatching between the stages, and the whole place was bustling. Once through those gates, there wouldn't be a single human face.

Like everywhere else in this town.

Hollywood was supposed to be part of the city. But the monsters, specifically the crawling eyes that owned the studios, kept Hollywood separate from Los Angeles. It was not yet a city on its own, not officially, but remained an unincorporated part of LA County. The real power lay in the tentacles of the studio heads and the paws of the Hollywood Sheriff's Department.

They were technically bound by the state's Fair Game Law, but absolute power didn't make for law-abiding monsters.

I parked down the street from Visionary's gates and got to wondering. It was already late in the day, the summer sun shining almost directly into my eyes. Talk my way onto the lot—there was one option. Sneak on; there was another. Bribe my way on. Almost laughed at that one. I could barely pay my secretary.

Just in front of the gate was a guardhouse, but since it was built for an ogre, it would have been a two-story palace for anyone else. The ogre sitting in there, stuffing whole lobsters into his maw from a barrel, was hardly watching anything but his lunch. Of course, if he looked over, he'd grab me in one of those turkey-sized fists, and... I don't know what, actually. I had an image of him sticking me in his mouth and crunching me up alongside those fish-stinking lobster shells, but I wasn't sure. Ogres ate people. Everyone knew that. Right?

How did ogres change people?

I mean, one day you're Larry Johnson, certified public accountant. You get caught across town with a flat or something, and one of the ogres wanders down from the neighborhoods in the foothills of La Crescenta and... what, exactly? Werewolves bite you under a full moon, zombies eat your brains, ghosts scare you to death, but ogres...? Did they club you over the head until you got giant and stupid? Did they make you drink some kind of yeasty *ogrebrau*? Or was it more like the manhood ceremony of a primitive and gigantic tribe of linebackers? It was the best kind of mystery: one I never wanted solved and prayed no one would pay me to.

So Larry Johnson gets a flat, and an ogre... ogrifies him, and he has to pick a rebirth name and goes with Kizok the Backbreaker, and now he's out of a job because no one will take financial advice from a man who thinks "subtlety" is the word for what's left after you hit a guy with a tree.

However he came to be, he was in my way. And when an obstacle packs a billy club as big as your leg, it pays to be cautious.

There's a benefit to being my size, especially when it comes to dealing with something his size. I just waited. Thankfully, I didn't have to wait long. A pickup truck rolled in carrying potted yew trees, all about ten feet high. I scampered up to the side while the driver, a carnivorous carrot, talked to the ogre security guard.

"Delivery for *Brittania's Huns*," he said in a bizarrely high-pitched and buzzing voice.

"Go on," the ogre rumbled.

I stayed alongside the back wheel, hunched over and moving slowly as the truck rolled through the gate. I followed it to the first side street and peeled off from there, straightening only when I was out of sight of the guardhouse.

The studio was bustling. Zombies carried props to and fro while doppelganger actors and extras rushed to their stages from costuming, dressed as cowboys, Roman senators, or Zulu warriors, their faces blurred between one shift and another. They'd probably settle right before the cameras rolled, but until then, it hurt my eyes to look at them too closely. Every now and again, a robot would clank past, spewing sparks and muttering to itself about how late it was and how it wanted to terminate all humans.

Each of the indoor sets had a removable placard with the name of the film on it. *The Winter of Bastogne, Isandlwana, The Vampire's Wife.* I remembered the script sitting by Imogen Verity's chair: *Love is a Many-Splendored Thing From Another World.*

A gremlin wandered by, wearing huge mirrored sunglasses

and carrying a massive parasol to keep the sun off his leathery olive and yellow skin. I stopped him, kneeling politely to look him in the eye. He had two massive white muttonchop sideburns. I kept the surprise under control; this little monster had been lurking outside my window last night.

His large ears went up, maybe in recognition. I got a look at my terrified face reflected in the lenses of his glasses.

"Do you know where *Love is a Many-Splendored Thing From Another World* is shooting?"

"Pfah!" he said, grimacing.

"Is that a... I need some help here, sir."

The gremlin spoke in a rasping snarl, "Gortran... *caca!*"

"Gortran is directing that one?"

The gremlin nodded, holding one long, apelike arm out and pointing with one huge claw from its three-fingered hand toward one of the buildings, careful to remain under the shadow of his parasol. "Gortran... hiiiii hooooo." He paused. Then, almost as an afterthought, adding, "Yum-yum."

"Um, right. Thank you. I appreciate it."

"Pfah!" The gremlin dismissed me with a swipe of his claw that nearly took my eye out, then waddled to another set, his parasol held high. It would have been nice to see some significance in his presence both here and outside my house, but there were only a few human neighborhoods left in Los Angeles. Weird coincidence, but not necessarily anything more sinister. Well, more sinister than him wanting to web me up in a snot cocoon and turn me into a three-foot-high monster with an uncontrollable desire to tinker.

A large motorcycle, all black and silver with plenty of chrome piping, was parked under the placard for *Thing*. Was this a biker movie? Didn't sound like one. Painted on the black gas tank in garish silver was a guitar and the words THE

DISASTERS. Didn't know that gang. Wonder how they had carved out any territory when all of Southern California was Howler turf.

I opened the door into a blind curtain meant to keep out the LA sun, wrapping me up like a spider. I swore, punched it, and got through. A zombie was on the other side, dressed in the casual coveralls of a grip. "Brains?"

"Brains," I said to him.

"Brains," he agreed and staggered away, pushing a loaded dolly.

The cement floor was a maze of cables, with a few canvas folding chairs set facing three-quarters of a house. Other sections of the house were stowed in the darkened part of the warehouse, along with what looked like a pleasant garden and a demolished city street. Zombies shuffled around, doing the grunt work of maintaining the set. A crawling eye sat behind the camera, one of its tentacles draped over the top of it, another resting on the crank. Even though the thing couldn't really display an expression, it managed to look bored. Sitting next to him was a shiny chrome robot, two antennae sticking from the top of his boxlike head, a thread of bright blue electricity climbing them.

Three actors were onstage: a younger, pretty actress and two older people playing her parents. Appearances were deceiving. They could have been any age, since they were all doppelgangers and could look like anything they liked. My client might have been any one of the three, but chances are she was the pretty blonde daughter, since that looked like the lead role.

They were in the midst of an argument. The girl said something about a human, and everyone gasped. "I love him, Father! I don't care that he's a human from another world!"

"More emotion, Imogen!" the robot buzzed and crackled,

gesturing broadly. His hands were nothing more than clawed clamps that he used to coax my client, so it really looked more like a threat.

"More emotion, Gortran? Please, tell me what you know about emotion."

"My programming recognizes sixty-four distinct emotional states, and right now, you are demonstrating none of them."

Imogen rolled her eyes, still in the character of the girl, so she looked authentically petulant. Or maybe actresses generally had a lot of growing up to do. "Tell me about my motivation—and you are *not* a good enough director to throw a 'paycheck' crack at me."

"You're telling your father, who is an old-fashioned werewolf, that you're seeing a human. And he's from space!"

"I've read the script."

"Have you?" Gortran snapped.

"I don't know why I'm not leaving."

"This is your *father*!"

"Oh, and you're close to your father after some robot put your brainwaves in a box?"

"Just because you think you're It doesn't mean I can't go down to the bus station and find a girl twice as pretty who will work for half as much."

"They're called whores," Imogen retorted. In the middle of theatrically rolling her eyes at the robot's gall for daring to gainsay her, she caught sight of me in the darkened stage. "Could we take five?"

"Why not? It's not like we're past deadline, over budget, and cursed with a prima donna."

At that moment, what I can only describe as a space octopus fell out of the rafters, slamming into the set. It would have crushed all three doppelgangers had they not scattered at the first cracking sound from above. As it stood, the giant, rubbery monster took a chunk out of the back wall and completely crushed a lovely end table that was nicer than anything I owned.

"Damn it!" the robot crackled, lancing an arc of electricity from his antennae that scorched the rug and sent a puff of white smoke toward the ceiling. "Will someone get that thing secured? Someone who can tie a decent knot?"

The zombies moaned and closed in on the prop octopus. It was hard not to flinch with all those stinking and staggering corpses moving past. I think I managed. At least, that's how I choose to remember what happened. They began the long and arduous process of hoisting the monster back into the rafters while Gortran, the director, telescoped up out of his chair and stormed off, the lights on his chest blinking erratically. His face was a fuzzy greenish screen, an annoyed human expression visible in the static.

Imogen came back into the dark with me. It was strange: she had all the mannerisms of the woman I saw earlier in the day, but she wore the face of a younger and more innocent girl. The role had been dropped, or perhaps she had put a different one on. She was also shorter than me now, which I thought was nice for a change.

"What brings you here, Mr. Moss? Checking in?"

"Actually, no. I spoke to your husband's secretary. Said he had lunch with Gortran on the day he disappeared. Did you happen to see him?"

"He just left. Probably headed for his office."

"Wait, your husband was here?"

"No, Gortran. He was the robot."

"Right, well, I meant your husband. Did you see him when he came here?"

Imogen shook her head. "No. He comes by every now and

again."

"He and Gortran are friends?"

"I wouldn't call it that, exactly. They know each other, but it doesn't seem like there are many warm feelings there."

"Are there usually with robots?"

"Not in my experience, no."

I gestured to the thing that the swarm of zombies was only now beginning to heft off the broken set. "What's that?"

"The thing from another world."

"Ask a stupid question, I guess."

"How did you get past Ugoth the Castrator?"

I had to let that sink in before I could speak. "The... the security guard's name is...?"

She nodded. "I felt it was a little gauche, but, you know, ogres."

I swallowed. "Oh. Well. I'm glad he didn't see me."

"Your voice is high enough as it is," she said.

"Wait, what's that supposed to..."

"Break a leg." And with that, she returned to her costars.

Gortran was around here somewhere. I followed his path around the side of the set and tried to hear the radio crackling of his voice, smell the sharp scent of his constant electric venting, or see the flashing greens, reds, and blues of his body. As I got farther from the persistent moans of "brains" coming from the giant alien prop cleanup, the avenues between set walls and equipment got slimmer until there was room for only one person.

I had gotten used to being around monsters pretty much all the time, so maybe the cold sweat that was presently covering my body was because it was dark, or because my only options were behind me or ahead into the unknown. And no matter how used to zombies you got, hearing them scrabbling on something and moaning about their favorite food was never fun. No matter how you sliced it, I was getting that hunted feeling.

As though the world wanted to make my fears manifest, the makeshift hallway in front of me was eclipsed by a humanoid silhouette, but one almost a full foot taller than me, carrying a box or something on one shoulder. Leather squeaked as he came toward me. We got a little closer and I made out his face: phantom. Milky goggle-eyes set in deep black sockets. Giant snaggleteeth, like a crocodile in desperate need of orthodontia. Waxy skin that looked pretty good for a corpse, but not so good for anything else. And to top everything off, a glorious raven-black pompadour, drenched in enough oil to run a cargo ship. The thing on his shoulder was an apple crate. I put my back to the wall and tried not to go for my whistle.

He muscled past me, never once throwing an acknowledgement my way, moving the crate from one shoulder down to his waist, and then up to the other. It was partly filled with circular gray film canisters. His leather jacket was covered in patches, including a prominent one on the shoulder depicting the screaming skull of the Howlers. On the back, he had the elaborate iconography of the gang: a skeleton playing the pipe organ, the actual pipes being bloody spears, with sections normally reserved for a motto replaced with bars of music. The phantom looked like the kind of monster whose love for motorcycles came not from a taste for freedom, but because he liked the opportunity to assault new and interesting people. I prepared myself for what seemed inevitable until he strode to the corner and was out of sight.

I stayed in one spot, getting my breathing back under control. With backstage still and quiet, I could just begin to hear the crackle of Gortran muttering to himself. I roused myself, moving back down along the makeshift hallway towards where the phantom came from until I could make out what he was saying. It was "terminate all humans," over and over. Nothing unusual there. Robots generally said something like that whenever their minds wandered. It was almost comforting, in a terrifying sort of way.

There was an office tucked in the back corner of the set, just in front of what looked like the back door, a small room with big glass windows in the wall and the door. The lights were off, with the lion's share of the light coming from the green glow of Gortran's televised face. He sat behind a desk, grumbling. Sitting in front of him was a film canister, spotlighted in green. I knocked on the half-open door.

He looked up. A second later, the face on the screen registered surprise.

"Mr. Gortran?"

"Just Gortran," he crackled primly, moving the canister to the side of his desk, under some papers. The surprised face blinked away, replaced with officious annoyance. "And what do you want?"

"My name is Moss. I'm a detective."

"Figured you for an agent," the robot said. The words were calm, and the tinny radio voice betrayed no emotion. The way his steel pincers clicked together seemed like nervousness, but it was tough to tell. "What do you want? I have a set to look after. One that keeps getting crushed by a giant alien prop."

I stepped into the office. The air was hot and close, magnified by whatever was simmering off Gortran's metal hide. "Yeah, I was wondering about that. It seems like you could have just hired a leviathan or bug-eyed monster or something."

"And pay overtime?"

"Might have a better sense of balance."

"Is that what you came here to tell me?"

"No, no. I wanted talk to you about Juba II."

The thin thread of lightning between his antennae seemed to be climbing a little quicker before fading into a spark and starting again at the bottom. "What about him?"

"You know him?"

The face on his screen flickered, went to static, and suddenly was the Indian test pattern. The voice was very carefully monotone, even tuned artificially to make it so. "Yes, I do."

"You had lunch with him day before yesterday?"

"We did."

"If you don't mind my, uh, what does someone like you ea... you know what, not important. You're friends, then?"

"Acquaintances. I'm working with his wife."

"What did you discuss?"

"His wife. She's been difficult." The Indian head flickered, bowing out on a line of white and showing Gortran's annoyed face before the staticky eyes met mine and the Indian head returned.

"Is that... is that what actually happened?"

The Indian head was stoic. "Yes."

"Oh. Oh, good." I needed a second to collect myself, to find some way to put the robot on his metal heels. I reached into my jacket and tried to shake a cigarette out out of the pack. They went all over the place. "Damn." As I collected them off my lap and chair, I said, if only to distract him, "Do you have a light?"

The face reappeared. "What? Here." He rummaged in his desk, removed a matchbook and tossed it at me. The Indian head returned immediately. I caught the matchbook and froze at what stared back at me from the cover: a silver snake coiled against a black background. I held it up. "Where did this come from? I mean, what club gives these out?"

The robot was silent for a second. When he spoke, the

monotone was gone, his voice cut instead with naked hostility. "Moss? Odd name for a werewolf, isn't it?"

"I'm not a werewolf."

"What are you then?"

"Nothing. I'm... uh... I'm human."

Gortran stood up in a huff, but the Indian head stayed plastered on his TV-screen face, the lightning surging up his antennae in waves. "I don't think I need to answer any questions from a human." I was impressed at how much scorn he slathered onto "human." It dripped down the sides to form a tacky lump on my ego.

"Oh. Sure. Well, sorry to have taken up your time." I stood up and headed for the door, with Gortran clicking and whirring in silicon fury behind me.

"I didn't know the police let your kind hold badges."

I stopped. "They don't. I'm a private investigator."

"Who hired you, human?"

"That's not... there's a confidentiality issue there, sir. Have a nice day."

I left Gortran's office, and believe me, it's tough to turn one's back on a robot. You never know when they've reached the last straw and just *have* to destroy all organic life in the vicinity. Not that there was any real record of this, but that didn't stop me from thinking it.

I stepped into the makeshift hallway, half expecting that phantom to be waiting for me. He wasn't, and I began the long trek back out to the sweltering late afternoon sun. My watch said I wasn't going to have a ton of that left, but I'd make it home well before dark.

By the set, the zombies were still in the process of hauling the thing from another world back up to the ceiling. Imogen was talking with her costars, and she waved me over as soon as she saw me. I was about to say something to her, if only to have another story that would make Serendipity squeak and lose all the water from her goggles, when the curtains separated, letting in a bit of light from the outside. Stepping onto the sound stage was a young woman with a whole lot of wavy red hair, wearing an old and patchy dress.

"You," I said, and winced, wishing I'd managed something a little better. "Can I talk to you, please? It's about Councilman II?"

She regarded me, and I thought I saw recognition in her eyes. Not necessarily unfriendly, which was better than I got from Gortran, at least. I jogged over to her, noticing too late as one of her hands disappeared into a pouch. She brought up her fist, and before I could do anything, blew a handful of powder in my face. She hissed a few words I didn't know and made a couple gestures, the last of which was obscene in any language. Then she pushed past me in the direction of Gortran's office.

I turned around to follow her, but somehow my feet got tangled up in the curtains by the door and I fell forward, smacking my chin hard on the ground. "Ow. Miss! Miss, I need to talk to you?"

She kept walking, her skirts nearly brushing the floor. I got up, feeling a little dribble of blood snake its way down my chin. "Miss!"

I stood up, and almost immediately, a zombie pushing a dolly of crates cut in front of me, knocking me backward into the curtains, which promptly ripped, sending me to thump through the now-open door into the middle of the studio street outside.

I heard brakes squeal, tempered by annoyed shouts of "Damn it!", "What's that?", and "Brains!"

I finally managed to get the black curtain off of me only after a great deal of struggling. There were flies who had easier times escaping spiders. When I tore the black caul off my head, I saw that, sure enough, I was lying in the center of the street outside, a truck's bumper inches from my head. I stood up and waved at the driver, who was headless. He shot me a rude gesture, and I heard a booming spectral voice shout, "Are you crazy? Get out of the road!"

"Sorry! Sorry!" I went back to the door, hoping I could still catch that witch.

It opened outward, right into my face. The explosion of white stars dropped me onto my ass.

"Brains," the zombie coming out said to me.

"Yeah," I said, cupping my palm to my eye. Wait, didn't that door used to open inward? I got up and almost went back to check it. No. If that witch had actually cursed me, and I kept doing what she didn't want me to, things were going to get worse and worse, and I was already working on a shiner and a bloody shirt.

The truck rolled past me, and I could tell, I could just *tell*, that driver was staring at me and shaking his nonexistent head.

Gortran

TEN

I t took me a little longer than I liked to start driving home, mostly because I wanted to be certain the curse had worn off before I got behind the wheel of a thousand pounds of fast-moving steel. My eye was unlikely to swell shut, but it *would* change color and it hurt like a son of a gun. The witch rang my bell, no way around that. By the time I started the car and turned toward Watts, it was getting on in the day. Not so late that I wouldn't make it. I could still—

They didn't use sirens in Hollywood anymore. I heard the howling as the sun was just starting to turn red. A large reddish-brown wolf hopped out from between two parked cars in front of me. I swerved to miss him, just in time to see a black wolf coming up big in my sideview, baying like the siren he didn't have.

Braking like my life depended on it, I squealed the car to a stop. Well, more like a stall. I had to restart it to get it out of the road, waving to the two wolves that I was, in fact, pulling over and not trying to flee. Great. Now I had trouble with

the Hollywood Sheriff's deputies. The black wolf paced beside
the car, tongue lolling out, his luminescent yellow eyes staring
straight through me. The brown wolf transformed.

Into a naked man.

He was a big guy, with stubbly cheeks and a touseled mop
of red-brown hair. I kept my eyes above his waist, focused on
the deputy's star tattooed over his heart. Finding just the right
place to look, that was the trick. Too high—well, making eye
contact with a werewolf wasn't the best of ideas. Too low just
didn't appeal on any level.

"Do you know how fast you were going?" he asked, bending
over to stick his head in my car. His breath smelled of blood,
but I still didn't envy the view from across the street.

I tried not to lean away too far and kept my eyes on the
dash, as though the speedometer would give me the magic
words to placate him. "Um... I think I was going... you know,
it wasn't that fast."

"Have you been drinking, sir?"

"No, no, nothing like that."

"You were driving erratically."

"You... uh... you jumped out in front of my car. I was trying
not to hit you."

"Stow the attitude."

"Attitude?"

"There it is again. You seeing this, Warg?"

The black wolf *woofed*. The sun turned even redder as it
fell toward the horizon to be momentarily eclipsed as a tripod
clanked by, using the streets as helpful suggestions on where it
might put its clawed feet. "I'm really sorry, officer..."

"Deputy."

"I'm sorry, deputy. Didn't realize how fast I was going. Just
trying to get home before dark, you know."

He squinted at the dying sun. "Oh, look. It *is* getting late, isn't it?"

"Yes, offi... deputy. It sure is."

He took his time thinking things over. Off to his left, the sun got lower and lower, taking with it my chances of making it out of here on two legs. "So what kind of business do you have in Hollywood? Didn't think the studios hired..." he leaned in and sniffed me. "Meatsticks."

"They didn't... I'm, ah... I'm a detective. Private. Detective."

"You hear that, Warg? This fella thinks he's a detective." He turned back to me. "Let me see a license."

"Sure, I can..." I reached into my jacket, which flapped wide open in the kind of snafu that seems to happen only after you pray for it not to.

"Gun!" he yelled, the voice turning into a snarl as he grew a big furry snout and clamped a huge jaw across my throat, teeth making little dimples in my skin. I couldn't be sure if the hot liquid dripping from my neck to my collar was blood or sweat, and in any case, I remained still. I took his little snarl as a prompt.

"I... I have a license for that, too," I squeaked. It's not easy to talk without actually moving your throat.

He growled.

"I'm... I'm reaching for it... and not the gun. Definitely not the gun."

The sun got lower. It was almost trying to limbo. I willed it to remain in the sky for a little bit longer.

I reached. Slowly. Glacially. Like two continents sauntering by one another, having a geological reunion. I was desperately trying not to annoy this werewolf, though it was difficult to know what would set him off when it seemed like my mere existence would do the trick. I pulled out my wallet , thick with every license I needed in this line of work. Private investigator, firearm, silver, salt, gold, blood, you name it. I held it out, and something snatched it from my hand like it was mortally wounded prey.

A moment later, a voice growled, "He's got all the paperwork, Beast." The other one, Warg, had changed back to human form.

My friend Deputy Beast let me go. I rubbed at my neck, watching him shift out of the corner of my eye. The paws scratching holes into my upholstery changed into dirty human hands. The snout shortened back into that pugnacious and oh-so-wolfsbane-able face. He held a hand behind him and his partner put the wallet into it, then turned back into the black wolf with the yellow eyes.

"So everything is in order—" Beast looked into the wallet, "—Mr. Moss. I'll remember that name, just in case you decide to make trouble in my neighborhood again."

"Oh, swell."

"Remember what we talked about. The attitude."

He threw the wallet back into my lap, and just like that, the two wolves loped back onto the sidewalk, presumably to catch more reckless drivers. I gingerly touched my neck, certain the hand would come away bright red. Nope. Just sweat. He'd had some control. Though I wanted to show him the same gesture the witch used on me, I knew that was a bad idea. I didn't have that kind of power, or any at all, really. And without power, confidence was a little lacking sometimes. The best bluff needs something to back it up, especially now that the Night War was over and my side had lost.

The sun was really low, and I had a choice. Either I could do what they were accusing me of and drive recklessly, or I could get home after dark. They had paddled me up shit creek and now I had to swim home. Well done, you just made a pumpkinhead very happy, you damn mutts.

And, of course, chances were, the two deputies would follow me to the end of their jurisdiction. So speeding was out, at least until Hollywood ended.

I did it anyway.

ELEVEN

I got to my neighborhood right as the sun dipped below the horizon. As soon as that happened, the cars lining the road opened up, spilling out monsters. Some were already by the houses, lurking by windows and doors. They were the ones who respected the letter of the law more than the spirit.

I hit the gas, making a gill-man dive for cover, sideswiped a brainiac's cart, and swerved into my driveway. A zombie turned from where he was pacing the line of salt by my roses and lurched toward me. Sam Haine was waiting on my front lawn, peering at me as though he couldn't quite picture me outside the house.

I got out of the car.

"Nick!" Sam called happily. He was about five steps away from me. As I was mentally sizing up that distance, he grew, thorns ripping through his suit, a long and viney tail tearing away the seat of his pants. Going home was going to be a little embarrassing. Maybe. Or maybe he kept spare trousers in the car.

The fire blazed up in his pumpkin head, tongues of flame licking from the angles in mouth, eyes, and nose. He reached out for me with hands that lacked clear joints. I dodged aside, his thorny claws swiping along the hood of my car, throwing angry sparks into the air. "Sorry, Nick," he said in a voice that sounded like roaring flames. "I'll pay for that if you just... slow... down!"

I sprinted for the house. The zombie lunged from the bushes, grabbing my jacket. "Brains!" His cold, stinking breath washed over my face as he tried to get his teeth on my skull to gnaw it open. I reached for the vial of salt, but that turned out to be unnecessary.

Sam was less than happy about the zombie getting fresh. My hero. He took a swipe and I went boneless. The zombie struggled to hold me up, raising his milky eyes at the last moment. I wished I could have seen them get big as saucers while Sam's massive, thorny paw slapped him. Zombies don't do head trauma, and the guy went tumbling head over heels to lay still next to my jacaranda tree.

"You okay, Nick?" It really sounded like Satan talking.

I didn't bother answering him, being much too busy dodging those huge mitts like tree branches. He reached forward, and I had no choice. I dove. Right at him. The claws scraped along my driveway and into my lawn, tearing furrows where I used to be. Great. At least now it was plowed, and I could plant, I don't know, maybe pumpkins or something. Thanks, Sam.

I tumbled, got up, and bumped right into Sam's leg. It hurt, but fortunately, it knocked me back on my ass in time to avoid Sam's next grab, which ended up tearing his suit even more. I thought about going for the powdered chicken blood in my coat, but I didn't trust the time it would take. Punch Sam's ticket to dreamland and there were twenty other monsters who would jump at the chance to turn me into something else. So I just crawled between his legs, his long dinosaur-like tail whipping around overhead. I got the distinct impression that if I wasn't turned into a weird pumpkin-headed plant monster, I was going to get squashed.

No pun intended.

I crawled three more feet, popped upright, and sprinted for the house. A vampire hissed at me from my porch. I flipped open my jacket to flash the holstered cross and kept running for the door.

I dropped the keys once, stooped, and hopped behind the line of chicken blood. Sam looked deflated, but the zombie, now getting up from Sam's hit, had his white eyes on me.

"Brains!" the zombie said, dragging himself to rotting feet.

"I'm flattered," I said, getting the key into the lock and falling into my living room, breath burning in my throat.

The lawn was quiet for a moment, and then came Sam's infernal voice, oddly plaintive. "Hey, Nick! Come on out. Let's talk about this."

"There's nothing to talk about! You tried to turn me into a pumpkinhead!"

"I can't turn you into anything else!"

"That's not the... oh, forget it."

The cat was sitting ten feet away, calmly washing itself. When it was convinced I was watching it, it languidly stared right through me and meowed.

"And how was your day?"

It meowed again, a little angrier this time. Like, *okay, I gave you a chance to unwind, now let's get to feeding me.* I blinked. It gave me another, even louder meow, this one accusatory.

"Right, sorry. Guess you almost had your head replaced with fruit."

Meow.

"Vegetable, whatever."

I went into the kitchen and opened up a can of food. The cat hissed when I set the can down, but apparently its feline hatred of me didn't encompass whatever I put in front of it. As I opened a can of tuna for my own dinner, a mummy staggered by my kitchen window. I nearly laughed out loud. Wouldn't that just be how this thing got solved? The missing guy found wandering through the dick's backyard. It really did look like all the pictures of Juba II I'd seen, though. Wrapped in bandages, of course, but there was also the nice suit and that snazzy Egyptian headdress. And Watts would be the last place anyone would ever look for the guy.

I spooned some iffy relish into the tuna and shook my head. No way. Whatever crypt he had found would be near Evelyn Farrell, presently lying in state in the monsternity ward of Los Angeles General Hospital, the same ward Juba himself had donated. After it was pretty obvious we humans weren't going to win the war and the monsters tried to sell us a peace we could live with, their best argument was that they couldn't have children the old-fashioned way; they claimed all of the changed people were like children to them. They were loved and wanted. Which was nice to hear, even if you *had* just become a giant eyeball.

The point is, if that were true, Juba would be close by Evelyn Farrell. I thought about that for a second. I was so unused to tracking actual monsters, something so obvious took awhile to get through. And besides, with everything else ending in dead ends and angry monsters, another tack would be good for the investigation and my continued existence. Might be worthwhile to check in and see if anyone matching his description had stopped by. Of course, if he had another one of those disguise hexes, he could look like anything he wanted. It was hard to find someone who didn't even have the decency to walk around in his own face.

I brought my sandwich into the living room. The cat followed, hopping up on the arm of my chair. I reached out to pet it, but a swipe of its paw said that wasn't what it was after. No, it was going after my tuna fish sandwich with the confident air of an alpha predator. It even glared at me with those big green eyes as if to say, *Yeah, punk, what are you gonna do?*

And I had one of the most sobering revelations of my life. If the cat wanted my sandwich, there wasn't much I could do about it. How's that for sad?

The doorbell rang, because if there's one thing shame loves more than misery does, it's company. I got up, leaving my sandwich behind, and the cat yowled with triumphant glee.

"Sam, look, this is getting a little..." I was saying as I peered through the peephole.

Standing at the threshold was Imogen Verity.

I yanked open the door. She was back in the form she wore at my office, the form she wore on the red carpet. The famous face of porcelain skin, shining blonde hair, and legs that seemed positively criminal. She was wearing yet another designer suit, although it being night, she hadn't bothered with hat or glasses, so I got her sapphire blues boring through me. "May I come in?"

"Uh... yeah... please do."

She moved past me. Sam was on my front lawn, back in his smaller form, wearing the tatters of his suit. "Oh, come *on*! That's not fair!"

I shut the door.

Imogen frowned at the sight of my cat eating a tuna fish sandwich off a plate, but was much too classy to bring it up.

"So... what, uh... what brings you here? Um, I mean, would you like something to drink?"

"I'm fine," she said, looking around for a decent place to sit and finally giving up and settling on my old couch. It seemed a little too small for a woman like her, and certainly didn't match her style. "May I smoke?"

"Of course, sure." I took the plate from the cat. It was momentarily upset, but I left the sandwich, so, really, the cat had nothing to complain about. I set the plate next to Miss Verity as an ashtray.

"You really like that cat," she observed, lighting her cigarette.

"Actually, no. I just keep it around for security. Jaguar people. Of course, werewolves like to chase them, so maybe it ends up being a wash."

"I suppose you have many security concerns."

"Well, yeah."

"I've never been to this part of the city before."

"Why would you?"

"Precisely. So, at the studio, I had wanted to ask you what you found, but you... kept falling down."

I blushed. It was tough, trying to keep my composure in front of a bona fide movie star, especially one who looked like an unholy combination of sex and elegance. "Oh. That."

"I would never get between a man and a healthy love of drink, but you seemed..."

"Cursed! I was cursed. The witch? You saw her. The redhead with the dress like an Amish quilt? I think she shook your husband down two days ago, and..."

"Shook my husband down?"

"Oh... uh..." I settled down on the other end of the couch, mostly because the cat had claimed my chair's section of the living room along with my tuna fish sandwich, splayed out in front of it like a kill on the African savannah. "Yeah, you remember how your husband is a hex addict?"

The glare said she not only remembered, but would like to cut it into my skin so I might remember as well.

"Right... um, well, I think that witch is his dealer."

"What was she doing at the studio?"

"I wanted to ask her, but... curse."

"And you started your best Buster Keaton impression."

"There was that, yes."

She sighed. "This is your only lead?"

"Well, no. Miss Verity—"

"Imogen, please. No need for formality in private."

"Imogen, right... uh... well, there's the matter of the matchbook. Gortran had one as well, and as soon as I asked him about it, he threw me out of his office."

"Why would he do that?"

"I don't know, not exactly, but it bears further investigation. You're sure you've never seen it?"

She shook her head, somehow managing to look perfectly innocent.

I sighed. Actresses. "Well, all right then." Only Gortran and Aria Enchantee had recognized it, and whatever it was was bad enough for both of them to suddenly bring up the racial difference and throw me out.

"Do you have any leads at all? Other than the matchbook, I mean?"

"Well, not as such. But he's got to be around here someplace, right?"

Imogen sniffed, a tear welling up at the corner of her eye. It was the most photogenic tear I'd ever seen. A few more joined it and then she was bravely crying like an Army wife waiting to hear bad news but keeping it together for the sake of the children.

I mean, why not. If you're going to have the ability to look like whatever you like, there's no reason not to go about everything in an attractive manner. Little tears ran along her cheeks, not mussing any of her makeup, because it wasn't makeup. She had perfect eyeliner and mascara and that rosy shade on her cheeks because she could simply change the color of her skin to fake it. I scooted a little closer.

"Don't worry, Miss Ve... Imogen. It's okay. I'll find him. I've found people with a lot less to go on." I left out the fact that sometimes I failed to find people with more to go on, since that didn't seem like the kind of thing that would make her feel better. Instead, I put a hand on the couch cushion between us.

She grabbed it immediately. "Thank you, Nick. You're very kind to say those things to me."

"Oh... uh... yeah, I know. I mean, it's my pleasure." All I was looking at was her graceful hand over mine, holding just tight enough to let me know that if I wanted to disengage, I'd have to yank. And I really didn't want to. This was Imogen Verity, and calling her merely perfect would have been an insult.

She looked up, the tears magnifying her eyes. They were literally impossibly blue. The Pacific Ocean should have taken notes on the proper look for a summer day. "Nick. Tell me, what are the chances my husband will be found alive?"

"Pretty good. Very good. Well over fifty percent. Maybe sixty... sixty-five?" No idea where I'd pulled those figures. Mummies don't go vanishing every day. Makes generating statistics a little dicey.

She pulled my hand toward her, forcing me even closer. We were well inside comfortable distance now. "Oh, Nick. I'm so worried about him!"

"Don't worry too much... I mean... are you... what are you doing?"

She had my hand close to her mouth, as though ready to kiss it. She stopped, turning, and very deliberately slid closer to me. "Hold me, Nick."

Now, when a woman who looks half as good as Imogen Verity tells you to do something like that, you do it instantly, and make a note to thank God later. Maybe send the big guy a fruitcake or something. I leaned in, finding her face not giving way for mine, instead poised there, practically begging to be kissed.

I leaned in...

I didn't notice right away. I think it had been going on for several minutes, maybe since I joined her on the couch. There was nothing in my vision except for her face. The edges were blurring, her features becoming more generalized, less distinctively her. Eyes falling into her cheeks, lips thinning into nothing, nose collapsing into a mere bump. And as this happened, I felt a buzzing in my own face. Reaching up, I knew I'd touch the bristles of my end-of-the-day beard, but scarcely felt it. As though the beard was nothing more than a layer of mist on my face.

Wait...

I jumped up. "You're trying to turn me!" My face ached. I could feel the bones and skin returning to where they belonged.

"And?" she said, leaning forward, her voluptuous curves a tantalizing lure. I had to admit, she had a point.

"No! No... wait. This isn't right!" I ran for my jacket, hanging by the door, to get the weapons hidden within, the protection it offered. She was up in an instant, pursuing me like a cat after something small and squeaky, and she would have caught me if not for my tuna fish sandwich. She slipped on mayoed fish and tumbled to the floor, the first inelegant thing she'd done since I met her. I scrabbled through the jacket's pockets and pulled out a woman's compact. "Don't make me open this!"

"Nick, be reasonable. My husband was having a child. I might as well do the same."

"You're turning me as revenge?"

"Not revenge. Think of it more like turnabout."

"That's revenge!"

"Then I'm explaining it poorly."

"Is that really the problem here?"

She calmed herself, her voice dropping to a throaty purr. "Just think, you can be taller. Not look so much like... how you look."

"What's wrong with how I—that's not the point! I invite you in, and you try to change me! This is not how you build trust!"

"Is that what we're doing?" she asked, elegantly unfolding herself from the floor. The bit of sandwich still stuck to the heel of her shoe sort of ruined the effect.

"It's what we should be doing!"

"The change doesn't hurt, you know. And there are... side benefits."

"You mean like se—no, wait. You're a married woman!"

"To a man who has not performed his marital duties in quite some time. At least, not with me." The last was said quite pointedly.

"Oh. Well, that puts us in a stickier moral place."

A languid smile spread over her face like the sexiest oil slick I'd ever seen. "Come now, Nick. Let me show you how easy it will be."

I knew I wasn't going to be able to resist her. Who could? So I just opened up the compact and showed her the mirror. She shrieked, hands going to her face, and bolted for the door.

Scrabbling against it, she couldn't find the knob. So I went over and helped her out.

When she was on my porch, she uncovered her eyes and glared at me. "How *could* you?"

"You tried to turn me!"

From my lawn, Sam yelled, "Good job, Nick!"

"I'm not dealing with you right now, Sam," I said.

Imogen, finally looking the slightest bit disheveled, smoothed her skirt. "That was horrible of you. I really thought we had something."

"Had. Had! You shouldn't try to turn people without asking!"

"And why not? I would think it might be a benefit in your line of work. All I'm offering is the chance to look like whatever you like, whenever you like."

"And the ability to be terrified of mirrors and die if anyone ever pokes me with cold iron."

"How often do you really encounter cold iron in your daily life?"

"I have a dagger in my jacket!"

"Oh. Well then, I appreciate you only using the mirror. As horrid as it was."

"It's okay. I'm used to it," I said, pointedly not looking at Sam.

"Well," she said, continuing to fix herself, "what is your next move?"

I let her change the subject, as long as that was all she tried to change. "Two things. First, I'd like to check on Evelyn Farrell. If your husband was having a child, he probably wouldn't abandon her. After that, I'm going to sit on Gortran and hope either the witch comes back or your husband pokes his nose out to see his old friend."

"So we might see each other."

"Well, yeah... but that's not to be taken as any tacit—I'm not leading you on here."

She sniffed. "Good night, Nick. Please, think about my offer."

I sighed. I was getting more "offers" than I was comfortable with today. "Sure. Good night, Imogen."

I leaned against the doorjamb, looking out into the nightly chaos of my street while Imogen got into the back seat of her white Rolls-Royce. Her headless chauffeur closed the door and drove north. Finally, I closed the door.

"Good night, Nick."

"Night, Sam."

TWELVE

Wake up. Shower. Shave. Notice that the aborted change had healed both the black eye and the cut on my chin. Feed the cat. Drink some coffee. Try to figure out why I'm so hungry, find a half-eaten tuna sandwich on the living room carpet. Clean up the sandwich. Get dressed. The green suit today. Check every single anti-monster item in my jacket to make sure it's there, even replacing the compact from the previous night.

Insane. What was it about humans that made monsters lose their damn minds?

At least it was just conversion. Some of them had a taste for long pig, and there wasn't much to dissuade them. The dark rumors coming up from San Pedro were just that as long as I didn't have to investigate them, although I couldn't help wonder how many of the people I didn't find wound up as monster poop.

I sighed. Not much I could do about that. Finding Councilman II was more my speed, since that lacked any semblance of a higher purpose beyond making sure I had enough tuna for me and the cat. It glared at me from the doorway, flicking its tail back and forth.

"See you tonight," I said.

I took the car out, waving to Will Hammond on the way, and headed up to the main drag. Long as I was sitting on Gortran before lunch, I should be fine. What the hell did that guy eat? Maybe I could get someone to hire me to find that one out. I pulled up in front of my office, ducking into the laundry quickly.

I put the shirt from yesterday on the counter while Mr. Rodriguez came in from the back. "You can get blood out, right?"

"*Si*, it's no problem."

"Swell."

He looked at the bloody collar, scratching at it with his thumb. "It's ready tomorrow."

"Thanks."

As I opened the door into my office, my secretary's eyes were huge. Bigger than normal, even. She wore a grimace that was wider than anything a human woman could accomplish, her needle teeth bared. Even the fish in the aquarium behind her looked agitated. "Is something wrong, Miss Sargasso?"

"Police!" she shrilled. "In your office!" Her gills momentarily frilled outward.

"Which... uh... which police?" I had an image of the Hollywood Sheriff's deputies padding around my office in full wolf form.

My office door opened. "Detectives Phil Moon and Lou Garou, LAPD," Moon rasped from my doorway. Inside, Garou was rifling through my files.

"Nice suit, Moon. Does Elmer Fudd know you're borrowing it?"

Moon chuckled, brushing some imaginary dirt off his pink checkered jacket. "Nice seeing you too, Moss. My partner said you and he came to a bit of an understanding."

I stopped about a foot outside my office. Moon was easily six inches taller than me, and probably had close to a hundred pounds on me. I could be slightly comforted that thirty of that was gut, and at least five was bad taste. "You two... you two aren't going to wolf out on me, are you?"

Garou, now sitting at my desk, said, "Depends on how cooperative you are."

"I love to cooperate with the police."

"Good," Moon said. "I thought so."

"Sit down, Moss," Garou said, gesturing to the chair opposite my desk, where I normally kept clients. When a wolfman tells you to sit, you sit without reflecting on the irony. Moon loomed behind me like a color-blind eclipse. Garou leaned back in my chair and put his feet on several files piled atop my desk. The detective narrowed his eyes. Something outside of my window whizzed by, but I would not take my mind off the predator across the room, to say nothing of the one right behind me. "How was your evening?"

I blinked. Of the millions of possible questions, that was not the one I saw coming. "Huh?"

"Your evening," Moon repeated. "How was it?"

"Not... uh, not great? My cat ate my sandwich."

Garou burst out laughing. "Your sandwich?"

"Yeah. It was tuna fish."

"Real tough guy, Moss?" Moon said. "Let a cat eat your sandwich?"

"It's a big cat. Like..." I held my hands out, then brought them in to show off how big my breadbox-sized cat was.

"You see anyone?"

"Other than the normal people in my neighborhood?"

"Other than them."

"Oh. Imogen... uh, Miss Verity. My client. She stopped by."

"When?"

"Eight, I think?"

"How long was she there?"

"An hour, maybe. What's this about?"

Garou didn't hesitate. "Evelyn Farrell is dead."

"What?"

"Someone went into her room at LA General, doused her in moonshine, and lit her up. We had to scrape up the bits for the coroner."

"Oh my..."

"And you're the alibi."

"You don't think Miss Verity did it, do you?"

"Who else? You got someone in mind?"

In point of fact, I did. Gortran. That witch. Both had connections to Juba, both had a reason to want to hurt him in some way. Something told me to keep that information quiet for now, but they already knew by my hesitation that the answer to their question was yes. So I stammered, "Wuh... what about Juba II?"

"II's dead, Moss. We haven't found where she swept him up, but he's a pile of dust just like his kid."

"You've got her tried and convicted already. What do you need me for?"

"Due diligence," Garou said. "She named you as her alibi and we have to check, even if we know her story's so full of holes it wouldn't even make good cheese."

"You had that one in your back pocket, huh?"

Moon's hand came down on my shoulder. "I like your sense of humor, Moss, but maybe you shouldn't get smart with my partner. He's not as friendly as I am."

I resisted the obvious short leash comment and instead nodded. "Right, sorry. I... uh... yeah, she was over at my place."

"I'm impressed, Moss. Making time with a movie star. Is that why you took this case?"

"Oh, there was no making of... there was nothing. All on the up and up. She wanted to know how I was doing finding her husband, and she was depressed that I'm not doing well—"

"...because she killed him."

"No... no... well, maybe. But I haven't found anything to, ah, to suggest that."

"Haven't found anything to contradict it, either, or you'd have said something."

Garou seemed a little fuzzy on how the justice system worked, but pointing that out, or using the word "fuzzy" around him, was a monumentally bad idea. "Well, no."

"All right, so you saw Mrs. II at your place last night. Why'd she leave?"

"I... uh... I chased her off."

"How did you do that?"

"A mirror. Doppelgangers hate mirrors, you know, like you guys hate wolfsba—"

"We know what we hate," Garou growled.

"Why did you chase her off?" Moon asked. "You have a pretty lady like that in your house, emotionally vulnerable, and you pull a mirror on her?"

"She tried to turn me."

Moon guffawed and even Garou cracked a smile. "You don't strike me as much of an actor, Moss."

"I'm not. I don't really know... maybe she was drunk?"

"You smell anything on her breath?"

"No. But different monsters get drunk on different things.

Could have been something that didn't smell."

Garou looked over my head, clearly sharing a thought with his partner. The wolfman nodded to himself and stood. "I'm going to offer you a hell of a deal right now, Moss. Prove Mrs. II killed either her husband or Evelyn Farrell and I'll turn you. You'll get a nice job on the force. Be a real detective."

I swallowed. "I actually don't want to be turned."

Garou grinned. "I'll turn you if you don't, too. The difference is, I'll put you on traffic."

THIRTEEN

I sat in my office with my heart pounding long after the two wolfmen left. Serendipity came in, her clammy hands pressing a coffee cup into one of mine and a doughnut into the other. "Nick, are you all right?"

"You know, I'm used to a certain amount of police harassment, but this is getting ridiculous." I dipped the doughnut into the coffee and took a bite, realizing I hadn't had a proper meal since the hot dog at Castle Frankenfurter. After that, the doughnut disappeared in two quick swallows, even though it was a little salty from Serendipity's hands.

"You thinking of giving up on this case?"

"I can't. I told her I'd find her husband, so I'm going to find her husband."

"You're a strange man, Nick."

"Thank you, Ser."

"I just know Imogen Verity would never hurt anyone."

"And how do you know that?"

Serendipity managed to look both painfully sincere and

ashamed of that fact. "Because she's my favorite actress."

"Since when?"

"Since I met her the day before yesterday, and she was so nice and beautiful."

"I don't know what that has to do with anything, but noted." She chewed her lip. "What's your plan, then?"

"I want to see what's left of Evelyn Farrell. Maybe I can learn something, and if I get really lucky, Juba II will want to come by to say goodbye to his daughter. Then I'm going to go to the studio and sit on Gortran. I know he's not telling me everything, but I don't have the slightest inkling as to what 'everything' is."

Serendipity got a hopeful look in her giant yellow eyes.

"Yes, you can have the day off."

"Oh, thank you, Nick!"

"But only because you bought me—are there more doughnuts?"

She pointed to a pink bakery box as she swept out of the room on a salt breeze. I really wished the cat were there to glare at me, if only so I'd have someone to talk to. Lonely business, this.

After a couple more doughnuts, I went to a nearby diner to pick up lunch; somehow, the pastries had only made me hungrier. The place catered to humans almost exclusively, with only a few things on the menu for the odd monster patron. The giant ant filet probably wasn't even real giant ant, just a housefly who drank his milk and got that Charles Atlas program. The waitresses here didn't bother with fright makeup, and everyone knew me. It was a nice reminder of what the world had been before we dropped the big one and everything had gone insane.

I ordered an egg salad sandwich, and they threw in a slaw cup, probably because it looked like I hadn't had my eight daily servings of mayonnaise yet. As the waitress, Ruth, spooned yellow-and-white egg mash onto whole wheat, she said, "You okay, Nick?"

"Been better. Tell me something, Ruth, you're local, right?"

"Yep. Over on 109th. But don't get too excited, honey. I'm married."

I wasn't. Ruth was about twenty years older than I was, and all of that could be counted like tree rings in the nicotine caking her wrinkles. "You have trouble with monsters at night?"

"Oh, of course. Not as much as I used to, of course. Monsters are like men. They like 'em young."

"I'm not exactly a bobby-soxer."

"You got an admirer?"

"Seems like I have all of them."

"Well, don't that just make you the prettiest belle at the ball. Thirty-five cents, Cinderella."

I paid the woman and accepted the paper sack with my lunch in it. It was probably good that both wars had gotten me used to not eating regularly. The first one, now almost ten years done and over, you never knew when or where you'd eat, or if Kraut artillery would be pounding you like drums when you finally got to. And with the Night War, well, shortages were pretty common then, too. I wish someone had told me at the time that both would end up being totally pointless. Might have stopped me from jumping out of that plane.

The Los Angeles County Coroner's office was on Mission, in an appropriately depressing industrial neighborhood, just a block from a shipping yard where old train cars were lined up like a housing development. Supposedly the current trains were getting retired soon and replaced by something else, designed by one of the better mad scientists we had now. I pictured something throwing arcs of lightning around or blasting along on a pillar of fire. It was an exciting and terrifying time to be alive.

Seen from the outside, the Coroner's office was a single story, with a lone basement level that was mostly refrigerated doors for the bodies Los Angeles dropped. I headed inside and shivered a little as the temperature fell precipitously with the air conditioning. I nodded to the receptionist, an older siren, her weedy hair gone greenish white.

I explained who I was and what I was doing there, but I left out the human part, and the "private" that went in front of detective. It was only a little dishonest, and the wolves *had* asked that I look into Evelyn Farrell's death.

"Er, Mr. Moss?" the siren asked, raising her fin eyebrows, ragged along the tips.

I nodded.

"Is there a reason you brought your lunch?"

I blinked, looking at the paper sack I'd forgotten I was holding. "It's egg salad. If I leave it in the car in this heat, who knows what it'll turn into."

She nodded to the corner of her desk, and once I put it there, gave it the uneasy look of someone who didn't entirely trust egg salad. "Take the elevator to the bottom."

"Thank you," I said, obeying her instructions.

At the bottom, there was a small room just off the elevator area, and beyond that, two swinging doors leading into a room of cabinets. The sublevel of the Coroner's Office was legitimately freezing. I could watch my breath coming out in big gusts of white. If it ever got wet in here, there would be snow falling indoors. That's not why I stopped dead in my tracks.

No, I did that because of the seven feet of white fur, yellow teeth, and curved claws that was messily devouring a human body on one of the cabinet drawers. The monster's face was grayish, like bloodless flesh, the skin stretched tight over a distended humanoid skull. White fur sprouted in clumps over his jowls. It looked like Santa Claus might, after you murdered him and dumped the body in a snow drift.

"Oh, sorry," the wendigo said, "you caught me in the middle of lunch." He stood up, sucking his spidery fingers and sticking his hand out. "Dr. Hannibal Winters."

"Oh, God," I said, unable to keep my eyes off the half-eaten corpse.

"Don't worry. John Doe. No one claimed him." The coroner's gaunt face split in a horrifying smile, showing off more teeth than I thought existed in the world. "One of the perks of the job. That and the air conditioning. What can I do for you, Mr..."

"Moss.."

"What can I do for you, Mr. Moss?" Winters asked, his glowing yellow eyes curious.

"I'm here to see Evelyn Farrell."

"Ah," he said. "Not much to see. She was a mummy. Put a flame to one of them and... whoosh!" He gestured meaningfully, but with that paw full of daggers, the only meaning I could figure for it was a threat.

"Can I see?"

"It's actually rather interesting." The wendigo straightened his lab coat, which had some disturbing red stains on the lapel, and shambled over to one of the drawers. His impossibly long fingers, tipped with curved, razor-sharp claws, curled around the drawer and opened it up. He unzipped the black bag, revealing long strips of a semi-opaque substance. "Glass," he said, carefully holding a piece up for me to inspect. "Kill a mummy, he turns to sand. Burn him hot enough, and the sand turns to glass. This unfortunate young lady was coated in high-proof alcohol before someone set her on fire. She burned very, *very* hot."

I swallowed. That had been Evelyn Farrell. She had been a pretty girl from Kansas City and now she was window material. No way for someone like that to go.

"You mind my asking how you know her?" Winters asked.

"I don't, actually. I found her. She was still alive then. Well, you know, undead."

The wendigo opened his mouth to say something when the doors opened behind us. We both turned. It didn't take a detective to figure out who the two nice-looking people were. They were dressed conservatively, both in glasses, and were clutching at each other in fear and uncertainty. The woman was on the edge of tears; the man was stoically bearing it for both of them. I felt horrible just being there, like I was intruding on their grief.

"Excuse me?" said the man who I knew must be Mr. Farrell. "The hospital said to come here?"

The woman sniffed.

"Evelyn Farrell?" Winters said.

The man nodded. "I'm her father, Dick Farrell." Winters beckoned them over with his claws. I backed off, wishing I was somewhere else. Anywhere else, really.

"The police called us yesterday," Mr. Farrell said. "We only just got to town and the hospital said to come here."

"I'm afraid your daughter is..." Winters gestured at the strips of glass.

Mrs. Farrell let out an agonized sob. Mr. Farrell, his voice quavering, said, "I don't understand. Where is my daughter?"

"Right here, I'm afraid. She was turned into a mummy, as it happens, and the fire that killed her had a rather interes..." Winters clicked his claws together, no doubt realizing how offensive he was about to be. "Well, it's terribly unfortunate. You should be able to claim her remains in a day or two when the police have finished their investigation."

"I don't understand," Mr. Farrell repeated. His wife wailed, collapsing into his arms. He tried to hold her up while looking at Winters with eyes fogged by tears.

I slunk out of the room, Mrs. Farrell's agonized sobs chasing me out the door. I didn't know who killed Evelyn, but whoever it was now had me to deal with. That probably wasn't much of a threat, but it was more than she had before.

FOURTEEN

I got back in my car just as the day was starting to turn, tossing the sack lunch into the passenger seat. Noon in the city was never pleasant: the sun would get high up in the sky, start baking the asphalt, and you'd get some cranky monsters out and about. Still, as long as one of them wasn't Ugoth the Castrator, I'd be all right.

Speaking of Ugoth, he was sitting in his guardhouse, this time eating an entire roast pig. I showed up in time to watch him shove the head into his massive maw and bite down. The cracking reverberated all the way across the street. I was beginning to see why the studio boss kept him around. Just by feeding the guy, they had the best security money could buy. Only a crazy person would try to sneak by him.

Which made me crazy, I reflected as I hopped in the back of a prop truck as it slowed down in front of the guardhouse. I ended up nestled between several fake cactus beds, the sand glued to wooden planks, the cactus made of plaster-of-paris. All my life, I've lived in a desert and it took me this long to really feel like it. With my sack lunch resting on my belly, I listened to Ugoth rumble at the killer zucchini driving.

I waited for the vegetable to make a couple turns before hopping out. The truck was barely moving by that point, slowed up by a parade of gladiators. The set wasn't too hard to find after a little looking, although I was a little disappointed to see that I had left no blood on the asphalt from my last visit. A guy likes to know he's made his mark. I poked my head past the curtains, half expecting them to betray me again, and found Gortran directing a scene with the same actors. Might even have been the same scene, for all I knew. The important thing was Gortran.

I slipped in and found a dark corner of the set to watch from. It felt a little odd spying on Imogen, both for the fact that she was my employer, and that the previous night, she had attempted to turn me. I put it out of my head. Dwelling would not help the investigation and would probably just create resentment. Resenting monsters for doing what they did was a waste of energy. Wouldn't get them to stop doing it, and might make me do something stupid out of some misguided desire for revenge. If revenge was really that important, I'd've let Sam turn me ages ago.

The crew zombies shuffled around me in the dark, but not one seemed to notice me, let alone question my presence. Zombies had lousy eyesight, possibly due to a lack of vitamin A in a strictly-brains diet. Meanwhile, Gortran yelled at Imogen and her co-stars for performances he deemed passionless and pedestrian. I wondered how much a robot really knew about passion or pedestrians. Probably a bit more about the latter, at least when it came to how to run them down.

The scene wrapped and Gortran ordered a set change as he headed back toward his office. Imogen had turned around, and I was worried she'd see me. Not that she'd try to turn me again—I just didn't want to deal with the awkwardness. Worse than a bad date. So I moved around the back of the set. The maze I'd stumbled into the day before continued there, albeit with more open spaces where the sets waited for their turn under the hot lights. I made my way through the destroyed city street. Above me, the tentacled Thing swung slightly from its perch in the rafters. That would have been an ironic way to go. Survive real monsters only to be crushed by a special effect. They'd have to put that on the headstone. NICHOLAS A. MOSS, KILLED BY THE ONLY FAKE MONSTER IN LOS ANGELES.

The shuffling of the zombies and the conversation of the doppelgangers faded a little as I moved deeper into the sound stage. Finally, I made it to Gortran's office. He sat behind his desk, leafing through a script, his metal claw ripping every page. I waited in the dark while the sounds of the set being struck— hammering, dragging, the sepulchral moaning of the cannibal dead—bounced around the studio. I found a comfortable spot, just inside the false front door, and stared through Gortran's office windows for what seemed like an hour before a gremlin hopped over and scratched at the office door. The little guy had huge white eyebrows.

"Come in," the robot crackled.

The gremlin did the usual routine of growls and sound effects with an occasional actual word thrown in.

"I'll be right out."

Gortran got up a moment later, clicking and whirring, the face on his television screen flickering. I let him move off and then went into the darkened office. That's when I realized there wasn't a light in there. Of course there wasn't. Robots didn't need light. They either walked around all lit up or they saw in some weird spectrum where they didn't need light. Meant they could sneak up on you pretty well, but the old bucket-of-water-on-a-door trick was a pretty effective deterrent. That was the fun part of the war, the way it was half terror, half Three Stooges movie. It really made the other war look bad. Hitler never had much in the way of a sense of humor.

So I flicked my lighter. The golden glow washed over Gortran's desk. The silver matchbook sat right where the director would have been looking at it, reflecting the light right back at me as if to say, *Hey, I'm the key to this whole thing. Too bad no one will tell you what I am.*

They'd tell a wolfman. Maybe I should call Garou, let him do what he wanted, and then just ask Gortran again. Unfortunately for her, Miss Verity's case wasn't important enough to me to spend nights peeing on fire hydrants and chasing cars.

I picked the matchbook up, hoping it might tell me something this time. The snake stared back, flickering in the dim light. I opened the book. Nothing written on the inside. Probably a little much to hope that the address to the mummy's safehouse was scrawled on the flap. Where would a mummy feel comfortable? A cemetery maybe. Or on the old Babylon set still rotting away on Hollywood Boulevard. Maybe a nice pyramid up in the hills somewhere. I couldn't see anything written there, though. Nothing at all.

Other than the matchbook, Gortran had two scripts on his desk, one a copy of his current film. I flipped through it, finding notes written in the margin with machine precision: "100111." "1110110001." "110101100."

Goddamn robots.

There was also that can of film he had tucked aside when I came in the day before. Could have been a reflex, just hiding the studio's next big hit from a possible spy. Or it could have been something more sinister. I rummaged through the papers, finding the can buried right where Gortran had left it. I set the lighter down, cracked the can open, fished the reel out, and unfurled a little of the film. Couldn't see anything.

I knelt awkwardly by the lighter, angling the movie to see the frame. It was a difficult operation, since one false move and the film would go up in my hands, and judging by the amount of wood around, I could add "Arsonist" to my list of occupations. I squinted at the strip, barely making out what looked to be a sepia-toned opera house, though not the only one I would recognize. Ugh. A musical.

"Call me when the set is done." Gortran's voice. Extremely close, buzzing with annoyance. I looked up, and through the glass, I could see the greenish glow from Gortran's television, barely illuminating the way into his office. I quickly returned the film to the can, jammed it back under the papers, and clicked the lighter shut. The glow outside was stronger. He was right there. If I tried to bolt, he'd see me. I cast around for a place to hide. The desk. That was it.

I crammed myself under Gortran's desk right as the door opened, pressing myself against the back as his heavy metal feet clomped over to his chair. He settled in, the chair squeaking in agony. Gortran's feet were sort of trapezoidal, his legs a ribbed and flexible black tubing. I had a lot of time to look at them, hoping he didn't feel the need to look under his desk. At least he didn't chew gum; it was clean as a whistle down here.

I heard him pick up the script and start muttering to himself as he wrote on it. "Terminate all humans." Crackle. Buzz. Hiss.

I wondered how long this was going to take. Technically, I was doing what I was supposed to be doing. Watch Gortran, check. I could turn my head to the right and watch his dented metal crotch. I had my robot deterrent in the breast pocket of my shirt, but other than that, I didn't have a way to take him down if he decided to make good on his mutterings. I tried to remember where the nearest fire hydrant was, in case my breast pocket protection didn't work. My only other option was the holy water, which probably needed to hit somewhere vulnerable to short him out effectively.

A knock on the window of the office almost made me yelp.

"What is it?" Gortran buzzed.

The door opened. The smell of saltwater wafted in; the voice belonged to a woman. A siren, most likely. "Mr. Gortran? Mr. Oculon wanted to confirm your meeting this afternoon?"

"It's just Gortran," he crackled.

"Of course, sir."

"I'm at Mayor Oculon's disposal, as always."

"Thank you, sir!" she said brightly. The door closed.

"Terminate all humans," he muttered. I knew he really meant "terminate all sea hags" or "terminate all crawling eyes." Just a nervous tic. A horrifying nervous tic.

It was then that I noticed Gortran had gone silent. No scratch of his pen, either. I might have thought he was asleep, if not for the fact that he was a robot. Did they even sleep? I had no idea. I was still pretty unclear as to how people turned into robots, and wasn't too keen on finding out. The only sound was the crackle of electricity climbing the Jacob's ladder sticking out of his head. From the sound of it, the arc was moving quickly, and from the steadily increasing glow, that line of lightning was thicker than my finger. The whole room had begun to smell quite strongly of ozone.

Had he somehow sniffed me out? Using not smell, but some weird robot sense, like radar, calibrated to sense weak flesh. Of all the myriad kinds of monsters, with new ones seemingly appearing every day, the robots were the ones I was convinced would ultimately decide they no longer needed humans. The others turned us, or ate us, or any number of things, but I always got the impression the robots were the only ones who were offended by us. Like they remembered when they were still flesh and blood and resented the hell out of it.

Of course, I could have been reading things into a perfectly innocent declaration like "terminate all humans."

I stayed right there, crouched under Gortran's desk as he buzzed and crackled and seemed to get angrier and angrier. Finally, he stood up and slapped the desk with his pincer hands.

The desk split in two, hatching me like an egg.

The robot looked down at me.

"Hi," I said.

FIFTEEN

You?" The face on the screen was momentarily baffled, but quickly turned angry, the static almost completely swallowing it up.

I reached into my pocket and whipped out my robot prevention: a postcard with M.C. Escher's *Relativity* on it. Gortran stopped in his tracks. The face flickered, spun, wiped, and suddenly was an empty prompt. His face said "LOADING..."

I quickly replaced the postcard in my jacket and stood up. He was going to be mad when he came to, which meant I had to make tracks, and fast. I gingerly picked my way between the halves of his desk, slipped out of the office, and scampered off the set as quick as I could. I only stopped running when I was safe outside and hidden amongst the rabble of the studio. There was a copse of potted palm trees probably waiting for some desert movie, and I took up residence with them.

As the day burned, I took the egg salad sandwich from my pocket, unrolled the bag, opened up the wax paper, and dug in. Not great, but then, egg salad's ceiling was "good" and this qualified, especially considering it had spent several hours in my pocket in the summer heat. I ended up eating the coleslaw off the blade of my dagger, which got me more than a few looks.

"What?"

But they were Teamsters, and cold iron wasn't going to do a damn thing to a bunch of killer vegetables. I think they were mostly just offended that I was eating cabbage.

So I waited. Gortran never poked his head out from inside, so apparently I'd either wrecked his brain or he wasn't as angry as I'd thought. I was fine with either. The business of the studio carried on around me. Doppelgangers rushed to their sets, zombies did the heavy blue-collar work, and an assortment of others went on their specialized errands. I saw the little gremlin with the puffy muttonchops holding his parasol and loping toward one of the sets. I didn't wave. That might be leading him on.

The afternoon wore on, baking me in my suit. I had already sweated through the undershirt and was working hard on the next layer. I passed the time practicing smoking, but still wasn't any good at it, and I'd gone through almost a whole pack. I had to be the only man in the universe who couldn't master that simple skill.

The sun was slowly sinking in the sky, offering me a little relief from the punishing heat of the day. Truth be told, I was toughing it out on the ghost of a hunch. Gortran might not get another visit from that witch, but Juba had been with him the day before he vanished, and Gortan had that matchbook. The robot was the key to this. Somehow.

The sun was getting dangerously low when a limousine pulled up right outside of the sound stage. The driver emerged, a headless horseman. They never could get the chauffeur's caps on them, which I thought was unfortunate. I stepped into the lee of the building where I was waiting, well-shadowed by the potted palms. A moment later, the chauffeur came back out, Gortran behind him. They stopped at the limo. The door opened and a blood-red tentacle beckoned the robot in. I might have been imagining it, but Gortran seemed a little scared. Or possibly hungry. I don't understand robots.

The limo started to roll toward the exit and I realized what I had to do.

I sprinted for the open gate.

In the guard house, Ugoth the Castrator was in the process of tearing a cow carcass in two. Better you than me, Bessie. I ran to my car and turned the engine over. I only had to hit the gas briefly to catch up with the limo. After dropping down to Sunset, they headed east. As the city got seedier, I wondered where they hell they were going. Slumming? In a limo?

Maybe that was how slumming was done.

Even before the war, my family wasn't really the kind who would go slumming. Or, more accurately, we'd have called it "homing." Dad used to like to joke that the family name came from the only green we'd ever touch. Sometimes I wish that statement hadn't become quite so ironic.

The limo cruised along Sunset, the buildings growing more dilapidated around it. Some of them still sported damage from the war: chunks of wall bitten out, black smears of soot, even lines of bullet holes. The limo didn't seem to care. Wherever it was headed, the driver knew the way. I was getting more than a little nervous—I was getting farther from home, and the sun was dipping lower and lower behind me until the shadow of my car kissed the limo's bumper.

Judging from my experience yesterday, there was no way I would make it home before the sun went down. A sane man would have turned around. But Evelyn Farrell made me stay out. In for a penny, I suppose.

And then, in a flash, I knew where the damned thing was going, even before it pulled up. Right on the corner of Sunset and Winona, the flashing neon sign said THE BOMB SHELTER. Lined up outside like soldiers on the parade grounds was a row of motorcycles. All black and silver, emblazoned over and over with the organ-playing skeleton of the Howlers. This wasn't just Howler territory; the Bomb Shelter was the beating heart of their empire. Supposedly, anyone who went in there who wasn't a phantom could expect their next appearance to be made face-down in the LA River. There wasn't even enough water in the river to properly float down it, especially in the summer. Insult to injury.

The limo parked and the driver got out to open the door for the passengers. Gortran was the first one out. Next was a crawling eye, slithering along on his clump of red tentacles. That had to be the unofficial mayor of Hollywood, Oculon. His iris was a deep burgundy that managed to convey a sense of elegant evil I was probably imagining. Actually, he was very pretty, as long as you ignored that he was four feet across. A lady phantom was last, wrapped up in a lovely evening gown, her hair immaculate over a ghastly face. Aria Enchantee.

I turned down the next corner and parked, assessing the situation. This was the lion's den. After dark was one thing, when any monster who recognized what I was had every right to turn me. Nothing I could do there. This was something entirely worse: the Bomb Shelter, where even being the wrong kind of monster could get your ass royally kicked.

The most tenuous of leads got me here, but that was all I had. Juba II just up and vanished into thin air. Evelyn Farrell had been burned to glass. And if I was going to find the guy and get some justice for her, my path led through the Bomb Shelter and about a hundred Howlers.

Fantastic.

I walked across the street as the sun was dipping out of sight. Look on the bright side. This was the last place anyone would be looking for humans. And besides, phantoms weren't known to identify humans on sight. Crawling eyes, sure. And Gortran and Aria Enchantee both knew me. But I was trying to make myself feel better, so I wasn't going to think about that.

There was no doorman. The place didn't need one. Who was crazy enough to enter that didn't belong?

The first thing that hit me was the smell of beer, permeating everything in the bar, baked into the floorboards and released with every booted stomp. Just underneath, leather, which everyone inside, with four exceptions, was covered in. Under that, the stale french fry smell of sweat. Packed in, almost shoulder to shoulder, were Howlers. Every one of them a waxy-skinned, snaggletoothed, hollow-eyed phantom, pulling on beers, pushing each other, glaring in the direction of the stage. The backs of their jackets were emblazoned with the skeleton at the pipe organ, the pipes dripping with threaded blood. There was an area of open ground, a buffer zone, around the three outsiders in the middle of the bar, the crawling eye flanked by the robot and the one elegant female phantom.

On the stage opposite, a band was setting up. Four phantoms, dressed in blue jeans or leather pants and sleeveless white shirts, showing off arms crawling with tattoos. One tuned a guitar, the other one of those new electric basses. One pushed his piano into place, another spun his drumsticks. The drum kit had two scrawled words across the bass drum: THE DISASTERS. That was the same heraldry I'd seen on the motorcycle at the studio.

And I recognized the lead singer. The phantom who

shouldered past me as I was on the way to Gortran's office for the first time. This was beginning to feel more and more like the correct call. Familiar faces were almost always a good thing. As long as I ignored the horrendous amount of danger I was in.

There were eyes on me. Bug eyes, some covered in a milky caul. I was safer moving, so I moved. Through the crowd, muttering to myself, hoping there wouldn't be too much hubbub over a little guy in a suit. I went through the only door I saw, the one in the back.

I found a dingy hall and a couple restrooms. At the end, the hall turned a corner into deeper darkness. I paused at the ladies room, almost overcome with sick fascination. Had it ever been used? Was it even a restroom anymore? Had they converted it into one of those weird deathtraps phantoms were supposedly obsessed with? Would I open the door into a pit of lions and collapsing chandeliers? And yet no amount of fascination could overcome the ingrained sanctity of the ladies room.

From the bar, I heard the singer say, "I'm Cacophony Jones, and we're the Disasters. This one goes out to all the kittens out there. This is 'Angel of Mayhem.'" Then, the music kicked in. Barely muffled by the walls, it was ear-splitting. I was tempted to call it noise, but it wasn't that. It was fast, it was driving, it was precise. Controlled chaos, it had all the complexity of jazz without the pretention and self-indugence. Before I knew it, I was tapping my foot and bobbing my head, my attention pulled inexorably back into the bar. Guess the Disasters were okay after all.

I shook my head. I didn't have time to appreciate music, and this was hardly the place, so I went to the corner of the hall. There was a bare bulb dangling from the ceiling, but it had burned out. A single door stood at the end, paint cracked over the heavy wood. I tried the knob. Locked. I paused. I could have sworn there was something moving behind that door, but couldn't hear it clearly over the sound of the Disasters. I reached into my jacket for lockpicks when the music suddenly got louder. Almost as quickly, it softened again. Through the din, I made out loud talking, out at the mouth of the hall.

"...went in here."

"You're sure he's still in here?"

"No way out."

That was not something I wanted hear as I pressed my back into the wall.

"Check the john."

There are very specific sounds that come with opening a door. A click of the knob, a creak, all nice and slow. I didn't hear those sounds. I heard a crash, a thump, and a second, softer thump. This was them kicking the door in. I pulled the compact that had frightened Imogen so, opened it up, and had a peek into the hall.

There were two phantoms in the hall covered in Howler leathers, both standing by the men's room and peering in. From the sounds of stall doors getting kicked open, there was another one in the can.

From the john, an agonized, "Goddamn it, Johnny!"

"Sorry, Apocalypse."

"You could've just knocked."

"I said sorry! Now pinch it off, we got an outsider back here."

I put the mirror away. Any one of those phantoms was bigger than me. And sure, I knew how to fight. But what they don't tell you is that no matter how good you are, three big guys pretty much trumps Golden Gloves any day of the week. And my gloves were aluminum at best.

Which left what I had on me that was anti-phantom. I racked my brain, amnesiac from fear. What was it? Salt? No, that was zombies. Cross? Vampires. Shit! My cat! No, that was the jaguar people and it was at home anyway.

"Not in there," said Johnny, the phantom kicking in the doors.

"Check the ladies?"

At least some of my curiosity would be assuaged. Small comfort, but I was willing to take whatever I could get. Now what the hell was it? Music? No, that was killer vegetables. Water? Robots and witches. No, wait, music. Music sounded right. Damn it!

The other door was kicked in, followed by the stalls, one at a time. Johnny had a heavy foot.

"Not in there, either."

"Must be over there."

"Door's locked."

"You hear me? You little maggot? I saw you come in. You listening to what we're saying? Your little maggot heart beating loud?"

They were getting close. I could practically smell them: leather and pomade over decay. What *was* it? Music. The Disasters continued to blare through the hall. It was a perfect sound, really. Every single one of those guys was a brilliant musician, never making a single mistake I could detect. Each song was flawless... and that was it.

The whistle was in a small pocket sewn into the lining of my jacket. I fished it out, my fingers shaking so badly it almost fell to the floor. I gripped it tightly and turned the corner.

The three phantoms were about four feet away, straightening suddenly as I looked up at them with what I hoped was convincing bravado. The Disasters stopped playing, maybe taking a little break.

"You a little small for a phantom, ain't ya?" the leader,

Johnny said. He was a big guy, larger than the two cronies behind him, and the greasy pompadour gave him another inch.

The guy behind him wore a rather jaunty leather cap. The other one had an improper ducktail hairdo. All three looked like half-rotten skulls, and were packing fists into leather-gloved hands.

"I'm a little small for a lot of things," I growled.

There was a long pause as we all realized that must have sounded better in my head.

Johnny peered at me. "What the hell are you? You ain't a wolfman or you'd have flashed a badge or wolfed out. You're too damn hairy for a vampire, and too alive for a ghoul."

"Maybe he's a meatstick, Johnny," said the guy in the cap.

"Dig that, Razz. Maybe he is. Still kinda small, though."

I put the whistle to my lips and blew. A single discordant note blared through the hall. All three phantoms dropped like stones, hands over their ears, moaning in pain. I grinned. Easy peasy.

I stepped through the writhing phantoms. "Not too small to get one over on the likes of you."

Just then, the men's room door opened to the sound of a flushing commode, and what I can only assume was Apocalypse stepped out. And kept stepping out. It seemed to take him about a week to fully emerge, like the sun rising up over my imminent and brutal asskicking. The guy was huge. He had to hunch to make it through the doorframe, and once in the hall, I swear he couldn't straighten up all the way. One of his fists was the size of my head, and his ham loaf of a face was crossed with more scars than your average meat golem. From the looks of him, he had picked a fight with a goddamn train, and I'd bet easy money he'd won. The grin spreading over his face made me feel like a bug that was about to get its legs ripped off.

I smirked back up at him. Didn't matter how big he was. One blast from the whistle and he'd be on the ground with all his friends. He reached for me. I put the whistle to my lips...

"This one's called 'Blasterade,'" said Cacophony Jones, leader of the Disasters. And right then, the band kicked in. Their sound, their perfect sound, rocketed through the hall, and as I blew, the shriek of the whistle was completely lost.

"Oh, shi—"

Apocalypse grabbed my shoulder and introduced me to the wall. Everything in me felt loose, like I was a jar of jellybeans shaken vigorously. I'm not sure how, but the whistle was still in my mouth. I blew, but the band was still playing. The other phantoms in the hall were getting up, rubbing their ears and looking like they might like to see exactly where in my body they could forcibly hide that whistle.

As Apocalypse geared up to slam me into the other wall, the song came to an end. Thank God their songs were short.

I blew as hard as I could.

Apocalypse dropped me and other phantoms fell to the ground with an agonized, "God dammit!"

I got up, the whistle still dangling from my lips like a cigarette, and opened the door into the club. The Disasters were onstage, playing something hard and driving, the audience of phantoms gazing up in rapture as they danced, drank, and, in one case, fought. Cacophony's grimace was the stuff of legends, sneering at his song, at the audience, at the whole world from the pedestal of his perfect song.

I looked around and barely caught the back end of Mayor Oculon slithering out the door. A quick squeeze through the crowd of giant terrifying bikers and I could be back on the trail of one of the most powerful monsters in Hollywood in the dead of night.

Until the Disasters made it to the end of the song. The phantoms started looking around, momentarily released from their trance. I held my breath, knowing that one would turn to me, point one of those fishbelly-white fingers, and every one of the Howlers would be on me like stupid on an ogre.

"This one's called 'Drink of Me,'" Cacophony announced, and the Disasters started playing. As I snaked between a couple of guys, I hoped this would be a good, long number.

The door to the back burst open, Johnny and his boys boiling out. Razz stopped, head moving to stare at the stage, mouth dropping open. Johnny slapped him, but Razz was done. Right as I looked, Johnny turned, his eyes meeting mine. "There!" he shouted. I could barely hear it over the exquisite racket of the Disasters.

They came after me, shoving through the crowd, and with Apocalypse leading the way, the phantoms parted. More and more of them turned to see what the problem was, and when they did, they saw me, the one guy in clothes that didn't come off the back of a cow. Pretty soon it was a sea of angry, half-melted faces pointed in my direction, ready to join Johnny in the righteous crusade of beating me halfway to next week.

Just then the Disasters stopped.

"Gentlemen!" I shouted. "I'll see you all later!" And blew the whistle.

Every one of them fell to the ground, clutching their ears, the Disasters included. I turned and ran from the club, looking both ways along the street. The limo was heading west on Sunset, back the way it came. I bolted to my car, starting her up just as the Howlers tore out of the club toward their bikes.

I slumped real low in my seat. Johnny pointed and shouted, and I was done for. Maybe I'd set some kind of record as the man who was killed the most.

They gunned the bikes, and I knew that would be the last thing I'd hear. The rumbling engines would get closer and that would be it.

The gang turned and roared in the other direction after a different car. My heart almost exploded with relief. Sorry, fella. Better you than me.

I tried not to floor it after the limo. The last thing I needed was to get pulled over by the Hollywood Sheriffs after dark.

The limo wound west, out of Hollywood and into the wilder areas. It disappeared for a second. I nearly panicked, but then there it was, heading north on Laurel Canyon. Up here, the houses were spaced out; most of the area was nothing more than scrubby hills. The limo and I were the only things on the road now, and the only lights were his, mine, and the occasional house.

I suddenly realized that I hadn't been outside in full dark for a couple of years. Not since the general amnesty and the Fair Game Law, around two years ago. Felt nice. For a little while, I could forget that I was the dream date for every monster out there. Besides, I'd made it out of the Bomb Shelter. I had the tools. They hadn't gotten me yet, and they wouldn't.

Sure, just keep telling myself that as I followed three incredibly powerful and connected monsters deep into the domain of the Hollywood Sheriff's Department.

Laurel Canyon turned onto Mulholland, a road that snaked through the foothills of the Santa Monicas. Houses were even farther apart here. This must be some party they were headed to, and with any luck I'd find Juba II there, sipping a cocktail or tripping a hex or whatever it was mummies did at parties. Telling pharaoh jokes, maybe.

I had no idea how far away my house was at this point. Sam was going to be worried.

Finally, the limo pulled into a driveway. I went past, checking to make sure it was just that and not another road. Yep, it was a long driveway, bordered on both sides by tall trees; at its end, barely visible from the street, stood a huge Victorian, painted dark colors that looked like shadows. I pulled over about a half-mile up the road, right around a bend where some trees would block my car unless someone was right on top of it, and started walking back.

Despite the scorching heat of the day, it had gotten cold up in the hills. That was the problem with deserts: always turning on you. Somewhere, off in the trees, something yipped and howled. I hoped it was only coyotes.

Then I heard a loud hiss and a pop, distant, but echoing. Clearly mechanical, but like nothing I'd heard before.

I made it back and went up the driveway, hugging the greenery along the side. Getting closer, I saw the limo with several other cars, all big, all expensive, all new, parked around the side of the house where the brick driveway created a lot. Past the screen of trees, there was a nice, if smallish, garden, decorated with a fancy fountain. Little stone gill-men frolicked in it, dragging nubile women into the watery depths. The house was enormous, and mostly done up in rich shades of burnished brown. As I stepped into the light of the porch, I looked up into the eaves.

There, looking back at me, was a silver snake.

Just like the matchbook.

No wonder no one knew about this goddamn place.

Cacophony Jones

SIXTEEN

I approached the house cautiously. It felt strange, almost like going up to a massive version of the matchbook in my pocket, ready for it to unfold. Along the way, I made a list of all the ways this was a terrible idea:

It was deep into the night.

I was somewhere along Mulholland.

I was standing in front of an old Victorian mansion.

The chances of it being haunted were close to a hundred percent.

The only lights came from the house itself and the antique streetlamps lining the walk.

And there were at least three monsters in there.

I sighed. What the hell was I doing? Trying to find Juba. For what, a check? For Evelyn Farrell? Find Juba, find who lit her up. Was that it? Was I really going that soft? One thought of the Farrells blubbering in the coroner's office answered that question.

As I had approached the mansion, it seemed to materialize

from the shadows, every step forward making it grow. Now that I was at the porch, the damn thing seemed to encircle the entire city. This place was big enough to get irrevocably lost in. I'd become the Donner Party, forced to eat whatever wall hangings and window treatments I could find. Hopefully it wouldn't come to that.

I put my foot on the first step up to the porch, and the front door flew open like it was on a pressure plate. I nearly screamed, but fortunately I had war-bred instincts to fall back on. Monsters loved screams: they made it easy to find humans, and during the Night War, you learned to keep your fear to yourself or you learned to live with some extra tentacles. Sometimes it was a little easier to hold back the yelling. In this case, the effort it took to stifle it nearly turned me purple, and what I saw was still going to be burned into my brain forever.

A bug-eyed monster stood on the threshold. Her flabby, potato-shaped body was covered in what was probably meant to be an evening gown, but the clumps of tentacles she had in the place of arms and legs spoiled that. Her noseless face was elaborately made up, including flanged designs painted on the corners of the bug eyes. She topped it off with a beehive hairdo that added a good two feet to her height. It was going to take a ton of self control not to punch her and run.

"Good evening, Mr..."

"Wolf."

"Mr. Wolf." She smiled, the most chilling grin I'd seen since my secretary's. "Mister? Officer? Or is it detective tonight?"

"No, nothing like that. I'm not here in an official capacity. This is completely, uh, recreational."

"My apologies, Mr. Wolf. Do you have an appointment?"

"I don't. Will that be a problem?"

"Not at all. Your choice is going to be slightly more limited than it would be otherwise, but I trust we can find something to suit you. Welcome to Fer-de-Lance."

"Oh, phenomenal. Thank you, Miss..."

"Miss Zoltar."

"Of course you are."

I followed her in, trying not to step in the mucus trail she left across the porch and the rug. Inside, the entry hall opened up into a huge living room draped with the kind of decadent furniture I remembered seeing one time in France. Wasn't too hard to figure out what kind of house I'd stumbled into. Pretty soon, there would be an array of ladies marched in, probably all in something silky and lacy, and I'd pick one and have an uncomfortable conversation with her about how I wasn't actually here for that, and she would be out whatever the johnnies normally paid.

I went over to the chair facing the entry hall, where a curving staircase went upstairs.

"Do you have a preference of location?" Miss Zoltar asked.

"Location? You mean, other than bedroom?"

"Bedroom might be difficult, though we do have one on the premises. You might have to wait. If you'd care to, we have films available to make your time more pleasant."

"What are the other options?" I asked, dreading the answer.

"Oh, you know. The usual ones. Cemetery, woods, old farmhouse, flying saucer landing." She ticked off the options on her masses of tentacles.

"These are usu... and where are they?"

"Out back, for the most part. We have a few in the house, although it is primarily for the staff."

"Can I see the, uh... the options?"

"Of course, Mr. Wolf. This really is your first time, isn't it? What's the occasion?"

"My, uh... my birthday. Commanding officer told me about this place."

"Sheriff Castle, of course. We're always happy to cater to his people. Please, come this way." Sheriff Castle. Had to be Hollywood. I filed that away as I followed Miss Zoltar along a lovely paneled hallway to a rear door. "I'm afraid a few of our sets are in use at the moment, although if one is to your liking, you're free to wait in the bar or theater until it becomes available."

"All right."

Her tentacle glommed into the door and pulled it open.

It's fair to say I wasn't expecting what I saw.

The mansion was perched on the tip of a small ridge, a gentle slope falling into a gully, then going back up in a lolling wave topped off with the night sky. Lights glittered from various structures dotting both slope and ravine. In a copse of pine trees, a few lights strung in the branches gave fitful illumination. Directly across from me, a glass ballroom was built into the side of the hill, gold light and piano music spilling from it. A small medieval castle built at the top of the ridge had torches burning in sconces. At the base of the gully, a flying saucer jutted from the ground, lit with carefully tended fires. Each one was some kind of bizarre theme room.

"So as you can see, many choices. Some fit naturally with a specific kind of lady or gentleman, but we're quite open to mixing and matching. Really, anything you desire."

"Uh... how about I see who's available?" So I can pick the one who looks the least angry. Or hungry.

"Of course. Please follow me back inside."

Right at that moment, a scream tore through us from the direction of what looked like a small schoolhouse. I tensed, and Miss Zoltar grinned. "Don't worry, tiger, you'll get your chance."

My chance to... what, exactly? I gave her a smile I hoped wasn't as queasy as it felt. She led me back in, to a new room, practically upholstered in red velvet. She moved over to the foot of the stairs, the suckers on her tentacles making little *plop-plop-plop* noises on the hard wood. Her tentacle touched a panel in the wall, which retracted, revealing a metal speaker attached to a glowing green rod. "We have a visitor!" Miss Zoltar purred into it, turning to me and flashing another terrifying smile. Was that what passed for charming amongst monsters? Footsteps echoed down a hallway, coming toward us from another room. As the mansion's employees came to greet me, I reflected that surprises were a dime a dozen tonight.

A meat golem—and a pretty one, as these things go—was the first in. The angry stitches pulling the disparate parts of her body into a single form were de-emphasized, hidden with what looked like makeup in the few places cloth wasn't covering them. The green skin tone meat golems got after being in the sun for more than a day was also concealed, although there were places—along the hairline, on the back of her neck—where the pancake makeup had not been applied quite right and she still looked like pea soup. She was dolled up as a cheerleader, in a short skirt and a sweater with a big scarlet A that I hoped was a coincidence.

Following her was an invisible man, though it took a little staring to see the clear areas around the mask he wore. He was in a letterman's jacket, pegged jeans, and a t-shirt, looking like every clean-cut quarterback in the city. The mask was pretty lifelike, considering. Unfortunately, the effect was ruined by the fact that the eyes were blank and shadowed. I tried not to let the fact that he was also a *he* bother me. I hadn't specified and, you know, Miss Zoltar was there to please.

The next one in line was a woman, a phantom specifically,

with the usual melty face, and I really didn't understand her character. She was dressed like a housewife, and not even a naughty one. Just your standard "hi honey, I'm home," type. She was even carrying a tray of muffins. I didn't remember seeing anything close to that in France. Not that I'd looked for it, so maybe I had just been missing out.

The parade continued. Most of the monsters were of the more human-looking variety, although there was a single gillman dressed in hip waders and a plaid shirt, carrying a fishing pole. I might have been imagining the faintly humiliated look on his fishy face. Mostly, though, it was zombies, phantoms, witches, and invisible people, the types who could pass as meatsticks with enough makeup, good costumes, and a prop or two. Oddly, no doppelgangers—most of them probably made more doing even less at the studios in town.

They fanned out as though posing for a class photo, all looking expectantly at me. I was trying to find the ability to speak when Miss Zoltar said, "Sherry, please."

The meat golem cheerleader stepped forward and chirped, "I'm Sherry Smith! It's late and I'm trying to make it home before curfew, and decided to cut across the old woods."

I swallowed.

Sherry stepped back.

"Steve?" Miss Zotar prompted.

The invisible man stepped up. "Hi, I'm Steve Smith. Practice ran late, and the guys want to go drinking in the old cemetery. Sounds like fun to me."

This was getting distinctly uncomfortable.

"Donna?"

"Hi, I'm Donna Brown!" said the phantom housewife. "I was working so hard on making these delicious muffins for my husband, I forgot the wards and now there's a way into my house."

It went on down the line like that one. Each one had a story about how they were wandering alone at night next to the old lake, or haunted house, or abandoned clown college, or how they were otherwise completely vulnerable to monster attack. Each one with a normal-sounding name and a nothing job.

Monsters dressed like humans. Helpless humans. All of them with their eyes on me, maybe seconds from realizing I was the only real human in the room. An actual helpless human with a nothing job who decided to wander into the woods and check out a haunted house.

Irony is hilarious.

"So, Mr. Wolf, do you have a favorite? If you're uncertain, Sherry specializes in werewolves, and if you're a bit of a classicist, we have a pretty convincing moors a short walk from here."

"Moors? I'm really more of uh... yeah, I guess, you know, when you're a werewolf, you really want to... get some peat under your paws. Growl a little. Maybe rip up someone's slippers."

Miss Zoltar's expression was frozen in something horrible and unreadable and possibly encouraging of the overwhelmed new client. Just as terrifying, albeit in a different way, a couple of the working girls and guys were beginning to look skeptically at me. One pretty brunette, dressed up as a medieval peasant girl, had begun sniffing the air. Uh-oh.

"Right! I should really, uh, pick. So you all can get back to work."

I looked over the assemblage with no idea which monster I wanted to go off alone with, and only the faintest idea of what to do when we did. What had a hard time detecting humans? Which ones could I incapacitate quickly and quietly? Not the phantoms—blow that whistle in here and I'd bring every werewolf in the place down on my head. Not the gill-man—he was about twice my size, and there were the claws to deal with. Not the invisible people—once they got naked, they would be impossible to deal with. Maybe the meat golem?

As I was frantically ticking them off my mental list, I finally noticed her. Standing up on her tiptoes, bugging out some big green eyes. A blonde, cute rather than pretty, and dressed up like some kind of lady adventurer, all browns and khaki. "How about her?"

"Mary, please?"

Mary jumped out of the crowd with a cheerful smile and did a little twirl. That's right. Mary Brown, on an expedition with her scientist father, separated from the group and now lost. "Uh, yep. Mary," I said.

"You may all go," Miss Zoltar said, and the other monsters filed out, although the sniffing woman gave me a last quizzical glare that I didn't like one bit. As the gill-man in the hip waders waddled out, one of Miss Zoltar's tentacles closed the door. "And your choice of venue, Mr. Wolf?"

"How about the... castle, I guess?"

"Wonderful choice. You can work out your scenario with Mary. Do have a *lovely* time. Happy birthday, Mr. Wolf." She opened the door for us, and Mary laced her arm through mine, rather forcefully I thought, and escorted me out into the night. She pulled us over to a stone path that led down into the gully and turned into steps on the other side, heading up toward the little castle. Behind the stone parapets of the castle, the moon was hanging low.

And full.

Oh, goodie.

When we were almost to our destination, Mary spun on me. "What the hell are you thinking?"

"I'm not sure. I thought... well, you *are* a prostitute, right?"

She slapped me. Hard.

"So that's a no."

"I'm not a prostitute! And you're not a monster!"

"Keep your voice down!"

She dragged me toward the castle, pulled a lever that dropped the drawbridge, and yanked me inside.

"You're not a monster," she hissed.

As she said it again, my blood got a nice shot of ice and my hand automatically went into my jacket for a weapon, but I realized I didn't know what to pull.

"What are *you*?"

"An actress!"

"You call this acting?" I glanced around. We were in what I guess was a courtyard, but it was only about half the size of a basketball court. The right-hand tower looked like you could actually go into it, but the left one seemed solid. She pulled me through a heavy wooden door at the far end of the courtyard. Inside was a small feasting hall, complete with prop food on a long table.

"Wow. This place is pretty good," I said, one hand still in my jacket, playing over my collection of possible weapons. "Wait. Why aren't you trying to turn me?"

"Oh, look at the ego on this one."

"It's happened enough in the past couple days for a pattern to emerge."

"Pattern, ego."

Still tensed, I stared at her, realization dawning over me like the false plasma sunrise of a death ray. "You're not a monster, either."

She shushed me. "You know what happens if any of *them* hear that?"

"The same thing that happens if they hear you say the same

thing about me. What the hell *is* this place?"

"Come on," she said. Mary led me out the back of the miniature great hall, through a bedroom made up like something out of an old Errol Flynn picture, out into a small chamber where a wooden ladder went up through a hole in the masonry. We climbed up, emerging onto the second-story walkway running around the entire castle. From there, she pulled me into the open tower and up the stone spiral staircase. Vertigo was a bit of a problem, since the cold desert wind slashed in through the open windows, and the view three flights down was almost directly into the gully and the fitful burning of the crashed flying saucer. Mary didn't seem to care. She peered out, scanning through the night, and pointed. "There."

She moved out of the way to give me a clear view. About a hundred feet away on top of the ridge was a miniature ski lodge, complete with a little gondola whose lines stretched back to the central house. The lights in the lodge were all on, and through the windows, I saw Mayor Oculon.

Well, I'm guessing it was Oculon. It was possible it was another crawling eye, but fortunately, they were pretty rare beasts. Maybe they were more common in areas of the country without so many sandy beaches to contend with. I could see a woman, dressed for cold weather, shining a flashlight around. Something about her looked off, but I wasn't sure what, exactly. It was likely some of her monstrous features peeking out through her costume, even if I couldn't see exactly what those were from this range. Tentacles materialized from the gloom behind her, always dancing out of the way of the light. Teasing, testing. Stalking. And then, they wrapped around her, and with a piercing scream, she fell out of sight.

"Holy—"

"And there," she said, pulling me over to the other window

and pointing to the ballroom. I couldn't be sure, but seeing it all lit up now, it looked remarkably similar to the place I'd seen on the film in Gortran's office.

A man played the piano, oblivious to the world around him. Just then, a masked phantom—Aria Enchantee; I recognized the dress—came in from behind him and spoke. The man stopped playing, tensing up as the phantom held out a hand. After a short conversation, he began to play and she began to sing. The act culminated when she slid beside the pianist and grabbed him. His wispy calls for help floated across the gully.

"And there," she said, pointing me farther down the ridge where sparks hissed from the windows of a distinctly German-looking lab. A young man in pajamas ran up to the window and screamed, then ran out of sight. Shortly after, a clanking box with lightning climbing his antennae waddled past the window, his pincers snapping at his prey. I couldn't see the image on Gortan's TV-screen head, but even money said it was the test-pattern Indian.

"Those people. They're not people," I said to Mary, unable to take my eyes off the now-still ballroom.

She shook her head.

"Monsters pretending to be people."

She nodded.

"And you're a person pretending to be a monster pretending to be a person."

She nodded.

"That's... uh... how do you get into this line of work?"

She ignored the question. "Monsters like to turn people. Or pretend to, anyway."

"And then what?"

"And then nothing. They stalk us, pretend to turn us, pay, and leave."

"Wait, you work in a brothel and don't have sex with anyone?"

"No!"

"That's sick!"

She looked to be plotting my death. Fairly elaborately. "Now, you want to tell me what the hell you're doing here?"

"Following them," I said, pointing to the dark ballroom and then to the ski lodge, then down to the lab.

"Why would you do that?"

"I'm a private eye."

"Following a crawling—"

"Yes, it's very funny. Do you know them? That group?"

"Juba's friends? Of course."

"Juba II? The city councilman?"

"You know him?" she said brightly.

"Not exactly. I'm trying to find him. He's disappeared."

"Oh no! What happened?"

"Well, that's sort of what I'm trying to piece together. Those are Mr. II's friends? Is that all of them?"

"They don't come together every time, but there's a group of them. Oculon; Aria something, that's the phantom. The robot in that lab over there, and there's a gremlin too. Sometimes Sheriff Castle is with them."

I didn't like that last part. "And how do you know Juba?"

She blushed. "I'm his favorite girl."

How was I going to break this to Imogen? *Your husband wasn't cheating with Aria Enchantee. They just go to the same brothel, where he was going after the monster equivalent of a younger woman.* But... wait. He was pretending to turn Mary and at the same time, actually turning Evelyn Farrell. Something wasn't quite adding up.

"Does he know you're human?"

She hesitated before nodding. "I told him eventually."

"And?"

"He promised not to tell anyone."

"How are you pulling this off? That werewolf in there was already sniffing me out!"

"Disguise hexes. Well, actually, that's just what I'm telling them. I bought a couple to keep on hand, just in case someone starts snooping around. I look, sound, and smell just like a human. Means I can practically name my price."

Pretending to be a monster by not pretending. Mary Brown was not just playing a dangerous game, she was beating the stuffing out of it like an All-American. I rummaged in my jacket, since my hand had been lodged there ever since I tried to figure out what Mary was anyway, and pulled out a battered container. I shook a cigarette out of the pack and managed to miss my hand. It rolled away into the dark, and I tried to pretend that had been the plan all along.

"Tell me about Juba," I said, wanting to change the subject.

"He's a really sweet guy. Most of the monsters who come in... this is some sort of back-to-the-grave thing for them. They can get a little... carried away. Not Juba. Sometimes in the scenarios, he doesn't even turn me, and when he does—well, pretends to—it's different."

I leaned forward, trying to look as sympathetic as I could. Either I was being played for a complete sucker, or she really liked the guy. "Different how?"

"He liked to ask my permission."

"And that's unusual."

She laughed. "It's unheard of! The whole point of Fer-de-Lance is to let monsters be monsters, and that means never asking."

I looked over at the fake ski lodge, but the flashlight had gone out, leaving blackness in the windows.

Mary kept talking. Guess she needed to confess, and I was

her priest. Role-playing, right? "Something was bothering him. I knew it. He never said anything, but I could tell. Eventually, he asked me if I knew any witches. He wanted hexes."

"Amnesia spells."

"Yes."

"And you gave him your dealer, the one who made those disguise spells for you. A witch. Redhead, right? Lots of hair, kind of curly? Wears a patched-up dress?"

"How did you know that?"

I gave her my best attempt at an "all-knowing detective" look. "What's her name? How do I find her?"

"Hexene Candlemas. She has an herbalist shop on Gower."

A name with the face, and now a location. Of course, knowing who and where she was didn't make it any safer to go after her, since she was, in all probability, the person who made Juba II disappear. Maybe even the one who turned Evelyn into glass. At least I'd have my evil eye ward and maybe a bucket of water when I got to her. That would even things up.

Mary noticed my grim look and said, "What? Does Hexene have something to do with this?"

"Thanks for your time, Mary. Good luck on the, uh, on the acting."

"Wait. You owe me fifty dollars."

I blanched. "I don't have fifty dollars."

"I could always start yelling about a human on the property."

"I could do the same."

We had what the local wits had termed a Human Standoff. Two meatsticks ready to sing a high note for some scaly attention, knowing it doomed us both.

I said, "Look. I'm trying to help Juba here. When I find the guy, I'll tell him he owes you another fifty, and he'll pay up."

"And if you never find him?"

"I'll add it to my expense report under 'unspecified bribes' and get his wife to fork it over."

She nodded, straightened, and belted out an ear-splitting shriek that probably melted the paint on my car.

"What the hell are you doing?" I hissed at her.

"Screaming," she said. "You hired me for a scene, and if we don't make a little noise, people are liable to get wise."

"You're serious."

She nodded, and somehow managed to find an even higher and more terrified note. I could see why she was able to charge so much. There was such a crystalline quality to her fear. I was so busy appreciating it that apparently I missed my cue.

"Now you," she said, nudging me.

"I don't think I can scream that high."

"No! You're supposed to be a werewolf, right? One of Castle's boys? That means you need to make wolf sounds."

"Uh. Woof?"

"Louder. And better."

"Better? How better?"

"Come on! You've heard wolves before."

I tried not to feel so self-conscious, since this was to preserve my cover. I tried to summon the howling in my head. During the Night War, the hills around the Los Angeles Basin were lousy with werewolves and wolfmen. I had done my share of hunting them with a bolt-action rifle and a German Luger I took off a dead SS officer I had fallen on top of on D-Day. Having an American paratrooper falling on him wasn't what killed the fella, but I can comfortably say I had never seen anyone look so surprised until a couple years later when that giant ape moved into Catalina.

The sound of their howling locked in place, I tried one. "Arooooooo." It died pretty quick because I felt like an idiot.

Mary nodded eagerly, though, and gestured at me to keep going.

I howled again, this time with a little more gusto. She nodded again, and screamed, pointing at me to howl in counterpoint. We did that a few more times until my throat was good and raw and she broke off mid-shriek.

"Okay," she said, catching her breath. "That should be good. Now let's get you out of here before someone figures out what you are."

"Good idea."

Mary led me back out of the castle, down into the gully, and around the side of the house. "Normally, we'd be going to the bar for a little drink to unwind," she said wistfully.

"Do mummies drink?"

"Well, no. But he's happy to watch me drink. Doesn't need his hexes then, either."

"I like to drink. Well, not a lot. I mean, I'm not a drunk or anything like that. I'm not opposed... you know, I'm no teetotaler..."

"You're a detective?"

"Yes."

She shook her head. "Good luck finding him."

"He ever make any promises to you? With regards to his marital situation?"

She stopped. "Just do your job, detective. You let his relationships alone."

I shrugged. "All right, then. Thank you, Mary. Have a nice evening." I turned and walked to the corner of the house, backpedaling quickly into the darkness at what I saw. Aria Enchantee waited on the porch, drawing on a cigarette ensconced in a long holder. A moment later, a cherry Rolls-Royce pulled up. A killer carrot in a chauffeur uniform got out, shuffled over to the rear door, and opened it. Apparently, Miss Enchantee didn't want to stick around with her pals and had called her own car. Aria nodded to her driver and slunk into the back. The carrot got into the driver's seat and started the car.

At that moment, the panels came off the car, supported by fully articulated arms made of the raw pistons and machinery of the automobile, revealing the two shocked and terrified monsters inside. The panels slammed down, pushing the car off the ground, while Aria Enchantee shrieked and her carrot chauffeur made that weird buzzing sound killer vegetables did. Irons clapped over both monsters as the car flipped over, then opened like a flower. Strapped to rails, the monsters zoomed to the center of the contraption's mass and the entire car collapsed into a tight ball. They went silent.

Carrot juice dripped onto the front lawn.

SEVENTEEN

The screaming started a second later. It seemed like a second, anyway. I was too stunned after watching a Rolls-Royce turn into a cartoon trash compactor to accurately measure time.

"What in the name of the twelve apostles is going on here?"

Crawling eyes don't really have mouths. I'm still not entirely certain where their voices come from. And they all have these radio-ready voices, glib, deep, and smooth. Always sounds like they're trying to sell you something, even when they aren't. Disembodied, too, usually emanating from thin air, ahead and in front of the massive eyeball that makes up their body.

Mayor Oculon had slithered out onto the porch and down some of the steps, his eye taking in the folded-up car. Miss Zoltar shrieked and slithered up next to the eyeball, a mass of tentacles over her face. She shrieked again, maybe concerned that the first one didn't take. Oculon wrapped her up in some tentacles and used another mass to rocket a slap across her face. "Get ahold of yourself, woman!"

Miss Zoltar screeched in theatrical distress.

"I need to know what happened, or so help me...!"

It took Oculon a minute or two to calm Miss Zoltar down, minutes I stayed crouched around the side of the house, my back pressed to the siding. There were entirely too many tentacles on that porch for my taste. When Miss Zoltar was relatively coherent, she stammered out exactly what I had seen, albeit with more swooning. Oculon listened. It was difficult to read his expression, considering he didn't have a face, or even a massive eyebrow to raise skeptically.

A moment later, a sparking and fuming Gortran tottered out of the house to join the crawling eye and the bug-eyed monster.

"After all day working and... what's that?"

"Aria's car."

"That's not a car," Gortran said. "You know how I can tell? I couldn't drive it."

"It *was* Aria's car. Now it's a depressing reminder of mortality."

"Oh, I can't possibly!" Miss Zoltar swooned, but when neither Oculon nor Gortran moved to catch her, she steadied herself.

"Where's Aria?"

"In her car," Oculon said in a tone that made me want to buy soap flakes.

Gortran's television face lost vertical hold for a moment. "Oh. So she's, hmm..."

"Extremely," Oculon confirmed.

"How?"

"Whoever did this waited for Aria to get into the car. The murderer might still be here."

Miss Zoltar fainted, for real this time. Neither Oculon

nor Gortran cared enough to catch her and her flabby body collapsed onto the porch.

"Call Lobo. Now," Oculon said.

Almost immediately, Gortran started crackling, "Gortran to Castle, come in Castle. Over."

Oculon turned toward the house and I slunk back into cover. Crawling eyes saw everything. If I sprinted into the wilderness, he'd see me clear as day and I'd be finished. He'd know I was human instantly, and then I'd be wishing I'd let Sam Haine turn me into a pumpkinhead while I lived out the rest of my days as a giant eyeball.

I hugged the wall, heading for the back, praying that I could maybe get far enough away to make escape possible. From the front of the mansion, I could hear Oculon keeping up his stream of orders, delivered in the same sonorous tones. He was telling some of the women to take care of the fallen madam, get her inside, and fix her a stiff drink.

I made it around the corner. The gully, dotted with its sets, dipped in front of me. Maybe I could make it up and over, then double back to my car. It wouldn't be pretty, but I could get out of there before—

The howls started from atop the ridge. I saw them in flashes, large furry shapes momentarily silhouetted against the night sky before surging over the rise to be invisible against the wall of the gully. Three of them. Coming right at me.

I nearly ran for the front of the house before remembering that Oculon would be waiting there, quite capable of seeing me for what I was, and probably more than happy to blame me for his friend's crushing death. So I went up the back steps and into the house, hoping to find Mary.

I didn't, instead running right into Sherry, the meat golem cheerleader. "Do you know where Mary is?"

"You looking for another round, wolfie?"

I rolled my eyes and let her go. Toward the front of the house, more and more of the monsters were milling around. Get too close, with everyone's blood up, and I was a goner. Maybe they'd sniff me out and blame the human for the mess on the front lawn; maybe they'd just attack and sort the mess out later. It was nighttime, after all—it wouldn't even be illegal. Right as I entered, the woman in the peasant costume whipped around, her nose sifting through the scents on the air.

I darted a hopeful look at the stairs and saw Mary's khakis retreating. I pushed through the crowd of monsters, each one giving me a glance or a glare, some staring longer than I would have liked. Outside, Oculon was trying to calm everyone down, though, to be fair, not everyone was panicking. A large gray wolf padded around the side of the house and approached him, turning into a naked man as he approached. He was shaggy, with a mane of gray hair, and lambent yellow eyes I could see from where I was. Hairy, though not as hairy as I would have liked.

"Thank you for coming, Sheriff," Oculon said.

Beyond, two more wolves paced around the perimeter. I couldn't see them clearly, as they kept to the perimeter of the light. So now I was cordoned in by werewolves, trapped in a house full of nervous monsters.

To hell with subtlety. I ran up the stairs. The second floor was plush and well lit, hallways lined with doors extending and turning corners. "Mary!" I whispered. "Mary, where are you?"

After a moment, a frowning Mary backed up around one of the corners. "What are you still doing here?"

I ran to her. "The phantom. Aria Enchantee. She was killed!"

"I know," she said. "Was it you?"

"Of course not! Did you see how it was done? I don't have the kind of mechanical know-how to do any of that. I doubt anything human does. If I had to put money on it, I'd say a gremlin was settling a score. Didn't you say they have a gremlin friend?"

She nodded. "Uh... Brows, they call him. Has big white eyebrows."

"Yeah, I put that together." Familiar, too. I'd seen a gremlin like that at the studio, calling Gortran to the set.

The murmuring downstairs got louder.

"All right, I want everyone to gather up, employees in one room, customers in another." The voice was rough and deep, and it didn't take a PI's license to guess that it belonged to Sheriff Castle. "Is there anyone upstairs?"

Miss Zoltar was out of breath, and I could imagine her fanning her terrifying face with a clutch of tentacles. "I think there might be. Would someone please...?"

I pulled Mary down the hall. "Mary, do you still have any of those emergency disguise hexes?"

"Why?"

"Why do you think?"

"So you can lie to the sheriff? I don't think that sounds wise."

"I'll pay."

"Oh, so you'll pay now?"

I opened up my wallet and emptied it out.

She looked at the money. "Sixteen dollars?"

"It's all I have!"

"You keep it. I'll add it to what Juba's wife owes me. You're keeping a tally, right?"

The thought of Aria, now so much phantom-and-carrot soup inside that car, made me want to speed negotiations up.

"Maybe you could invoice me?"

"Come on." She jogged down the hall to one of the doors, opening it quickly. Inside was a bedroom, though it wasn't one that looked like it got much use. She opened the closet, revealing a large walk-in lined with costumes ranging from the ridiculous to the bizarre. She knelt under the clothes, rummaging around, until she found a shoebox. Inside, nestled amongst other keepsakes, were little squares of parchment exactly like the ones I saw in Juba's secret room. "I keep a couple used ones just for appearance's sake," she explained as she sifted through a few faded pieces. "Here we are."

She handed over a square with the spell on it. "When you say the words, picture exactly what you want to be, all right? Everyone will react to you as though you're the image in your head. But you have to believe it completely. The more you doubt it, the more it slips. Understand?"

I nodded, thrusting my hand out for the hex.

She handed it over. "*Caveat emptor.*"

"No thanks, I've already eaten."

"It means 'buyer beware.'"

"I'm bewaring. I haven't stopped bewaring since Miss Verity hired me." Glancing at the script, I couldn't help but wonder how much the actual words mattered. "You're sure this woman is literate?"

"It's not in English."

"Yeah, I can tell."

"Read it like it's spelled."

So I did, trying not to stammer, which for me is a tall order. I pictured a monster in my head, and maybe it was because of the Bomb Shelter earlier, but I pictured a phantom. Me as one, anyway. Nick Moss with a melty face, milky eyes, and snaggleteeth. Probably good at some kind of instrument. How about the sousaphone? All right, that works. I was a sousaphone player for the band down at the Gloom Room. Spending time with my favorite girl, Mary Brown. I looked up from the paper, the words still bouncing around my head.

She blinked. "You play the sousaphone?"

"What? I... I mean, yes. Perfectly. How did you know?"

She gestured at the air around me. "One appeared around you for a moment. Like a ghost."

I wished I'd seen that. Just then, there was a knock at the door. "Mary? Mary, are you in there?"

"Yeah, Ida. In here with a client."

"Sheriff is downstairs. Wants everyone in one place to be questioned."

"We'll be right down." Mary turned to me. "Ready?"

I nodded. I could do this. I just had to completely, utterly believe that I was a sousaphone player with a dead face. Mary opened up the door and I followed her downstairs. There were three naked men standing in the front hall, the sheriff stars tattooed on their chests only semi-visible under the rugs they called chest hair. They looked up at Mary and me, and I knew, just knew the sons of bitches could sniff me right through the mask. I clamped down on the thought. Couldn't think like that. Had to believe. This was the same disguise Mary pretended to wear night in and night out and it was so good no monster ever questioned it. It wasn't a disguise. Who I am. The sousaphone player at the Gloom Room.

So I smiled at the sheriff and his deputies.

"Employees in there," Sheriff Castle said, gesturing to the front room now filled with a mixture of bored and frightened monsters. "Customers in there," he added, gesturing to another door off to the side.

I nodded to them—*just a citizen cooperating here, a normal phantom like any other*—and headed into the room indicated. The door swung open to a smaller sitting room. Gortran was in there, pacing and sparking, as was a pumpkinhead, lounging on a sofa and tapping an irritated and thorny hand on an end table. I took a seat and tried to look as inconvenienced as they did.

The pumpkinhead nodded to me, the flames behind his eyes dim as candles. "You see anything?"

I shook my head. "I was upstairs, picking out a costume."

He nodded. "Someone got killed, I guess."

"Someone," Gortran sparked. "Aria Enchantee, you philistine. Terminate all humans."

The pumpkinhead shrugged, giving me a look that said he and I were in this together.

"Shouldn't even be in here," the robot muttered.

We waited in silence while Gortran seethed palpably from the indignity of being treated like everyone else. Abruptly, I did not envy Imogen. Even though she'd tried to turn me, I couldn't help but sympathize: working with this guy must be a nightmare.

A moment later, the door opened and one of the deputies poked his head in. He glanced around, settled on me, and said, "Sir, would you come with me, please?"

Not "meatstick" this time. What a difference a face makes.

The deputy herded me into the kitchen, a fairly large room toward the back of the house. Sheriff Castle waited, leaning against the sink, arms folded and looking rather angry. He was a big man, maybe even a full foot taller than me. Broad, too. The guy looked like he could throw me like a football. As I walked in, he fixed me with a dark gaze. *I'm not human. Just a normal, everyday phantom.*

"What's your name?"

The one goddamn thing I'd forgotten. "Uh... Angelo. Angelo

Music."

Castle shook his head. "What is it with phantoms and that name? 'Course, if I had a nickel for every guy on the force named Wolf... it's like meatsticks with 'Smith' and 'Rodriguez.'" He sighed. "And what are you doing here, Mr. Music?"

"The, uh, the usual, sir."

"What do you do for a living?"

"Sousaphone player for the band at the Gloom Room. I come here once a month. To blow off steam." I was getting into this. That sounded like something Angelo would do.

"Uh-huh." Couldn't tell if Castle believed me. How do you read a werewolf? He wasn't wagging his tail. He didn't even have a tail at the moment. Couldn't think about it. I had to be Angelo Music, who didn't read anything other than sheet music.

"Did you see anything?" he asked.

"I saw a little bit when I came downstairs. Looked like someone stepped on a car and then put some legs on the side."

Castle stared at me and sniffed the air. Just once. I tried not to let the worry show on my face. My melty monster face. What was he smelling? What did a phantom smell like to a werewolf? Rosin and strings? The sewer underneath an opera house? Did that smell different than a normal sewer? Of course. I knew the answer to that, because I was a goddamn phantom. A phantom of the Gloom Room.

"Tell me something, Mr. Music, do you have a favorite performer here?"

"Mary. Mary Brown."

He nodded, like he pulled her from memory. "And if I asked her, she would know you?"

Not by that name. "Yeah."

"You're sweating, Mr. Music."

My hand went to my forehead to mop up the flop sweat before I realized how truly guilty that made me look. "It's hot in here."

"No, it's not."

"Well, you're naked. So, you know, uh, you feel the cold a little more."

The werewolf grinned at me. "Tell me, Mr. Music, why did you kill Aria Enchantee?"

"I didn't!"

"I know a phantom trap when I see one. Don't think this is the first time one of yours got a little obsession and a poor innocent girl ended up dead in some bizarre contraption."

"That was a gremlin kill and you know it."

"Thought you said you didn't see it."

I was gobsmacked. Rookie mistake. I should have known better. I was the one that sprang things like that, not the stooge who fell for it.

Castle squinted. "Are you all right, Mr. Music?"

"I" meant Nick Moss. Goddamn it. I was supposed to be... what was it? Angelo Music. Saxophone player? Son of a bitch. I could feel the face fading under the werewolf's attention.

"You don't look so good."

"Well, you know, zombie complexion."

"You're a phantom."

"What's the difference?" I tried a laugh, but it sputtered and died. Bad choice of expression.

He took two steps toward me, form already shifting. Pretty soon he'd be that big gray wolf I'd seen earlier and things would get very bad for me. Without thinking, I reached into my jacket, pulled the wolfsbane, and flicked a nice pinch right into his lengthening snout.

With a howl, the sheriff dropped to the ground, snuffling,

pawing at his face with hands that weren't quite hands anymore. Caught halfway through his change, he could not have looked more awkward writhing on the ground. Not that this helped me too much, not after assaulting an officer of the law in the commission of his duty. He was making a sound that was almost a dog's yelp and almost a man moaning in pain.

I rushed out the door, knowing the noises he was making were loud enough for all the werewolves to hear.

"Hey! Stop right there!" a deputy called after me. I kept running for the back, getting a glimpse of my terrified face in a window. Half-phantom, half-human, and melting like this afternoon's ice cream. Oh well. It almost worked.

I plowed through the back door into the cold night and ran for the gully.

In the house, one of them howled. Then another, finding a different, discordant pitch. And then the third, joining the other two. Three werewolves, ready to run me down. They knew the hills. They could see in the dark. They had badges.

I was a dead man.

If I was lucky.

Sheriff Lobo Castle

EIGHTEEN

There's a problem with running from werewolves, and that's the fact they're faster than humans.

And when I say "werewolves," I mean the ones who turn into actual wolves. The wolfmen are another kind, and both claim to be the original version of the monster. There's a bit of a schism between werewolves and wolfmen, and while I might not understand it, I am grateful for anything that makes monsters pay more attention to each other than me.

For the lay person, wolfmen are the ones that usually join the LAPD; when they shift, they sort of lope along, hunched over and awkward. They look a little like a drunk college freshman trying to evade campus police. You can outrun those guys if you stick to straight lines and sprint in the early going. They tend to rely on natural terrain and the ability to use doorknobs to catch their prey, and they might brag about their animal senses, but I've never seen any one of them do something with their noses I couldn't.

But the werewolves, the ones in the Hollywood Sheriff's

Department and probably all the other ones, too—those were pretty much impossible to outrun. You could tire them out, sure, assuming you could avoid them long enough. A human being can run a horse down if you give us the chance. I learned that in Basic, when they made me run while wearing a pack that weighed as much as I did. The problem is, put a man and a werewolf on open ground, and within five minutes, the werewolf is going to have the man on the ground crying uncle. And there was the fact that the wolves hunted in packs and had trained to do this at the Police Academy.

I broke out into the night, running downhill because I wasn't exactly thinking straight. Right at the bottom of the hill was the fake crashed saucer, glowing a faint green in the dark, little fires burning safely in pits in varying intervals around it. As I came to a stuttered stop at the bottom of the gully, the arc of the saucer protruding from the ground right in front of me, the wolves howled at the top of the hill, out under the night sky. I cursed, slapping a hand on the smooth metal before me. With a soft scrape, like someone opening an old can, a portal opened in the side. I jumped in and touched the wall until it slid shut.

The lights were on in the flying saucer, but no one was home. Tubes carried a luminescent green liquid that provided the odd light. The entire thing was tipped up on its side, sloping down toward a chintzy cockpit. Well, okay, that wasn't fair, I realized as I moved deeper into the thing. This set was easily the equal of anything I'd seen at Visionary. Even better, since I could actually crawl through the thing without the illusion breaking.

Outside, the wolves howled again, getting closer. I considered my options. I could plug them with silver bullets, sure. No safe way to get all of them, and that made me a murderer besides. Killing police wasn't a good way to get popular, and being a human killer? The trial would only last long enough to fit me for Old Sparky's cap.

I checked my wolfsbane. A little left, but nowhere near as much as I'd like. Those kinds of things were stopgaps, anyway. A way to keep a monster at bay for those extra seconds you needed to get somewhere safe. Not something to incapacitate three cops.

The saucer's interior was a single hallway wrapping around a core. A doorway on the other side of the cockpit—really, just the foremost section of the saucer—led into the core, and I found a hinged lid there. Peeking inside, I saw a tank of glowing green liquid, the source of all the light in here. It smelled artificial, like engine degreaser, and was strong enough to make my eyes water. That was a good sign. Not the most pleasant place, but with the wolves so close, I didn't really have another option. I put a hanky over my nose and climbed up to the tank.

The stuff felt like cold snot and there was a ton of it. Wasn't caustic, and maybe in the right mood, I could have even found it pleasant. Well, as pleasant as bathing in cold, glowing green snot was going to be.

Outside, the howls turned into snuffling, followed by the scrape of the door. "Fan out." Castle's voice, turning back into a snarl as he changed again.

The hairs on the back of my neck would have stood up, but they were tacked down with goo. I could hear the werewolves sniffing around the saucer, following my trail right to the vat of stuff.

I would be caught in moments.

I reached into my jacket, my hand closing around the revolver loaded with silver slugs. Three shots, right? Cramped quarters meant not much chance of missing. Pop all three cops, and then, what, a thousand years in jail? That's if they didn't just string me up instantly from the nearest streetlamp.

My hand left the revolver. Moved over in the gloppy confines of my jacket to the whistle. I pulled that out, stuck it into my mouth, covering the slot in the top, and totally submerged myself. Now I could breathe.

Kind of.

There wasn't much air to be sucked through that tiny thing. Hopefully I wouldn't suffocate before they decided to kill me.

I decided against opening my eyes in the goop. That could be seen as tempting fate. Instead, I listened to the sound of canine nails clicking on the metal floors, punctuated by growling turned deep and muddled by the tank of stuff. I kept wondering just how visible I was, while desperately sucking for air. My lungs could have used more.

Two loud clicks said one of the wolves was up on its hind legs, forepaws resting on the tank, sniffing. Then, a yelp of pain. I was starting to get short of breath.

There was a short, muffled conversation I couldn't follow, and the clicks got quieter and quieter until they were gone.

I surfaced and inhaled, nearly throwing up at the artificial wind in my lungs. There was no werewolf staring at me over the top of the tank. So, victory, I guess. Well, victory until they figured out my gambit and started tracking me again. I got out of the tank and the gunk fell off me in thick, folding waves. That would be fun to explain to Mr. Rodriguez when I dropped the suit off tomorrow. I shook a little more off me and gingerly made my way to the door. No werewolves.

The howls were distant, doubling back to the castle. My scent was all over that place. As was Mary's, but I had to trust she could take care of herself. I went back out into the night, the air freezing on my slime-coated skin. I felt like a snail. And then there was the fact that I was still glowing slightly. Yeah,

I'd be real hard to find.

I figured it was better to find some cover than to be out and fluorescing in the open, so I looked around for somewhere to hide. The next closest set was that opera room, so I headed up the slope for it, slipping on my own glowing green footprints. One side was almost entirely glass, a sphere made of trapezoidal windows set into the side of the slope. Inside, there was a darkened stage, and beyond, some seats. The room had been given over to shadows, the chandelier barely hinting at the gold light that once illuminated the set. The entryway was in the side of the building, where the glass windows gave way to some normal wood paneling.

I opened the door and wiped my feet, getting most of the glowing gunk off. Wouldn't baffle the noses, but maybe I'd be leaving less of a literal trail to follow.

A hallway led around the side of the theater, with two aisles tracing three seating areas. A piano sat onstage, waiting for another phantom to take up the song. The location made me think of the last person I'd seen here. Aria Enchantee. The woman's car went crazy and squashed her. Hell of a way to kill someone. Monsters couldn't even commit murder like normal people.

I kept moving through the darkened theater, getting to the other side and back out. The place definitely looked a lot like what I'd seen on the film stashed in Gortran's office, but I couldn't be sure. After all, it wasn't like I had a ton of opera houses to compare it with.

Ahead, near the top of the slope, was a miniature high school. Just then, the howls echoed, much closer than I would have liked. I sprinted for the fake high school. Behind me, the wolves swished through the underbrush. How long would they be hung up in the opera house? Not long enough.

I got to the door of the school and pulled the wolfsbane from my jacket. After shaking a little glowing gunk off the bottle, I took a couple sprigs out and crushed them on the doorknob. Merry Christmas, Sheriff.

The door opened up into a hallway lined with lockers. It wasn't as long as the hall in a real high school; like every other one of their weird theme rooms, they made do with a miniature version of the genuine article. Two doors on the other end of the hall led out into the night. The wolves were back on my scent. I could hear them eating up the turf with their loping strides, little growls and huffs coming from between bared teeth. I picked a door along the hall and shouldered it open, revealing a science classroom. It wasn't entirely unconvincing, either. Plenty to get the weird johns of this place in the mood.

I picked up a beaker and it crumbled in my hand. Sugar glass. So that wasn't going to be useful.

There were more beakers of more stuff, but there was no way a brothel catering to monsters was going to have dangerous substances like salt, or wolfsbane, or powdered silver, or anything useful to me. There wouldn't even be salt or sand. I picked up a beaker and sniffed. Baking soda.

Well, if there was some vinegar, I'd be in business, because nothing frightens werewolves like grade-school science projects.

There was a yelp at the back door. Someone had tried to use the doorknob, and would spend the next several hours shaking his paw helplessly and gimping along after me.

I went back to the racks. Baking soda. Flour. More baking soda. Pepper. Flour. Wait, pepper. That might work. I grabbed that beaker and ran back out into the hall. Outside, I could hear the werewolves rushing for the other door. My shoes squeaked on the floor as I skidded to a stop. I sprinkled a little pepper right in the doorway, then shrugged and just upended the whole thing, making a couple little piles of it. Then I sprinted back the other way, chucking the sugar-glass beaker over my shoulder.

Right as I was sliding into the door at the far end of the hall, the one I'd originally entered through, the other door opened. A black wolf padded in, sniffing around, followed by two more, one holding up a paw like it hurt. The first one took a big whiff of the floor.

And sneezed. Powerfully.

The one right behind him sniffed, I guess without thinking, and pretty soon he was sneezing too.

I burst out into the night and doubled back, running as fast as I could down the hill, passing a small colonial church probably meant for the headless horsemen clientele, toward a pond. Back at the high school, one of the werewolves let out a howl that was almost immediately choked off by a sneeze. Maybe I allowed myself a little arrogant smirk, but the truth was, that trick had bought me almost no time, and I knew it. At the end of all this, I was still going over uneven ground with three werewolves behind me. And now I had pissed them off.

Still, them mad was better than me dead. It was a question of degrees, really.

I followed the slope down to a pond surrounded by reeds. Pushing a couple aside, I could feel they weren't real, just plastic stems and coarse cloth leaves, secured to the bottom in metal trays. A little pier had a boat that couldn't have been more than a dingy, but it was built up like one of those shrimping boats that tooled around the Gulf of Mexico. Dogs couldn't track you over water, right? I read that somewhere. Or saw it in the movies. That's why people on a jailbreak crossed a river. Worth a try.

I splashed into the shallows and started to swim. The water

wasn't more than four feet deep at any point. I was grateful for that, since I was pretty sure there was something swimming around in the murk. Hopefully nothing worse than some Japanese goldfish.

The wolves did another howl-sneeze, this one a little closer. I made it to the other side of the pond, splashed out, and kept running along the floor of the valley. Up ahead, the natural dip opened up, a fold emptying into the Hollywood Hills. Right at the exit was one final monster fantasy.

A goddamn carnival.

And they hadn't skimped on this one, either. It wasn't full-sized, but you couldn't call it little. The Ferris wheel was at least forty feet across, and there were a number of tents fluttering in the night air. The midway had games; there was a freakshow and a funhouse. As I got closer, there were even the right smells: popcorn, french fries and vinegar, cotton candy and funnel cake. Clearly, this was Miss Zoltar's big attraction, no pun intended.

I chanced a look behind me. The werewolves were streaking toward me like furry bullets. Apparently, the pond gambit had been a complete waste of time. I'd note that down for the future. If I had one of those.

I had to wrestle every breath into burning lungs. My feet weighed about a thousand pounds apiece. Sure, I'd been exhausted before, mostly in France and Belgium, but the nice part about war is that ninety percent of it is incredibly boring. And say what you will about the Krauts, none of them could turn into wolves back then.

They were coming up fast. Two of them were, and were stumbling every four or five steps to sneeze loudly, while the reddish-brown one was still limping slightly from the wolfsbane trick.

I ran up the midway. As much as I had managed to slow them down, they were still going to get me before long. The real question was, what were they going to do? Arrest me? Turn me? Or had I pissed them off to the point that they were simply going to kill me? Hey, it was after dark, and I was outside of my home. Anything was legal. And even if it wasn't, who was going to say boo to the Hollywood Sheriff's Department?

The next howl, punctuated by a violent dog sneeze, was a little too close for comfort. I broke left, where there was a bottle game set up. I reached into my jacket, pulling out the vial of wolfsbane. There was about a pinch left, enough to distract a single werewolf for the amount of time it would take his buddies to air out my guts.

With a snarl, the wolf lunged for my arm, grabbing a mouthful of my sleeve, which promptly tore away in his slavering jaws. Another one jumped, and I gave him a kick to the head. Wasn't expecting that, was he?

I opened the vial, shook out the sprig into my hand, and flung it at them. They yelped and recoiled long enough for me to hop the counter of the bottle game and head for the back of the tent. The first wolf, the one with the bum paw that seemed to be getting better with every step, leaped easily over the counter. His tongue lolled out of his mouth as he closed in.

Oh, what the hell. I scooped up a baseball from where it lay next to the bottle pyramid. "You want the ball?"

The werewolf perked up.

"You want the ball?"

His ears quirked.

I threw it.

The werewolf deputy instinctively turned and jumped out of the booth before giving an annoyed yelp, and was back over the counter again in a few seconds. By then I had gotten out the back of the tent and was running hard for the biggest building I could find in the place: the funhouse.

Of course it was the funhouse. If there was anywhere a monster would want to stalk some nubile young thing, it would be a place like this. Right? At least that's what it seemed like, though to be perfectly fair, I was viewing it from the outside and didn't have the best opinion of monsters after being hunted through the Santa Monicas.

The wolves had recovered, the sneezes growing a little more infrequent. At this point, I was down to silver bullets. Six of them. And a werewolf's sense of smell was admissible in court, which means either I killed all three cops or I got sent up the river for a long time. Shooting all three of them was getting really tempting. And if I had an M1, a foxhole, and about fifty feet of open ground, I might do it. A revolver, five feet, and six shots wasn't going to cut it.

I ducked through the doorway into the funhouse. The calliope kicked in immediately, filling the cold air with a disjointed carnival theme. Canned screams and ghoulish laughter reverberated down the narrow halls. A mechanical reaper tried to take my head off. Did real reapers find that offensive?

Two hallways led into the funhouse proper, probably two ends of the same pathway. I picked the right-hand one, since it really didn't matter once the wolves had my scent. They'd be in the funhouse soon enough, which begged the question of what the hell I was going to do next.

The corridor was narrow, the walls painted black, some weirdly colored lights shining on the special effects. Mostly dummies of what we thought monsters looked like before we knew any, or what monsters remembered us thinking monsters looked like. Things got very complicated for so many reasons after the war.

Canine claws clicked on the ramp leading up into the funhouse. Then a sneeze. Sheriff Castle would be in the lead, those two deputies right behind.

I moved quicker, trying to keep silent, my aching lungs fighting me for every measly breath. I slid along the hall, past a meat golem dummy, touching the walls when I could, getting tangled up in a number of fake cobwebs.

The panting of the werewolves was getting closer. Or maybe that was me. Hard to tell, really. I was thinking about the breathing so much I nearly missed it. But something rang a bell in my brain and my hand went back to what I'd touched. A doorknob. My hand closed around it. I turned, opened it. A maintenance room. Pretty big, too.

It'd have to do.

There was a growl. Too close.

Desperate times, desperate measures. I undid my belt and opened my pants. And lo and behold, I couldn't piss. I was going to be the first man who died because he couldn't get a stream going. Okay. I had to think. Sea travel. Noah's ark. The Hoover Dam? That was it. A ton of water, building up behind that barrier, just waiting for the chance to burst forth and flood...

...there we go.

Not my finest moment. And the stench was a bit hard to take. Oh, well. The worst part was that I couldn't hear the approaching werewolves over the sound of my own stream.

I caught the motion out of the corner of my eye. I ducked into the alcove between the meat golem and the wall, not even daring to breathe. And, not to be indelicate, but a breeze was tickling my nethers. Didn't even get a chance to shake.

Time to see if the gambit worked.

The werewolves padded down the hall, snuffling at the ground, their sneezing growing softer and more infrequent. Castle paused, sniffing the air. He woofed, low and menacing.

Come on, guys. Take the bait. See how scared I was? Wet myself, even!

The wolves growled at each other, one whining softly.

Goddamn it. Don't make me die with my dick out.

Castle stalked into the maintenance room. The deputies stayed in the hall. They were only a couple feet from me. I really hoped that piss smell was masking the fact I was literally soaked in sweat, pond water, and maybe leftover goo from the flying saucer.

Finally, the other two wolves slunk into the room after their boss.

I burst from hiding and slammed the door, then tipped the dummy over to barricade it. Wouldn't hold them for long, but it would have to do.

I ran, trying to get my pants buckled. Along the way, I grabbed a zombie dummy and tucked it under an arm while wrestling everything back into place. Behind me, the wolves howled, battering into the door. After a moment, the howls turned into loud swearing.

Back on the midway, I pounded toward the center of the carnival. The Ferris wheel rose ahead of me. I plopped the zombie in a seat, slammed my hat down on his head, and cast around. A loud splintering came from the funhouse. Well, that hadn't taken long. I took off my jacket and rubbed an armpit across the safety bar on the dummy's seat, then yanked the lever.

I sprinted up the midway right as the shapes emerged from the funhouse: all three wolves, eyes flashing in the dark. I followed my nose for the first time, and found what I was looking for.

The tub had enough left in it. Might as well make the best of it. I stuck my hand in and drew out sticky strands of cotton candy, smearing the confection over my body, where it collected in wispy pink clumps. Whatever smells I had been covered in were now nothing more than candy. I hoped.

The wolves charged.

Here's where the rubber hit the road. The Ferris wheel spun slowly, the dummy going upward. I was frozen behind the cotton candy cart, my pink Santa beard less than dignified. Well, if I was going to die, I hoped they would lie and say I died like a soldier or something. At least not covered in piss, goo, and cotton candy.

The wolves stopped at the Ferris wheel, heads craned upward. Castle shifted, becoming human-shaped once more. He called up, "Hey! We have you treed. Come quietly and you won't be hurt."

Damn right I won't.

I slunk away, down the midway, into the lip of the miniature canyon, and down the slope. A dirt path spilled me down into Mulholland. I tried not to kick up too much dust, stepping lightly until my feet found pavement. Up above, the wolves bayed. Must have finally gotten a good look at my decoy when it came back around. I refused to smirk.

The howls got farther away, splitting up. *Now* I let myself smirk.

Couldn't go back up the road and fetch my car. That would be too close to Fer-de-Lance and the Hollywood Sheriffs. I sighed and started heading down Mulholland, trying to figure out how I would get to Watts in the middle of the night without a car.

I made it back onto Hollywood Boulevard an hour or two

later. My appearance probably helped me move around without getting harassed. Haggard, covered in cotton candy, lurching, I was just your average zombie after a hot night with a killer clown.

Fortunately, the red car still ran at night, now that the majority of the populace no longer had much need for sleep. I dropped a dime into the till, and the driver, a zombie, said, "Brains."

"Brains," I said back to him. I felt we made a pretty deep connection there.

Only a few folks were riding the red car. A zombie. An old gill-man and his sea hag wife. A young vampire. No one gave me so much as a second glance. Even when I couldn't help myself and ate my fluffy pink beard. It was late, and I was hungry and exhausted, so I don't think God or anyone else should judge.

I got off near Watts and lurched home, hoping no one would recognize me. Let Sam take the night off for once. Maybe he got it through that pumpkin head of his I didn't want to be turned. Right, and maybe all the gremlins would go get suntans.

The air was getting lighter blue. Morning was just over an hour away. My street had mostly cleared out, with only a few stragglers hanging around. That carrot that was always bugging Mrs. Henderson, the killer robot who had it in for the Schroeders. And, of course, Sam Haine, sitting on my front lawn, looking all viney and pumpkiny and forlorn.

Waiting him out was a possibility, but I had already gotten lucky. Getting home from Hollywood was a goddamn miracle. Now was not the time to tempt fate.

With a resigned sigh, I went around back, where a narrow alley ran between the streets. There a few shadowy shapes lurking about, but I kept up my shuffle and groaned an occasional "Brains" to keep them happy. Best camouflage in the world. Who expected a human out in Watts? Might as well carry a sign that said "Bite me."

And in the post-Night War world, climbing some human's back fence was the least suspicious thing in the world. I jumped down onto the little patch of grass that was my backyard, went to the cracked concrete steps leading up to my kitchen door, and let myself in, locking the door securely behind me.

Only then did I let out the long, long sigh I'd been holding since the red car passed Sunset. Then, a laugh. I'd made it. All the way home, and the best part? Castle still didn't know who I was. Sure, he had my scent, but not a name to go with it.

I opened up the icebox, grabbed a beer, and wandered into the living room. Might as well watch the sunrise with a...

I dropped the beer onto my carpet.

Because sitting on my sofa, petting my Judas of a cat, was a redhead in a patchwork dress.

NINETEEN

I yelped and immediately reached into my jacket for the evil eye charm. The witch—Hexene Candlemas—sighed and scattered a handful of powder at my feet while spitting out an incantation, following it up with a rude gesture. She used the finger like punctuation, almost to let me know she was done speaking. I pulled the charm a second later, but lost my grip on it. It tumbled end over end to land in the corner of the room.

Witches weren't immune to bullets, were they? I went for my revolver, but as soon as I leveled it, the cylinder fell out, dropping silver bullets all over the carpet.

She rolled her eyes. "Would you cut that out please?" The cat yawned.

Water! Witches and water. Throw a bucket on her, and that's the end. I turned and bolted for the kitchen. The linoleum was slipperier than I remembered, or at least that's how I justified it when the floor decided to throw me down on my face. I lay there, gasping for air, and sensed the woman behind me.

Barely rolling over like a turtle, I saw her standing above me, stroking my cat, which seemed to think I was to blame for interrupting its terribly important feline business.

"Damn it, detective, I want to stop beating you up."

"Wuh... wuh... wuh..."

"Is that a yes?"

"*Witch!*"

"Oh, toil and trouble—"

I scrambled to my feet, ran to the cupboards, and yanked open the one where I kept the pitcher. The shelves collapsed, hitting me in the face with nearly every dish I owned on their way to shattering on the floor.

"Detective. Look, just—okay. Stop! Or I'll turn you into a newt!" A final dish clocked me on the head and broke on the floor next to me.

Dazed, I fought to my feet, only to collapse in a heap myself.

Hexene Candlemas stood by the door, my cat headbutting her hand to demand more petting. Traitor. "Done?"

I nodded.

"Promise?"

"So this is where it ends, huh? You're going to turn me?"

She snorted. Not very ladylike. "You're a man."

Oh. Right. "So this is a hit? Who hired you?"

She shook her head and sauntered calmly back into the living room. After a moment, I was able to get my feet under me and carefully shuffled through the broken ceramic. Hexene had resumed her position on my sofa. I sank into my chair, and immediately popped back up when something bit my ass.

A green-and-brown toad, about the size of a saucer, glared up at me with peaked eyes. It ribbited, displaying a set of teeth that had no business being in the mouth of any amphibian. It reproachfully hopped off the chair and made its way over to

Hexene, eventually hopping onto the sofa, and from there onto her shoulder. My cat studiously ignored it, as though that were a solution.

I took my seat. If there was any consolation to the display earlier, she'd already had ample time to kill me.

"How did you find me?"

"Trudy Alvin told me who you were."

"Trudy Alvin?"

"Mary Brown," she clarified. "She called me after the business at Fer-de-Lance. Apparently, the Hollywood Sheriffs are combing the hills looking for you. What did you do to them?"

"I... uh... there was some cotton candy. And a dummy."

She giggled. Somehow that was more frightening than any cackle.

"Why are you here? And how did you get in?"

"Your evil eye ward on the bedroom window was turned the wrong way. Also, your allward was kind of old, so I went ahead and touched up the line around the house for you."

"Oh. Thanks."

"A pumpkinhead was quite upset with me. Kept saying that I didn't understand you. And that I didn't care about you like he did." She shook her head.

I massaged my brow. "Yeah... um... he's sort of got his heart set... see, there's a pumpkin patch out in San Berdoo..."

"I'm sorry. I didn't give you the impression I wanted to know, did I?"

"Right."

She shifted in her chair, scratching my cat's head. I never saw that thing look so happy. I didn't even know it *could* look happy. It took me a second to catch on, but then I realized: Hexene was extremely uncomfortable. "I came to apologize," she finally blurted.

"You what?"

"Apologize. To you."

"Which you chose to do by beating me up?"

"After you pull an evil eye charm? And a gun? And then try to douse me with water?"

"After you broke in!"

"Your window wasn't warded. "

"You see? This is what's wrong with you monsters!"

"'You mons—'"

"*I'm talking!*"

Hexene started in shock. I had the briefest moment to consider the fact that I was haranguing a hex-slinger in my living room after dark, but my mouth was already going and I was pretty much just along for the ride at that point. "Just because my window is open-ish doesn't mean you're allowed to just break in! And okay, I know what the law says! But that doesn't make it not rude! You could have come by the office! But noooooooo. You had to barge in here, curse me, destroy all my dishes, and make me sit on a goddamn toad, who's giving me the crazy eyes! And I'm not crazy here! This is not a nice thing to do!"

I caught my breath. Hexene looked a little sheepish. Finally, she mumbled, "You broke your dishes."

"Right, well, usually I'm not all that butterfingered. I made it through the entire war without breaking a single dish."

She was quiet, her freckled cheeks going bright red. "I thought you were Oculon's bagman," she blurted.

"What?"

"That's why I cursed you at the studio."

"Why would I be doing shakedowns for Oculon?"

The blush deepened. Her green eyes searched the cat, like

it had anything to say on the matter. "Because of Gortran. Possibly Juba, too."

"Too or II?"

"Uh... both, I guess. Juba II as well."

"You're dealing to both of them?"

She looked up at me, defiant. "What if I am?"

"No, I mean that as a question. It might help me with my investigation."

"Oh! Oh. Then yes."

"What is Gortran getting?"

"I don't think I should say."

"There's no such thing as dealer/customer confidentiality, Miss Candlemas."

"Well, there should be. Let's say you came into my shop and wanted a love spell for, I don't know, the pretty... waitress? Sure, waitress, the pretty one at your favorite coffee shop. I wouldn't go around telling everyone that Detective Nick Moss is a deviant who can't get a date."

"Wait. How did we end up there? I'm not—look, I can get dates. It used to be easier, you know, before the—none of this is relevant! What is Gortran taking?"

She glanced at the toad, and I swear by all that's holy, the damn thing shrugged. "It's hard to explain. The hex is supposed to disrupt the flow of electricity. Causes blackouts and the like. Robots enjoy the sensation."

"Huh." I thought it over. "How long has Gortran been a customer?"

"Around a year. Juba referred him to me. I guess he was having trouble with his last dealer. Something about blackmail."

"Gortran was being blackmailed." I tasted it, seeing if it fit with the rest of what I knew. "Still?"

She shrugged. "I have no idea."

"And Juba?"

"Gortran is one thing. He's brusque and rude and doesn't believe in tipping."

"You're supposed to tip your hex-slinger?"

"There's an understanding."

"What's the, uh, I mean... is there a percentage?"

"Ten percent is considered polite."

I filed that away, just in case I needed her later. She had a point about the whole dating thing, although I wasn't planning on dating anyone who was on hexes. Seemed like a can of worms I didn't need to open. "I already know you're feeding Juba amnesia hexes. What I want to know is why."

"I don't know."

"Wonderful."

"Let me finish. Juba is a nice man, but he owes me money."

"Which is why you came by his office. To shake him down."

"I wasn't shaking anyone down! I just told him that he should pay me what he owes, or I'd curse him."

"That's the definition of a shakedown."

"It is? Good to know. Okay, then, yes, I suppose I was shaking him down for the money, which he promised me tomorrow. Um, the day before yesterday, I think? But that's not the important thing. A couple days ago, two nights before I went down to his office—"

"Before the shakedown."

She scowled. "I get a call at my shop. My coven," and here her lips turned into an irritated line, "was getting ready for some weather ritual. Bringing rain to the southland. But who pays for that? No one, that's who. And who cares that witches are doing it? No one! Why? We're dames. Skirts."

"Luh... ladies. I always say ladies."

"Ladies," she sneered. "Or that. No, I'm not fixing the

weather for you people. Either it's a bunch of monsters who won't let us join their little clubs or it's humans thinking we're going to turn them or curse them or boil them up in a cauldron and eat them, I don't know, as soup." As Hexene got worked up, she was petting my cat harder and harder. I thought that should have upset it, but the purring only got louder.

"You weren't going to change the weather," I prompted.

"No, I wasn't!" She settled herself, closing her eyes and taking a couple of deep breaths. "All right. Anyway, I received a telephone call as I was closing my shop. It was Juba, and he sounded desperate. More so than usual. When he calls me, he's always a little... agitated. He needs his hex yesterday and so on."

"How much was he using?"

"When you use hexes regularly, you sort of build up a tolerance. Same way for all curses. So he was needing more and more to stay normal."

"All curses?"

"It's why witches like to switch things up. Or make sure we don't have to curse the same person too many times."

"Oh. Go on."

"So, the beginning of every call is me trying to calm him down. Only this time, he wasn't going to be calmed. He snapped at me as soon as I tried, and, well, I'm not going to take the time if that's what I get. Anyway, he wants me over at Visionary *toot sweet*, as they say. I grab my broom and Escuerzo and—"

"I'm sorry, Escuerzo?"

She nodded toward the toad, who let out a loud and, I'm assuming, fly-scented belch.

"Right, you grabbed your broom and Escuerzo. Like you do."

"Right," she said blithely. "It was a clear night and there were very few flyers out, so I went low. More fun that way, when you have things to get out of the way of. Not recommended if you're trying to get somewhere fast and... are you falling asleep?"

"Huh? No. No, I'm awake. Been a long night. I was, uh, I was resting my eyes."

"I could still curse you."

"That might undermine the sincerity of your apology."

"I thought you were one of Oculon's bagmen!"

"Which is an explanation we'll get to... when, exactly?" The sun was beginning to light up my front lawn. It was officially illegal for her to do anything to me now, which wasn't going to get me another dinnerware set.

She made a couple gestures, but I was pretty sure they were just obscene and not in any way magical. "As I was saying. I arrived at the Visionary lot, and I just skipped over that ogre they have guarding the front."

"Ugoth the Castrator."

She paused. "Really?"

I nodded.

"Oh dear. Well, Juba had told me they were on Stage Eight, so I headed in. And immediately, Escuerzo croaked. Not his 'I'm hungry' croak. His 'danger' croak."

I looked at the toad. He croaked.

"That's the 'I'm hungry' croak."

"Of course," I said, nodding, desperately faking some sincerity.

"I let myself into the stage. There were voices, deeper in. I could recognize Gortran and Juba, and there were a couple others. A woman, a man, and a gremlin. They were arguing."

"About what?"

"The bus station."

"The bus station? Why would they be arguing about the bus

station?"

"Herbalist," she said, pointing to herself. "Detective," she said, pointing to me.

I really wanted to throw some of those earlier gestures back at her, but I couldn't face the ethereal disappointment of my mother if it ever got back to her.

"They stopped arguing as soon as I came around the corner. Oculon saw me first, of course, and he had a tentacle on each of the people present. I later found out the phantom was—"

"Aria Enchantee."

"Right! And they called the gremlin—"

"Brows."

"Right, because of the—" she supplied the eyebrows with hand gestures that implied the gremlin was carrying around the equivalent of an albatross's wings on his face. "Juba and Gortran rushed over to me instantly, and Gortran paid for his hex, but Juba didn't. He asked for credit, which I don't do, then just tried begging me. So I'm turning him down, and things are getting more and more uncomfortable. His eyes actually turned indigo, and he's shedding sand all over the place. Then, all of a sudden, Oculon booms out, 'Just give him the hex!' And I knew, right then, I was in real danger."

"You? You're a witch."

"I know what I am. I also know what Escuerzo was telling me. And that was to get out of there immediately or not get out at all. So I gave Juba the hex and he promised to pay me, which he never did. And I got out of there, back on my broom, and flew away. But if you want to know what I think? If Juba vanished, it was one of them who nabbed him."

I nodded. Things were pointing in that direction. They didn't come much more powerful or well-connected than Oculon. His "mayor" title might have been unofficial, but it was also dead serious. If I was going to go after him, I'd need solid evidence of something. Anything, really, would have been nice.

"And when we... met... in the studio, you thought I was Oculon's bagman, coming to... what?"

"Blackmail me? Attack me? I don't know. Just... nothing good. It didn't help that I had just been scryed on. I was a little on edge."

"That was also me." To her confused look, I offered, "I know the Salem Sisters."

"I don't know who they are, but they're not very good witches."

"I think they're more interested in singing."

She looked me over. "Are you planning to sleep?"

"Maybe later. I really have to solve this thing and I'm sort of on the clock." I stood up, somewhat unsteadily. "I do need a shower, though."

"That's a good idea. I didn't want to say anything, but you smell like you've been eating cotton candy out of the toilet."

TWENTY

Hexene was waiting in the living room when I got out of the shower. She had my cat on its back and was rubbing its rapturous belly. My living room stank of beer, and that's when I remembered the bottle I'd dropped when I found her. I picked it up, poured the remains out in the sink, and chalked up a rug cleaning as yet another thing this job would have to pay for.

I made sure everything was refilled when I put on a clean suit. Especially the wolfsbane. Things got a little uncomfortable when I picked up my revolver and reloaded it, but Hexene was nice enough to ignore me. Her manner got icier when I retrieved the evil eye charm and stuck that back in the tiny pocket under my left armpit, but I wasn't taking any chances. Better impolite than dead. I took my spare hat off the rack, momentarily disappointed I'd lost the other one to the werewolves.

When it was obvious I was ready to go, she put the cat down, causing it to angrily squawk at her, and announced, "As part of my apology, I'm buying you breakfast."

"Oh. Well, thank you, but I'm the, uh... as the man, I should be buying the breakfast."

"And I'm the monster. When we take humans out, we pay."

"Is that in some monster etiquette book?"

"Are you going to complain the whole time?"

"Probably. But I won't turn you down."

She scooped up her toad, who looked like a cow patty with eyes, and put him in her satchel. A moment later, the saturnine face poked up to peer out with disinterested annoyance at the world. She went to the door, picked up her broom from where it leaned against the wall, and we went out into the morning.

"Where's your car?"

"Up by Fer-de-Lance. I had to get out of there on foot."

"You walked home from there?"

"There was a red car involved."

"That's still a long walk."

"Seemed even longer when I had werewolves chasing me."

"Tell me about it."

I blinked and gaped at her.

She gave me a sheepish shrug. "Hex-slinger, remember?"

"Right. Listen, after breakfast, you think I could get a lift back up there?"

Her eyes lit up. "Of course!"

"I wasn't exactly expecting enthusiasm."

"Are you kidding? You've never flown before, have you?"

"Sure. In a plane."

"Spells and hexes," she said in a tone that made me think she actually meant something like "apples and oranges."

"Okay..."

"The city is beautiful from above. I can show you a few things."

That did not exactly fill me with confidence. "Come on,

there's a pretty good diner not far from here."

She sat down on her broom and looked hopefully at me.

"It's two blocks. We're walking," I said.

Hope curdled to disappointment, but she fell into step next to me, carrying the broom over one shoulder. I was unpleasantly muzzy. The shower hadn't cleared my head too much, and things were starting to ache from last night's terror run through the Hollywood Hills. I could tell the day was going to be a hot one. Add to that, I was about to have breakfast with a self-confessed hex-slinger. A witch powerful enough to slap my closest witch allies silly. Although to be fair, only one of them actually liked me.

She deflated a little more when we got to the diner. It was a sleek aluminum bullet with fragrant smoke billowing from the top, sitting in the corner of a small lot. A old married couple worked the grill and took orders at the outdoor counter. There was only one customer, a man in a light gray maintenance jumpsuit, sitting at the end of the counter, plowing through a double order of ham and eggs.

"Good to see you, Nick," the old lady, Henrietta, said with a smile.

"Mornin', ma'am. You too, Clarence," I called back. He waved the spatula in one gnarled hand as acknowledgement, not bothering to turn from the grill. It was already the longest conversation I'd had with the man.

"And who's your lady friend?" Henrietta asked, pulling the pencil from behind one ear and leaning in.

"Hexene," answered Hexene. "And I'm not his lady friend."

"She's not even friendly."

Henrietta looked Hexene over, and a little light went out in her eyes. She knew Hexene was a monster, and not a nice, pretty girl I was having an unseemly breakfast with. Still, she tried, bless her heart. "Oh, too bad. This one's a catch, miss. If I had a daughter, her daughters would almost be young enough for him."

I coughed.

"What can I get you, Nick?"

"How's the steak?"

"Not green yet."

"Steak and eggs. Toast and coffee."

"And you, Miss Hexene?"

Hexene peered around. "I haven't seen a menu."

"Same stuff here as anywhere, miss. You want it, Clarence can make it."

"Make me something without any meat, then, please."

"Well, almost anything."

"Everything has meat?"

"Everything worth eating. And whatever doesn't gets bacon grease."

"It's what gives the whole thing its flavor," I explained.

"Whatever you have that has the least meat."

"Think we have some salmon back here."

Clarence shook his head.

"No salmon. Sorry."

"Salmon is mea—" Hexene started. "Um. No meat. Or fish. Or fowl."

"Eggs ain't fowl yet. How about those and some toast and hash browns?"

Hexene nodded, a queasy look washing over her face.

"You get all that, Clarence?" Henrietta called back. Clarence waved the spatula again. I never knew why Henrietta bothered with the order pad. Clarence never looked at it once. Never had to. And even if he did, I refused to believe the weird symbols Henrietta scratched on it were in any way related to English.

Hexene set her toad on the counter between us.

"So Trudy... I mean, Mary Brown tells me you're looking for Juba."

"Mmm-hmm," I said. The toad was watching me with uncomfortable intensity.

"How close are you to finding him?"

I looked around. The guy at the end of the counter was desperately trying to ignore the witch sitting three stools down. Henrietta had a very interesting crossword to scrape at with the stub of a pencil. And Clarence would have probably been unaware of a gamma-ape trashing Normandie Avenue if he had frying bacon in front of him. To be fair, the ape thing happened only one time and I'm pretty sure it was a zoning issue.

"I don't think I'm looking for him. I think I'm looking for a pile of sand."

Hexene blinked. "You think he was murdered?"

"Keep your voice down!"

"Sorry." She thought it over. "Shouldn't you go to the police?"

"I don't have any evidence, and they have it in their heads that his wife did it. I go to them, and she's in cuffs."

"And why would that matter? She probably did do it."

"His wife is my client."

"So you have a vested interest in her innocence."

"It's not like that! I mean, sure, I'm much more likely to get paid if she *is* innocent, but I'm going wherever this thing takes me. Right now, what little I've found is saying that she's the least likely suspect, and that's not just because a pair of LAPD bloodhounds are on me like stink on a gill-man. It just doesn't add up."

"You can't just tell them it wasn't her?"

"I'm human. They won't listen to me."

"Why wouldn't they?"

"Aren't you the same person who told me monsters don't respect women? Well, humans are the women of the monster world." I tried to parse that. "Or something like that."

"Steak and eggs," Henrietta announced, sliding the plate in front of me. "No meat breakfast," she said with a martyred sigh, placing it in front of the witch.

Hexene picked at the fried pile of potatoes. "Why do you think he was killed?"

"A gremlin killed Aria Enchantee—"

"Juba's friend is dead?"

"Very."

"You know it was a gremlin?"

"Only one of those crazy bastards could gimmick a car like that."

"Phantoms do that kind of thing, too."

I shook my head. "Believe me, I've been on the wrong end of both, and there's a difference. Phantoms go more for old-style, baroque deathtraps. They like trapdoors, spike pits, wild animals... the kinds of things you'd find in a castle or something. Gremlins are more like saboteurs. They like to take a device and change it. They're all about technology gone awry. You ask me, something like that happened to Juba II. And there's been one gremlin rearing his ugly, eyebrow-waggling head."

"Brows."

I nodded, mopping up my yolk with some toast. "I think Oculon and Gortran are next."

She thought about it. "Why?"

"Don't really know. I know there's blackmail happening, and something about a bus station. I'm going to warn Oculon and Gortran because that's all I can do. If studio security can deal with it, so much the better. And maybe once they have, I can tell Juba's wife what happened to her husband."

We finished breakfast in silence, and Hexene placed a few crumpled bills on the counter. Henrietta counted them out. "You gave me too much, miss," she said, handing a few back.

Hexene held up a hand. "It's all right. It was very good." There was still half a plate of food in front of her, but the lie felt good that early in the morning.

The witch put her toad back in her satchel and sat down on her broom. "No more avoiding it, Nick. Time to ride."

I wanted to back away—from the broom, from her, from everything. Nothing about this seemed safe. "You know, I jumped out of a plane over France."

"What?"

"In the war. You know, the one before the other one. They—the Germans—were, you know, shooting at us. And as soon as I hopped out, there was this flash. Flak, popping off the wing of the plane I just jumped out of. And I thought to myself that I was never going to get in a plane again. I mean, that's a sign, right? The last plane you get out of, and it loses a wing?"

"Well, you could chalk that up to the Germans. There aren't any Germans in Los Angeles, at least none with anti-aircraft guns. And besides, this isn't a plane. It's a broom. Totally safe."

"Right. Because who needs a nice enclosed bit of metal when you can get on a cleaning device."

"Just get on, you big baby."

Well, now Henrietta was looking, and so was the guy at the end of the counter, although he was adept at pretending he wasn't. I couldn't very well back out now, no matter how much the whole idea terrified me. So I got behind her and straddled the broom.

"You're going to want to hold on. Wrap your arms around my waist."

"I don't see how that—"

The wind ate the rest of the sentence, because the broom zipped upward into the clear blue. I grabbed Hexene about the waist with one arm, clamped my hat to my head with the other, and buried my head in her back. She smelled a bit like jasmine, but it was tough to dwell on that, what with my life flashing before my eyes. She soared up and over the buildings, the valleys of Los Angeles spilling out all around us. A few other witches zoomed through the sky, as did a couple of human flies, a gargoyle or three, and your odd flying saucer. That air traffic would be one of the primary consequences of the Night War was wholly unexpected.

"Where are you parked?" she yelled back to me over the howling wind.

I looked down, where Hollywood was presently passing under my feet. I clamped onto the broom a little harder and Hexene let out a barely audible huff.

"Down there!" I shouted, not wanting to actually point at anything, since that would mean either letting go of Hexene or my hat.

She was getting closer to Mulholland, and I guess she took that as free license to go spiraling down toward the earth. I was pretty sure if I looked to my left, German flak was going to be shearing off a heretofore unseen wing. We were headed straight down toward the winding blacktop. Safe, my ass.

At the last instant before impact, the broom pulled up and we were streaking at car height along Mulholland. I didn't have to wonder for long what she'd do if a car came along. It honked, the terrified phantom behind the wheel bugging his eyes out even more as he yanked on the wheel. Hexene calmly zipped over him, kicking the roof of his car on the way over for good measure.

The broom whistled through the morning air, and with every second, I was more and more certain I had survived werewolves only to perish in a broom accident, when we began to slow. I opened my eyes, blinking away the oily colors, and saw that we were right in front of Fer-de-Lance, hovering about ten feet over Mulholland.

"Here?" she said.

"Actually, maybe a hundred feet up," I told her, which I regretted as soon as she pushed that broom the whole way in the space of a few seconds. And there was my car, just below and to the side of us, parked mostly out of sight unless you were right on top of it.

The broom settled down, my nerveless feet making contact with the road. I resisted the urge to fall to my knees and kiss Mulholland, but I had never before been that happy to see it. To make matters worse, my ass was more than a little sore from resting on top of a stick of wood. How did she handle that? Witches.

"Th-thanks for the ride. And, uh, and breakfast."

Hexene Candlemas gave me a sunny smile. "Good luck, Nick."

"I'll need it."

She darted back up into the sky. I waited until I stopped shaking, got into my car, and drove very carefully down into Hollywood. I had gone without sleep before, of course, but I had gotten to that age where it wasn't a trivial matter anymore. Still, had to warn the robot and the crawling eye that the gremlin was going to kill them. And then hate the fact I lived in a world where such a sentence was said with a straight face.

Hexene Candlemas

TWENTY-ONE

I drove up to the Visionary lot and, for once, had sort of legitimate business there.

Ugoth the Castrator sat in his guard booth, stuffing whole live chickens in his mouth. As I pulled up, he crunched down on one. "What you want?" he asked, every word raining a plume of feathers down on me.

Not chicken. Ever again. "I'm here to see Mayor Oculon."

Ugoth peered down at me, and that's when I realized his little piggy eyes were the size of baseballs. "Have appointment?"

"No. Uh, no, sir. No appointment. But it's an urgent matter."

"No appointment, no get on lot."

"I assure you, sir, that this is a matter of life and death."

"If Ugoth let on everyone who had life and death matter, Ugoth get fired. Ugoth no want get fired. Ugoth like job. Ugoth live in studio bungalow. Get Christmas bonus."

"And there is no way I'd want to, uh... to interfere with Ugoth's Christmas bonus." Not sure why I thought that the ogre was going to let me past. "Can you call... call Imogen

Verity. Tell her Nick Moss is here to see her."

"Oh, now want talk Miss Verity? Think Ugoth reborn yesterday?" He popped a clucking chicken into his mouth. "Just another pervert want leer. Well, Ugoth not having that either!"

"No, she knows me. I'm her employee."

"And if Ugoth ask Miss Verity, she say same thing? She not say, 'Who this puny man? Ugoth, castrate intruder!'"

"I can guarantee she will not say that."

"Because Ugoth good at that. That Ugoth's name."

"Yes. Yes, sir. I know."

Ugoth watched me closely, eating three more chickens like potato chips. "Ugoth trust puny man. Hear do anything—ANYTHING—Ugoth not like, then," and he mimed something I think he intended to mean castration. If so, he had a generous idea of what I was packing, but I was not going to correct the man. He picked up another chicken and used it to wave me into the lot. "Ugoth check later. If puny man not meet with Miss Verity, we do what Ugoth talked about earlier."

"Got it. Yes, sir. Don't you worry."

"Park on left. Don't disappoint Ugoth."

I really didn't want to disappoint Ugoth. There was a whole barrel full of clucking reasons not to. I pulled into a narrow parking lot. First step would be checking in with Imogen, just so if Ugoth asked, all of my parts would stay attached.

I headed toward her sound stage through the wandering throngs of costumed monsters. The stage was bright, and Gortran was running through another scene with Imogen and her fake family. The ceiling was to fall in, and the tentacle monster puppet was supposed to come through to threaten everyone. Looked like the climax of the film, or close to it.

"I want fear," Gortran buzzed at his stars. "I want emotion!"

I started across the open stage. Might as well warn Gortran

while I was at it. The robot kept up the direction, his green and fuzzy television face unreadable from my distance. "And Brows, make sure the damn puppet works, will you?"

"Bah! Yum yum," came the raspy growl from the rafters.

I froze, neck craning upward. There, amongst the purple tentacles of the octopus, was the olive-and-yellow body of Brows, easily identifiable by those massive white eyebrows sweeping skyward over his beady red eyes. He climbed over the thing, his clawed three-fingered hands tinkering.

I turned around as smoothly as possible. Pissing off Ugoth was worth it if a murderous gremlin was climbing around. And so we lose Gortran. The world could maybe do with one less junkie robot, right? And it's not like his movies were that great. *On Silicon Pond* was overlong and emotionless. Or maybe I'd just come back later and hope Brows hadn't dropped that incredibly oversized puppet on Gortran while I was gone.

The executive offices were over on the other side of the lot, a collection of bungalows with bright lawns and little plaques on the doors. Oculon's wasn't hard to find. I just went to the edge of the lot. There I found a small courtyard with a little fountain, the figure in the center something between Cupid and a crawling eye. It was just as disturbing as it sounds, made all the worse for the apparent purpose of being decorative.

Oculon's office was bigger than my house, complete with its own yard and stand of trees. It could not have been more secluded, even though it was in the heart of the entertainment capital of the world. And right there on the front door, a little gold plaque: OCULON, PRESIDENT.

I opened the door into a waiting room. A sea hag looked up from her desk, her goggles much sleeker and nicer than Serendipity's; they even had little cat-eye flourishes on the end. "May I help you, sir?"

"Hi, yeah, my name is Nick Moss. I'm here to see Mr., uh, Mayor Oculon."

"And do you have an appointment, Mr. Moss?" she said, opening up a book.

"Uh, no. No, ma'am. Wasn't sure how to get one, and it won't take long."

She closed the book with an authoritative snap. "Well, then, I'm sorry, sir. Mayor Oculon is a busy individual."

"I completely understand, ma'am, and I wouldn't be here unless it were important."

"If you would like a meeting, I would be happy to schedule one for you."

"It can't wait."

"How is a week from Thursday?"

"That would be waiting."

"It's the best I can do."

"You're not listening!"

It's fair to say I regretted shouting almost immediately, because two shapes materialized on either side of me. Both semi-translucent, glowing, and slightly greenish. One was a man with bleeding eyes and knives sticking out of his chest. The other was a man with a noose around his broken neck. They grabbed me under the armpits and started to drag me to the door. Hitting them would have been a waste of time. Ghosts were only as solid as they wanted to be.

"I'm here about Juba II! Aria Enchantee! And Brows!" I shouted on the way to the door.

The front door opened without either ghost touching it. "Best go limp," said Knives.

"Or grow wings," suggested Noose.

The door into Oculon's office opened. The man standing in the threshold was dressed in a three-piece suit and had no head. Probably Oculon's chauffeur from the other night, but it was tough to tell without a face to see. He held up a hand, flipped it around, and waved me in before turning back and disappearing into the office.

The ghosts dropped me and I hit the floor. "Looks like you get a stay," Knives said.

"Execution-wise," Noose said.

I got up and rubbed my ass. "Good to know."

"You can go right in," the sea hag said pleasantly.

"Thank you, ma'am."

Oculon's office was dark. Probably because, as a giant eyeball, he could pretty much see everything he wanted no matter how dim the lighting. The shades were drawn over the picture window behind the desk. Still, two lamps, one on Oculon's large mahogany desk, the other across the room with a bar, gave off a gold glow. The headless horseman stood by a bar, and as I looked closer, I noticed that the crystal decanters all had large rubber-tipped eyedroppers in them. The carpet was thick, and on one wood-paneled wall hung a portrait of Oculon, standing behind a chair with one tentacle draped over the back. Two chairs faced the desk, and right as I approached, the leather chair behind the desk turned, revealing Oculon himself, blood-red tentacles spread out. Some on the floor like feet, others on the desk, tapping like hands. The massive burgundy eye stared at me, and there was no way it was going to blink first.

"Please, have a seat, yes, yes." Oculon's voice was deep and sonorous, unmarred by any of the fear I had heard the previous night. Had he slept since Aria Enchantee had died?

"Thank you for seeing me, sir," I said, doing exactly as he asked. Quick mental count: a crawling eye, a headless horseman, two ghosts, and a sea hag, all within shouting distance. Best keep this as polite as humanly possible. No pun intended.

"You mentioned the names of three of my friends. This is naturally of interest to me."

"Um, yes. Yes, of course. Do you know who I am?"

"You told Miss Kalah your name is Nick Moss."

"Right, I mean beyond that. I'm, uh, I'm a private investigator. One of your contract players, Imogen Verity, hired me to find her husband."

"I was under the impression the police were handling that."

"They're handling one angle. I'm following up on others."

"Such as?"

"Well, um, you understand that right now, this is pure supp... I'm here to warn you, sir."

I could not tell a single thing Oculon was thinking. It was just an eye. Even the tentacles, writhing around the desk, told me nothing. Maybe there was an edge to the eye's pleasant voice, but I couldn't tell. This was the head of a studio, one of the most powerful beings in Los Angeles. I started to watch one of his tentacles out of the corner of my eye where it tapped on his desk blotter. "Warn me?"

"Yes, sir. I'm beginning to think Mr. II wasn't kidnapped. I think he might have been murdered."

"Oh?" The tone was light, but that tentacle stopped tapping for a second. "And what gave you that idea?"

"Well, sir. Aria Enchantee was killed last night."

"And how would you know that?"

"I have contac... that's not really, uh, germane to any of this, sir."

"I suppose it's not."

"That's two of your friends, sir."

Oculon was silent for a moment, the only sound the tapping of his tentacle. "I'll admit some concern when one member of the New American Benevolent Society vanishes and the other is killed."

I remembered that name. Bloody Bridget had told me they were philanthropists. "Right, the various members of the NABS should be warned. It's why I'm here."

"Well, I thank you for the warning, Mr. Moss. Tell me, do you know the killer's identity?"

"Uh... this is a little difficult. I think he's an employee of yours. I mean, I don't know for certain, but I think it's Brows."

The tentacle, which had stopped moving while Oculon asked the question, tapped the desk in time with his laughter. His laugh was a distinct, patrician "ha ha ha" with a clear demarcation between syllables, and when he was finished, there were no aftershocks. "Mr. Moss, I assure you, Brows is quite innocent of any wrongdoing."

"How can you be sure?"

Oculon ignored the question. "What motive do you ascribe?"

"Well, um..."

"And evidence, sir?"

"None right now, but I thought—"

"And you were very thoughtful. I appreciate the warning, Mr. Moss, but there is no one trying to kill me. Now, if you'll excuse me, I have the business of a movie studio to run."

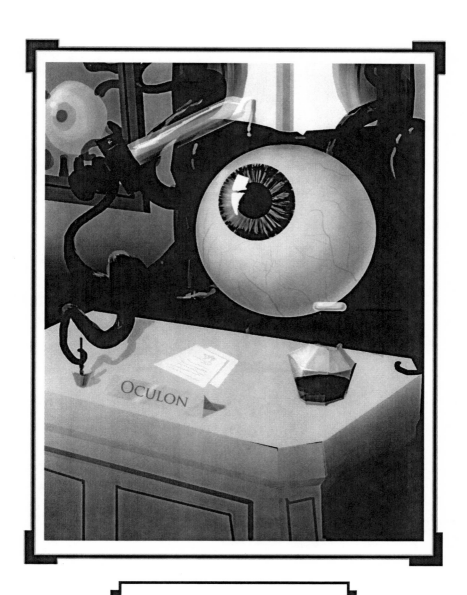

Mayor Oculon

TWENTY-TWO

My pride was kind of wounded, sure. No one likes getting dismissed like that. Even if it was by a giant monster in his office. Still, Oculon had a point. I didn't have evidence against Brows. Might be I'd get the evidence when he struck again, and wouldn't that be fun? Who would be left holding the bag when another monster bit it? Why, the one human in the vicinity.

Which meant I had to get my ass in gear and prove Brows did it.

The gremlin struck at Fer-de-Lance, but that didn't mean he was there. Aria had called for her car, and *that* got her. It was just possible Brows had gone into her home and gimmicked the car there. The problem with that was her place was liable to be crawling with LAPD, and Moon and Garou still had it out for me and my client. Didn't fancy another run-in with them, especially since I was officially out of local law enforcement to go to. It was a case of robbing Peter to get eaten by Paul.

Retrace their steps, maybe? Aria left from the studio with

Gortran and Oculon. No Brows, although he would have had access to Oculon's car. Maybe that headless horseman of Oculon's was really observant and the gremlin couldn't get to the mayor's limo. Their first stop had been that biker bar on Sunset. The Bomb Shelter. Seemed like an odd place for three uptown monsters to go, but who was I to judge? Maybe they just really liked that band.

The last time I'd gone, I had almost gotten a surprise boot party from the Howlers, but then again, that was after sundown. It wasn't as though bikers were known for being law-abiding citizens, but in broad daylight, chances were the bar was closer to empty. And there was the little matter of that locked door in the back.

Wouldn't hurt to check it out. Probably nothing. Yet something was nagging at me. Something I hadn't pieced together, but that was right there in front of my face. I'd get it when I least expected it. Hopefully not while dealing with a pissed-off phantom biker gang.

Sure enough, the Bomb Shelter's neon sign was off. There were no motorcycles out front. I pulled in around the corner and got out. The sun was climbing and with my luck, it would soon be a scorcher. I checked my jacket, brushing fingertips over the whistle and the lighter. Good a time as any.

I walked across the street and into the cool darkness of the Bomb Shelter. It still stank of beer, but that oppressive leather scent was gone. The place was almost empty, except for a couple of oldtimers drinking at a back table, a bartender half asleep against the back bar, and a shabby man sweeping up.

The bartender was a phantom, old and beaten up, but the janitor was a zombie, and apparently a fairly fresh one. The phantom fixed me with an odd look. I figured bravado was the best course of action, so I put a bill down on the bar. "Beer."

He squinted at it, shrugged, and pulled me a mug of stuff that looked like liquid jaundice. I'd had more alcoholic water in France. After a couple courtesy sips, I got up and shuffled in the direction of the can. No one took much notice, and I was in the back hallway, right where I wanted to be. I opened and shut the men's room door just in case anyone was listening, then went around the corner. The mystery door was waiting for me.

I took the lockpicks from my pocket and, with a nervous glance over my shoulder, got to work. I'm not very good with this aspect of the job, but good enough to get things done. I might have preferred a little dynamite, but as liberal as the laws were about what I was permitted to carry, TNT was sadly not on the list. Despite the fact you could make a compelling argument that it was the one thing almost every monster had an allergy to.

The irony was, I'd learned how to work locks during the Night War. We veterans were pretty prized back then, mostly because we'd gotten a lot of our fear done back in the other war. I'd never had to actually pick locks before that, since standing doors don't really matter after artillery takes out a wall, so it was a new experience for me. In the early going, when the monsters first started showing up, things were chaos. Then battle lines formed and it started behaving like a proper war, albeit one where the other guys were a mite uglier than I was used to. Then, in the latter days, when we were just a grimy resistance, locks became important again. The monsters I worked with on a daily basis now probably didn't want to know how many of their kind I took out over the years. But the Treaty of St. Louis gave us all amnesty for anything we did in the war, so there wasn't much they could do about it.

Still, the extralegal things I learned in that war, starting with lockpicking, gave me a bit of a leg up in my current career, even if it's something I wasn't about to advertise too loudly in mixed company.

The lock clicked and I opened the door.

I was expecting a storage room stuffed with boxes, some open and showing off cheap bottles of booze. I was expecting a keg or two. I was expecting a mop and bucket, along with some industrial cleaners. I got those things. I nearly closed the door, dismissing it all as a red herring that had already consumed far too much time and energy.

Something barely glimpsed made me open the door back up. On one of the shelves was a line of mason jars, filled with what looked like water. I picked one up and unscrewed the top. The rippling wave that hit me in the face said I shouldn't inhale from closer than three steps. Moonshine. Pure moonshine.

Evelyn Farrell had been soaked in grain alcohol and set on fire. Not damning evidence, but circumstantial enough to prod my desire for a little payback. I screwed the top back on and replaced the jar. Giving the room one last look, I prepared to get out of there.

From deeper in the room, a soft whimper.

I frowned. The storage area wasn't big enough to hide anything. Shelves were in the way. I took another two steps into the space, my head cocked. Silence.

I nearly turned and left, chalking it up to an overactive imagination and lack of sleep. And probably those moonshine fumes getting me good and drunk before noon.

The whimper sounded again. This time I was sure of it. Here and, more importantly, close. I followed it, weaving though some boxes stacked waist high, and ran into a shelf. Another whimper.

I moved some of the boxes on the shelf and peered through.

Tucked in the narrow space between the wall and the shelf was a young man, bound and gagged. Looked about twenty, brown hair and eyes, tall and athletic. Scared, too, flinching as soon as I revealed myself.

I held a finger to my lips and whispered, "Human," nodding encouragingly.

He frowned, eyes big, and nodded back.

I undid the gag. "Who are you?" I whispered.

"Charles. Charlie Lewis."

Hadn't heard that name before. "All right, Charlie. I need you to tell me what happened."

As he talked, I started on the restraint. It was actually a leather belt, which had been wound around his wrists, soaked, and dried, constricting his circulation and turning his hands blue. Getting him out would take time, and after poking my head into the makeshift prison, I saw his legs were tied the same way.

"I got jumped by some bikers."

"Somehow I was expecting more of a story than that, Charlie."

"Oh. I'm from Fix, Oklahoma, originally."

"I've never heard of it."

"It's near Sweetwater?"

"Not helping. How did you end up in a biker bar on Sunset?"

"I came to Hollywood to be discovered."

"This might not be the best place for that."

"I got off the bus, and I was heading toward some rooming houses I knew about, and these bikers just surrounded me. Then one of them drops a hood over my head and I hear engines, then everything gets muffled. Then, I don't know how much later, I'm here. They tie me up and leave me here."

"When was this?"

"I don't know. A day? Maybe two?"

"Why?"

"I don't know! Just get me out of here! Please!"

"Yeah. Yeah, of course. Don't worry."

I took my knife to the bonds, but the leather was tough. The challenge was trying to work the blade into the reluctant belt, cutting it enough for Charlie to do the rest. I was making a little headway when I heard a door slam. The door at the end of the hall, meaning that my only avenue of escape was effectively cut off. Thinking fast, I pulled the gag back over Charlie's mouth with a "sorry" and hauled myself into the alcove next to him. Times like this, I was grateful I was built like a Norway rat. There was a narrow alley of space stretching the length of the room back here, bordered by some boxes, stacked almost as high as the shelves. A solid ten feet to get lost in, but not enough space to bend over or square my shoulders. I nearly breathed a sigh of relief before remembering to cover my tracks. I put the box back in just as the door opened.

Standing up in the narrow space, I slowly inched away from Charlie, trying to cram myself in the far corner, the darkest place I could find. Muffled voices reached back, and as I moved, I could see little glimpses of leather-wrapped phantoms.

"Which one of you mugs left the damn door unlocked?"

"Wasn't me, Cacophony," said another voice.

"Had to be Raven. Probably left the light on, too," said a third voice.

"Fathead."

The one bossing the others was Cacophony Jones, the lead singer of the Disasters. I moved a little farther down the narrow space to get a better look and put some distance between me and Charlie. There was a crack in the boxes here, and I could see more of the storage closet. The first man I saw—who, if memory served, played the piano—was a shorter, beefy phantom with the same drawn and rotten face most had, only he topped it off with a jaunty leather cap set at a rakish angle. I shifted a bit to get a glimpse of Cacophony. There he was, sneer and all, over six feet of possibly undead muscle and murderous intentions.

"Bring him out," Cacophony said.

"Raven? He's in the car," said the guy in the cap.

"No, you dumb shit, the meatstick."

Removing that box would make me visible. All they had to do was turn a head and there I'd be, standing right there, probably waving sheepishly. Because what the hell else are you supposed to do in that situation? I reached into my pocket for the whistle, something to keep them at bay. Maybe give me that snowball's chance in hell.

Right as I was bringing the whistle from my pocket up to my lips, it hit one of the shelves and tumbled from my hand, tinkling across the floor.

"What the hell was that?" said Cacophony.

I froze.

"What was what?"

"Something fell. Did one of you mooks drop something?"

I wanted to swear, but that probably wouldn't help. Through the space between the boxes, I saw Cacophony hunting around the floor, trying to determine what was lost. The other two phantoms were a little less focused, checking the walls and ceiling.

"Nope."

"I might have dropped a quarter," the piano player said.

"Might have or did?"

The phantom paused. "Might have?"

"Get the human. But be careful. That could have been

him moving around back there. Maybe slipped his bonds."
Cacophony dropped to his hands and knees to ferret out the
source of the sound.

The box in front of Charlie Lewis scraped over the shelf
and light spilled over his terrified face for the second time.
Rough hands clamped over Charlie's shoulders and dragged
him out into the room. Cacophony looked up from the ground,
where he was still hunting for my whistle. He couldn't see it,
and so I had no prayer of locating it.

"You alone back there?"

Cacophony pulled the gag off Charlie. "Yeah. Yeah! I'm
alone."

The phantom fixed the human with milky bug eyes. Finally,
"He's lying. Largo, you check he's telling the truth."

The one in the leather hat, the piano player, dropped down
and out of sight. In moments, he'd poke his rotting face in and
peer up at me.

Up was the solution. He'd be looking over, right? I hoisted
myself up onto the shelves, taking care not to scrape around, but
to set my weight down deliberately. The boxes weren't light, but
I knew that they would hear the slightest nudge as cardboard
slid over wood. I climbed up one shelf, my index and middle
fingers finding a place between two boxes. My big toes were all
that kept me aloft. Another lesson learned from the Night War:
how to be extremely quiet when you had to be.

Largo would still see my legs without much trouble. At this
point, he would be within inches of the hole. I had to move.
My toes had other ideas. They wanted to drop me back to the
floor, preferably with a nice, loud thud that the rest of the
band would hear. I reached for the next shelf upward, my toes
making a smaller and smaller platform. My fingers scrabbled
on the shelf above, searching for some purchase. The phantom

would be almost in. I pushed off, slipping, ready to fall, but my fingers curled around the shelf, holding me up.

Carefully, I inched along to the right, toward the opening, hoping I wasn't moving fast enough to notice in the dark spaces behind the boxes. I knew if I moved too quickly, they'd hear me scraping along. But if I didn't move fast enough, Largo was going to catch me and someone would have to invent a new machine just to measure how deep in the shit I was.

"I don't see anything." The voice came from below. I looked down to see Largo's leather cap poking into the space between shelf and wall. He was peering around, but not directly up.

"You sure? Someone dropped something," Cacophony said.

"I'm telling you, it was a quarter," said the other phantom.

"Did you see a quarter, Harley?"

"No."

"Did it sound like a quarter?"

"Not really."

"Then if you say quarter again, I'm going to shove your bass so far up your ass, you're going to have to play by patting your stomach."

"Okay." Harley paused. "What if I need to buy a hamburger or something?"

Cacophony was silent for a moment, and from my vantage point, I could clearly see him weighing his options. Finally, he said to Largo, "You sure? Nothing back there?"

"I think I saw a rat."

"Okay, then. Get this meatstick loaded up. They're waiting for him."

Largo popped back out, and the box of liquor closed up the way into my little hidey hole. Harley put a bag over Charlie's head, then, with a grunt from both of them, threw the human over his shoulder. I was relieved, since my fingers and toes really wanted nothing more than to give out. The pain was increasing every second, the muscles and tendons wobbling. At least it was almost over.

Cacophony followed his men to the door, turning around at the threshold to glare inward. I was certain his buggy phantom eyes would pick me out in an instant. And even if they didn't, my own body was conspiring to give me away. I tried to force Cacophony out the door with the power of my mind alone. *Go on. Take the guy wherever you're taking him. Just get the hell out of your storage closet.* The phantom didn't care about what I wanted. My fingers shivered with the strain of holding me up. The ache running from my toes up to my shins was getting unbearable. I bit my lip and waited.

At last, Cacophony hit the light and closed the door.

I dropped to the floor as lightly as I could in the confines of the alcove and awkwardly got to the bottom shelf, pushing the box out of the way. I had to move quickly if I was going to tail the Disasters to wherever it was they were going. There was no time to look for the fallen whistle, and even if I decided to chance it, there was no guarantee I'd find anything. The Disasters hadn't spotted it. No reason I would. I went to the door, listened, and, hoping Cacophony wasn't waiting just outside, pushed it open.

The bend in the hallway was empty. I was in like Flynn. You know, as long as tailing a biker gang that was part of some kind of kidnapping ring was something Errol Flynn might consider. Might be the most generous definition of that phrase there was.

I nearly whistled as I headed toward the door back into the bar.

It started to swing open. My heart tried to strangle me, and I thought as quickly as I could under the circumstances.

Jumping forward two steps, I grabbed the door to the men's room, opening it.

Largo peered in, his milky, buggy eyes narrowing slightly at me.

"Uh. Hey. You might want to give it a minute." I waved a hand under my nose.

Largo looked me over. I really wished I had that whistle. For a moment that took a little longer than forever, Largo simply stared. The murder in his eyes might have been imagined, but it was tough to see anything else in a face that looked like a half-finished skull. He ran a gray tongue over his protruding yellow teeth and gave me a final once-over. After what seemed like seven years, he turned around, letting the door swing shut.

I exhaled a long-held breath. By the time I made it into the bar, the door was silhouetting Largo's back, spotlighting the Howlers patch on his jacket.

Nodding to the bartender, I exited, turning left and jogging to my car. A black hearse pulled out of the small lot next to the Bomb Shelter, Raven and Cacophony on motorcycles riding next to it. I followed, keeping several cars between me and the bizarre phantom convoy.

Before we got there, I knew where we were headed. As they pulled in, I shook my head. Time to talk to Ugoth the Castrator again.

TWENTY-THREE

The hearse and bikers rolled through the gates of Visionary with barely a word from Ugoth, who was now thoughtfully masticating half a swordfish. As I pulled in, he glowered down at me, but after a second, his expression softened. I might not have noticed the subtleties in his simian face had I not spent time earlier trying not to become his next improbable snack. His breath washed me in a hot, fish-scented wind.

"Puny man back," Ugoth opined.

"I know. Those phantoms who came through, do they come in often?"

"Why puny man want to know?"

"Uh... curiosity?"

"This have anything to do with earlier visit?"

"Um..."

"Look, puny man, Ugoth the Castrator no dummy. Know maybe you work for Miss Verity. Know maybe even have business on lot. But Ugoth know one thing as sure as he know sound bone make when chew it—" Ugoth the Castrator held up an index finger that was bigger around than my arm. "Know Disasters bunch of hoods."

He waved me through.

"Don't make Ugoth regret decision."

"Ugoth... uh... *you* won't. I'll be like a mouse."

Ugoth's eyes widened. "Mouse? See mouse? Where?!"

"No, no. Nothing like that. Just, an, uh... simile. Possibly a metaphor. One of those."

Ugoth calmed down, snapping off the swordfish's blade between gnarled thumb and forefinger. "Oh. Ugoth know that. Just testing puny man."

"Of course. Thanks, Ugoth."

He waved me on, and began picking his tusks with the fish's bill. I pulled into the parking lot. The rumble of the Disasters' bikes reverberated through the narrow streets of the studio, bouncing off walls at random, making them hard to track, but at least there was no way they could go faster than a slow walk, what with the crowds of studio personnel milling around.

I jogged to the mouth of the main strip through the center of the sound stages, where a steady parade of actors and crew headed to and fro on their errands. The hearse and bikes weren't part of it, so I kept moving along the aisles. The foot traffic lessened, but Visionary was a busy place, and there would always be at least one zombie going about his work. The sun beat down on me, raising a fresh coating of sweat under my suit. As I walked, the sputtering bikes went silent. I ran to the final whitewashed wall and poked my head around the corner into the sun.

The black hearse was parked outside a familiar sound stage in the corner, the motorcycles nearby. Of course it would be Gortran's stage, where he was shooting *Love is a Many-Splendored Thing From Another World*. Largo leaned against the wall outside the door, smoking and staring off toward the line of trees just on this side of the wrought-iron fence. Dealing with a phantom guard was the last thing I wanted to do. If I had the whistle, I could have gotten in no problem, although it would probably alert Cacophony and the rest of the Disasters inside. Maybe I could get a rag into the gas tank, turn the hearse into a bomb. Another option was stealing a bike and doubling back after leading the phantoms on a little chase.

I don't know what possessed me to start jogging at Largo, my right shoulder parallel to the sound stage wall. He turned his ugly phantom head right as I picked up speed into a dead run. I think he smiled first, a confused baring of teeth that might have been a greeting, which quickly turned sour. His eyes bugged out, even more than usual, and he shook his head no. That's when I rocketed a right hook that landed flush on his jaw. Lights out: his body keeled over, thumping to the baking asphalt. His whole body was stiff as a board, his left leg hovering off the ground a little, his too-small eyelids trying to flutter closed.

The pain bled into my knuckles slowly as I cradled my hand and realized I'd just punched out a phantom biker. Shame no one saw that.

I opened the door into the sound stage quickly, went through, and shut it behind me in a single motion.

A grinning demon was waiting for me on the other side. I didn't scream, mostly because I was expecting *something*, but I did go for my pistol. Took me a second to realize this was one of several demon faces, all made of fake stone, decorating the pillars of a Bronze Age temple taking up most of the space in here. So they were rebuilding Babylon, even though it was still rotting after being pulverized by artillery near Hollywood and Vine.

I peered into the dark and saw that the Babylonian temple had been hastily put up in front of the living room from Gortran's other film, a quick coat of paint turning suburbia into Old Testament times. The octopus puppet swayed in the rafters above. The floodlights were off, so the sound stage was nice and cool after the brutality of the sun.

Voices bubbled out of the back, coming from the direction of Gortran's office. I ducked behind some stacked cases and waited. Gortran's crackling radio voice was the first identifiable. "In a Babylonian temple? That doesn't seem to fit."

"Bah! Hi ho," said a rasping, gremlin voice.

"Can you settle this?" Gortran buzzed.

"Above my pay grade, Daddy-o. Where do you want him?" This was Cacophony, a voice I had become very familiar with in the last hour or so.

The monsters came into view, first Gortran waddling along unsteadily, then Cacophony following with Raven and Harley behind, carrying a limp Charlie between them. As they moved into the open area in front of the mock temple, I saw another figure, the owner of the rasp. It was Brows, hopping along next to Gortran and apparently not killing him. It was hard to read body language in someone who was basically several silvery metal boxes connected with varying lengths of industrial tubing, but the robot didn't seem at all discomfited by the gremlin. And as worrisome as they were to humans, gremlins were about a thousand times more dangerous to robots, something they could freely tinker with.

"Put him on the altar," Gortran said. "I still think this is silly."

"Pfah. Gortran caca," Brows said.

"Fine. This is a waste of time and a perfectly good human. Terminate all humans."

Raven and Harley deposited Charlie on the fake stone altar beneath the grinning demon faces. Brows hopped up next to him, poking the boy with a large claw. Only then did Charlie start moving, although he barely made any noise. Poor kid was probably all screamed out.

"Yum yum," Brows rasped, his large ears pressing into his back.

"Camera equipment. You three, come with me." Gortran was already shuffling back toward his office, assuming the Disasters would follow his lead. They exchanged a look, then a shrug, and trailed the robot.

"Hi ho," Brows said, rubbing one of his white eyebrows thoughtfully as he hopped down and followed them out of the room.

I barely waited to see the gremlin's olive-and-yellow back before rushing to Charlie's side. He whimpered while I sawed at the bonds. "Don't worry, kid. It's me," I said, yanking off the hood.

Even through the gag, Charlie managed to look as relieved as it's possible to get in his state. The leather straps came off his hands and I went to work on the ankles. He pulled the gag off. "Thanks, mister. I thought you were going to leave me behind."

"I considered it."

"Oh."

"Kidding. Jesus, let me do this. They're only going to be gone for a little while."

The knife flashed, cutting through the last of the leather. Charlie rolled off the altar and onto his feet unsteadily. Just by the way he was standing, I could tell he had nothing but spiders in those legs.

"What the hell are you doing?" said a voice.

We looked up. Raven was standing in front of the stage,

holding a couple cases and gaping with his buggy phantom eyes, Harley moving up fast behind him. Cacophony, Brows, and Gortran hadn't yet showed, but it was only a matter of seconds. And the only two exits to the sound stage I knew about were either through Raven and Harley or right by Gortran's office.

"Funny story," I began.

Harley picked up a shortened boom microphone. I didn't like where this was going.

"You know what, meatstick? Why don't you save it. They're going to be jazzed when we double the human quotient."

And Harley cracked Raven across the back of the head. The phantom went down and kissed the floor, lying still.

I blinked. "Harley. I didn't know you cared."

Harley's features melted away like they had been threatening to, reforming into those of a perfect blonde bombshell. She dropped the boom and stood imperiously over the fallen biker. "I don't. But I can't have my employees getting killed, can I?"

"Doppelganger!" Charlie squeaked.

"Imogen," I corrected him. "And I'm glad to see you, we—"

"Did you hear that?" Gortran buzzed, only a few steps from emerging into plain view.

"Bye bye?" rasped Brows.

Imogen ran past me to the mouth of the temple, turned, and beckoned. Sounded good. Shouldering Charlie's weight, I made it to the entrance. The green glow of Gortran's television face illuminated the floor just as we rounded the corner.

"What the hell? Raven! Raven, what happened?" Cacophony's voice. I peeked out, seeing the singer kneeling down by his drummer.

"Whuh? Huh?" Raven's voice was wobbly.

"Yum yum?" Brows said. "Meatstick bye bye."

"How does a tied-up human knock out one of your men and

escape? He *was* tied up, wasn't he?"

"He was," Cacophony growled. "He must have had help. Rave, where's Harley?"

"Ruggle... right behind me. Oh, hey. Time for rehearsal?"

Cacophony picked Raven up.

"Where the hell do you think you're going?" Gortran said.

"I'm putting Raven in the car. Then Largo and me are going to come in here and find Harley."

He was not going to like what he found when he got outside.

"No, you don't!" Gortran snapped. "You work for me. You get back here!"

Cacophony gently laid Raven back down, took two big steps, and put his drawn and decayed face right into Gortran's, the green glow making the phantom look even more rotten. He bared teeth that, due to receding gums, looked much too large for his head, and with a hint of the rock star grimace he had on stage, spoke quietly in Gortran's face. The menace in his tone made it carry, and it was like Cacophony was talking directly to me. "I don't work for you. You forget that again, and you're a new muffler on my bike."

Gortran's face flickered, turning into the test-pattern Indian.

"Yeah, I thought so."

Cacophony, victorious, picked his fallen bandmate up and made for the door. This left me with a killer robot and a gremlin in a giant sound stage that I wasn't even supposed to be in. I could vanish and no one would even know where to look, and that's if there was anyone who felt like bothering.

I turned around, and Charlie shook off the offer of support. The kid could move under his own steam after all. Good, because I was getting a little tired. I nodded toward the back of the sound stage, in the direction of Gortran's office. Everyone was in the front of the stage, as Cacophony would be when he got back. That left a clean exit out the back. I couldn't help but wonder what the universe would do to make a lie of that, but what is life if not the continued search for new ways to invite fate to empty her bedpan on your head?

The back of the temple was bare wooden walls, back just enough for the camera not to get a hint of how shabby the whole thing really was. If there were hallways, they were somewhere else. We emerged into the street set of *Love is a Many-Splendored Thing From Another World*.

"There's a back door by Gortran's office," Imogen whispered.

I nodded. "Yeah. Follow me and stay close."

The broken street gave way to a little bit of open ground, and then we were in the living room, with the octopus overhead. The living room had been turned all the way around, and now what had been open was facing the wall. Imogen led us through a door. A wall and another door, this room twisted the other way, and we were in an office set. Something small and cozy. Up ahead, I could see the real office, the wood-paneled room at the back of the stage, windows looking out over the exit.

I ran for the door back out into the studio, ready to tear it open.

The knob turned. I wanted to swear. Instead, I bolted for Gortran's office. I didn't even have the time to look for Imogen or Charlie. I could only hope they took the hint and hid.

The door opened just as I slid into Gortran's office. The desk he had cracked in half was still lying there; nothing had been cleaned up. I dropped like a stone, with no time to even shut the door. Cacophony came in from the outside, and, peering over one half of the desk, I saw him turn and lock the sound stage. I could try to pick the thing, but the lock was a heavy-duty one. It would probably chew my picks in half if I tried.

"Gortran! Locked the back door. If the meatstick's still in

here, there's no way out."

From back in the stage, Gortran crackled back. "Good! Get to looking."

Cacophony made an obscene gesture, none of the venom reaching his tone. "The guy we left outside was knocked cold! So the human might have help."

I wasn't sure if I'd exactly call myself "help" at this point, but sure.

I glanced around Gortran's office, terrified of moving enough to draw Cacophony's attention, searching for something that might give me an edge. There wasn't anything that looked even remotely like a whistle. Gortran had pens. That might do. I looked over the halves of his desk. The reel of film from the other day was peeking out of some scripts that had fallen into the corner.

Cacophony began to move back into the sound stage. I kept the low wall between him and me as his shadow passed by. I grabbed the reel off the floor, stuffed it into my jacket, and went back to the door, peering into the gloom of the collected stages. Like prairie dogs, first Imogen poked her head out, looking faintly ridiculous as a blonde ice queen in Howler leathers, then Charlie, his fear rendering him drawn out and exhausted. I risked a look around the corner to see Cacophony's broad back disappear out of sight. Hunched over, I joined the human and the doppelganger.

"Change of plans. We're going out the front."

"Where the Howlers are?"

"There's only one Howler."

"Yeah, the big one!"

"He's moving around. We can give him the slip."

"I don't like this plan," Charlie said. "Let's just kick the door in."

"That thing is thick. Steel, too, from the looks of it. So we'd have broken ankles by the time the robot, gremlin, and phantom show up to kill or turn us. There's one way out, and it's back the way we came."

With Cacophony around one side, I led the group back into the sets, first to the fake office. Out in the sound stage, we could hear the rattling of the monsters: Cacophony swearing and knocking things over, the gremlin muttering and clanking in the rafters above. I paused, straining to hear Gortran. The loudest of the monsters, he was always accompanied by the buzzing of his antennae, the faint whine of his joints, and, of course, his constant unconscious mantra of what he wanted to do to humanity. There was no sign of him.

I tried not to let that bother me as I wished for a nice big bucket of water.

I peered across the angled bit of open ground, trying to penetrate the gloom inside the false living room, getting a momentary shock at the television set, convinced it was Gortran crouching in the middle of the rug. It wasn't, being too large on one hand and lacking terrifying clawed arms on the other. I paused at the front door to the fake house, just to make sure the TV wasn't going to try anything, and kept moving.

There was a clatter from the far end of the stage, Cacophony spitting out a stream of curses. We hugged the wall, hoping Brows wouldn't see us from his perch above. He was somewhere not too distant, judging by the rattle of the catwalks.

We had to make it through the living room, then onto the outside set, and from there, follow the line of the wall to the exit. I stepped out onto the darkened set of the street broken by lovesick alien invasion, and Gortran powered up right in front of me, venom-green light from his chest and face washing over me. His face flickered to a still smile, the electricity climbing his antennae.

"It's you. Probably should have known," he said.

Charlie squeaked behind me, Imogen remaining quiet. I backed up; Gortran advanced with a heavy tread, his claws clicking.

"Detective, had you stuck with finding Juba, we wouldn't find ourselves in this position. Terminate all humans."

"Can't help where the trail leads me," I said, continuing to back up. I was in the living room, positive I was about to take a tumble over the coffee table. That would probably be the end of things.

Gortran got to the door. One of his tubey arms came up, the claw clacking together in a way that just seemed unnecessary. "You probably don't even know what's going on."

"I know that someone is knocking off the members of the New American Benevolent Society one by one."

Gortran's expressions never changed smoothly. They cut from one extreme to the next. So one moment he was glaring, then the head on the TV screen was thrown back and laughing, then back to the glower. "Is that what you think? Good thing I'm not a member, then."

I kept backing up. The wall hit me. I wanted to look for Charlie and Imogen, maybe mouth a pathetic "help" in their direction, but I couldn't take my eyes off the robot and I was fresh out of space to back up into. Gortran kept advancing, now reaching out for me. "You know, we could have turned you. You might have made a good gremlin. You ever think of that?"

"I'm already pretty short."

I looked around, desperate for anything. And then I looked up.

"Well, it's too late now," Gortran said.

"One thing. I've always thought, Gortran: love is a many-splendored thing."

The face snapped into the Indian test pattern. I threw my

whole body against the back wall. It shuddered, the wave of force climbing upward.

The thing from another world fell from the rafters. I jumped away, landing in the center of the room and curling into a ball, protecting my head. Gortran might as well have been nailed to the spot as he looked up. A colossal crash echoed through the sound stage, followed by a few lonely sparks. When I scrambled to my feet, there was only a giant purple octopus alien sitting in the middle of the set.

Imogen stepped up next to me. "I warned him about that thing."

"Come on." With Imogen and Charlie, I ran. Cacophony and Brows would be converging on the alien dummy, so we had no real reason to be quiet. We made it into the open part of the stage, running hard for the exit. Charlie tore the door open and was out into the hot sun with Imogen right on his heels. I was almost into the light when something hit me in the back, pushing me to the ground.

"Meatstick, caca!" rasped the gremlin, his claws digging into my back and neck as he tried to throttle me. I reached for him and got a nasty bite on my hand. I pried at the monster's claws, trying to get the vises off my neck. The stage door was open, throwing a pool of light on the floor a few feet from my head. Behind me, I could hear what was undoubtedly Cacophony getting closer.

The gremlin's claws squeezed, wringing the air of my lungs. I had to fight the instinct to wrestle with him. That wouldn't work at all. He had all the leverage and the grip strength of a guy twice my size. I pressed down, flopping forward like a fish while the psychotic little monster choked me. One flop. Two. The light should have been getting stronger, but it wasn't. Black was closing in on my vision, like someone drawing the curtains at a movie theater. I flopped again. Once more. Sunlight splashed across my face and body.

"Bright light!" the gremlin hissed.

And suddenly there was nothing on me. I clambered to my feet and turned to see the creature glaring at me with his red eyes, the lips curling over needle teeth as his claws smoked. I gave him a wave as Imogen pulled me outside.

TWENTY-FOUR

We joined the streams of monsters going to and fro around the various stages of the Visionary lot. Cacophony was nowhere to be seen, but then again, he had a scorched gremlin, a crushed robot, and two knocked-out phantoms to deal with.

Which reminded me. "Imogen, how did you... where's Harley?"

"At home. In that room of my husband's?"

"How did you... why did you..."

"Those bikers had been hanging around the studio for the last several days, and I got to wondering. Besides, there *is* a motorcycle movie in development, and if I'm to convince Oculon I'm right for the role of Switchblade Stephanie, I need to do some research."

"So you thought you'd kidnap one of them?"

"Well... not in so many words."

I almost demanded elaboration on the point. It was pretty clear Imogen was living in this famous-actress wonderland where her actions didn't have much in the way of consequences. "You know what? I don't think I want to know what words you *would* use."

The main drag through Visionary was busy, with trucks tooling up and down the middle of the road. We didn't even stand out. Not Charlie in his ragged teenager clothes, me in my torn and bloody suit, or Imogen in a man's biker outfit. There are times when working in Hollywood has definite benefits. We rushed to my car, arriving just as I started hearing the sputtering cough of the Disasters' bikes.

As we drove through the gate on the right-hand side of Ugoth the Castrator's massive guardhouse, the ogre raised a paw in greeting.

"Hey, puny man," he boomed. "See Imogen there. Ugoth's trust pay off."

I tipped my hat at him. "Say, Ugoth, the Disasters might be coming through the gate, and they've been bothering Miss Verity..."

"Say no more, puny man. Now see who dumb-ass ogre."

The grin that spread over Ugoth's backhoe of a jaw was the same smile that had once been on Genghis Khan's face when he looked out over Europe. He waved us through and shut the gate. Behind us, the hearse rolled up with the bikes, and Cacophony started angrily shouting at Ugoth. Not the smartest thing I'd ever seen a phantom do. The ogre cracked his knuckles, sounding like pistol shots, as he stood up. I was nearly disappointed I couldn't stick around and see the fallout.

"Smoke?" I asked.

Both Imogen and Charlie took one from the squashed package, Imogen delicately, Charlie like a half-dead robot groping for a generator. I watched in admiration as both of them lit up with no problems and eased back in the seats of my

Ford with effortless cool. I shook a cigarette partly out, tried to retrieve it with my mouth like I had seen some people do. It ended up in my nose.

I drove east on Hollywood, heading vaguely in the direction of Imogen's house. "So, Charlie, where do you want to be dropped off?" The cigarette wouldn't light. I finally dropped it out the window and hoped no one would notice.

"Shouldn't we go to the police?"

"Well, if you want to. I don't know if they'll believe you or not."

"But what about you?"

"I know they won't believe me."

"What are we supposed to do?"

"We're humans, kid. We're supposed to grin and bear it. Now where do you want me to take you? Where were you staying?"

"Nowhere. They grabbed me right from the bus station."

"There are a couple human-only hotels around there," I said.

"What on earth would possess you to come to Los Angeles at night?" Imogen asked.

"What? I didn't."

"Your bus, Charlie," I said. "You left... what was it, Sweetwater, in the daytime. But you got here at night."

"It's Fix. And no, I didn't. I got here in the afternoon."

"Wait. The Disasters jumped you in broad daylight?"

"Yeah. Of course."

"What do you mean 'of course'? Don't you have laws where you're from?"

"Sure we do. But I was alone, so it was fine."

"What?"

"In Oklahoma, if you're alone, they can grab you if they

want," he explained patiently.

"In California, in Los Angeles, if the Disasters did what they did after dark, yeah, no problem. But if they lay one hand on you in the daytime, they're criminals!"

"Are we going to the police, then?"

I shook my head. "They're hoods, sure, but they have someone's ear at Visionary. Or more accurately, someone's eye."

"Oculon?" Imogen asked.

"Who else? From what Gortran said, this isn't about a series of murders. This is about something different. Something about grabbing kids like Charlie from the bus... station..." The words came out slow as I remembered what Hexene Candlemas had said the New American Benevolent Society was arguing over when she brought the hexes for Juba and Gortran. The bus station.

"The Disasters are grabbing humans in the daytime and they're giving them to the New American Benevolent Society."

Imogen gasped. "The Society would never do that! It's illegal and the sheriff of Hollywood is one of the founding members."

Right, the picture on the wall of Juba's house. A crawling eye, a gremlin, a phantom, a mummy, and a werewolf. Oculon, Brows, Aria Enchantee, Juba himself, and Sheriff Lobo Castle. Philanthropists. Humanitarians, meaning they ate humans. "They would and they did," I said, still distracted by the revelation.

"Why? What could anyone possibly gain from something like that?"

"I don't know."

We dropped Charlie off at the bus station. I gave him the rest of my smokes as a consolation prize. It was his word against all four Disasters about what happened, and they could probably afford some expensive lawyers with the money of Visionary

Pictures behind them. Then I drove into Echo Park toward Imogen's stately Victorian, and I was left wondering first what sort of madness I'd found myself in the middle of, and also what kind of lunatic I had for a client.

As we climbed up the sunny steps, the door opened of its own accord. In the gloom of the hall beyond, Bloody Bridget waited. Would it have been so hard to manifest legs? Or to stop bleeding from the mouth, eyes, and hallway? Probably. Ghosts. There was no dealing with them.

"Welcome home, ma'am. May I get you something... *to drink?*"

"A couple glasses of lemonade, I think," Imogen said, without asking me. Since it got Bridget out of the room, it was fine by me. "And something for Mr. Moss to eat. He must be famished. Nick, would you wait for me in the parlor? I need to get out of these clothes."

"Oh, yeah. I was going to... not that you don't look fab... right. Parlor, was it?"

Imogen arched an eyebrow, the tiniest smile tugging at her lip, and headed upstairs.

"Sir? Would you like a... *ham sandwich?*"

"Uh... yeah, please."

"With... *hot mustard?*"

"Now you're just doing that to annoy me. But actually, yes."

Bloody Bridget faded from view while I went into the parlor. On the way, I paused at the New American Benevolent Society picture, a bunch of rich monsters making things better for other rich monsters who didn't really need it. Be nice to have one of those groups for humans, but I wouldn't see that in my lifetime. I sighed and settled into the parlor. The script was gone, so I watched the street out of the nice bay windows. Sleep buzzed in the back of my head, as this was the most comfortable chair I'd been in and the first time I'd been able to relax since the day I'd spent shadowing Gortran.

"Detective... *your sandwich.*"

I yelped and jumped up. The lemonade floated in front of me, gripped by a pale gray-green hand. In the matching appendage, there was a plate with a ham and cheese on rye, some carrot sticks next to it. Bloody Bridget grinned at me, the corners of her mouth dripping blood that vanished before hitting the floor.

"Th—thank you, Bridget."

"Anytime. *Detective.*"

Ghosts.

She set another glass on the end table by a weird-looking asymmetrical sofa. I got to eating, devouring lunch in a few quick bites. I might even have remembered to chew once or twice. A moment after I polished off the last corner of the sandwich, Imogen came down in a pale blue dress, looking as immaculate as always, ready to step in front of a camera. Doppelgangers never had to reapply their faces. Or had to constantly, depending how you thought of it. She took her place on the couch, tucking long legs under her.

"That's an odd sofa."

"It's a fainting couch."

"Is there, uh, is there much fainting around here?"

"Depends on how persistent Bridget is."

We sipped lemonade in silence for a while before I couldn't ignore the obvious any longer. "Are we going to talk to the phantom in your basement?"

"He's not going anywhere."

"You do know kidnapping is still a crime when the kidnappee is a monster, right?"

"I'm worth a great deal of money to Visionary. I doubt they'd let my name get dragged through the muck."

The fact that she was right was obnoxious. All around me, monsters were doing whatever they pleased, and the one actual crime that I knew for certain had happened, Charlie Lewis's abduction in broad daylight, was pretty much unprovable. I stood up. "Let's go talk to him."

"If you like."

As angry as I was, I took the lemonade. It was actually very good. Never thought ghosts would be much for summer drinks, but live and learn. I had been down in Imogen's basement the day before yesterday, but it seemed like longer. Probably what happens when you spend a couple of days in mortal terror. Imogen opened up the secret door, and sure enough, there was Harley the phantom, lying in the sarcophagus, bound hand and foot and with a gag in his mouth. He was stripped to his undershirt and boxer shorts, which I was disappointed to learn weren't decorated with tiny pipe organs.

"How did you nab him?"

"Same way I got Raven. Snuck up behind him and bap."

"Bap?" I marveled at how such a silly word could become chilling when used in the right context.

"You know, with a truncheon of some kind."

"That wasn't my sticking point."

"He's all yours."

Seeing I wasn't going to get anywhere with Imogen, I knelt over Harley and undid the gag. He spat out a glob of phlegm that smelled like grave dirt and shot me a defiant glare.

"Hi," I said.

That pretty well derailed whatever hate train he had been planning to board. "Uh. Hi?"

"So you play bass in the Disasters."

Harley nodded.

"And you're a Howler, too, from what I understand."

"Yeah, what of it?" He was getting belligerent again.

"I thought you bikers were anti-establishment types. Thought you were about freedom, the open road, that kind of thing."

"We are."

"Then why are you Oculon's little errand boys?"

"The hell we are! We work for us, and he pays us good money—" Harley stopped, the realization dawning over that cheesecloth face of his.

"Yeah, so you realize I got you there, right?"

"And who the hell are you? Cop?"

"Uh, yeah. And you best remember what happens if you get me angry. Grr."

Harley flinched a little bit.

"So speak up, see? What are you doing kidnapping humans in broad daylight?"

"I don't know."

"You don't know why you're kidnapping humans or you don't know why you're doing it in the daytime?"

"The first one. We do the second because it's almost impossible to get meatsticks at night anymore. They take precautions, you know? Wind chimes, half songs, sometimes even open flame..." He shuddered.

My heart was breaking for him. Really it was. Hard to get humans at night. At least he'd given me a couple new ways to distract a phantom.

"I don't know what the eyeball wants with 'em, and he don't tell us. Maybe he tells Cacophony, but not me. I'm just the bass player."

"Lead singer stuff?" I said sympathetically.

He nodded.

I stood up and went back to the door.

"Wait! Aren't you going to arrest me? Or her? Or get me out of here?"

"Nah." I shut the door and turned to Imogen. "He does have a point. Are you just going to keep him?"

"Don't be silly. Bridget is washing his clothes now, and once those are done, I'll have her take him out of here." She waved in that special vague way only the wealthy have truly mastered. "What do we do now, Nick? We're no closer to finding my husband." Juba II's five canopic jars sat on the shelf next to me, each one containing a little bit of the missing man.

I kept my mouth shut at the very real probability that we had already found her husband, and he was that little bit of sand on the windowsill. "Not to be rude, but *we* are not doing anything. *You* are a client and should let me do my job."

She sighed. "Which is what? I like to know what I'm paying for."

I reached into my jacket, removing the reel of film. "Don't suppose you have a projector?"

She pursed her lips in amused aggravation, snatched the can from my hand, and calmly sashayed up the stairs. I jogged after her. "Bridget! Bridget, set up the screening room!" she called out.

"Right away, ma'am," Bridget said, manifesting as nothing more than a chill up my spine and the feeling of someone tapdancing on my grave.

"This way, Nick," Imogen commanded. We passed a more intimate study, then stepped through a doorway and into a smallish room. A projector was in the back, and the translucent maid loaded the film while Imogen and I sat in large, comfortable chairs that were nearly entirely covered with doilies. We faced a silver screen pulled down from the ceiling. It was nicer than most movie theaters I'd been in.

"What is this?" Imogen asked me over the clicks of Bridget working the projector.

"I don't know. It was in Gortran's office, and Cacophony delivered it, I think. It seemed important."

"It's ready, ma'am."

"Thank you, Bridget." The ghost turned the projector on, then stepped through the wall to give us privacy. The projector threw a countdown onto the screen. I wasn't sure what I was hoping for. A western, maybe. I always liked those. Even the modern ones; you could sort of ignore that Billy the Kid was a vampire now for some reason. Horror movies were the worst, since you had to sit through a bunch of monsters moaning about nonexistent persecution.

The countdown clicked off and the screen went dark, then light, showing a static establishing shot of an old-timey opera house. I was right. It was the place at Fer-de-Lance. Even if I couldn't see the other side of the gully through the windows, I'd know that place anywhere after having put glowing footprints through its small lobby. The curtains drew, and onstage was a grand piano, a man tied hand and foot to the bench.

Imogen gasped. Scandalized, sure, but there was a little more to it: the sound of someone who was enjoying being offended.

The man on the bench was right around Charlie's age, and the same general type. Athletic and handsome, although he had more of a greaser look to him. Here was where a certain amateurishness betrayed the production, in that there were no cuts. The camera moved in to linger over the captive, but it was unable to cope with the boy's clearly unrehearsed struggles. It captured his terrified face in isolated moments. There was no sound, but my mind supplied his terrified whimpers. It had Charlie's to work off of.

The camera settled into another static shot, still never cutting.

A woman stepped into frame from behind the curtains. She wore a long and elegant evening gown, showing off pale, smooth arms. As she got closer, I recognized the sallow skin, the buggy eyes, the oversized chompers, and the patch of decay on her cheek. This was Aria Enchantee.

She danced closer to the struggling young man, her creepy corpse eyes fixed on him. Imogen wasn't gasping. Probably because she was as horrified as I was.

Once she reached his side, she began to sing, and the keys of the piano depressed as though an invisible player was at work. Whatever she was singing had to be good; phantoms knew their music. The camera moved again, trying to keep both the singing phantom and the young man in frame; it wasn't easy, because the kid's struggles had grown more desperate. His head jerked back and forth, and, before my eyes, I watched his skin tighten against his bones and begin to rot away in places. His gums receded over his teeth. His eyes turned milky and bulged outward.

The boy went limp and I recognized his new, altered face. It was Cacophony Jones, leader of the Disasters.

The camera panned out a final time to show Aria Enchantee sit beside her new creation and stroke his hair. And then the screen went white as the film flapped against the projector.

In the sudden quiet, I could hear Imogen breathing rapidly. That wasn't quite what I was expecting, so I turned. Her shiny blonde hair had fallen to cover her expression. "Uh, Imogen? Miss Verity? Are you all right?"

She turned to me, revealing blank skin where there should have been a face.

I cursed, falling out of my chair and backing up until I hit the wall.

"Oh, Nick," said Imogen's voice, sounding weird and echo-y

now that it no longer issued from a mouth. "Why fight what we've known all along?"

"Known? We haven't known anything! I'm completely clueless!"

Imogen got up, the the projector splashing light over her featureless visage. The skin was flushed bright red all over, with no differentiation of where she should have had cheeks or eyes or anything else.

"Don't play coy, detective. When I tried to change you at your house, you were letting me."

"I was, uh... that is, I wasn't, um, expecting... that." I inched along the wall in the direction of the door while Imogen prowled toward me. I knew any second now, I'd start seeing her edges blur, start feeling my face drift away like mist.

"Just let it happen. You know you want this, Nick. All those things you were talking about—getting ignored by the police, treated like a second-class citizen—that stops. All that stops. And I can guarantee you a contract at Visionary. Or maybe you keep your current job, or join the police force and become the greatest undercover officer who ever lived."

"I'm, uh, I'm actually fine with the way things are. Being human, I mean."

"Don't be silly. Who would want to be human?"

"Uh... well, there's me. This sweet old couple who run a diner near my place, and..." My hand closed over the doorknob. "Possibly Evelyn Farrell, but we'll never know."

Imogen jerked backward, and her ice queen mask rippled over the blankness for a second like a wave over a pond. I opened the door, ducked through it, slammed, and leaned.

On the other side, Imogen worked the knob and pushed. "Nick! Nick, come on, let me out! It doesn't hurt, I promise! It'll be so good for both of us!"

I'm a small man, but I still have some of the muscles I

found in Basic. Never wanted to thank my drill sergeants more than I did right then, although they couldn't have foreseen all those pushups being put toward keeping monsters from eating my face. Well, considering some of the things they told us about Krauts, maybe they did.

Imogen slammed into the door. "Nick! Any man would die for this!"

"Not any man, apparently!"

"Don't be crude! Open the door!"

"No means no, Imogen!"

"Mr. Moss, I must insist you... *release my employer.*"

I turned to find Bloody Bridget floating next to me, and she had found a way to replace her face with snakes. I screamed and lost my grip on the door for a moment. Imogen slammed into it, nearly knocking me down, but I dropped a shoulder and hammered it back.

"Bridget! Thank God," I said.

"What?" The snakes stopped writhing for a moment, regarding me with confused and beady eyes.

"Your boss has gone cuckoo."

"Yes, but you can't just—"

"She's trying to turn me! That's illegal, last time I checked. And I'm the kind of man who holds a grudge."

"Yes, but—"

"Look at her if you don't believe me! She's gone stark raving mad!"

Bridget's face returned to normal, which for her was still ashen and bleeding from the eyes. "Well, all right. But if this is something else, I will throw you out of this house."

"Good!"

Bridget stuck her faintly glowing head through the door to peer into the other side. Slightly muffled, Imogen said,

"Bridget! Thank goodness. Would you tell Mr. Moss to open the door?"

"Miss Verity, maybe you should put your face on?"

"Don't you get cheeky with me, you—"

Bridget pulled her head back to my side of the door. "Hm. You were right. She's insane. What happened?"

"We were watching that film, and she lost her mind."

"What was the film?"

"A phantom turned a human."

"Oh...!" Bridget's eyes got bigger as she fanned herself and the walls started to bleed.

"Great, now *you're* all hot and—"

"Mr. Moss!"

"I'm sorry." Imogen slammed into the door again, knocking me in the head. "You think maybe you could lock this until she calms down?"

"Oh. Oh! Of course!"

Bridget vanished, reappearing moments later with a key. I held the door while she locked it. "I'm so sorry, Miss Verity! You're not yourself! I'll let you out soon!"

"Bridget! So help me, if you don't let me out this instant, you'll be haunting a tenement on Traction before week's end!"

"She doesn't mean that," I said to the ghost.

"How long do I have to keep her in there?"

"I, uh... how long does she normally take with, you know, maritals..."

"Mr. Moss!"

"This isn't pleasant for me either!"

I stared at the ghost for a long moment, then took a deep breath. "Look, just keep her in there for now. I'm going to—"

And nothing derails a train of thought quite like an explosion.

TWENTY-FIVE

What was that?" Imogen asked from behind the door.
But Bridget and I were already running downstairs. The entire house thumped like it had been punched in the gut, and when we got to the main floor, we found that every window had been shattered, pictures knocked to the floor. I envied Bridget her lack of feet as I picked my way through the glass and out to the porch.

Off to the left, about two blocks away, probably on Kensington, a single pillar of greasy smoke stained the blue summer sky.

"What the hell?" I said, steadying myself on one of the columns on the balcony.

Bridget shook her head helplessly. All along the street, other monsters were emerging from their homes, dazed and cut up from the sudden violence. Welcome to my world, guys.

"Bridget!" She wouldn't focus, and when I tried to slap her, my hand went right through her face and whacked the pillar. "Ow! Dammit!" That got her attention.

"Detective?"

Shaking out my throbbing hand, I asked her, "Is there anyone else in the New American Benevolent Society who lives in the neighborhood?"

"What?"

"Is there anyone—"

"Miss Enchantee lived on Kellam and Mr. Brows on Kensington."

Naturally. "Stay here. I need to check this out."

She nodded and I made my way unsteadily to the car, driving the two blocks toward the smoke. As I neared the explosion, things got worse and worse. Windows were blown out, some trees were smoldering, and one palm had gone up like a match, spilling embers onto lawn, sidewalk, and street. Some houses showed damage, from panels torn off to debris sticking out of rooftops. I turned onto Kensington, a wide, curving residential street, bordered with Craftsmans and Victorians, and the source of the smoke was soon clear.

On a large lot, where there had probably once been a lovely home, was some burning wreckage scattered in and around a blackened crater. The police had arrived, and were only just roping the area off. There were only two uniforms securing the site; the dicks hadn't shown yet. I just had to play it big and hope for the best.

So I pulled the car up and walked toward the rope. "Officer, what do we have?" I flapped open my jacket briefly so he'd get the glint of something and hoped his brain would complete the picture.

"Wow, you're here fast, Detective..."

"Wolf."

"Detective Wolf. Well, sir, looks like someone blew up the house."

"I can see that. I think all of Los Angeles can see that." I walked past him and into the wreckage. There wasn't a whole lot of the house left. Seemed a bit of overkill to me, but who was I to judge? After all, I'd seen someone else get squished by a death-car, so it seemed like when a New American Benevolent Society member died, they died in a manner sure to interest the good people at Ripley's Museum. "Whose residence is this?"

"Uh," he said, searching the name out on his notepad. "A 'Lord Craven the Bringer of Destruction and Despair.'" He paused. "The neighbors said most people just called him Brows."

"Gremlin."

"Yes, sir."

The blast looked like it had a source right in the center of where the house had been, and from the scorching, it had exploded outward and upward. I'd seen enough bombings to know what one looked like, though I couldn't for the life of me say exactly what explosives were involved.

The smoke mostly blotted out the sun. Who would blow up Brows's house when he wasn't even home? He could have gotten home from Visionary in the time since I'd left there, but it seemed unlikely. Which meant that whoever was knocking off the New American Benevolent Society was getting sloppy. I stood there, sweating in the premature twilight, breathing in the outdoor wood-stove aroma when a car pulled up in front of the bomb site.

Two men got out and I recognized them immediately. Detectives Lou Garou and Phil Moon. My heart fell into my shoes. They looked up at me and broke into broad, sadistic smiles.

"Hey, rook, usual practice to give private dicks the run of the place?"

"Private... what? Sir, he has a badge."

Garou called over to me. "How about it, Moss. You got a badge yet? Because I can haul you in for that."

I shrugged. Not much to say when a couple cops wanted to mess with you. Garou came up the cement steps and onto the lawn, Moon following. "So what are we to think, hmm? A close associate of Juba II's murdered in a bombing, and who should be here but Juba's widow's bagman. Tell me, Moss, what was it you did in the service?"

"Killed Krauts, mostly. I had a rifle."

"He had a rifle," Garou said to Moon.

Moon guffawed. "You can understand why we're suspicious."

"I, uh... look, detectives. If I was trying to kill Brows, I did a piss-poor job. He wasn't even here."

"And where was he?"

"Visionary Pictures. You can ask anyone there. He had to have been seen."

"You snooping around the studios, Moss?" Garou said. "Looking for another rich sugar monster to bankroll you?"

"Nothing like that."

Moon stared at the crater. "So what *are* you doing here? Not like you get called when something like this happens."

"The II household is right over there," I said, pointing over the tops of the blackened and shredded neighboring houses. One of them was missing a good section of one wall, giving us a view into a bombed-out kitchen.

"So it is. Pretty convenient for you and Mrs. II."

"Are you going to arrest me?"

"Haven't quite decided yet."

"But you'll know when we do," Garou growled, "by the feel of my shoe in your ass."

"Right. The Dresden Hello."

Garou laughed at that. "See, Moss, I don't know what the problem is. If you're not in Verity's pocket—and who'd blame you if you were—you're a halfway decent detective."

"We looked into you," Moon said while peering at the wreckage. "Got a good reputation. For a human."

"Thanks. I run on word of mouth, mostly."

Garou went on: "Decent investigator, not a whining nancy like most of your kind—hell, we could use a man like you on the force. Once you get in touch with your wild side."

"I, uh, I don't really have one."

"Not yet you don't. But one of us bites you, you wait till the full moon, and you're an animal."

"And I have to throw out all my good silver."

"He's got you there, Lou," Moon said.

Garou's expression hardened, which was a little nerve-wracking when discussing a wolfman. "You make do with tin," he said, a trace of bitterness in his voice. "Now let's get back to earlier. What were you doing at Visionary that you saw this Lord Craven?"

"Looking into things? Juba II's disappearance. Still working that case."

"Any closer to finding the guy we all know is dead?"

"Actually... actually, I think you two are probably right on that one."

Both Garou and Moon were stunned, Moon looking up from his inspection of some blackened boards. "You what?" he said.

"I think Juba's probably dead. I still don't think the wife did it, though."

"And why's that, Moss? Because she really fills out a sweater?"

"No. Because another member of the New American

Benevolent Society has been murdered."

"The what?" Garou said.

Moon spoke up. "Before your time. Right when the war was kicking up, a group of monsters was sort of working for mainstream acceptance. New American: you know, monsters. Benevolent Society, like a charity. Who was murdered, Moss?"

"Aria Enchantee. Phantom. She was a composer over at Visionary."

"Yeah, that sounds right," Moon said. "How'd she buy it and why is this the first I'm hearing of it?"

"Because she died in the Hollywood Hills."

Moon and Garou exchanged a look and I swear that Garou's lip curled with a soft growl.

"Goddamn Hollywood sheriffs," Moon said. "How is it you know this?"

"That's, uh, that's not really... look, I couldn't have done it even if I wanted to. You can look into it. Her car folded in on itself, ended up crushing her and her chauffeur to death. Looked like a gremlin trap to me. And before you start, Brows here was also in the Society."

Garou blinked in surprise. Moon's tired face settled into a squint. "Thought you said Brows ain't dead."

"Well, he's probably not. I mean, maybe he is. But this does seem to be an attempt, at the very least."

Garou spoke up as Moon went back to looking at wreckage. "For a minute, I'm going to overlook that you just admitted to being on site for not one, but two murders. So long as you tell me everything you know about the Enchantee murder."

"All right. She was at a place in the Hills, a place called Fer-de-Lance. They have monsters dressed up like humans, and the clients—monsters—hire them to pretend they're victims. Her car arrived, she got in, and the thing just folded up into a little cube. Squish. Like an orange."

"Who do you like for it?"

"Him," I said. "Brows."

"But Brows is dead."

"Right, well, if he actually were, that would put a dent into the theory, but all I see is a crater. I don't see a body. I see a gremlin who just faked his own death."

The weird thing was, Garou was actually listening to what I was saying, letting out a whistle as he looked over the black lawn. "Hell of a theory, Moss."

"Holy shit," Moon mumbled. He was standing at the edge of the center of the crater, looking down.

"What do you have?" Garou said.

"Better come here and look."

Garou and I walked over and followed Moon's gaze down. Beneath the house had been a small basement, a fifteen-foot cube of earth taken out. In the center, what looked like a small fallout shelter. The bomb had cracked a large hole in the ceiling, a greasy stain showing exactly where the device had been placed. The staircase was partially intact, shielded from the full brunt of the blast by the shelter itself.

The sun shone down into the shelter, revealing a cot sized for a two-foot creature. One wall held a shelf stuffed with candy.

"So much for your theory, Moss," Moon said, gesturing.

A shaft of sunlight illuminated a puddle of lazily bubbling yellowish goo: the clear remains of a gremlin. "That might not be..." I clambered down to the edge of the crack for a closer look. Perched on the jagged edge of the fallout shelter, I could see the parts of the gremlin the sun hadn't hit: a bit of arm, his foot. In the center of the puddle, two giant white caterpillars.

His eyebrows.

"No, that's him all right. Brows is dead."

TWENTY-SIX

hey didn't laugh at me, really. Even the intimidation seemed a little perfunctory after that. Garou and Moon made a couple threats about turning me, but their hearts weren't really in it. I couldn't blame them. I'd just shown how good my detective bona fides were by detailing an elaborate theory that revolved around one particular guy not being a puddle of snot.

Brows could have gotten back. Driven a car with suicide tint, or else one of those enclosed flying machines gremlins seemed so fond of. He could have beaten me to the neighborhood. Then gone into his fallout shelter... and then what?

Leaving Visionary like that? Leaving Gortran, who was in bad shape, if not outright dead? Leaving Cacophony, who seemed about five seconds from turning on everyone? Something about that seemed wrong. But there was no escaping that this was Brows. The cops had even fished the eyebrows out of the goop, and those were not fake. Still had a bit of gremlin meat on them that promptly melted away as soon as Moon held it up to the light.

What remained was the location on that stag film. Although "stag film" didn't seem to be the right term. There probably wasn't a word for what it was. A brand-new invention for the New American Benevolent Society. Their true claim to fame, a legacy-builder that right now would not be revealed.

While this whole case was murkier than a bachelor gill-man's pond, one thing, at least, was clear. If I was to find the killer of Evelyn Farrell, Aria Enchantee, Brows, and probably of Juba II, there was just one place to look.

Fer-de-Lance.

Miss Zoltar had mentioned something about films during my visit. This had to be what she was talking about.

There was a chance Oculon and Sheriff Castle didn't yet know they were the last monsters standing. Once they did, there would be a scramble, and in it, I'd lose whatever would prove what happened. Prove what happened to Juba II. And let me get some goddamn sleep.

I went by my office first. Serendipity looked up from her gossip magazine when I walked in. "Nick? You look terrible."

I grunted at her and went into my office.

"Um, are you all right?" She was standing in the doorway, wringing webbed hands.

I rummaged through the filing cabinet, finding my spare whistle and putting it in the pocket of my jacket. As I went out the door, Serendipity got out of my way quicker than she ever had before. I must really have looked a fright.

"Don't wait up," I told her.

This time, daylight shone on the golden hills over the City of Devils. I was no longer following the taillights of a limousine filled with monsters. The destination was now familiar, etched in my brain for the rest of my life. Yet for those differences, it somehow felt more dangerous. I knew the score, at least some of it, and that made me an actual threat. A threat to powerful monsters, and a threat to whoever was killing them one by one.

I parked where I had the night before, turning my car around to face downhill and hoping I wouldn't need to call on Hexene for another ride.

Fer-de-Lance looked different in the daytime. The sordid grandeur it held at night was replaced with an oppressive sense of normalcy. It was merely a house, albeit a large one. Knock and find a normal family of wealthy monsters inside. There was no printed sign marking it as closed, though the silence in the air and the darkness of the windows told that tale eloquently. A breeze rushed through the Santa Monica Mountains, drawing a shiver from my sweat-covered skin as I headed for the front door.

An oil stain on the driveway glimmered, along with little pieces of Aria Enchantee's car. Some of the stains were probably blood; I didn't look too closely. Some of the others were probably carrot juice, which was funny or tragic, depending.

I knocked on the heavy wooden door.

The house seemed to hold its breath. I knocked again. After more time than would have been allowed had this been operating hours, the door opened. It was the sullen gill-man, still in his flannel, though, thankfully, he had ditched the hip-waders for a pair of blue jeans. He blinked in fishy surprise at the sight of me.

"Uh... can I help you?"

"Yeah, you probably can. May I come in?"

He stepped aside out of trained politeness, and I bulled in before he realized he'd made a mistake. I turned around to find him looking flustered. "We're, uh... we're closed."

"This is a business?"

"Oh, um. I don't know that—"

"I'm just joshing. I know. I'm a regular customer."

The gill-man gave a shuddering sigh. "We're still closed. Soon as the sun goes down, we can fix you up with whoever you like."

"Mary? I usually see Mary Brown."

"Mary is booked solid," he said quickly.

"The last time I was here, Miss Zoltar pointed me in the direction of a screening room. I was wondering if maybe I could kill a little time in there. I'll pay, of course."

"Actually, I don't think that's such a good idea." He reached out to put hands on me, and since these were gill-man paws, webbed and clawed, I took it as a threat. I reached into my jacket and pulled the flashlight, clicking it on right in his eyes. As the beam reflected off the multiple gill-man lids, I could swear the damn things were red. He scarcely blinked, getting his claws over my shoulders and yanking me toward the door. I barely had time to be impressed by what a tough bastard this guy was; instead, I ripped a punch right to his liver, which he had graciously left unguarded.

He didn't react. I made a mental note that either gill-men no longer had livers, or else their scales were thicker than I had previously imagined. A shove sent me stumbling onto the porch as he slammed the door.

Well, that made things a little more difficult. I peered at my suit, thankful to find that his claws had not torn little holes over the shoulders. I sighed. Mr. Rodriguez got enough of my money as it was; at least I'd only be paying him to get the fishmarket scent out, instead of patching the thing, too. I went around the side of the house, where I had watched Aria Enchantee get betrayed by her car, and emerged on the lip of the gulch. The sets looked smaller in the daylight. The castle, standing on the opposite ridge, was dark and shabby. Below, the wrecked flying saucer wasn't any grander than a junked car, the fires not yet lit. I peered down the ravine to the west where it spilled out and could barely see the Ferris wheel glinting in the afternoon sun. I gave it a little nod of thanks. It was the most any amusement park ride had ever done for me, with the possible exception of the bumper cars at the Santa Monica pier.

I could feel every step of last night's chase in my legs, as though in arriving at the site, they were preparing for another one. At least it was a little closer to home field advantage if it happened again.

The back door was locked, but around the side of the house, I found a window propped open to let in some air. I hoisted myself up and balanced on some pipes that came from the ground in a lazy L shape. Peering into the gloom beyond, I saw a small sitting room on the far side of the house from where I had originally waited to pick out my fake victim for the evening.

I nudged the screen and the damn thing popped out. I braced myself for a loud clatter to the floor, but hadn't counted on one thing: brothels have nice, thick carpets. The thing was almost silent as it hit the rug, tipped over, and leaned against one of the plush red velvet chairs. Not about to look that particular gift horse in the mouth, I boosted myself up and in.

The house wasn't quiet. People moved around with muted footsteps, having muddy conversations. But there also wasn't any shouting or running. I picked up the screen and replaced it on the window, went to the door, and had another listen. Still nothing to indicate I was about to be descended upon by a bunch of angry not-prostitutes.

I opened the door to find myself in a long hallway. Fer-de-Lance was huge, like several houses mashed up into a single building. Inside, it was a maze. On my last trip, I had a guide: Miss Zoltar first, and later Mary. I knew I could spend all day looking for the movie room and never even come close to it. Meant I needed someone to show me.

Very quietly, I followed the hallway toward the foyer. I finally found it through a large parlor, where I stopped in the doorway to check my path up the stairs. In the opposite room, the gill-man who had given me my walking papers was sitting calmly, reading a book. For a second, I was overwhelmed with curiosity about what a gill-man might read. Would it be something thematic? *The Old Man and the Sea* or *Moby Dick*? Or would it just be some trashy detective novel?

Though he was facing the front of the house, he would see me out of the corner of his eye when I came out to turn the corner and go upstairs. I rattled off the choices in my head. Make a noise, get him to investigate, then double back and get upstairs. Problem with that was, he knew the house better than I did, and odds were he'd get back to his place before I could use the distraction.

Throw something over his head to hit the opposite wall. No, his head would go here, and then whip back around. He'd be even more aware of something moving than if I had done nothing.

Which left doing nothing. I slunk out of cover, moving fast as a snail, back inching along the wall, eyes glued to the gill-man. I hit the first step, the carpet eating the sound. The gill-man stared at his book. One step. Pause. Wait. Be positive he'd come after me. Come on over, maybe rough me up a bit this time before throwing me onto the lawn. Or worse, hand me over to the denizens of the house. No way Mary could help me then. He coughed, a wet, blubbery sound, and turned a page. I waited. Another step, move the leg up, settle, shift weight, push, settle, and wait.

The fins on the side of his face fluttered for a moment. Claws scratched across the page as he turned it. I got a little more confident. Every step was getting me farther and farther from his peripheral vision. Every step was getting me closer to my goal. I grinned.

And then there was a knock on the door. He looked up. I froze. With those big black fishy eyes, it was hard to tell where he was looking. It was possible he was regarding me. Possible he was just checking the door. I stayed frozen until he picked.

The gill-man got up, putting his book down on the table beside him and shuffling from the room. There was a moment when I thought he would suddenly turn for the stairs, haul me down, and give me the beating of my life. I kept seeing those big claws of his tearing me up. I held my breath as he reached the foyer. He turned his back to me and went to the door. I disappeared upstairs.

Fer-de-Lance was a maze on the second floor as well, but I could remember the general path Mary had used.

From downstairs, I heard the gill-man inviting the new guest in.

I followed the hallway, trying to sort through the jumble of memories muddled up by the stress of the previous night. How many doors had it been? It was right past a bend in the hall, wasn't it? I pretended Mary was with me again, putting my mind back about sixteen hours. I finally got to where I was more or less certain Mary was and knocked on her door.

Muffled sounds greeted the knock, cursing going from murky to crystal as the door flew open. And there was Mary, a housecoat wrapped over a nightdress, her hair in rollers. Perfectly made up, too, including heavy eye makeup. She opened her mouth to screech, but I clamped a hand over it.

"Please don't." She fired a slap over my cheek. "That's all right, though." I took my hand away.

She made sure the housecoat was shut tighter than Fort Knox and planned my murder, every step obvious in her eyes. "What do you want? I'm trying to sleep. I work nights."

"I've seen you work."

"And why are you even here? We're not open."

"Yeah, the gill-man downstairs let me know that on no uncertain terms. I'm, uh... I need help. Miss Zoltar mentioned something about films when I was waiting to see you."

"We have a screening room downstairs. Next to the bar."

"I never actually found it."

She rolled her eyes. "Between the bar and the swimming pool?"

"There's a p... no, I never found that, either."

"Can I get dressed?"

"I'm sort of on a—"

She slammed the door.

"—clock." The problem with humans is that we don't have a perfectly mundane item that terrifies us. Everything is pretty logical. Guns scare us; sharks, too, and heights. But any one of those has the potential to kill us, and only the most cretinous heel would actually threaten a woman with a shark. Assuming he had some way to get it on land, but what with those proposed aqua-pneumatic subways, it wasn't out of the realm of possibility. The point is that, with monsters, there's always something basically harmless that causes them to shriek, hiss, and get out of my face. Humans, not so much.

So even after the Night War changed almost everything, I was still at Mary's mercy. Something was wrong, though. She didn't seem like she had been asleep. Her eyes weren't puffy, her makeup was perfect, and she smelled like perfume. But why would she bother to pretend? Like she said, they weren't even open.

Five minutes later, the door opened. Mary had changed into a nice blouse and some pedal pushers, but the glare remained intact, made all the more intimidating by the heavy and ornate eye makeup. "What do you want the screening room for?"

"I think there's something in there that might tell me what happened to Juba."

"Getting close?"

"Not really. I'm sorry. I think he was murdered."

"Oh," she said, turning away.

We walked in silence until I realized she was leading me directly to the front stairs. "Wait, no. We can't go down there. There's a gill-man in the way."

"He's harmless."

"To you, maybe. He already threw me out once."

She sighed. "Come on, then." We turned around, and if I didn't know better, I would think she was trying to get me lost. Hell, maybe I *didn't* know better. We went down hallways, turning and turning again, passing doors and windows, leaving me wondering how anyone could ever live in a place so large. The simple answer was, start a brothel for monsters. Finally, the hall turned to a narrow staircase, probably originally for use by servants. This spilled out into the large kitchen where Sheriff Castle had questioned me ever so briefly the night before while my disguise hex melted around my ears.

We went through the kitchen, this time into the back hallway and through another. We seemed to be getting into the center of the house, and at the turn of a hall, I saw I was right. A wall of latticed windows looked out over an indoor pool, a skylight streaming down sun. Several monsters were swimming, including that werewolf who had given me the stinkeye. If I ever brought up dog paddling around her, she'd probably eat my face.

We turned away from the bite of chlorine to find a single door at the end of a long hallway. "There's the screening room."

"Okay, good. And where are the actual movies?"

"You know they're not what you have in mind. It's not *On the Waterfront*."

"I always preferred *Marty*. Look, I know they're, uh, they're... stag films? Do you know about tho—uh, okay, some men like to watch..."

"I know about stag films."

"Of course, you work here. Wait, I didn't mean how that sounded. But the movies in there, they're still of the, uh, blue variety?"

"Monsters turning people, yes. I know."

"Oh. Then you know what it does to them."

"Yes. What does this have to do with Juba?"

"He knew the men making them, and those men are turning up dead."

Her eyes got huge. "Oh my..."

"Yeah. So I need to see what I can..."

"First door on your left. Can you see yourself out?"

I nodded. "Worst comes to worst, I'll just find that gill-man and have him throw me out."

She didn't smile. Just turned and rushed off. I had other things to look for. I went down the hall toward the screening room. As I got closer, I starting hearing the clash of film reels smacking into one another. I opened the door carefully and found a large room, lit softly by an antique fixture above. There were racks of films, all of which had been rifled through, reels covering the floor and shelves willy nilly. I peeked around the corner to see the source of the sounds.

Sheriff Lobo Castle knelt in front of the shelves at the back of the room, an apple box stuffed with films next to him. He had one can open and was peering at the frames. With a grunt, he threw it into the growing pile in the box. Castle paused. Then turned.

He regarded me with cold eyes. I tried to remind myself that the last time he saw me, I was a phantom. A tuba player or something. He knew me as a musician. Not a human. Not a private eye. "Sorry," I said. "I was looking for the restroom."

Castle waved me off, attention back on the films.

I turned to leave, relief bleeding from my pores. A phantom, not Nick Moss.

Castle sniffed the air and let out a thudding chuckle.

"Cute trick with the Ferris wheel last night, meatstick. Want to tell me what you're doing here?"

TWENTY-SEVEN

That was a shot of pure glacier into my veins. Sheriff Castle was already standing, making his way toward me, when I turned around. "It's like this," I said to him. And ran.

The sound of ripping followed me and it wasn't hard to figure out what he was doing. Pretty soon, I'd have Sheriff Castle on my ass for the second time in twenty-four hours, which was the opposite of something I wanted to turn into a habit. Lose him again in the maze of sets? Would that even be possible? Fool me once, shame on me; fool me twice, and I'm werewolf food.

I made it to the hallway bordered by the indoor pool when Castle growled that growl of his that sounded like the tread of a Tiger tank. I turned around slowly. He was a gray wolf, easily four feet at the shoulder, with yellow eyes that would convey hate if they were capable of showing anything so pleasant. The snarl rippled along his lips, displaying teeth that I could readily picture tearing big chunks off me. Slaver dripped from his jaws as he padded forward.

"Sheriff Castle... I think we, uh, got off on the wrong foot, um, paw... or something."

He lunged, jaws open. And I knew, beyond any shadow of a doubt, that I was going to end my career in a tightly coiled pile on the lawn.

I went for my gun. No way I'd get to it, let alone plug the mutt, but why not? Might as well die like a man.

That's when I heard a loud whine, like a circular saw against battleship plating. Something glittering flew past my head. I threw myself at the wall in time to see a spinning hunk of metal fly straight at Castle and bloom like a flower made entirely of razors. It came apart more and more as it got closer, hitting him, the metal sizzling into his flesh. The wolf howled, and I realized then that it was silver. The metal plates, as though alive, kept moving through the poor bastard, linking together, breaking him down and boxing him up. The sounds of slicing and howling stopped and a little silver box thumped to the ground. It whirred, and a red metal ribbon spooled out and tied itself into a nice bow.

I took a second to gape openly at the remains of the former Sheriff of Hollywood. I felt eyes on me, breaking through the haze of what had just happened. I turned, slowly, to regard the pool.

Four monsters in bathing suits were staring at me with mouths open in abject horror.

"Wait. Do you think I—I didn't do it! And even if it were, that's, uh, that's self-defense!"

There was a long moment of silence. Then the sea hag screamed.

I turned to run in time to see a little three-toed foot scampering ahead of me around a corner. Gremlin! Of course. A gremlin killed Aria Enchantee, and probably killed Brows.

Or whoever that was. Who's to say there wasn't another gremlin out there whose patches of white hair could be shaved into eyebrows?

"Hey! There's the real murd—oh, never mind."

I sprinted after the fleeing gremlin.

The screams of the monsters at the pool followed me, bouncing around the walls until it sounded like I had a horde of shrieking banshees on my tail. Fortunately, none of them were actual banshees.

A scaled backside disappeared around the next bend as I rounded the corner. I barely had time to consider the fact that the little guy was running from me. Had to be a good sign. Otherwise, he'd just stand and kill me. That put some air under my feet. With my longer stride, I'd have him in no time.

I turned the corner. The gremlin, this one sporting white stubble on his cheeks like a pair of muttonchops just growing in, was waiting at the next turn, barely ten feet away. He bared little yellow teeth, his red eyes lighting up, brandishing something like a dull aluminum bazooka over his shoulder. "Bye bye!"

I hit the deck. The circular saw whined over my head, and I pictured that horrible metal flower blooming and whirring and slicing. With loud crunches, the thing slammed into the wall, chewing into the wood, plaster, and wallpaper, showering me in multicolored excelsior.

The gremlin's mad cackle disappeared around the corner. I rolled over, squinting into the snowfall of what had recently been a wall. The blades shifted, fell into place, and a box tumbled from the freshly bored hole. As I stared dumbly at it, the ribbons popped out and wrapped it up.

I knew those muttonchops anywhere, even half-shaved. That gremlin had been outside my window, and later on had been at the Visionary lot. Now that he was trying to kill me with his terrifying death gift-wrapping machine, I could scratch coincidence off the list, as well as five years off my life.

All right, Chops. I won't get cocky. I got to my feet, sprinted to the corner, and this time merely peeked around. Catching the monster was going to be difficult, but I really didn't want the sheriff's murder pinned on me.

The way the halls wound through the house, it was difficult to see where he was headed at first, but after several turns, it became clear he was going for the back. Not sure why. This was broad daylight. If he went outside, he'd end up as a couple of sideburns floating in a puddle of goo.

As he ran, I caught glimpses of him fiddling with the bazooka. Reloading, maybe, but I wasn't about to test him. There was no real rhyme or reason to how gremlin inventions worked. Made as much sense as vampires turning into mist, or the way gill-men kept raising antediluvian horrors in San Pedro Bay. Becoming a monster meant getting powers that didn't always make sense. Made up for developing a sunlight allergy so bad you turned into Campbell's soup on the first summer day.

I peeked around the corner. The gremlin, all two feet of him, had the cannon leveled at me, his huge ears back. "Hi ho!"

I ducked back behind the doorway. There was no whine. Nothing horrible and whirring flew past my head. So he was holding his fire. Wanted to make sure he got me this time.

"Hey? Uh, Chops?" I said.

"Cure blood," the gremlin rasped.

"Right. Um... look, we don't have to do this. I'm not one of them. I'm not in the New American Benevolent Society."

"Kill, kill."

"You really have your heart set on this, huh?"

"Hi ho."

"Talk to me. This doesn't have to end with me dead."

"Take sides."

"Right! Right, I'm not on their side. You saw it! Castle was going to kill me until you showed up."

"Kiss feet."

"Right now? Well, I was thinking, uh, more that we could... you know, if it keeps you from turning me into a bloody Christmas present, maybe we can work something out. What's dignity, really?"

"Die, die."

"I thought we were making headway here, Chops."

"Hi ho."

"I don't see how that... oh, come on." I risked a look around the corner, and in the middle of the hallway was a cobbled-together radio speaker, dented and partly rusted. The sound quality was excellent. When it babbled, it was completely indistinguishable from the gremlin. I kicked the little thing and it fell over, ticked twice, and exploded. I yelped, jumping backward, but it was just spewing confetti. Cute. Very cute.

Behind me, there were the cries of hysterical monsters, although those were far enough back that I wasn't too worried about them catching up with me. Ahead, the gremlin couldn't stifle its raspy giggling. I played the hunch and made my way toward the back, past the kitchens, and to the back door. Outside, the sets were where I left them. I scanned the little gully for Chops, who might've been retracing my frantic escape from the night before. Even though most of the bottom was shrouded in gloomy shadow, he would have an umbrella, bobbing down the slope as he hobbled along in that odd, ape-like gait gremlins had.

There was no such sight. I looked upward for a glinting flying machine heading away from the house. No such luck there, either. I turned around and headed inside. The giggling was faint. Almost impossible to tell where the little bastard had gotten off to. And impossible to tell if it was really him and not another one of those speakers. I pulled my flashlight, just in case, and headed into the kitchen.

Distantly, I heard a cackle. Couldn't be sure, but I'd lay even odds it was bouncing downstairs from the staircase Mary had shown me. I peeked around the corner and, not seeing two feet of grinning green death, made my way up the stairs as quickly as I could. Pausing at the top, I strained my ears. The cackle sounded again, this time a little louder. I'd made the right decision for once in my life.

Of course, now I was back in the maze of the upstairs. Endless halls lined with doors, and Chops could be behind any one of them. He didn't know I had an ace in the hole.

I moved quickly in the direction of Mary's room. Whatever it was she was doing, she could put it on hold for a little while longer. Up ahead, at a bend in the hall, a window looked out onto the ravine beyond. I turned the corner to find Chops at a heating grate, tearing it from the wall with his claws. The bazooka lay on the thick carpet next to him. "Hey, Chops."

The gremlin turned, his beady red eyes widening. "Caca!" he rasped, reaching for the gun.

I clicked the flashlight on. He threw up his claws and hissed, falling over on his ass. I clicked the light off. "Now, we can be civil about this—"

He lunged for the weapon again. I hit the light, sending him sprawling backward, crawling over the carpet, trying to get the light out of his eyes. "Bright light!"

"Damn it, Chops. I don't want to do this, but if you keep

trying to turn me into Dracula's Christmas present, you and I are going to have some problems."

The gremlin cautiously lowered his arm to peer at me. It's hard to get emotions other than homicidal rage out of vertically slitted red eyes, but I'd swear Chops was scared of me.

"Do we understand each other?"

"Hi ho," Chops said, nodding. His ears, which had been down over his back, raised up to their natural more winglike position.

"Good. Now, you just killed Sheriff Castle. I want to know why."

"Castle caca!"

"That's, uh... that's not really much of an answer."

The gremlin shrugged.

"Okay. Tell you what, you can nod, you can shake your head."

Chops nodded.

"All right. Did you kill Castle for what's on those movies downstairs?"

Chops was silent. His ears went back and a snarl rippled over his snakelike lips. He nodded.

"And you killed Aria Enchantee?"

Another nod.

"Same reason?"

Nod.

"Brows?"

Nod.

I looked him over. "That was you, earlier. At the studio. Shaved the chops and wore fake eyebrows. Only you're a gremlin, so the hair is already growing back."

Nod.

"You tried to kill me. Why?"

"Gortran caca!"

"Oh, right. Uh, you wanted to kill Gortran."

Nod.

"And I guess I beat you to it. Which made you mad."

He was still. And then he nodded.

"Sorry about that, but he was trying to kill me at the time."

He nodded, relaxing the tiniest bit.

"Now, why were you outside my win—" Movement pulled my attention away from the gremlin and to the other end of the hallway. Mary had stepped out from the other end, holding a revolver. "Mary! It's all right. Chops isn't going to do anything. Everyone is doing great."

Mary looked up at me. Leveled her pistol at me.

And fired.

Chops

TWENTY-EIGHT

I should thank my lucky stars she was a terrible shot. The first shot threw some plaster in my face, sending me staggering backward. The second smashed the window behind me. The third shattered the frame. The fourth tore along my upper arm, and that was right when the low wall under the window threw my feet up over my head and there was sky above me and apparently nothing below. I hit the ground on the slope, tumbling down into the gully, ending up flat on my back and skidding to a halt on the dirt. Just below me was the flying saucer.

I looked up at the open window where the few shards of glass still hung in the frame like rotten teeth. Mary appeared at it and put two more bullets into the dirt near me. Well, it definitely wasn't a misunderstanding, then. I thought about running along the ravine, repeating my escape from the previous night. I had slipped three werewolf cops; I could probably do the same with a crazy prosti-actress. But that left the movies Castle was trying to destroy. The whole reason I'd come to Fer-de-Lance again in the first place.

Meant I had to go back into the house. While someone who knew it better than I did hunted me with a gun, and plenty of time to reload. Well, no one said this was supposed to be easy. I shook the dust off my hat and plopped it back on my head.

I quickly checked my arm. Just a graze. Nothing to get too worked up about, but it'd burn like hell in the shower later. Rushing to the door, I reflected that three people trying to kill me was probably a record for any trip to a brothel. Something to hang my hat on.

I picked the lock on the back door and got back into the kitchen. I could already hear Mary's feet on the stairs. She'd shot without good aim, but also without hesitation. She was ready to put me in the ground. Meaning if I pulled my gun on her, the best-case scenario ended up with her dead. And maybe I'm a sucker, but killing a human wasn't really something I wanted to do. Getting close enough, disarming her? That risked another shot, and even she wasn't so bad she couldn't plug me from two steps away. And the worst part was, I couldn't just show her a cross and scare her off.

That left running, so running is what I did. Trying to remember the path Mary had taken me on the first time, I slipped deeper into the house. The route was already fuzzy in my memory, so I tried to follow the sounds of the pool and the scent of chlorine. There weren't really any splashes, but of the second, there was just enough.

Mary's footsteps dogged me, but it's possible those were in my mind. The carpet was thick—should have swallowed every one of them. Yet there they were, pounding into my head. I'd cheated death so many times in the last couple days, maybe this was how I was supposed to go out. Killed by a human. That's irony for you.

The smell of chlorine got more insistent, soon joined by the murky sounds of conversation. I was getting close. I turned a corner and found three monsters clustered around the small silver box containing the mortal remains of the former Sheriff of Hollywood, gazing at it in terrified wonder. They looked up at me: the werewolf who had spotted me earlier, a zombie whose prosthetic left eye fell out of her skull, and lastly a pale woman with a widow's peak who could only be a vampire.

"Uh... hi, ladies."

The vampire bared her fangs. The zombie opened her mouth to reveal broken and yellowed teeth. The wolfwoman began her change, muscles swelling, hair growing, face turning bestial. Made the polka-dotted bikini a little incongruous.

They were about ten feet away from me. I was going to have to be fast, but this was a problem I knew how to deal with. I sized the three of them up. The zombie would be slow. Vampires tended to like to scare first. That left the werewolf.

And sure enough, she was loping at me, ready to rip me up with those distressingly muscular arms of hers. The wolfsbane vial was in my hand without even having to think. I flicked open the top and tossed a sprig right in her face. She yelped like a hound, falling down and pawing at her face, desperately trying to sneeze it out of her sinuses.

The vampire was next, doing that weird thing where they seem to get to you without crossing the distance in between. I was ready and drew the cross like I was Wyatt Earp converting the heathens. The vampire stopped like she'd hit a wall, hissing at me. "Take a powder," I suggested.

She backed off pretty quickly, which left the zombie lurching toward me, ready to make a nice meal. The salt was easy, and she got a big pinch right in her mouth. She fell over like a plank, next to the yowling and pawing werewolf.

"Bye, ladies."

I stepped over the other two, scared the vampire into the pool, nodded to Castle's boxed-up body, and went into the movie room. The sheriff had thoughtfully already packed what I needed. I picked up the crate and went to the door. Something stopped me from going through it. A sound, maybe, or just the sense of sure danger.

Someone was right outside, and it didn't take much to figure out who. I was trapped in this storage room; no other way out. Six bullets between me and freedom, and more than enough space not to miss. I set the box down and hid behind one of the shelves. The place was still as chaotic as Castle had left it.

Hunkered down amongst the films, I was suddenly struck with a thought: I was in a room full of reels Castle hadn't wanted. This begged the question of what was on all of them. Were they more of the same, or were they normal films? I didn't have the imagination to come up with an answer or the stomach to check. Or the time, really, because the doorknob was turning.

Her arm was first, holding a black bit of murder that glinted under the soft lights of the room. Her face was next, drawn and frightened, tears streaking her face and making her thick black makeup run down her cheeks in inky slashes. What did she have to cry about? I was the one getting killed here. She opened the door wide, taking a step inward.

"Moss? Come out. It'll be—"

Her gaze fell on me. The gun came up. I pushed the shelf over. The gunshot was deafening. The light fixture shattered, dropping us into darkness and showering me with broken glass. The shelf tipped up and over. Mary screamed, and there was a cacophony that almost drowned the memory of the gunshot entirely.

Then, silence.

"Mary?"

No answer. I clicked on my flashlight, and found Mary, under the shelf, a cut on her head, eyes closed, but breathing slowly and evenly.

"Sorry about that, Mary." I picked up the box of stag films. "You understand. I hope."

And with that, I made my way out of Fer-de-Lance.

TWENTY-NINE

Knocking on this particular door was awkward for a variety of reasons.

The first, and most obvious, was that I had an old apple crate stuffed with films that could not be discussed in mixed company. Even though no one could tell what was on them without holding them up a foot from their face, I had lived in terror for the entire ride. The reels went into my trunk, of course, but during the drive down Mulholland, and from there south into Torrance, I was convinced the police would pull me over, pin me down, search the car, and start asking a lot of very uncomfortable questions. While I was still in Hollywood, out of every shadow, leaping between every two cars, I saw Deputies Warg and Beast, the two who had pulled me over the other day. And of course, they would sniff Castle's blood on me somehow, and I'd get hauled in for that. They wouldn't listen to a meatstick about a cop killing, and any protestations that it was self-defense would get contradicted by the girls at Fer-de-Lance, who were probably into the Hollywood Sheriffs for a couple hundred each.

Once I was out of Hollywood and into the open parts of South Los Angeles, past my neighborhood, the paranoia switched over. No longer was I worried about those two; I became convinced that Moon and Garou would suddenly be working traffic, and they would be prowling the streets for me. Pulled over for being human, of course, detained until after dark while they tore my car apart. And then how to explain the reels in the back? Wouldn't have to, because both cops would be in a frenzy to turn me.

When I crossed into Torrance, the cops became a nebulous image. Werewolves, but instead of the wolfmen of the LAPD or the big wolves of the Hollywood Sheriff's Department, they were something in between. A new nightmare form, huge and oddly apelike, with an animal's snout and a man's hands, albeit with claws the size of my fingers and covered in fur. These things wouldn't even bother with the standard harassment. No, they would go straight into wearing my intestines as boas.

I parked on the street. With any luck, I could just pass as a monster, but what monster was soaked in flop sweat? I was positive that the people I passed on the street knew what dirty little secrets I was carrying in my trunk. I wanted to tell them, especially the prudish-looking vampire women out with their parasols, that I didn't even like what was in there. It was for work. I was a detective, and it had nothing to do with any *proclivities*.

Despite the anxiety, I stopped into the automat on the corner. A few of the tables had monsters at them, a gill-man sipping coffee in one corner, a sasquatch eating a ham and cheese on rye. Everyone looked glum, and of course knew instantly about the crate in my trunk. The cases had normal foods: sandwiches, pieces of fruit, covered glasses of iced tea and lemonade. There were also things for the monster clientele, like glasses of blood, frozen hearts on popsicle sticks, living fish swimming around in a bowl, and large rawhide bones. I kept my eyes front, dropped a quarter in the machine, and lifted out a tuna sandwich wrapped in butcher paper. I dropped that in a paper sack and returned to my car, grabbing the crate and dropping the sandwich on top of the films. Climbing the three flights of stairs to the apartment in question was just as nerve-wracking.

The second reason actually knocking on the door of Apartment 17 was awkward was a matter of decorum.

I am not an old-fashioned guy by any stretch of the imagination. There's a nice English woman I met on a weekend pass who would tell you that. Still, there was something wrong about going to a woman's apartment in broad daylight. Especially carrying a crate of what I was carrying. Sent the wrong message, the kind that would get me drummed out of whatever corps there was for men who still liked to show a little respect.

And lastly, this was the wrong context to be seeing her.

The door opened on my secretary, Miss Serendipity Sargasso. She blinked in surprise, first the inner, clear lid shutting vertically, then the opaque one shutting horizontally. "Nick? What are you doing here?"

"This isn't what it looks like."

"It looks like you brought a crate of movies to my apartment."

"I take it back. You still have your projector, right?"

"Well, yes, of course."

"Can I come in? These are a little heavy."

"I suppose." Serendipity moved aside as I lugged in the box. Her living room wasn't huge, but it was decent-sized. I knew she had two roommates, one a doppelganger extra trying to break in as an actress, the other a ghost who worked as a maid at one of the beach hotels. Your average single girls making it in the big city. "You can put them on the sofa."

I did as she asked.

"I only came home a little early," she said.

"What?"

She repeated herself.

"Oh. It's all right. I have all I can handle right now with this case."

"Then I came home a lot early," she confessed.

"And you sat in that drugstore, didn't you?"

She twisted her fishy lips. "It's a cafe. The Top Hat Cafe, and I only sat there for an hour."

"Two hours."

"Two and a half hours."

"Did you get discovered, at least?"

"I did. That's why I'm at the Visionary lot right now with Mira." Mira Mirra was her doppelganger roommate.

I grinned, handing over the bag. "I brought you a tuna sandwich from the automat down the street. I remember you said you liked them."

"I'm on a diet," she pouted.

"Since when?"

"Since Audrey Hepburn."

"What's an Audrey Hepburn?"

"A sidhe or something. They took her out of the chorus line, and now she's *it*. And she's *tiny*," Serendipity finished with palpable disgust.

"Does this mean less eating fish in the office? Because you've been known to make some of our human clients a little nervous with that habit."

"If you know a better way to get fresh fish, you can tell me."

She pulled the sandwich from the paper bag and unwrapped it resentfully.

I turned to look for her projector. Serendipity gave me a sympathetic hiss when she saw my arm. "Oh my! Are you all right?"

"Huh? Oh, yeah. I got shot."

"You got *shot?*"

"A little, yeah."

"You got shot a *little?* How does one get shot a little?"

"Well, you start out with someone who can't shoot very well, and then you sort of fall out of a second-story window."

"You what?"

"I fell out a window."

She shook her head, trying to count everything up. "You were shot and then you fell out a window."

"A little, yeah."

She put her hands on her hips like a stern and blue schoolmarm.

"Ser, trust me. I was in the war. I took a bullet in the rear end in Normandy. I know the difference between getting shot a little and getting shot a lot."

"Well, all right, then. Just don't make a habit of it. I don't want to have to look for another job."

"Visionary will call. Assuming the diet holds."

She had just taken a bite, and was chewing and glaring at the same time. When she swallowed, she asked me, "Who did it?"

"A German. I never got his name."

"A German shot you? In Los Angeles?"

"No, a German shot me in the rear."

"In the rear in Los Angeles?"

"She might have been German. I didn't ask."

Serendipity shook her head in frustration, her gills

momentarily frilling out over her neck. "Who shot you *today?*"

"Her name was Mary. Well, Trudy, actually. Trudy Alvin."

She made a "go on" motion with a webbed hand while taking another bite of her sandwich.

"Her real name is Trudy Alvin. She works at a place called Fer-de-Lance under the name Mary Brown."

"That's her rebirth name? Seems awful plain."

"It would be, if she were a monster. Mary Brown is a stage name, Trudy Alvin is her real name, and I'm guessing she probably has a fake rebirth name somewhere, too, that I never actually caught. Anyway, Fer-de-Lance is sort of like a... uh... I don't know the delicate way to put this, seeing as you're a nice girl—"

"Bordello?"

I blinked. "That'll do it. Only they don't do what you'd think they'd do at a bordello. It's all monsters who work there, only the monsters pretend to be humans. Helpless coeds, damsels in distress, probably lady reporters, that kind of thing. Then the, uh, the clients pick a scenario, and pretend to hunt down the disguised monster. And turn them."

She wrinkled her small nose. "That's repulsive."

"I thought so too. Anyway, Mary is one of the employees, but she's human. She's a human pretending to be a monster pretending to be a human. It's dizzying."

"And she shot you?"

I nodded.

"Why?"

"It was probably something I said."

She searched my face, her eyes enormous under the goggles. "Are you pulling my leg? I can't tell."

"I'm completely serious. I don't know what I could have said to her."

"Well, who is she?"

"She's a human pretending to be a monster pretending to be a human. Did you miss all that from earlier?"

"No, who is she really? Why did your paths cross?"

"Oh. Good question." It really was. I thought about it, finding the sofa and collapsing into it. Serendipity made a little dismayed noise, reminding me I was covered in dirt. "Sorry."

She made a face and shrugged. "Llorona can deal with it."

"Okay, so it turns out that Juba II and several of his friends—powerful and well-connected monsters—were all regulars at Fer-de-Lance. Mary was Juba's favorite girl. He was sweet on her, apparently. Her on him too, from what I could see."

"What was the last thing you said to her before she shot at you?"

"Let's see... okay, before she shot at me, I was chasing Chops through the bordello—"

"I'm sorry, 'Chops'?"

"Uh, yeah. There's a gremlin, as well. Killing people. Tried to kill me, even, although that seemed more like a misunderstanding."

She shook her head again. "You're chasing Chops through the bordello..."

"Right. He had just killed the sheriff."

Serendipity's eyes almost bugged out far enough to knock the goggles off her face, but she stayed quiet.

"The sheriff wanted me dead, because he recognized me from the night before. And I had caught him with the movies. After Mary led me to the room where they kept them."

"These are those movies?"

I colored. "Um, yeah. We'll get to that."

"Okay," she said slowly.

"And I told Mary that someone was killing the members of

the New American Benevolent Society."

"Who are?"

"Oculon, Aria Enchantee, Sheriff Lobo Castle, Lord Craven a.k.a. Brows, and Juba II. As of now, three of them are dead and one is missing."

"Killing them why?"

"Because of what's on those reels. I have a hunch I'm going to see every one of them. The monsters, not the movies."

"And what's on there is a crime?"

I nodded. Then shook my head. "It's a bit of a gray area."

"How gray?"

"I don't know. Charcoal? Look, if it *is* a crime, this means that whoever's on them would be implicated, meaning Juba might still be alive. And if he is, that might be enough to get Mary to try to kill me for sticking my nose where it doesn't belong." My train of thought rolled to the next station. Mary knew where Juba was. That had to be why she tried to kill me. To keep him from being found. I had left my best bet of wrapping the case up unconscious on the floor. Wonderful.

"So what's on these?" Serendipity asked, picking one up and unspooling it to get a peek. I popped up and snatched the film away.

"That's, ah, that's where this gets awkward. More awkward."

She blinked again, and I was probably imagining it, but those giant eyes seemed to be judging me. "How awkward?"

"They're... uh, see... this group... um, so, you know how when you turned into a sea ha... uh, a siren, that is. When you turned into..."

"Mr. Moss, I do have things I would like to do before retirement."

"Right, well, all right. It's like this. You have... needs, I guess you'd say. It's all about babies. Little monsters. You know how you monsters can't, um, make babies?"

Her gills extended, even redder than usual. "Of course."

"So you turn people, right? Well, it stands to reason this might be, uh, appealing to monsters. To, you know, watch."

Serendipity blinked, her brain trying to make the connection. Her eyes widened, which behind the goggles, made them look like they took up half her face, and her gills somehow managed to find a shade past red. "Oh my."

"Yeah."

"Why did you bring them here?" she squeaked.

"I need to watch them. There's something on them that's important. They'll implicate all of them, every last one."

"Uh, you don't want to, um... you don't want to watch them together?" It's always strange to hear a monster sound completely horrified.

"No. No! The last time... see, I watched one of them with Imogen Verity earlier—"

"You can't show one of these to her!"

"I know that *now*! We didn't know what was on it at the time, and, well, she went berserk. No face, coming after me and trying to turn me. Which she already tried once, but this time, she wasn't going to take no for an answer."

"Imogen Verity tried to turn you?" Serendipity asked in amused disbelief.

"Why is that so hard to believe?"

"She's a star. You're... you're you."

"I take care of myself."

"You're not exactly Rock Hudson."

"Well, I'm also... uh... look, I'm just telling you what happened, all right? The last time I watched these with a monster, she completely lost control, despite the fact that I am not Rock Hudson. So I need to watch these. Alone."

Serendipity thought it over. "So you came over to my apartment... to watch stag films?"

"It's not like that!"

"I'm just trying to understand."

"All right, it's like that. But I have no plans to enjoy a single minute of it, and believe me, this is just as bad for me as it is for you."

"It's actually kind of funny for me."

"Ser... please."

"The screen is in the hall closet, and the projector should be right next to it. Have fun, Nick," she teased. "And we'll talk about what kind of raise you'll be giving me tomorrow." She disappeared into her room and never once looked back to see the daggers I was staring into her back.

Grumbling, I retrieved the equipment, setting up the screen against one wall. I took the projector from its case and set it up on the table behind the sofa. There was a whole crate of the things, so I just picked the top one, spooled it, and hit the light.

The countdown ran, and I was in the castle at the top of Fer-de-Lance. I'd know that thing anywhere. In the left corner of the shot, I could even see the place where Mary and I had our whispered conversation. The scene wasn't something to be shocked by, which in itself was an indictment of what I was expecting. A pretty girl—and she was just that, a girl no older than nineteen—was in the frame, dressed in medieval peasant garb and shackled to a stake planted in the middle of the castle courtyard. She was looking into the camera, silently crying and begging.

A wolf padded in from offscreen, and even though the whole thing was shades of gray, I knew the wolf was Lobo Castle. He circled the stake three times, tongue lolling out, looking up at the girl with eyes that even on the film seemed to glow. Her attention was torn from the camera, desperately following the massive predator as it circled her.

My heart climbed up my throat. I wanted to scare the wolf off, put a silver bullet in the dirt by those big paws. It was a stupid impulse. I'd just watched that same wolf get turned into mulch. And this crime happened who knew how many years ago.

The wolf stood on his hind legs, the snout and fur receding into his flesh. Castle was a big guy, and he brought to mind cavemen. The nudity didn't help with that. He leaned in, stroking the sobbing girl's cheek as she cried, and I could see the tattoo of the sheriff's star on his chest. Now scaring him off wasn't enough; I wanted to kill him, but Chops had done that for me. I kind of wanted to buy that gremlin a drink, and even felt a little bad for the flashlight trick.

Whatever she said, however she begged and pleaded, he just nodded sadly and fell to all fours, body warping until he was a wolf. He jumped up, almost like a hound greeting his master, but instead of happy licks, he savaged her. Biting her face, neck, and shoulders. I winced and looked away before forcing myself to look back.

Castle had padded away a bit and was watching the girl convulse on the stake. He gnawed the ropes, and she fell to her knees. The change was on her then, warping what was once a girl into a large wolf. Then the two of them howled at the full moon, and the film cut out.

Disgusted, I got up and picked another reel of film.

This time it was a lab. Hadn't seen that set out behind Fer-de-Lance, but then, I had only gone in one direction along the gully. A young man was strapped to a medical table. The same kind of thing, and the repetition of subject matter already jaded me. This time the star was Gortran, and it was with some amount of morbid curiosity that I watched him hook the young man's head up to a machine, then the machine up to a robot body. He flipped a breaker, and electricity coated both boy and robot.

The robot body rose, and the boy was still.

There were other reels. In each one, I saw one of the dead monsters taking some poor sobbing kid and turning them. Juba wrapped women in bandages beneath the gaze of Anubis and enacted the rites to turn them into mummies. Aria Enchantee sang her angels of music into existence. Oculon slithered and slimed his victims, making one eye swell while their body dissolved away. Castle and Gortran took others. And there was Brows, immediately identifiable by those huge bushy white eyebrows. He cocooned his victims, and when they hatched, another gremlin emerged, each one with a shock of white hair somewhere on them.

My stomach was revolting on me as I pulled the final two reels from the box. I didn't want to watch them. I'd already seen more than anyone should ever have to. I had to remind myself that these monsters were scum, and watching the movies wasn't as bad as what the poor people they tortured and turned went through.

In the second to last reel, Brows had a pretty young thing in what looked like an old toy store. She was younger than the others, and dressed to look even younger than that. My stomach turned over. Sunlight had been too good for the son of a bitch. He webbed her up in that snotlike casing as she begged and cried. And when her cocoon split and the new gremlin emerged, it had huge, bushy muttonchops.

"Son of a bitch." There was motive, and a damned good one.

I picked up the last reel, not even certain I should watch it. What else was there for me? No, I'd started. I would finish this, come hell or high water. I threaded the final film and sat back to watch.

The girl in the sarcophagus was dolled up like an Egyptian princess. She had the headdress, the makeup, and even a wig. I leaned in closer to the screen, searching her features. She was sobbing like all of the others, silently begging for help that would never come. It was disturbing, but worse was the fact that I'd seen it so many times it barely registered anymore. But something about her face bothered me.

It wasn't until Juba came in and started his ritual that it clicked. For a moment, she went from crying to frozen fear. And that's when I knew I'd seen her before. Smiling on a driver's license. Evelyn Farrell.

Juba went about the ritual as he had done on several other reels, but this time, his motions were not sure and swift. It wasn't inexperience, as this was manifestly the most recent. He kept glancing up, his eyes glowing decidedly dimmer than they had in the other films. He was doing this to Evelyn reluctantly, reacting to each one of her sobs with a flinch. Still, he went through with it, wrapping her up in bandages, intoning the spells, and right before the film stopped, his shoulders slumped.

I heard the door open behind me and I bounced up immediately, fumbling to turn the projector off.

"What are you doing?"

A pretty girl stood behind me, dressed in an Egyptian-flavored chorus girl outfit. "Nothing!"

She cowed me with a suspicious glare, but she was also fanning herself, breath coming a little more quickly than I would like. Her features stayed as strong as ever, for which I was grateful. I grabbed for the reel, getting it off the projector and tossing it into the crate. Her eyes, elaborately made up like Cleopatra, never left mine. "Ser? Llor?" she called.

Eyes made up like Cleopatra.

Serendipity's door opened and she poked her fishy head

out. "Mira! Sorry. This is my boss."

"Hi," I said.

Eyes made up like Cleopatra.

Mira spoke with admirable elocution, every word perfectly formed and clipped off at the edge. "Do you have any idea what he was doing?" Her tone, however, was pleasantly scandalized.

"Uh... yeah. That's for, um, for work."

"I didn't even know such things existed," Mira said, looking me over.

"Really? I mean, I figured you would have heard of casting cou... uh, that's not really..."

Serendipity swept in to rescue me. "I told him he could. And it's for work, Mira. Honestly."

"Well, warn me next time your boss wants to watch filth in my living room."

Her eyes were made up exactly like Evelyn Farrell's. Really close to Mary's, who had been interrupted in the middle of putting her face on. Mary was getting dolled up to be turned into a mummy. Not only did she know exactly where Juba was, he was coming to her.

"I should, uh... I should be going." I picked up the crate, not able to look into the doppelganger's judgmental, slightly too bright eyes. "I'm... ah... you have a lovely home."

Serendipity walked me to the door and opened it. "Did you get everything you needed?"

I nodded. "I have motive. Now all I need is a mummy, and I'm pretty sure I know where I can find one of those."

"It'll have to wait until tomorrow," she said. "Sun's going down within the hour."

I looked at the golden light filtering in through her closed blinds and my heart sank. I really wanted to get this thing nice and wrapped up, no pun intended. Couldn't change the world, either to get monsters to leave us humans alone or to keep the sun in the sky for the hour or so it would take to finish this. "Good point. Thanks, Ser. See you tomorrow."

I rushed downstairs, barely concerned with the huge box of monster stag films cradled in my arms. I opened the front door to her building with my back, turning into the sun with a huge smile on my face, thinking about how I'd cracked the case.

The sun went into shadow. Cacophony Jones eclipsed it, sneering that rock star grimace. "Hey, meatstick."

His punch flipped on all the lights, then turned them out.

THIRTY

I realized it was a dream too late, as it went with all dreams. Not sure why any conscious mind would suddenly think it's back in a farmhouse on the French border, which was also my childhood bedroom. Or why I would be surrounded by werewolves who all had blank faces like Imogen Verity in her worst moment. Or why I had neither mirror nor cold iron nor silver bullets to get rid of the monsters who barked like artillery fire.

Turned out the artillery fire wasn't that. It was a pounding in my head, going in time with my heartbeat. I chose to look at the bright side: I had a heartbeat. I had, however, gone blind.

After blinking a few times, a dim bluish light convinced me I was just in a very dark room. Trying to rub my head showed me I was tied up, and as soon as I realized that, the spiders got going across my hands and feet. I was on my side, acutely aware of all my weight pressing down on my right arm.

Struggling didn't help much; the bonds were tight. The best I could manage was a wormlike flopping that didn't do much more than upset a bunch of things I was better off leaving alone. The light, diffuse as it was, seemed to be haloing something just in front of my head. I craned upward, putting my forehead against whatever it was.

A cardboard box. I nudged it. It sloshed and clinked in response.

I was in the storage room of the Bomb Shelter. Of course. Knowing where I was didn't really help much. It's like knowing you were about to be fed to a leviathan rather than a behemoth. Either way, you were about to become an *amuse-bouche*.

A little more struggling blew the remaining dust off my mind. I was lucid enough to realize two things. The first was that there was no way I could get these bonds off. My sleeves were still a little wet, which said these were most likely the same restraints that had been used on Charlie Lewis: leather belts cinched up tight and doused in water. The second thing was even more troubling.

My jacket was light. Very light. And quiet. While I was struggling around, the vials should have been clinking together, the dagger, cross, charms, and pistol swinging around with minds of their own. There was none of that. It was like I was just wearing a normal jacket for once, and it scared the living hell out of me. Meant I was so far beyond helpless, helpless was a distant and comforting memory I'd return to someday.

I lay there in the dark, wondering what to do. Wondering if there was anything to be done. Or if I was just waiting for the Disasters to come in, throw a bag over my head, and drive me to Fer-de-Lance to star in one of the New American Benevolent Society's sick little movies. Or they might just take me up Mulholland, put a bullet in my head, and send my body to the bottom of the gorge. The Bellum mob had been doing that to rats for years.

Great.

I struggled anyway, knowing it was useless. I must have made noise, because I didn't hear anyone coming until the door opened up with the sharp protest of metal. The light was blinding. The sound coming from the open door was an odd hissing I couldn't quite identify, despite being familiar. I tried to make myself small, as though that would somehow help. Whoever was coming in was doing so to see me.

The door shut quietly, but the light remained, a flickering gold that made shadows jump.

"Nick?"

I knew that voice. Sam Haine, the pumpkinhead who wanted nothing more than to turn me. So now I had two choices. Wait here for whatever the Disasters would do to me, or let Sam do what I damn sure knew he wanted to. I sighed.

"Hi, Sam."

"Nick! Where are you?"

"Down here. There's a space behind the shelves."

The hissing of Sam's viney skin sliding over itself grew louder. He knelt, and through the cracks, I saw the blazing candleflames behind the triangles of his eyes. "Nick!" The choppy mouth looked huge this close up. His thorny fingers pulled the box out and set it aside. "Thank God you're all right."

"How the hell did you find me here?"

"You didn't come home last night, so I was worried, of course. I stopped by your office, but you weren't there either. I started to get really worried then. I thought maybe your secretary knew where you were, so I followed her home, and you showed up with a crate of apples. I figured she must be baking something."

I didn't correct him.

He went on: "This biker must have already been following

you. He went to a phone booth, and a little while later, a whole gang arrived. And then, well, you know. They put you in a hearse, and I followed them here."

"Great! Now untie me."

Sam didn't say anything, his pumpkin face screwing up in something that might have passed for sheepish guilt. "I don't know about that, Nick. I mean, what if you run?"

"I'm *planning* to run. We're in a biker bar filled with Howlers who want me dead."

"No, I meant, run from me."

"Oh, right."

"I've been coming to your place for six weeks now, asking to change you, because I think you'd make a really great pumpkinhead. But you won't come out of your house, or let me in. And then you had that doppelganger over."

"She was a client. And I kicked her out when she tried to turn me."

"Figures."

"You know why I did that?"

Sam looked up, hopeful. The flames in his eyes and mouth were glowing blue. "Why?"

"Because I thought of how that might make my pal Sam feel."

"Really?"

No, not really, you crazy bastard. I'm telling you what you need to hear so you'll let me out of here, even though I need a shovel to keep from drowning in all the shit I'm shoveling in your direction. "Of course!"

"It doesn't hurt, Nick. I mean, you feel a little pinch with the killing part, but the getting buried in a pumpkin patch is totally painless. You wake up and you're crawling on out!"

"Sounds swell."

"And then, you and me, we grow pumpkins, we punish the wicked, and you don't even have to give up your job. Finding missing persons, hey, there are wicked people involved in that sort of thing sometimes. You never know. You just have to keep a positive mindset and put on a happy face."

"A pumpkiny happy face."

"Exactly." To describe Sam's grin as bone-chilling was an insult to fear.

"Well, are you going to untie me or not?"

Sam thought about it. "I suppose I have to. Trust being what it is and all."

He'd managed to make me feel slightly guilty before I remembered he wanted to kill me and bury me in a pumpkin patch. I flopped over, and his hands found the bonds. The thorns scraped along my wrists. His skin was odd, not quite as warm as a human being's, and extremely dry. Outside of one drunken night in Toccoa during Basic, I'd never actually punched a plant. Looks like that was yet another thing I'd get to do sober.

His fingers, which lacked bones and yet were surprisingly strong, made short work of the belt. Sam tossed it aside as I sat up and massaged some feeling back into my hands. "Thanks, Sam."

I got the damn belt off my ankles, then crawled through the open place in the shelf, stood up, and stretched. I had felt worse, but that time had involved a bullet in the ass and a farsighted medic. "All right," Sam said, "what now?"

"What do you mean, what now?"

"You're a private eye. You must deal with this kind of thing all the time."

"Uh, yeah. Of course. All the time. Me and the Howlers go way back."

Sam nodded expectantly. So he wasn't much for sarcasm.

"Okay. Well, first I need to know how many Howlers are out there."

"Maybe ten or so? Plus there's the ones I saw earlier. They're some kind of rock and roll band."

"They would be the Disasters."

Sam nodded like it meant something to him. "I think things haven't really gotten going. The ones in the bar are just drinking, and the band is clowning around onstage."

"That might make it difficult going out. I'm guessing you were the only pumpkinhead?"

"We pumpkinheads don't really go to bars. Oh, right. You'll have to give up liquor. Hope you're not much of a drinker."

"No, not especially. But... ah, why is that?"

"Reacts badly," he said. "Nothing to be worried about. Doesn't really hurt like the blood of innocents or anything like that. But it *is* rather unpleasant."

"Oh." I looked around, and my eyes fell on a neighboring shelf. "Hey, Sam?"

"Yeah?"

"I'm really, really sorry for this."

"For what?"

I opened up a jar of moonshine and threw it in his face.

The flames exploded from his eyes and mouth. He shrieked as what looked like a flamethrower spurted out of his face. I stumbled backwards, arm up, momentarily dazed. He flopped around, falling, the flames thankfully starting to die out quickly. I yanked open the door and shut it back up behind me. A hinge lock had been put on hastily, the padlock hanging from the hook. I slammed that shut, clicked the lock, and turned. A phantom was coming out of the can, buckling his belt.

"Shipping irregularity," I said.

The phantom shrugged and went back into the bar. I breathed a sigh of relief and followed him to the door. Peering into the Bomb Shelter, I saw exactly what Sam had described. The Howlers who were there early were mostly milling about and drinking, hardly paying attention to the guys onstage. It was the Disasters. All four of them, meaning Harley was still Imogen. I hoped she forgave me for the thing earlier, but chances are she was just as embarrassed as I was. Being seen with a guy like me could do irreparable harm to her career. I felt like there was something else I should be remembering, but it kept getting swallowed up by the ringing in my head.

Their instruments were resting untouched on stands. In the middle of them, sitting on an amplifier, was a collection of objects I recognized immediately as my stuff. My gun, my dagger, my cross, my salt, my holy water, my Escher postcard. The musicians were laughing, sifting through the pile, picking out individual objects, and cackling.

If I could get up there, I would be in much better shape. Not home free, but not in nearly as desperate a position. Which was in a biker bar, filled with the aforementioned bikers, and the sun was either already down or rapidly sinking below the horizon. So I had to get my stuff, starting with the whistle. In the middle of a bunch of phantoms, all of whom had several inches, thirty pounds, numbers, and monster powers on me. I slunk out of the back room, hugging the wall without looking like I was hugging it, heading for the small area backstage shielded from the bar. Some ratty black curtains hung from the rafters there, giving me a place to hide. I was close enough to hear the Disasters talking.

"Ha! Lucky we're not zombies, I mean, could you believe it?"

"Scared of salt. Hey, Duke! Come here, I want to show you

something."

"Brains?" The zombie janitor shuffled forward, then moaned while the Disasters burst into cruel laughter.

"We should take this shit up to Oculon's along with that meatstick in the back, dig?"

"There's some wolfsbane. Throw it in Castle's face. See what the little puppy thinks of our bikes then."

"What's that stuff?"

"Smells like pennies."

"Didn't a pumpkinhead come in? We could try it out on him, see what happens."

"Hey, this gold coin, let's mess with Oculon's driver."

"When do we get there?"

"Party's after dark. Oculon's got that place on Beachwood."

"What does the old man want with the meatstick, anyway?"

"Not my problem."

"They want him in one piece?"

"Nobody got specific."

"Maybe we go back there and rough him up a little." That was Largo. Probably still upset about me knocking him cold.

"Maybe we do," Harley said. Well, at least Imogen cared enough to go along with them, probably to make sure they didn't hurt me too bad.

I earnestly wanted to avoid a beating and so backed deeper into the shroud of cigarette-stinking curtain. Even though if they walked past me, there was no hiding from them. Instead, I heard the sharp rapping of their shoes as they hopped off the stage. That left my things unguarded, plus an easy way out. Pick up the whistle and the Bomb Shelter was as good as an open door.

I stepped out of hiding. Cacophony Jones looked up at me from where he was still sifting through my stuff, his ugly phantom face splitting in a picket-fence grin. "Well, look who's up."

"Can't keep a good meatstick down, I guess."

Cacophony moved around the amplifier, cracking his big knuckles. "So you got anything to say before I kick the everloving shit out of you?"

I glanced back at the bar. The phantoms there were barely paying attention. "I saw your movie."

He paused, and for a moment, I thought I saw a little fear in his milky eyes. "What'd you say?"

"The movie where Aria Enchantee turned you into a phantom. I saw how scared you were. Saw the look in your eyes. You didn't want to be turned, but she did it anyway."

Cacophony's head whipped around to the bar, but no one seemed to care about what was happening. "Yeah. But I was also scared before my first fight. Wasn't so bad. Now I do it just to get my blood up."

There was the pounding of feet from the back. "Cacophony!" shouted Raven. We both turned. "The meatstick is gone."

"Yeah, Raven. He's right here."

"Oh. You want we should give him a boot party?"

I made eye contact with Imogen, standing in the back, still wearing Harley's face, and nodded to her. She frowned. "What?"

"Now," I said, hoping she'd knock out Raven and maybe even Largo.

Imogen blinked. "Now? Now what?"

I mimed a knockout blow.

"Meatstick, she let me go," Harley said clearly.

Right. That would be what I was trying to remember.

Cacophony started toward me. "All out of options, pal."

I reached over, my fingers curling around something, and

brought it up like a club. It was a bass guitar.

Cacophony's eyes narrowed. "I forgot how rough you like to play. That works for me." He picked up a guitar, holding it in one hand, far more easily than I held mine. "Axes at sunset," he said.

"Actually, I didn't think this through…"

Cacophony swung the guitar overhand and I jumped aside. It cracked into the wooden stage, putting a nice dent where I had been. I poked at him, like this was a rifle with a bayonet. Not a strong hit, but enough to send him stumbling back and rubbing his eye. I glanced at the bar. Looked like we had everyone's undivided attention now.

"You ever wonder where it all went wrong for you, meatstick?"

"Probably the same time you soaked a helpless woman in moonshine and burned her up."

The phantom's grimace turned into a growl. I ducked his swipe and lunged for the stuff on the amplifier. Cacophony saw what I was after and swung the guitar in a nice arc that would have clipped the side of my head had I not gotten the hell out of the way. Of course, that change of direction sent me stumbling into the drum set. The cymbal clash was a rimshot for the impromptu comedy routine of my last evening on earth.

Cacophony followed it up with an overhand cut. I stumbled aside and it cracked down the center of Raven's bass drum, chopping the scrawled DISASTERS in two. I planted my feet and swung. He jumped back.

We circled each other, guitars choked up high on the necks, the strings cutting into my hands. "You're pretty quick for a meatstick."

"It's not my first guitar fight."

Cacophony brought up the guitar for another crack. I jumped backward, only to find he had expertly put my back to a wall. I had nowhere to go. He grinned, ready to split my head open. I brought the instrument up. The blow landed on the body of the bass, sending shudders up my arms. He picked his guitar up for another swing, so I barreled into him, hitting him in the gut with my shoulder. There wasn't much gut to speak of, but there wasn't much of me, either. We both went sprawling across the stage, him toppling over the remains of the drum set.

I stood up a little quicker and swung without hesitating. He stood up directly into my hit. The bottom of the bass cracked him across the jaw, snapping his head around. He went down, spitting teeth and blood. I stood over him for a moment, making sure he wasn't going to get up. Not for a while, it seemed, and he'd be eating through a straw when he did.

That's for Evelyn.

I turned around to the rest of the biker bar. They were all staring at me in wonder.

"Okay! Now I'm walking out of here and—"

They charged. All of them. Not just the Disasters, either—every single Howler in the place rushed the stage with an animal roar. I brought the bass up, ready to send every damn phantom to the la-la land Cacophony Jones was presently enjoying. The first hit tumbled Largo on his ass and off the stage. I'd knocked the guy out twice in a day; chances are I would be to blame if he forgot how to spell his name. The second swing dropped Raven, just because why not. Harley got his hands on me before I could make it a clean sweep of the Disasters and I had to drop the bass, which at that moment, I absurdly realized was his.

I threw a rabbit punch into his side. He loosened his grip, but more of the Howlers had gotten to me by then. It was a mob of half-rotten faces angrily yelling and flying fists cracking into me. My legs wobbled and gave. As I dropped to the stage, I realized the fists were still swinging, and the cracks were still sounding. Now it was just the phantoms pounding at each other.

I quietly army-crawled out of the scrum to Largo's unconscious body, pulling his keys from the pocket of his jeans. I stood up, looking directly into the bartender's eyes. He went for the baseball bat under the bar, and I broke for the door. "Hey! Hey, he's getting away!"

Sunset Boulevard was dark except for the streetlamps and I was completely unarmed. Largo's bike was right ahead, a heavy machine with the Howler pipe organ painted on the fuel tank. I started her up, let her rumble through me, and hit the gas, shooting off into the night. Moments later, what felt like every Howler in Los Angeles was following me.

To Oculon's house, where a host of monsters awaited.

I should really charge more.

THIRTY-ONE

I burned down Sunset as fast as the bike could move me. Hadn't ridden one in years, and it seemed about ready to tip me over at any moment. The wind in my hair said I wasn't wearing a helmet; my hat was probably lying on the pavement in front of Serendipity's apartment. My jacket flapping freely behind me said I was unarmed. A gang of phantoms on my ass said I was a dead man as soon as I slowed down. I redlined Largo's bike, figuring car accident or phantoms, it didn't really matter once I was pushing daisies.

I glanced backward. I had about ten Howlers following me, and all of them were spitting death.

We roared past the few cars on the roads, drawing confused rubbernecking from the monsters behind the wheel.

Everyone knew where Mayor Oculon lived: a lavish mansion, practically a ranch, in Beachwood Canyon, in the corridor leading right to the refurbished Hollywoodland sign. It's why he was so keen on turning that eyesore into a landmark. The mansion was famous, and an invitation there was a status symbol amongst monsters I would normally never know. Humans, of course, would never be allowed. A gatecrasher trailing a biker gang was probably even less welcome.

But when you've solved the case, it's a good idea to get things done as fast as you can.

I was operating on a couple of assumptions, a couple of shaky leads. I'd had my brains scrambled by a phantom, been shot at by a gremlin and by a human, beaten up by ghosts, and attacked by a doppelganger. It had been a rough day. And now, to finish things off, a phantom biker gang was ready to remodel my face. Fortunately, there was one thing I was absolutely certain of: Oculon had security.

I'd met them.

I gunned the engine, but the phantoms still ate up the little distance I had between them and me. One whistle and I could send all of them spinning out. Of course, if I had a whistle, or anything else, I wouldn't be in this jam.

The howling sirens—or at least I hoped they were mostly sirens—didn't come up behind us until Beachwood Drive was within sight. I hit that turn, the front wheel wobbling for a heart-stopping moment. I straightened it, but lost precious ground in the meantime as we went up the gentle slope toward the sign, glowing luridly against the dark outline of the hills and vomiting sparks into the air. Harley pulled up parallel to me.

"Hey, meatstick! We're gonna kill you!" he shouted at me.

I waved at him, making a bunch of gestures with no real meaning. Hexene would've been proud.

His eyes on me, he kept shouting. "You got a problem? You want to say something?"

I just pointed in front of him. I like to think he turned around in time to see the back of the car he plowed into, but it was really enough that he did it. Probably surprised the hell out of the driver. I saw Harley get airborne out of the corner of my eye, sailing through the summer night with something almost approaching grace before slamming into the street with a wet thud.

The Howlers backed off a little after that, falling behind and acting as a cushion between me and the cops. The street twisted, mansions lit up on either side like Christmas. I wasn't sure where Oculon's place was, but I knew I'd know it when I saw it. At the end of the street, the Hollywoodland sign shone, lighting up even brighter in sequence. HOLLY WOOD LAND, each syllable punctuated by a cannon-shot of sparks. The magical kingdom where anyone could be a star, as long as they could act, had connections, and got turned by the right monster.

A giant glass eyeball gleamed on the top of the house on the hill, the lights trained on it scattering in a blinding halo, linking it with the Hollywoodland sign like a garish rainbow bridge. I recognized it on sight; thank God for Serendipity's gossip magazines. The gates were open, limousines parked along the streets, headless chauffeurs leaning on the quiet vehicles. I slowed down only when I hit the flagstone driveway. Behind me, the headless horsemen were already converging to block the Howlers. The phantoms screamed curses, but good luck getting past the Prussian efficiency of the horsemen.

I dropped the bike, walking quickly up the wide staircase toward the house and trying to pretend that wasn't me who had just done all that. Stone statues lined the walkway and steps, but instead of cherubs, it was all crawling eyes, holding bows and arrows, tentacles curled into a pose that might be intended as coquettish. I didn't know for certain, but it was a fair guess they were all modeled on Oculon. I wanted to find his sculptor and beat him mercilessly.

A tuxedoed invisible man strode down the steps to meet me, the place where his head should be marked with a pair of almost certainly unnecessary glasses. He was just giving me a convenient place to look so I didn't have an entire conversation with his nostrils. "Sir, I must ask that you park your... *conveyance*... on the street outside."

"It's actually not mine."

"Excuse me?"

"I stole it."

"Sir, this is a private party, and unless you have an invitation, I must ask you to leave."

I sized the poor guy up. Looked paunchy. Probably middle-aged behind the transparent body. But he was just doing his job, and I was precisely the kind of riffraff Oculon did not want at his fancy party. "Well, Jeeves, you can worry about me, or you can worry about the Howlers outside, and the wolves they dragged along with them."

The glasses whipped around to peer over my shoulder. "Stay here," he commanded. I was running before he made it two steps. "Wait! You—"

I took the large steps two at a time, then bolted through the front door into the quiet Spanish mansion. The place was cavernous. Hardwood floors and antique ceilings made my footsteps reverberate all around me until it sounded like the Howlers were in here, and right on me again. Oculon's furnishings matched the Spanish exterior, and even the knickknacks looked like they came off some conquistador's flagship.

I glanced over my shoulder. Jeeves hadn't come back this way; hopefully he was out front, negotiating the surrender of the Howlers to the police. I moved quickly through the house, keeping to the Persian carpets when I could, and stepping lightly when I could not. The hall opened into large, high-ceilinged rooms at various points, but I ignored these for the straight shot into the back.

That was where the party was. Oculon had a beautiful garden, stone paths veining perfect lawns and flower beds. A stone deck complete with little pavilions took up one side of the yard, while a jazz band played on the stage. I felt a surge of hope that it was the Salem Sisters, because some backup would be nice, but no such luck. The singer was a siren flanked by a zombie combo.

The guests sparkled about, having whatever conversations rich and powerful monsters had. And they *were* that. These were the cream of LA's crop. Mummy politicians, doppelganger movie stars, vampire agents, and others I couldn't identify. All the men were in tuxedoes, all the women were in shimmering evening gowns. Not only was I out of place, I was severely underdressed in a suit ripped and filthy from my long day on the case.

In the center of it all was Mayor Oculon, slithering from guest to guest, gladhandling with a serpentine tentacle. My bile rose at the sight of him. This was the one guy who had escaped so far. Running a ring of abduction and forced change, and doing it for the jaded tastes of the monsters at Fer-de-Lance. I wanted to tell everyone there what kind of thing Oculon was, but I didn't have the evidence. That was back at the Bomb Shelter, probably. And who would believe a human over the word of a crawling eye?

As my blood started pumping at a saner speed, I picked out familiar faces amongst the guests. I knew the attractive wolfwoman on the arm of the ginned-up mummy. That vampire with the regal-looking meat golem was someone I'd seen. Same with the gill-man holding the rubbery pink pseudopod of that blob. I didn't recognize all of them, but I caught enough to know the dates of the guests were all employees of Fer-de-Lance.

The crowd parted around one of the flagstone patios, and who should rush into the middle but Mary Brown, looking as scrubbed and beautiful as always. *That,* I was not expecting. Point of fact, I never thought I'd see her again. She was dressed like a college coed, or at least the conception of one the monsters had. Tight sweater, short skirt, blonde hair in a ponytail, all of which took five years off her already young age. The cut on her forehead from where the shelves knocked her silly was bandaged up. Guess she woke up late enough to miss her chance to leave the city. She was a parody of wholesomeness as she ran, looking over her shoulder, and right as she hit the middle of the ring of monsters, she faked a trip and fell gently, gracefully to the ground.

A moment later, out of the dark, came Miss Zoltar. This time, her flabby body was covered in shiny silver fabric that crinkled with every movement of her tentacles. She looked like a horrifying baked potato. She brandished a raygun, and if I knew anything about the weird brainpower bug-eyed monsters got, that thing was a fully functional death ray. She slimed closer to Mary while the girl cowered.

I looked away, to the enraptured faces of the monsters. And there she was amongst them, my employer, Miss Imogen Verity, once again clothed in elegant white. I had to talk to her.

I opened the door, the pleasant night air of the Hollywood Hills giving me gooseflesh. I might have been a little too eager, taking the stairs just a tad too quickly, because when I hit the bottom, the ground chose that moment to lurch away, flinging my heels up in the air and dumping me on the plush lawn. I lay there, momentarily stunned. A large toad hopped over to my face, glaring at me. He had a distinctive pattern of green and brown over his lumpy back, and when he opened his mouth to croak at me, he showed off teeth like broken glass.

"Is that you, Escuerzo?"

Ribbit.

"Right, because I know so many toads in my life. Uh... if I pet you, would you bite me?"

Ribbit.

"Because I was hoping for a yes or... you know what? Never mind."

I straightened, gently picking up Escuerzo's warty body . He struggled, but it was only to resettle himself. "Where's Hexene? Can you, ah... you're just going to..."

Ribbit.

"Yeah. All right, I realize I'm talking to a toad, here. But I need you to go find Hexene for me. Go find mommy, Escuerzo. Can you do that?"

Ribbit.

"I'm going to call that a yes."

I set the toad back down on the grass, and sure enough, he hopped away with a purpose. Of course, he was a toad, so that purpose could have just been some tasty-looking flies. A few heads had turned my way, but quickly turned back in favor of the show taking place on the patio. Probably thought I was another one of Fer-de-Lance's people. "Harried private detective." Or possibly "Beaten-up insurance adjuster." Worked for me.

Imogen smoothly slipped from the crowd, stopping next to me as I stood up, dusting my suit off.

"Nick, I'm so glad you're okay."

"Uh, yeah. Looked worse than it was and the grass broke my fall."

"No, I mean from earlier, when I... oh, I'm so embarrassed."

"I think we can go ahead and blame the, um, the movie."

She blushed, which on a movie star is rather fetching. "Well, I'm terribly sorry. I hope you can forgive me."

"Already forgotten."

"Thank you, Nick. Might I ask one thing?"

"Sure."

"The toad? Is that a clue?"

"Kind of. He's sort of a friend of a friend."

"I see." She plainly didn't, but was too polite and uncomfortable to further pry. "What are you doing here? It's after dark. You're in a great deal of danger."

"Oh. I solved the case. I know where your husband is, and he might not be where he is for too much longer, so I thought you should know. Plus, the Howlers were kind of trying to kill me, so I had to go somewhere where they, you know, wouldn't."

"The Howlers are here?"

"Yeah, and you could have told me you let Harley go. I thought he was you!"

"I'm sorry. I'd mentioned I was going to. I called your office, but there was no answer."

"My secretary is trying to get discovered."

"How is that going?"

"You tell me. One of the biggest movie stars on the planet telephoned her, and she was out."

Imogen allowed me a small smile. "So where is my husband?"

"Oh, he's..." I peered into the crowd, right into the seething burgundy eye of Mayor Oculon. He pointed a slick crimson tentacle at me, and the headless man standing at what would have been his shoulder started toward me, reaching for something hidden at the small of his back. Two ghosts faded into view next to him. "Uh... I have to get some holy water.

Right now."

I ran back for the house.

"Nick! Nick, my husband?"

I stopped short. "Look, I'm trying not to get killed by Howlers, which is exactly what's going to happen if Oculon's men get me. So either you help me find some holy water and a gold coin or..." I snapped my fingers in realization and ran. Imogen came after me, and even hurrying on high heels, she somehow managed to look practiced and graceful.

Oculon was with his men, slithering along with all three of the apparitions. Probably wanted to enjoy seeing a persistent thorn like myself thrown to the wolves. Metaphorically speaking, for once. I ran to the eye's living room, rummaging through his cabinet of knickknacks. "Come on," I muttered. "Spanish decor."

"What are you doing?" Imogen asked.

"Look, your husband's disappearance... he was involved in some bad things. You saw the movies, right? Well, it was about guilt, I think. Not the movies, those were about... you know... baser..."

"Nick!"

"Your husband was feeling guilty about them, and had been for a while. Only he was in too deep by then. He leaves, and now he's made an enemy of Oculon and Sheriff Castle. Of course, one of those things isn't really a problem anymore. Juba wanted to get out of there, start a new life. I think a gremlin came by to settle a score that night, and Juba somehow got away, but not before being wounded. He's been hiding ever since, waiting for the chance to skip town."

"Why hasn't he left yet?"

"He had to be certain he was in the clear. And, uh, there was one other thing. This is where it gets awkward."

"Awkward?"

"You know, uncomfortable?"

"I know what the word means, Nick. Just not in this context."

"Yes, Mr. Moss," Oculon said, slithering into the room. His headless chauffeur was next to him, slapping a billy club into his gloved palm. The two ghosts, Noose and Knives, were flanking him. "Do explain to Miss Verity what awkward means in this context."

"Actually, this situation sums it up pretty well."

"You can imagine my confusion. I don't recall sending you an invitation to my party, and yet here you are."

"Cacophony Jones invited me."

I'd like to think Oculon would have raised an eyebrow had he had one to raise. "I'm afraid I don't know anyone by that name."

"He's your bagman, if that helps ring a bell."

"I'm a studio head. Even if I knew what a 'bagman' was, I can assure you I don't employ any."

"The hell you don't. I saw the movie. Aria Enchantee, your pal, created him."

"And tell me, Mr. Moss, was I in this movie?"

"No. But you were in others."

"And where are these movies now?"

"Uh... not here."

"Then it sounds to me like you have precisely nothing. Now either you can leave my home, or I can have my men throw you out."

"Well, there's the matter of the, uh, of the Howlers."

"I'm afraid none of that matters to me. Good night, Mr. Moss."

The three heavies came at me, Oculon following a few paces

behind. I backed up toward the front door. Imogen hovered nearby, unsure of what to do, but reluctant to get thrown out with her pet human. I couldn't quite blame her. That kind of thing could kill her career, and for what, really?

"One thing, Oculon. I really like your collection of Spanish things. In particular, these *ocho reales*." I held up the piece-of-eight in front of the headless horseman. He threw his arms up as though to shield a head that wasn't there, stumbling backward a step.

"Nice move, meatstick," Noose said.

"But we're not scared of gold," Knives added.

The ghosts advanced. The shadows seemed to collect in their wakes, clinging to their shoulders and arms. Noose grabbed me under the right armpit. Knives threw a punch into my gut, then grabbed the other armpit. They dragged me from the house. Oculon slithered to the door, his tentacles emerging in veiny masses. Imogen was behind him, hands over her mouth.

"You know," said Oculon, "I think perhaps I was a little hasty. Gentlemen, if you'd like to rough Mr. Moss up before throwing him to the Howlers, be my guest."

Noose grinned, dropping me and throwing two into my chest. Would have been nice to throw back, but fistfighting ghosts was the definition of futile. They hit me, and there wasn't a lot I could do, other than hearing the little dismayed noises Imogen made. Unconsciousness might have been nice, but the ghosts were good at what they did, working the body until it literally didn't work anymore. But in staying away from my head, I felt every last thudding blow.

And then a toad hopped across my field of vision.

Ribbit, he said to me.

"Escuerzo?" I croaked.

He didn't answer. Didn't have to. Because all of a sudden,

the fists weren't falling anymore. Blearily, I propped myself up to see that the ghosts were fading, their greenish glow fitful, their faces terrified and silently screaming. Hexene Candlemas stepped over me, brandishing a ward.

"I never thanked you for breakfast," I muttered at her.

She helped me up. "Are you all right? Escuerzo said you were in trouble."

"Better now, thanks. What are you doing here?"

Hexene's pink cheeks flushed even pinker. "It's a party. They wanted... uh, help."

"Right. Of course." The ghosts were cowering, flickering a little. Oculon had advanced, his headless horseman next to him. Imogen was still in the house, still unsure of what to do.

"They were beating you up for the case?"

"Is there another reason they should be beating me up?"

"You can be abrasive. And needlessly violent."

"I, uh... is that what you think of me?"

"Mr. Moss," Oculon said, "this changes precisely nothing. You are still leaving and you can take your witch with you."

"I am no one's witch!"

"Yeah, probably not a good idea to poke the toad, Mayor."

Hexene glared at me. "You know, just because I saved your life doesn't give you license to wolf-whistle at me. I've cursed men for a lot less."

"I know! One of those men was me! Twice! Wait, wolf whistle? I'm not... Hexene, get down!"

I tackled Hexene. I hadn't yet heard what she had. Didn't matter. I'd been shelled enough times to know if someone heard something, you hit the deck first and worried about what it looked like later. I wound up with Hexene underneath me, trying to cover both of our heads from the explosion.

But there wasn't an explosion.

And then, there it was: the sound was an actual whistle, which, as it neared, seemed to split into several distinct sounds. A keening wail undercut with a buzzing hum, all wrapped up in the fire-engine whistle of incoming artillery. I reflexively tried to clamp my helmet down, but only got a handful of my increasingly frizzed hair.

It was actually sort of beautiful. I felt it first or, more accurately, felt the wake of hot wind whipping over my back. Then I saw it. Something like the blooming silver flower of death that spelled the end of Sheriff Castle. Now it was a singular metallic organism unfolding, sharp tendrils coming from a central source, and spinning hateful revenge. With a thwack, an errant swing chopped one of Oculon's statues in half. A tentacle passed through the two ghosts, splattering ectoplasm over the lawn and momentarily disrupting their smoky bodies. Another glittering metal tentacle slapped the headless horseman into two equal parts.

Oculon's eye didn't widen. It was already pretty big. The metal folded around him, and there was a wet sound like someone squeezing a very large grapefruit. The device turned into a perfect sphere about two feet across, clunked to the stone, and began rolling gently down the stairs toward me.

I hopped up, pulling Hexene to her feet and getting the hell out of the way. The sphere bounced past me, stopping in front of a gremlin a few steps down. She regarded me, running her claws through the fluffy white muttonchops that had already regrown from earlier in the day.

"Didn't see a thing," I said to her.

She nodded, rasping, "Yum yum."

"So... you've been following me, haven't you? That's why you were at my window."

She grinned. "Hi ho."

"You've been using me as a distraction. With me around, they'd never see you sneaking up behind them. How did you know I'd find them?"

"Nick the dick."

"Is that what you're calling m... can we not... how about just Nick?" I held out a hand.

She hopped toward me, taking my hand with her three-fingered claws. "Billie."

We shook. Felt strange not being in danger from the little creature. "So what now, Billie?"

"Juba, caca."

"I'm about to tell his powerful, rich, and influential wife he's been cheating on her. She suspected all along, but it's worse than she thought. I think we have him chalked up for a fate worse than death."

Billie rubbed her hands together and chortled gleefully.

The ghosts were reforming, pointing at Billie and shouting silently.

"Make tracks. I don't know you, I can't tell the cops a damn thing."

"Hi ho, Nick."

"Hi ho, Billie."

She took the hint and loped down the stairs.

"What was *that*?" Hexene asked me.

"Revenge. According to gremlins, that's a dish best served with whirling angry death."

"Oh." She looked after the departing monster. "Well, then. Do you need a ride?"

Crap. "I do. But first, I have to do what I was hired to. There's a case needs solving."

"I'll wait here." Hexene turned to face the gates, where the wolves and phantoms still tangled outside. There would be a lot of arrests tonight, meaning a lot of lawyers could afford expensive new capes and coffins.

Imogen stood in the doorway, openly gaping at me. "What... what..."

"Remember when I said your husband was into some bad things? That gremlin is the result."

I kept walking through the house. Imogen had to delicately prance alongside me to keep up. I'd almost be worried about her falling on her face, had she ever taken an ungraceful step in her life that wasn't assisted by an errant tuna-fish sandwich. "I don't understand. Where's my husband?"

"The sad thing is, Juba wasn't really that bad a guy, not when you compare him to his pals. He needed help forgetting the horrible things he did, and got hooked on those amnesia hexes. Unfortunately, he used them so much, he built up quite a tolerance, and he had to get out of it. The life. Everything."

We emerged from the back door into the party, still blissfully going on with no clue the host had just been inventively murdered.

I went on: "So he got himself a disguise hex and hid out with... uh... this part is a little embarrassing." I lowered my voice. "Your husband was having an affair."

"I told you that already. But it was discreet."

"Not with Aria Enchantee. He was seeing a prostitute. Well, she doesn't think she's a prostitute since she doesn't have sex, but I thought that was sort of splitting hairs."

"Nick. Get to some kind of point."

I was still walking quickly across the lawn as I explained. "That matchbook you found is from a place called Fer-de-Lance. It's a specialty brothel where monsters pretend to be human and let other monsters hunt and pretend to turn them. Your husband was a regular, and he just happened to pick the one girl in the place who wasn't pretending. He was going to turn her. I'm pretty sure Evelyn Farrell was both a dry run and the final straw. After which this prostitute and your husband were going to run off together."

"Then where *is* he? Nick!" She screeched my name, losing just a little bit of her ice queen veneer. Maybe it's weird, but I felt safer with an angry Imogen than I did with an amorous one.

I stopped right behind my target, grabbing the gill-man by the shoulders and spinning him around. "See, Miss Verity, it took me awhile, but I remembered something very important. Gill-men have livers. Mummies don't."

"What?"

The gill-man looked surprised, but then with those fishy eyes, he always did.

"Well, mummies *do*, but they're on a shelf at home. Makes it hard to punch them there."

"No!" That was Mary, pushing through the crowd toward us.

"It's not important," I said. "This is your husband, Miss Verity. Drop the hex, Juba."

"I... I don't..." The gill-man sputtered at me, and that's when I saw the glowing red behind his huge black eyes. Saw that once before, come to think of it, back when I mentioned I wanted to see Mary.

I grinned. "Knock off the ruse, Juba. We can see right through you. After all, this is your wife, the woman who knows you better than anyone. You're Juba II, city councilman, known associate of Mayor Oculon, Gortran, Brows, Aria Enchantee, and Sheriff Lobo Castle. You're making movies where you turn people you've had abducted in broad daylight."

"I... I..." The hex came off in sheets, the scaly green flesh giving way to old bandages. The mummy looked at the ground, his eyes a contrite blue.

Mary threw her arms around Juba and shot us a defiant glare. "So what are you going to do, huh? Arrest us?"

Imogen Verity removed a cigarette from her silver case. "I was thinking divorce."

Juba II

THIRTY-TWO

I rejoined Hexene out front. The monsters just let me go, either because they hadn't realized I was human, or because the drama of famous actress Imogen Verity icily tearing apart the political career of her glum mummy husband was much more fascinating. I reached for my cigarettes, and was relieved to find I didn't have any. Right, I had given the pack to Charlie Lewis, who maybe got a little justice when I laid out all four of his kidnappers.

Hexene didn't turn when I stopped next to her. "How did it go?"

"You should see the other guy."

Escuerzo, now home in her purse, croaked at me with something almost like affection. But then again, I had been hit on the head a lot and was reading moods into the faces of toads now.

Hexene sat down on her broom. "Climb on, detective."

"Don't mind if I do." I sat down and barely had time to get used to the feeling of balancing on thin air before we whipped into the sky. The Hollywoodland sign shrank behind us on the way to Watts, and I was glad for it. And not just because I was halfway convinced it would start spitting flak at us.

I enjoyed the flight a little more this time. The city was a glittering blanket underneath me, and other than the Martian tripod clanking down Beverly, or Korguz, the Tar Tyrant, rising from the bubbling depths of La Brea, I could almost pretend it was before I had left for Basic and the world had only gone halfway insane.

Sam Haine was on my front lawn, looking more morose than usual. Hexene dropped altitude and darted over to my porch, where I dismounted.

"I can't believe you have the moxie to show up after what you did!" Sam yelled at me.

"You want me to do something about him?" Hexene asked. Escuerzo regarded the pumpkinhead with amphibian dispassion.

"No, thanks. I'll be fine."

She nodded, and looked ready to spur her broom back into the sky.

"Hexene?"

She turned.

"Your shop... it's on Gower, right?"

"Just south of Melrose."

"You carry powdered chicken blood?"

"It's on special," she said, with just the ghost of a smile.

"I'll, uh, I'll stop in soon then."

Hexene shot away and was soon gone. I opened my door, ignoring the hissing monsters just out of the range of my wards. I was unarmed, sure, but I was also tired, and I had gone through all the fear I had for one night.

"Nick! Don't go in. Please? We have to talk about this!"

"We don't have anything to talk about, Sam."

"You really hurt me!"

"Good night, Sam."

I slammed the door.

Muffled, about three seconds later: "Good night, Nick."

I fed the cat and went to sleep. The next day, just as I was trying to eat lunch at my overfilled desk, I got a visit in my office from Moon and Garou. They barged in, trying to blind me with badges and bad fashion sense.

"Heard there was a bit of a dustup in Hollywood last night," Moon said.

"A certain city councilman found alive at a party where the eye of a studio got his ticket punched," Garou continued, leaning in so I could smell his breath. I could have sworn I caught a hint of biscuit.

"What, do you like Imogen for that too?"

"Maybe we do," Moon said.

"Or maybe we like her human bagman."

I almost laughed, but that probably would have only made things worse for me. I didn't really have the energy to deal with either monster. "What do you two want?"

"You. On the LAPD," Garou snarled.

"But it'll have to wait," Moon said, putting a hand on his partner's shoulder, drawing the younger wolfman back. "Full moon's coming. Maybe we pay you a visit, maybe we don't."

"You'll need some crime to get me out of my house without tripping the Fair Game Law," I pointed out.

"We can tie you to... how many murders was it? I lost count."

"A gremlin did those and you know it."

"A gremlin no one can find. Besides, Moss, if we wanted, we could tie you to whatever we liked, and who's going to believe a meatstick?"

"They don't have to," I said, nodding toward the door.

Serendipity was standing there, holding a coffeepot, her gills frilled outward. "Any... anybody want coffee?" she stammered.

"And there's a certain star who owes me a favor. You might have heard of her. You were trying to nail her for a murder that didn't even happen, and she just might be keen for a little payback."

A snarl pulled on Garou's lips. He looked ready to sprout fur and claws. Moon pulled him back. "Well played, Moss. Next round, we'll see how you do." The wolfmen left and I let out the breath I'd been holding the whole time.

"Ser! I could use a little bit of that coffee now."

Later that day, Imogen came by and drew up a check. "And should you require a lawyer for any trouble, Mr. Moss, do let me know."

"Thank you."

"No, thank *you*. I believe I will be getting quite the settlement out of this." She was silent, and I swear I could see a blush blooming in her alabaster cheeks. "About the other day. In my screening room."

"I don't think we need to talk about it."

"I feel terrible. I wish there was something I could do."

"Well, now that you mention it, there is something."

Imogen leaned forward slightly.

"One of your publicity photos? If you could autograph it to 'my friend, Miss Serendipity Sargasso,' that would be kind of you."

Imogen smiled and was in imminent danger of laughing. "Consider it done. And the offer still stands. My lawyer is yours, should you need him."

When the photo arrived by registered mail the following day, Serendipity was so overcome that she lost the water from her goggles.

Two months later, I still periodically found myself thinking of the missing mummy while working the same futile missing persons cases that were my bread and butter. I was between jobs at that moment, and settling in for a nice, quiet day, staring at the flight traffic zipping through the sunny Los Angeles morning. Lunch was starting to creep up on me, and I considered just letting Serendipity head to that drugstore she liked so much. She poked her head in, proving that she could sense a half day off through the walls.

"Mr. Moss? You have a walk-in."

"Send him in."

She nodded, looking far more distressed than usual, then withdrew.

I smiled as Hexene Candlemas appeared in the doorway, but that smile died as soon as she spoke. Her skin, always pale, had lost its former glow. Her eyes were similarly dull, and her shoulders were slumped.

I popped up out of my chair. "Hexene? Are you all right?"

"No," she whispered. "You find people. Do you find toads, too?"

And now—

A WORD FROM OUR SPONSORS...

Are ordinary cars giving you a headache?

Use Your Brain!

Just *think* about it and you'll realize ———
There's no better way to get around than the

OLDSMOBILE
Brainwave!

Cerebral Roadster
from **$350**

A General Motors Value

Thinking Man's Sedan
from **$325**

Oldsmobile Power . . . Oldsmobile Styling . . . In the Size that's Right for You!

Now you, too can drive the car that makes distance an exciting adventure!

Drive an Oldsmobile — the *only* car with the smoothest "power package" ever built — the "Rocket" Engine and new Whirlaway Hydra-Matic Drive!

Drive the car with superb new sweep and flow in its styling — glamor in the finest Futuramic manner!

Command the car that wings you to your destination with brilliant, obedient response — "Rocket" Engine response!

Thrill to the car that delivers "Rocket" Engine power with incomparable smoothness — *Whirlaway Hydra-Matic* smoothness!

Drive the "Rocket" and Whirlaway --- in a new Futuramic *OLDSMOBILE!*

Business Coupé
from **$300**

Cerebellum Convertible
from **$360**

Oldsmobile Brainwave

. . . a decision you'll never have to *think twice* about!

Sometimes...

You're more **CRAWLING** than **EYE—** sluggish, red, and everyone knows it.

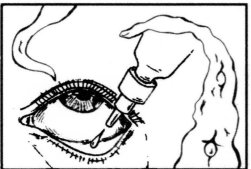

Reach for
Ocutol
from the makers of
Geritol™

Ocutol gives you the
PEP you require
and the
moisture
you crave!

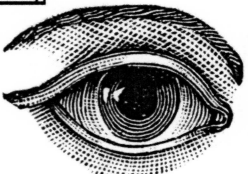

Ocutol.
For eyes.

TO PROTECT AND SERVE MAN

JOIN THE
LOS ANGELES POLICE DEPT.

THE ONLY PACK YOU WILL EVER NEED

Requirements: High School Graduate
Between 21-30
At Least 5'8" (When Human)
Wolfman, Doppelganger, or Invisible Man

APPLY ROOM 5, Los Angeles City Hall, or call MAdison 4-5211 and ask for Civil Service

The Los Angeles Minion

-personals-

Are you human? Are you looking to see the world in a new way? The eyes have it! I am a handsome crawling eye, green iris, red tentacles, like Christmas every day. I am looking for a human to share my "view." **Box 010**

SMG 4 SFW. LEP. F4F. XYQ7. **Box 235**

The ocean is a lonely place. This leviathan is tired of singing songs no one will ever hear. Looking for a fun-loving partner, human or monster, who enjoys travel, music, and damp. This is where the blubber meets the road. **Box 603**

You are: pale, widow's peak, caped, sunlight-averse. I am: young, beautiful, pale, human. Would like to open my life and veins to you. **Box 947**

Photographer looking for art models. Tasteful fashion shots. No gremlins please. **Box 722**

I am a human who would very much like to join the police force. I am a varsity wrestler at my school and I have maintained a B average. Please contact for information on which full moon I should go out during. **Box 451**

I am a bogeyman seeking new closet to hide in. Just friends for now, but we'll see how things go after a few late night scares. **Box 824**

Date, good. Fire, bad. Bride, good. Commitment, good. Love, good. Ankles, good. SMG S SFH **Box 126**

Mad scientist seeks witch for experiments in love and technomantic world domination. **Box 508**

Human twins looking to start a real life as different kinds of monster. Would prefer a vampire and a wolfman, but any are all right. Turned eighteen last week and all our affairs are in order. **Box 575**

I HUNGER FOR COMPANIONSHIP AND ORGANIC MATTER. **Box 398**

Looking for your bathing beauty? Your skin might be scaly, but your heart beats pure and true for your beloved. Will be out on a boat all week after dark. Find me there, or at **Box 838**

Need someone to cross running water for me. Lost my Hessian cavalry sabre on the wrong side of the LA River. **Box 035**

Gets lonely in my belltower sometimes. Looking for a pretty human to obsess over and defend from local law enforcement and clergy. **Box 882**

Was that you leaving spectral footprints on my lawn? Did you make my walls bleed? Are you stacking my furniture in unlikely-yet-intimidating arrangements? Want it to be you? Let it R.I.P.! **Box 449**

Coven needs a new maiden. Need someone responsible, intelligent, and not prone to running off with the first vampire who flashes his bedroom eyes. Red hair preferred. Cooking and herbalism lesson included. **Box 777**

Sing to me, my angel of music! Aspiring opera singer seeks skull-faced loner who will torment callow noble suitors and hit some high notes. Will provide own chandelier. **Box 914**

Heartbroken pumpkinhead looking for someone who likes to make jam and punish the wicked. **Box 066**

MWAHAHAHAHAHAHAHA! **Box 203**

Gorgoth the Destroyer want woman. Turn into ogress. Rule hill tribes. **Box 690**

Newspaper typist seeks career advancement, preferably in the form of multiple limbs or tentacles. **Box 73**

ACKNOWLEDGEMENTS

For those who don't know the name Kate Sullivan, you soon will. She's the head of Candlemark & Gleam, the fine publisher of the book you hold in your hand and hopefully just finished reading. You're going to know her name because people like Kate Sullivan don't stay anonymous for long. They do big, scary, world-shaking things and when Kate gets around to that, I hope to have a place in her regime.

In the publishing world, literally everyone you meet is remarkable in some way. Kate is remarkable even by those inflated standards. She possesses a terrifying intellect, a dizzying array of skills, a work ethic to rival most social insects, and most importantly for someone like me, enough of a suspect taste in literature to have published two of my books. But she is no mere publisher, content to throw a newborn book into the world to see if it splats against the wall of destiny. Oh no. Kate makes sure the thing is gussied up in its finest suit, ready to meet new friends, and hell, packed with any extras she and I can think of. Working with Kate has spoiled me irrevocably. She has become the impossible standard I measure others against.

This is my long-winded way of thanking her for this book. Thank you, Kate. I'll try not to let you down.

Without Kate, there would be no book, but without my readers (that's you, whoever has this book in their hands and totally just looked around to see if someone was watching them) there would be no story. Books can exist in a vacuum, but stories, what's really valuable, can't. I need you guys, every last one of you, and I remain grateful when you read and horribly flustered when you bring it up to me. Thank you all. You rock.

Photo by Leora Saul

ABOUT THE AUTHOR

Much like film noir, Justin Robinson was born and raised in Los Angeles. He splits his time between editing comic books, writing prose and wondering what that disgusting smell is. Degrees in Anthropology and History prepared him for unemployment, but an obsession with horror fiction and a laundry list of phobias provided a more attractive option.

FOLLOW THE AUTHOR ONLINE

www.captainsupermarket.com
Twitter: @JustinSRobinson
Facebook: http://on.fb.me/JustinRobinson

CPSIA information can be obtained
at www.ICGtesting.com
Printed in the USA
FFOW04n1336100216
21353FF